sweet
dandelion

Cover Design © Emily Wittig Designs

Editing: KBM Editing

Formatting: Micalea Smeltzer

sweet
dandelion

micalea smeltzer

PROLOGUE

"My sweet, Dandelion. May you always be as free as the birds, as wild as the flowers, and untamed as the sea."

I close my eyes, feeling my mother's fingers glide through the strands of my hair.

It's a familiar sensation.

"I love you," she whispers, pressing her lips gently to my forehead.

Her tears fall onto my skin.

I love you too.

Shots ring out again.

A thump.

And then nothing.

CHAPTER ONE

I PICK AT THE CHIPPED YELLOW NAIL POLISH LEFT ON the edge of my fingernail.

I can't even remember when I painted them. There's barely any left.

Across from me there's one window in the room. It should open easy enough, and if not I can throw the chair against it, hopefully shattering it quickly.

There's a door at my back, but the window … that's where I would escape.

"Are you listening?" My brother's tone is nothing if not exasperated with me.

I feel bad for him.

He's only twenty-five.

And now he's my guardian.

"S-Sorry," I stutter, forcing my eyes away from the window.

Clearing his throat, the principal leans forward. "This is your schedule." He slides the paper to me and I rub my finger against the smooth surface. He's an older man, his face lined with wrinkles like he's laughed and smiled a lot

3

in his lifetime. His hair is speckled heavily with gray, but with the underlying hint of brown still there. He laces his fingers together, laying them on the wooden table in front of him. The gesture disturbs the perfect straight line a stack of folders was in. I itch to perfect it once more. "We're aware of your situation, so we've made provisions for you to spend your fifty minute daily period with our school counselor, Mr. Taylor."

I look at the wall, at the thick-framed college diploma, then the icky dull colored painted vase of flowers hung beside it. What a bland room to have to work in. I would lose my mind.

"Dani," my brother prompts, desperation in his tone. "Is that okay with you?"

It's not, but in the last nine months I've learned to do what makes everyone else feel better. I don't think anything can heal me, but if it'll make Sage happy I'll do it. Even if all the therapists and counselors I spoke to in the hospital couldn't help at all. They tried, but they didn't know how to get through to me, and I didn't know how to tell them it was impossible.

I nod, resting my elbow on the arm of the chair.

"That's fine." My voice is soft, deeper than it used to be. There's something missing from it and I haven't been able to figure out what it is.

Perhaps it's innocence.

The principal, Mr. Gordon according to the plaque sitting dangerously close to the edge of his desk, starts going over more things but I'm not listening.

It's not that I mean to ignore him, but I find myself retreating more and more into my head. It feels safer here, but it's not. It's not safe anywhere. My brain is full of terrible memories, while the world is full of terrible people who do horrible things, every single day.

Principal Gordon finishes his speech and holds out a stack of papers to me.

I don't lift my hand to take them.

Sage grabs them instead, shaking the principal's hand. He stands and I follow suit.

"We hope you'll enjoy your time here at Aspen Lake High."

I don't respond. I don't even force myself to give a tiny smile. Frankly, I don't have the energy to.

Out in the empty hall Sage shuffles through the papers, reading them over. His light brown hair is longer than normal. He hasn't had time to get it cut because of me.

I've often wondered what he thought when he got the call I was in the hospital and our mom had been killed.

She died protecting me and other students, doing what she could to save lives. She was a teacher and in her final moments she went above and beyond what a teacher is supposed to do.

We lost our father when we were young to pancreatic cancer. I don't remember him much, but Sage is older than me so I'm sure he does.

In less than eighteen years four has become two.

I don't know what I'd do if I lost Sage too.

"Looks like your locker is this way."

"I probably won't use it." I toe the dirtied white edge of my yellow Vans against the tile floor.

His exhale echoes through the hall. "Do you want to see where your classes are?"

"I can figure it out on Monday."

His hazel eyes are tired when they meet mine—nearly the color of his, though mine are more green and his more gold.

"Dani, I'm trying here."

I know he is. He's trying hard. The problem is I hate him trying so much when I know he has a life.

He moved to Salt Lake City, Utah for college, stayed for a job and a girl. The girl didn't work out, but he says he likes the job. I don't believe him, not when he comes home looking weary and older than his years. We grew up in Portland, Oregon and I had plans to stay there, until someone else with a gun decided my fate for me.

Now I'm the girl who survived a school shooting. Who walks with a limp. Who barely speaks.

"I know you are, but you're missing work." I barely give breath to the words, my eyes reluctantly meeting his.

He softens, grasping a piece of my long light brown hair and giving it a playful tug. I used to get mad at him for pulling on my hair when we were little, but now I relish in the familiar gesture.

"I'm right where I want to be. Come on."

As much as I want to protest, I know he wants to help in any small way he can.

My fingers twist in the bottom of my shirt as I follow Sage. He looks intently at the schedule, then the map, before heading off in whatever direction he thinks we need to go like some bloodhound.

I think this helps him feel in control.

While I was in the hospital there wasn't much he could do to help me other than to encourage me not to give up.

God, I wanted to.

I often got angry, wondering why God took my mother but not me. Why did I have to endure the pain of getting shot and nearly being paralyzed?

I wasn't sure I'd ever walk again.

The doctors, too, were doubtful.

But Sage ... he was determined to see me walk again.

But running?

I think running is out of the question for me.

Once upon a time it had been my life. I thought I'd go to college with a scholarship. But things change and now I walk with a limp. I try not to let it bother me, after all I'm very lucky to be on my own two feet, but sometimes I feel like a bird with a broken wing, destined to never fly and it hurts all over again.

It takes the better part of an hour for Sage to locate every classroom and point out the quickest routes there.

Back at our starting area at the front of the school next to the administration section, Sage clears his throat. "Do you remember where everything is?"

I don't. "Yeah, I'll be fine."

And I will be.

I always am.

Fine seems to be my permanent state of being anymore. I'm growing quite comfortable with its dullness.

Sage blows out a breath, rubbing his fingers over the golden stubble on his jaw. His brown locks have always had that caramel-golden tint and his facial hair matches. My brown hair on the other hand has always been lighter, a little duller compared to his.

"I want this to go well for you." His voice lowers, shoulders drooping. "You ... God, Dani ... you've been through a lot." His hazel eyes glisten with unshed tears. My big brother has had to keep his shit together, to be the rock to protect me against the storm, and the wear of it is beginning to show.

I take a step forward, wrapping my arms around his middle. "We both have."

I might've had to heal physically, but we both had to deal with the grief of losing our mother in such a tragic way.

He hugs me back, his arms warm and strong. I don't

think he'll ever know how grateful I am for him coming to my aid. He stayed with me in the hospital, able to work remotely in order to be there, before I healed enough to come to Salt Lake City.

"You could've died, Dani." His gruff whisper tears at my heart, especially when my thoughts spear through me.

Sometimes I still wish I had.

CHAPTER TWO

THE FOUR WALLS AROUND ME ARE BARE WHITE.

They're not the sunshine yellow of my childhood bedroom. There are no photos of me and my friends taped to the walls, no posters, just nothingness. The sounds of the city can be heard through the window beside my bed. They say Manhattan is the city that never sleeps, but so is Salt Lake.

I sit up in bed, swinging my legs around. I pause before standing up, applying pressure slowly to my feet. Sometimes, when I've been lying down for a while I'll have trouble standing, like my body has forgotten all over again how to stay upright. When I feel certain my feet and legs won't give out on me I get up.

It's a strange thing to be thankful for something as simple as standing or walking, but I know how lucky I am to have made this progress.

I take careful, slow steps out of the tiny bedroom and down the hall to the equally small kitchen.

My brother's condo is a sleek modern masterpiece. It's nothing like the chaotic, eclectic home we grew up in. He offered to sell the condo and buy a home in the suburbs but I refused. This was his home and while I might hate the blank white walls, I wasn't going to have my brother uproot his whole life and move to another place because he got saddled with me.

Opening the refrigerator door, I pour a glass of milk and grab two chocolate chip cookies from the box he picked up at the grocery store.

Carrying them over to the living area I place everything on the coffee table so I can sit down. Grabbing the soft blue blanket from the back of the couch I wrap it around my shoulders before turning on the TV, careful to keep the volume low. I browse through the movies on Netflix, putting on Wedding Crashers. Picking up the glass of milk and cookies I settle in, letting my body sink into the comfy couch. Hopefully, I'll drift off to sleep out here.

I don't sleep a lot these days. I find it annoying lying in bed for hours on end staring up at a blank white ceiling. Back home, on the rare occasions I couldn't sleep I'd go out and run — probably not the safest thing and my mom is probably rolling in her grave — until I was utterly exhausted.

I startle when I hear a noise and look up to find Sage in the doorway to the hall, stifling a massive yawn. His hair sticks up wildly in the back like he lost a fight with his pillow.

"Couldn't sleep?"

I shake my head, taking a sip of milk and then a bite of cookie.

"Me either." He lets out an exaggerated breath, padding into the kitchen.

I fight a smile as he pours a glass of milk and grabs two cookies.

He joins me on the couch, plopping down with a groan.

"Wedding Crashers? I haven't watched this in ages," he sighs, stretching his legs up onto the coffee table.

Mom used to yell at him for doing that at home, but this is his place and he can do what he wants.

As if he senses my thoughts he slowly, one leg at a time, lowers his feet to the floor.

"Cheers." He clinks our glasses together.

I wonder what he thinks about the fact that I don't talk much anymore.

I used to be a chatterbox and he was always telling me to shut up—to which our mom would tell him those weren't nice words and to say be quiet instead.

Sometimes, I miss that girl. I think I'll always miss her. I might still be here, alive in the literal sense, where oxygen still circulates in and out of my lungs and my heart still beats, but who I was died on that bloodstained tile floor in the cafeteria.

I dip my half-eaten cookie into the milk, leaving it there for a moment before popping the last of it in my mouth.

Beside me Sage is doing the exact same thing. It makes me smile seeing the little similarities between us. He's seven years older than me, which is kind of a lot of space in between kids if you ask me. Still, we grew up fairly close. He was always looking out for me even if I was his annoying little sister.

Clearing his throat he wipes the back of his hand over his lips, rubbing away crumbs. "Are you nervous about school tomorrow? Is that why you can't sleep?"

I stifle a humorless laugh, flicking a stray hair from my eyes. "No."

His head droops.

He doesn't want to ask. To talk about that day, or mom, or what I remember from those final moments, which admittedly isn't much. But even though the memories are foggy my body still knows.

"I'll be okay."

He winces, because he knows my words imply I'm *not* okay. Not right now, maybe not ever. I'd like to think there's some mystical day in my future where I will be okay, but I'm also old enough to know this trauma isn't something I'm going to forget. It's simply something I'll learn to live with.

Slowly, he turns to look at me. A cookie crumb is stuck in his scruff. Normally I would laugh and make fun of him for it. Not tonight.

"Maybe the counselor at school will help you."

It's such a naïve assumption, but I love that he has hope.

"I doubt it." I want to be realistic with him. "I mean, this is a school counselor. They can't be that great, right? Otherwise they'd be doing something else?"

He sets his unfinished cookie and glass of milk on the coffee table.

I finish mine.

He brushes a crumb off his sleep pants, but one is still stuck in his prickly stubble. "Do you want me to try to find a therapist for you? Someone who specializes in this kind of thing?"

I let out a snort. "None of the therapists helped in the hospital. They ... they wanted me to talk about it. To relive it. Sage…" I close my eyes, blocking out the terrible memories. "I can't do that."

His brows furrow, lips drooping. "I wish I could take it all away. I wish none of this ever happened. I wish mom was still here, those kids, everyone…"

He doesn't voice it, I don't either, but wishes are nothing more than a figment of a child's imagination.

"Come here, Dani." He opens his arms, allowing me to dive in.

He hugs me tight, resting the side of his cheek against the top of my head.

I know getting stuck with me has been a burden on him. How could it not be? He's a young guy and for the last nine months his life has revolved around me. Not dating. Not friends. Just me.

"I know this is rough," he clears his throat, emotion clogging his vocal chords, "but you have me. You can always come talk to me, D."

I know he means it, but I can't. My brother is too good, too kind, to ever have the horrors that haunt my thoughts darken his heart.

At some point I drift off to sleep, and when I wake up on the couch, the blanket is tucked in around me, with a pillow slipped under my head.

CHAPTER THREE

MY BROTHER DROPS ME OFF FOR MY FIRST DAY OF school. I'll be stuck riding the bus for the foreseeable future. I have my license, but driving hasn't been one of those things I've wanted to conquer, especially not in a new city.

"Text me if you need anything," he calls after me as I get out of his car.

"I will."

Closing the car door, I turn and face the school, exhaling a weighted breath.

The three-story brick building with a banner inlaid proclaims it as Aspen Lake High School.

The lawn is teeming with students, dressed to the nines for their first day. I feel like I stick out like a sore thumb in my ripped black jeans, baggy t-shirt, and yellow Vans. I didn't even try, just threw on the first thing my fingers touched. At least I managed to brush my hair, which is a win in my book.

Ducking my head to let my hair shield my face, I head inside, navigating the halls to the best of my ability. I should've paid more attention when Sage was taking me through the school.

I bring up my schedule on my phone, careful to keep my head down and not make eye contact with anyone since I don't feel like talking. My first period class is art. I've never taken art before, or found myself to be the most creative type but I got stuck with it since I was enrolled late and couldn't pick my own classes.

Heading down the corridor, eyes still glued to my cellphone I bump into someone. I nearly fall over from the impact, but a strong hand grabs ahold of me. My eyes settle on that hand, the long fingers, veins cording up into his arm, before I finally look at the guy.

"Sorry about that," he says, letting me go even though very obviously I'm the one who plowed into him. Straight brown hair is pushed back from his forehead. He's pale and thin, but with some muscle. His eyes are an eerie blue so light they almost look white. He adjusts his messenger bag and I don't know whether to flee or keep standing there.

Finally, I blurt, "It was my bad. Sorry."

He tips his chin at me and returns to talking to two friends I didn't notice either.

I only spare them a brief glance before continuing down the hall at a clipped pace. Remembering the room Sage pointed out on his tour I practically run into it, grabbing a seat at the back table.

In the next few minutes the room fills up around me. The teacher at the front, a plump older woman with blonde hair sits behind her desk, eyes narrowed as she appraises every student who comes through the door.

Thankfully, no one sits down beside me. It's a big school, but everyone seems to know everyone, at least in this room, but maybe it only seems that way since I'm the odd one out.

The teacher gets up to close the door, but before she can another student breezes inside. It's the guy I bumped into earlier and my cheeks heat as I realize the only free chair is beside me.

"Thank you for joining us, Mr. Caron." She closes the door and waddles back to her spot behind her desk. "Welcome to Advanced Drawing and Painting. You all should be established artists at this point and I'm looking forward to the masterpieces you create this year." She clears her throat. "I'll be passing out the syllabus and rules for the classroom for you to read over. The most important rule is to not be late." Her eyes narrow on my table partner.

"You love me, Mrs. Kline."

She harrumphs, but gives him an almost tender smile.

I don't think my tablemate is lying.

She gets up, passing out the papers. She reaches our table and pauses beside the guy.

"Don't give me trouble this year, Ansel."

"Never." He winks, uncrossing his arms to take the papers from her, easily passing me one without taking his eyes off the teacher.

She doesn't look convinced, but heads back to her desk nonetheless.

"Don't let her scare you," my tablemate utters under his breath. "She's a big softy."

I don't reply.

"I don't recognize you."

Again, I don't give a response.

"What's your name?"

I sigh. I hate telling people my name, people usually laugh thinking I'm kidding.

"D—"

"Dandelion Meadows?"

I close my eyes, raising my hand. "It's Dani," I tell the teacher.

She marks me off on her roster.

"Dandelion Meadows," the guy, Ansel, muses leaning back in the chair. "Interesting name."

The chair squeaks against the tile floor when I move. "It's a name like any other."

"Definitely not like any other."

Our conversation is hushed, but I'm sure Mrs. Kline will notice at some point.

"Your name is Ansel," I accuse. "That's hardly normal."

"My dad is French, so my parents wanted me to have a French name."

"Can you speak French?" I level my eyes on him, trying to listen to what the teacher is saying, because God knows I'm not advanced when it comes to any type of art.

"Quels sont tes parents?"

"Hippies, they were hippies."

"Tu parles François?"

"Juste un peu."

"Je suis impressionné."

"Merci."

Switching to English, he holds out his hand. "It's nice to meet you, Dandelion Meadows."

"Dani. Just Dani."

He smiles, his sharp cheekbones softening with the gesture. Sliding my hand into his, he gives mine a shake.

"Welcome to Aspen Lake High, home of the Jaguars."

"Ansel. Dandelion." Mrs. Kline narrows her deadly gaze on us. "Quiet or I'll move you."

"It's Dani," I reply automatically. She doesn't even hear me. Admittedly, I don't speak too loudly.

Ansel blows a kiss at her and tilts the chair back, lifting his legs onto the table and crossing them at the ankles.

She shakes her head, turning back to the chalkboard where she's writing down different styles of drawing and painting.

"You seem to get away with a lot."

Ansel leans over, for a moment I fear he might fall from the chair but he's completely unconcerned. "Don't tell anyone," his voice is a hushed murmur, "but she's my grandma."

"Is she really?"

"Yep." His legs drop back to the floor. He seems unable to sit still for long. "I'm her favorite grandkid." He winks.

"Are you sure?"

He lifts his shoulders. "Probably not, but close enough."

We spend the rest of the period on our best behavior, although Ansel continues to move non-stop, always shifting his legs or drumming his fingers.

When the bell rings he slings his messenger bag over his shoulder. "See you later, Dandelion Meadows."

Before I can correct him he disappears as if he wasn't there at all.

CHAPTER FOUR

I SPEND LUNCH IN THE LIBRARY BEFORE TREKKING across school to spend my everyday period with the school's counselor. Probably some stuffy old fart, balding with bad breath and too big glasses who will pretend to know how I feel, to insist I can talk about my feelings and promise this is a *safe* space.

I pause outside the door. It's near the administration offices, but off by itself. The blinds are closed on the window inset into the door.

Tentatively, I raise my fist and knock. My heart thunders in my chest, the telltale feel of perspiration beginning to pebble my skin.

The idea of someone expecting me to sit down and talk about my trauma fills me with a kind of dread I can't explain.

"Come on in."

Wrapping my hand around the handle, the doors emits a low whine as it swings open. In front of me I'm met with the nicest, most firm ass I've ever seen.

Please do not let this guy be some nasty old man, because that ass is incredible.

The counselor is bent over, fiddling with a filing cabinet.

"Take a seat," he instructs, cursing under his breath. "Just trying to fix this."

Something clangs and he whoops in victory, crawling away from the cabinet. It closes easily.

I stand, staring at the counselor, Mr. Taylor. He's knelt on the ground, a pair of navy dress pants hugging his legs and ass. His pale blue button-down shirt is fitted and my God this guy is ripped. He looks like he should be a personal trainer with a body like that, not a high school counselor. From his profile I can tell he has dark scruff, a sharp nose, and full lips. His hair is a tumble of black messy waves.

When he stands up I squeak.

My high school counselor is Superman. Give him the glasses and he's got the Clark Kent look down too.

He's young, I doubt even thirty yet, and *hot*.

God, I know I didn't want a creepy old man counselor but this one … he's too beautiful for words. Normal would've been nice.

He brushes his large hands down the front of his pants and then sweeps one at the chairs.

"Take a seat."

I'm pretty sure he already told me that once, but I was distracted by him bent over. It should be illegal for a butt to be that firm.

Removing my backpack, I set it on the floor before taking a seat in the hard plastic chair.

He sits down behind the desk. Neither is anything fancy, but the desk is neatly kept, though it is only the first day and I suppose that could change. There's a diploma on the wall from the same college Sage attended.

"I'm Mr. Taylor and you're..." He looks down at a piece of paper.

Before he can say that dreaded word, I utter, "Dani. It's just Dani."

He uses the tips of his fingers to scoot the paper to the edge of his desk. "All right, Dani. Looks like we're going to be spending the whole year together." I pick at the edge of my fingernail, looking down. He might be easy on the eyes, but that doesn't mean I want to spend an entire year talking about my feelings with him. "Do you want to talk about why you're here?"

I look up and one dark brow is arched elegantly as he waits for my response. I wonder vaguely how he does that. I can't move only one eyebrow, if I tried I would like I was having a seizure.

"I'm sure you know why I'm here."

There's no way he doesn't know who I am. The shooting was all over the news after it happened. It's ironic though, that those who were quick to rush to the scene with their cameras to cover the horror never did any real thing to help any of us. They only wanted to profit off our pain, to use our trauma as a political tool instead of trying to rally us all together as what we are—people. There cannot be change without understanding.

"Yes, Mr. Gordon briefed me on your history."

My history.

The pain, fear, determination, and horror of everything is summed up in two simple innocuous words.

"Then you know all you need to know."

It takes me several tries to swallow my saliva as my throat closes up. I feel the telltale beating of my heart speed up slightly. My fingers drum lightly against my legs.

Mr. Taylor's eyes flick down like he can see the tick, but I don't think he can, not with his desk between us.

I look around the room, at the standard school issue posters on the wall with smiling kids and stupid sayings on them that are meant to motivate but only sound ridiculous.

"I know what I've been told," he replies, voice deep. "But not how you feel, or what you think."

I wet my lips, staring steadfastly at the wall to my right. My pulse jumps from the feel of him staring at me. Waiting. Waiting for words, waiting for a reaction, just waiting.

"Let's start simple." Out of the corner of my eye I see him get up. He walks around his desk and in front of me. His leg brushes mine that's crossed over my knee and he sits in the chair to my left. "Dani?" He prompts.

It's for the simple reason he calls me Dani instead of Dandelion that I turn my head from the opposite direction and face him.

Fear is crawling through my body like some sticky syrup clogging my veins, ready to suffocate me.

"How are you doing?"

The standard reply would be good. Or fine. It's what everyone answers with whether it's true or not.

I press my lips together, hoping he can't see how badly I'm shaking, but I'm sure he does. It's obvious after all. I'm quivering like a leaf, or as my Mom would've said, swaying like a dandelion in the wind.

"Bad."

"Bad." It's not a question. "Why?"

My eyes scan the room once more, looking for the thing that's missing.

"There's no window."

My admission comes out of me in a barely audible whisper.

He looks around the room, as if he didn't know there wasn't one. For someone else I'm sure it's not a big deal.

My fear of not having window access is silly, even to me, because that day the cafeteria had plenty of windows, but in an open space we were nothing but sitting ducks anyway. Ripe for the picking.

"Well," he stands up, holding a hand out for me, "let's go somewhere with a window then."

My brows furrow and I stare at his hand. It's big and tanned, the kind of hand that looks capable and strong, like he could build a house with his bare hands if he wanted. "Really?"

He tilts his head. "If you're uncomfortable in here without a window, then yes, we're going somewhere else."

"O-Okay," I squeak in surprise, placing my hand in his. He hauls me up and releases me before grabbing my backpack and swinging it over his wide shoulder.

"Come on," he opens the door and waits for me to leave, shutting and locking it behind us with a key, "we'll use one of the conference rooms today."

Today. Meaning in the future I might not have this luxury.

I breathe a little easier as we walk down the bright white hallway, past cherry red lockers. He leads me into the main office, past Principal Gordon's office housed inside it, nodding at the secretaries as we go.

He reaches a door and swings it open, flicking on a light in the process. Inside the room is a wall of windows, a hedge of trees coming up about halfway. There's one long table with at least twenty chairs. I pick the one farthest away from the door.

He follows me inside and places my backpack by my feet before sitting down in the chair across from me. Behind him I look out the window at the front lawn, breathing a little easier.

"Better?"

I nod. "A little."

My heart still hasn't calmed down and I can't figure out if it's to do with the claustrophobic office of his or just him.

"You don't have anything to write on," I accuse, pointing to the empty table space in front of him.

He shrugs, leaning back in the chair a bit, but not as far as Ansel did in art class this morning.

"I won't be writing anything down."

"You won't?" Surprise colors my tone.

He shakes his head, threading his fingers. Dark hairs sprinkle his knuckles. "I'm not here to judge you, Dani, or try to figure you out. I'd like to help you, but you have to be willing to let me."

"I don't know how to do that," I admit, picking at the stubborn piece of polish still stuck to my finger. I need to repaint them, but I haven't felt like it. Yellow is my favorite color, and my usual go-to, but right now it doesn't feel like what I need. Maybe a purple or a blue, something soft but gray in tone.

"Start by talking." Mr. Taylor interrupts my thoughts.

"About what?"

"Anything. Whatever you want. It can be as simple as what you ate for breakfast."

My eyes drift to the view out the window once more. The American flag billows in the wind. Other than that it's empty, the lawn eerily still.

"I didn't eat breakfast."

"Lunch?"

"A turkey sandwich. The bread was stale and the lettuce rubbery."

His lips quirk like he's trying not to laugh or smile.

"Don't get the turkey here, it sucks. Try the chicken salad." I open my mouth to protest because a school chicken salad sounds like the most disgusting thing I could possibly ever eat, but he cuts me off. "Mrs. Norris the head cafeteria lady makes it herself. It's good, I promise."

I think I surprise him when I scoot forward, holding out the pinky on my right finger. "Pinky promise?"

He stares at my outstretched finger contemplatively before wrapping his much larger finger around mine. "Pinky promise."

Our fingers drop and I sit back. "I'll try it tomorrow then."

He smiles, a genuine pleased smile.

I'm trying. I have to try. If it takes one day at a time to get better, I have to start somewhere. A simple conversation, a potential ally, I can do this.

The bell rings and I stand up, shouldering my bag.

"See you tomorrow, Dani."

I don't reply, instead I slip out the door and to my next class, thankful the day is almost over.

CHAPTER FIVE

THE LIGHTS IN THE WALGREENS ARE OBNOXIOUSLY
bright.

*Do they keep them like that so people will buy faster and get
the hell out of here?*

I peruse the shelves of nail polish. Every shade of blue
and purple imaginable, but suddenly I'm not feeling those,
instead gravitating toward the oranges. Maybe it's the fall
lover in me.

I pick up a few shades, reading the names—a polish
has to have a funny name or I won't buy it. Finally, I settle
on a retro rust orange from O.P.I. called Chop Sticking To
My Story.

I wonder who gets hired to make up these names and
how I could get their job.

My Heart Is In Smither-Greens.

Yellow, Mate.

I should start keeping a list of my ideas.

My phone starts ringing in my back pocket and I slip
it out. Sage's name stares back at me and I wince, starting

down the candy aisle—I can't go to the drugstore and not buy candy, that's insane.

"Hello?"

He exhales in relief. "You're okay."

"Yeah."

"I just got home from work, where are you? There's no note, and you didn't text. I was worried when you weren't in the condo."

"I'm sorry." I truly am, because I should've been more considerate. I forget that while Sage's trauma is different, he's been through a lot in these last months. "I ran down to Walgreens. I wanted to get a new nail polish."

"Dani, you have like a million."

"I wanted another. None of those were right."

"Well, do you want me to pick you up?"

"I'm a block away. I'll get some candy, check out and be home in a few."

"I brought Chinese home for dinner."

"Sounds yummy. I … I love you, Sage."

"Love you, too, D. Just … let me know next time where you're going, please?"

"I will. Promise."

I hang up the phone, tucking it carefully into my pocket.

I grab a bag of Hershey's Kisses for myself and a box of Milk Duds for Sage.

It doesn't take me long to check out and I make the short trek back to the building. That's the plus side of my brother living in a condo, I'm in walking distance to everything.

I enter the sleek building and head up in the elevator to his floor.

I use my key attached to a keychain that says I HEART NY from a trip when we went there when I was very young, before my dad died. I don't even remember the trip, but the keychain was his and now it's mine. It's one of the only things of his I have.

The door closes behind me with a loud bang like a heavy hotel room door. The smell of Chinese food wafts from the plastic bags on the counter. A yellow smiley face decorates the front of them.

"Sage?" I call out. "I'm back."

Walking down the hall to the bedroom area, I hear the shower running in his master bathroom.

I put the nail polish in my bathroom—aka the hall bathroom—and the Hershey's in my room. The Milk Duds I decide to put in front of the bags of Chinese food. I didn't get it as a peace offering but I guess it kind of is.

The shower squeaks as it's turned off. I pull some plates from the cabinet, fixing our favorite foods on each, then pour us each a glass of water.

A few minutes later Sage strolls in, his golden-brown hair damp from the shower.

"I'm starving," he remarks, opening the fridge and grabbing a beer.

Sage rarely drinks, so when he does I know he's either had a hard day at work or it's because of me.

My gut tells me tonight it's the latter.

We sit down on the leather barstools at the sleek black granite countertop.

"How was work?" I ask at the same time he questions, "How was school?"

"You go first," I tell him. It gives me time to form a response.

He swallows some beer, staring down at his plate of pork lo mein. "It was good. Same old, same old."

"Come on," I force a smile, bumping him playfully

with my elbow. "You gotta give me more than that. I barely know what you do."

All I know is my brother is a tech nerd and *very* good with computers.

"It's not all that exciting." Another swig of beer, maybe I'm not the culprit for his alcohol consumption tonight, after all. "I mostly keep the computers and system up and running."

"Sounds interesting to me," I muse, spearing a piece of breaded shrimp.

"Now tell me about school. Did it go okay with the counselor there? He emailed me about meeting later this week."

I nearly choke on my food, coughing until the piece of shrimp is dislodged. Taking a sip of water, I blurt, "Why would you meet him?"

"Are you okay?" Sage looks at me with narrowed brows and eyes filled with concern.

"I'm fine."

"He thought since he'd be counseling you for the school year that we should meet so I know who you'll be seeing."

"Oh."

"If you don't want me to, I don't have to."

I shake my head. "No, that's fine, I ... he promised anything I shared with him would be confidential. I don't ... I don't want to trust someone and have that trust broken."

Sage flinches and my chest pangs. I'm sure he wishes I would talk to him, open up. He has to see I'm a different girl, a different sister, than the one he grew up looking out for.

"He won't tell me any of your secrets, Dani." His tone is a smidge harsh.

"Sage—"

He shakes his head, picking up his beer and draining what's left. He gets up and tosses the empty bottle into the trash before grabbing another and popping the cap.

I might've not been the reason he was drinking before, but I sure as hell am now.

CHAPTER SIX

Sitting in my second period class of the day, Government, I decide school is a big joke. The teacher, Ms. Spencer spends the first ten minutes looking at her phone, the next five minutes naming off the rules of her classroom—one of which, ironically, being no cellphone use—and then the rest of the ninety minutes she leaves us to our own devices. In her words, "It's only the second day, no point in working."

Yeah, what could possibly be the point in that?

"This is going to suck," the girl in front of me drawls. She turns around, looking at me. Her long blonde hair is curly, well past her shoulders. "Hi."

My nose crinkles. "Hi."

"I'm Sasha."

"Dani."

"Nice to meet you." She smiles and it seems genuine. She looks like the cheerleader type, preppy and cheerful, but at least she doesn't seem snooty.

"Same."

I'm great with words.

Her smile widens. "I think we have another class together."

"I don't know." I'm not trying to be particularly shady. I genuinely don't know since I haven't paid attention to anyone in my classes.

"Yeah, I'm pretty sure you were in my Statistics class."

"Probably. I wasn't paying much attention."

She cracks another smile. "That's okay. What other classes do you have today?"

I rattle them off and we discover we also have Sociology together at the end of the day.

Looking over at the teacher I find her filing her nails, not paying any attention to us.

"Well," I say to Sasha, picking up my backpack from the floor and slipping it over my shoulders, "I'm out."

"What do you mean?" she asks in confusion.

When I walk out of the room and the teacher doesn't even notice, I think she gets it.

There's a chance I could get in trouble for this, but it's better than the alternative of being stuck in class for another hour doing absolutely nothing. I doubt Ms. Spencer will even notice my departure.

Strolling down the corridor I stop to look out the massive row of windows. It floods the hallway with light and I pause, soaking it up. The sun has always warmed and soothed my soul.

"Dani?" I startle at Mr. Taylor's voice.

I turn from the window and find him walking toward me, only a few feet separating us now. He's dressed similarly to yesterday, except today his pants are gray and his shirt white. My eyes zero in on his hand, noticing the carefully wrapped sandwich.

"Chicken salad?" He looks confused. "The sandwich." I point to the one in his hand. "Is it chicken salad?"

"Uh, yeah, it is." He shakes his head as if throwing off the fog of my question. "Shouldn't you be in class?"

"Shouldn't my teacher be teaching?" I jest.

He presses his lips together with no clear response.

I look back out the window, resting my hand against the warmed glass.

"My mom always said I lived up to my name. I needed the sun to thrive and the freedom to move." I look over at Mr. Taylor and he's studying me carefully. He doesn't say anything, but I can tell he's thinking. "I can't move like I used to, not anymore."

I walk away from him, the slight limp I still have slowing me down.

He doesn't tell me to go back to class.

I think maybe he knows that was me trying.

Trying to be honest. Trying to give a truth. Trying to get better.

You have to start somewhere, one small aching step at a time.

———

"Meadows, the library is for books, not food."

I look up from my chicken salad sandwich and find Ansel grinning down at me.

"Mind if I join you?"

I motion to the empty table. I can't keep him from sitting where he wants even if there are plenty of other places to sit in the library. He pulls out the chair across from me, slapping his messenger bag on top. He pulls out a paper bag for his lunch, a sketchpad, and pencils.

He digs into his sandwich, peanut butter and jelly I note, and says to me around a mouthful, "You know, if we're going to be friends you're going to have to start to talk more."

"Pourquoi devrions-nous être amis?"

"Why wouldn't we be friends?" he counters easily. He stuffs another bite of sandwich in his mouth and flips the sketchpad open. "I'm awesome. Everyone wants to be my friend."

"That so?" I nibble at my sandwich. Mr. Taylor was right. It's way better than the turkey and homemade. Unfortunately, I don't have much of an appetite at school.

"I'm fucking great," Ansel decrees, adding shading to whatever he's working on. I can't tell exactly what it is upside down but I think it's a close up of an animal's eye.

"If you're so great why are you in the library with me?"

He flicks a piece of hair from his eyes and I'm reminded of a young Leonardo DiCaprio in Titanic.

"Because, you didn't come to lunch yesterday, and I saw you head in here today. I didn't want you to eat alone."

"I'm fine if you want to go back to your friends."

"I'm good here, thanks." His tongue sticks out slightly as he bends over the sketchpad, working on his creation. His half-eaten sandwich sits lonely and forgotten beside him.

"Suit yourself. I'm kind of a bore." I pop the last bite of sandwich in my mouth.

I open the bag of chips I swiped from home, tossing a salt 'n vinegar chip in my mouth. Sage makes fun of me for loving them so much, but they're the best chip in my book.

"What are you working on?" I figure it's best to try to make polite conversation with him.

He flips it around so I can see.

There's an eye like I thought, but I still don't know what it is.

"It's a bear," he explains. "A personal project. I was watching a wildlife documentary one day and thought the bears were cool." He turns the sketchbook back around.

"I wish I could draw."

He looks at me with his strange pale blue eyes. "If you can't draw why the fuck are you in an art class? That makes no sense."

"I didn't get signed up for classes until late. So, I didn't pick any of my electives."

"Shit, that sucks. What else did you get stuck with?"

"Sociology and Food and Nutrition."

"Sociology," he shudders, "no thanks. But Food and Nutrition is awesome. I took it last year. We made pancakes."

"I'll probably burn the school down. I'm not the most skilled when it comes to the kitchen."

He laughs, rubbing his finger on the edge of his drawing to smudge some of the pencil into the page. "I would pay to see that."

"Don't worry it'll be a free show." I offer my bag of chips to Ansel and he looks up, shaking his head.

"I'm more of a sour cream and onion guy."

I pretend to gasp. "That's tragic. This friendship will never work."

He arches a brow. "So, are we friends now?"

The bell rings.

"I guess we'll have to wait and see."

―――――

MR. TAYLOR WAITS outside his door for me.

I tilt my head, giving him a quizzical look.

"I thought we'd go to the meeting room again, until I can work something else out."

"Work something else out?" I repeat his words, puzzling them over. "If it's a problem I'll..." I close my eyes, taking a grounding breath. "I'll be fine."

He shakes his head. "Don't worry about it. This isn't a big deal at all."

I feel like he's lying. Or maybe that's the guilt nibbling at the back of my mind that I should be fine in a room with no alternate escape route.

We head down the hall in silence, through the office, and to the same room as yesterday, taking the same exact seats.

He still doesn't have a notebook.

It's not that I doubted him yesterday, but ... I guess I did.

I'm so used to these people trying to *fix* me as if I'm a broken toy that only needs some new batteries to work again—pop them in and I'll start right up—that I'm not accustomed to someone wanting to *listen*.

"How was your lunch?"

Conversation. I can do conversation.

"It was good. I tried the chicken salad sandwich. You were right. It was yummy."

He smiles, his eyes crinkling at the corners. His eyes are the most unique color of blue-green ringed in gold. I've never seen eyes similar to them. Like a Caribbean sea dotted with islands.

"How's your second day going?"

I laugh softly. "I think you know how well it's going."

His lips downturn as he recalls finding me in the hall-way. "Regardless, you need to stay in class."

"I need to do a lot of things," I mumble.

"Like what?"

"Decorate my room. Talk to my brother more about real things, my real thoughts and fears. Make friends." I lean over the table, gesturing with my hand to drive home my point of what I have to say. "I have to carve out a sketch of the new version of me that fits in this world now that the old me is gone." Mr. Taylor doesn't give me a sad, pitying look like most people would. "You know what sucks about a sketch?"

"Tell me."

"They're easily erased."

CHAPTER SEVEN

I STARE AT THOSE BLANK WHITE WALLS.

Those God-forsaken blank white walls in my bedroom.

Sage said I could paint them when I moved in. Decorate the space however I wanted. But I haven't bothered to, because I don't know how.

The girl I was and the girl I am now are two totally different people.

I still like yellow, but the cold oppressive white seems somehow a better option.

Yellow means joy.

Vibrancy.

Happiness.

I'm not happy. I don't want my room to make it seem like I am.

The door to the condo opens, slamming closed a second later. I hate that door. It's so absurdly loud.

"D?"

"In here," I call out.

His dress shoes clack against the floor. It's so dumb to me that he works on computers all day, but has to dress up. My door cracks open a moment later and he finds me lying on my stomach, browsing the internet.

"You hungry?" he asks me, tugging at his tie and taking it off in one swift movement. He loops it around his hand, waiting for my reply.

"One of us is going to have to learn how to cook."

His lips tug into a grin. "You know I can't cook."

"Neither can I, bro."

"Well, until one of us caves, want to get pizza?"

My stomach rumbles. "Yeah, pizza would be good."

"Let me shower real quick and we can go."

He disappears down the hall to his room.

Closing my laptop, I roll out of bed and brush my hair. It only helps my appearance a minimal amount. Grabbing one of the few lipsticks I own, I fill in my lips with the nude color. Looking in the mirror it's impossible not to see how much I've aged in the last nine months. True, I don't have wrinkles, or sagging skin, or discoloration. But it's in the eyes, and I think that's the worst part of all. I'm afraid the haunted look in them will never go away and is a permanent thing I'm going to have to get used to.

It doesn't take Sage long to shower and change. He ushers me out of the condo building and down the street. The pizza place is the smallest I've ever seen. There are only three tables, all high-top with only two seats. The maybe ten feet of standing space is crowded with people either waiting to order or pickup.

"Grab that table," Sage directs me to the table in the corner where a couple is leaving, "I'll order."

I push my way through the people, holding my breath as I do, not because anyone smells but because I hate the suffocating feeling of their bodies pressed against mine.

I finally make it to the table and sit down. There are crumbs and red pepper flakes dotting the table. I brush them onto the floor, watching them drift away. It's ten minutes before Sage places the order and joins me. The receipt with our order number is clasped in his hand.

We sit across from each other, but we're worlds apart with no idea how to breach the distance. We try in little ways. Small, everyday questions. Nothing too deep. Tiptoeing around the trauma we've both endured. Sage might not have been in the building that day, but he's had to shoulder the burden of many things because of it and it couldn't have been easy.

"I got you the white pizza."

"It's my favorite." I look at my bare nails. I haven't painted them yet. I should do that tonight. "What'd you get?"

I squint at the menu hanging above the register.

"Meat lovers."

"Of course." I roll my eyes playfully. "What is it with guys and having to have meat on or with everything? Is it the caveman in you?"

"Probably." He picks up the shaker containing the powdered cheese and shakes it around, furrowing his brows as he stares at a chunk that's clumped together. "Want to do something this weekend? You haven't done much since we've been here and that's partly my fault. I should've shown you the city more, taken you exploring or some shit. Fuck," he presses the heels of his hands to his eyes, "I'm the worst brother ever."

I was only well enough to leave the hospital in May. It's almost September, which meant he spent six months away from his home, working remotely, so he could be with me in the hospital. Once I moved here with him, seeing the city was the last thing on my mind and I definitely wouldn't have expected him to take more time off to show me around.

"No, you're not, Sage."

He blows out a breath.

"You've done a lot more than most siblings ever would. You stayed by my side in the hospital—my God Sage you moved into my room and slept on the couch for months so I wouldn't be alone, I don't think you could've gotten away with it if the nurses hadn't had a major crush on you." He chuckles, ducking his head. He can deny it all he wants, but flirting with the nurses was practically his part-time job while he was there. "You moved me in with you. You've bought me clothes, school supplies, a new computer. You've never made me feel alone and that means more than you'll ever know."

My brother looks like he might cry. I reach across the table and place my hand on his.

He doesn't say anything. He doesn't have to.

When our order is called he slips off the chair silently and returns with two fresh pizzas in boxes.

"Want to head back to the condo?" I ask him. "We could put a movie on."

"No." He shakes his head, looking out the window at the passing cars and pedestrians, all of them oblivious to the simple horrors that can shatter our lives in minutes. Seconds. "Let's stay out for a while."

"Okay." I open my box of white pizza, inhaling the heavenly scent. It's my favorite food and I swear I could live off of it. Honestly, the food pyramid is a triangle, so is pizza, therefore all you need for a balanced diet is pizza.

I take a bite of the ooey-goodness stifling a moan.

"This might be the best pizza I've ever had."

Across from me Sage grins as he dusts more cheese on his and then a thick coating of red pepper flakes. "It's my favorite."

"This could be dangerous," I warn him around a

mouthful. "This place is only down the street and I could live off of this."

"It has spinach on it. It's practically a salad." He winks and I laugh.

It feels nice for at least a moment to feel happy. That's the thing about trauma, fear, grief—all of it—you don't feel those emotions fully twenty-four-seven. There are brief moments of reprieve, and when you have them you learn to cherish them.

Sitting in this hole in the wall shop, eating pizza with my brother, is one of the simplest things in the world but I know this memory will stay with me forever, because in the darkest time of my life this is a bright spot.

CHAPTER EIGHT

IT'S THE LAST DAY OF MY FIRST WEEK OF SENIOR YEAR and it's dragging.

More than usual anyway.

But at least I've survived the first five days even if they've tried my patience from the sheer monotony of it all. Honestly, the whole day could be condensed into a few hours, yet they subject us to nearly seven hours of this. Is that even humane?

"I don't know why you won't eat in the cafeteria. There's plenty of room at the table I normally sit at with my friends."

"Then go sit with them," I say, letting go of the library door. He catches it, following behind me to the table that's become mine this week. I'm thankful none of the librarians mind me, or us, eating in here since we clean up.

"Nah, I'm cool here with you, but if you're afraid of not having anywhere to sit that's not true."

I know Ansel would gladly pull me into his friend group. Even Sasha, who I've gotten to know more in our shared classes, would probably let me sit with her.

"I prefer the quiet and solitude." I give him a pointed look as I set my sandwich, the chicken salad, on the table before removing my backpack. I drape the straps over the chair and sit down.

Ansel fumbles with his messenger bag, pulling out his lunch and sketchpad before he finally sits down as well.

"I can be quiet, Meadows. You won't know I'm here."

He opens his sketchpad to a page with a barely started drawing and unpacks his lunch. He sets everything out in a neat row. Today he has an apple, protein bar, and yogurt. His drink is a blue Kool-Aid, one of those in the plastic bottles with a twisty top. He sets out his pencils and picks one up.

"What are you working on now?" I nod my head at the pad.

He flicks a piece of hair from his eyes and looks up at me. "Shh, this is quiet and solitude time."

"Touché," I laugh lightly, unwrapping the saran wrap from my sandwich.

Ansel works on his sketch, taking bites of his lunch in between. I eat, but don't have anything else to occupy me. I've never been much of a reader, but looking around at the shelves I wonder if maybe I should start. Homework and browsing the internet can only take up so much of my time now that I can't run.

Ansel looks at me between strands of his hair. "I was kidding, you know. We can talk."

I follow a grain in the wood of the table with my fingernail. "I have no idea what we'd talk about. We don't even really know each other."

I'm not being mean, but I don't know Ansel well enough yet to easily carry on a conversation and I loathe small talk.

He lays the pencil down and it starts to roll away. He

catches it before it can fall. Scooting the sketchpad to the side, he crosses his arms on the table leaning closer to me.

"If you want to get to know each other it's best to ask questions."

I frown. "I don't like questions."

He presses his lips together, fighting a grin. "Oh, Dandelion Meadows, how you amuse me."

"Dani," I correct automatically, tucking a piece of hair behind my ear.

"Dani," he mimics.

We finish our lunch and I clean up the trash while he folds his sketchpad and sticks it in his messenger bag. I return to the table to grab my backpack, but Ansel stops me. He grabs my arm and before I can ask him what he's doing he scribbles ten numbers on the inside of my forearm in black Sharpie.

He looks up at me with ghost-blue eyes. "If you decide you like questions."

The bell rings and he winks, flashing me a cocky grin before he disappears leaving me standing in the library stunned and confused.

———

I DON'T bother meeting Mr. Taylor at his office, instead heading straight for the conference room. When I enter the school's main office one of the secretaries stops me.

"Oh, no, sweetie. Mr. Taylor got all moved into his new office. You won't be meeting in here anymore."

"Where—"

"Dani." At the sound of Mr. Taylor's warm voice I turn around. His body leans halfway into the main office and he flashes the secretary a winning smile. "Thanks, Glenda, I've got her." He motions for me to join him, his arm flexing as he does. Considering he works at a high school all day five days a week I wonder when he has time to workout.

I follow him out of the room, confused as to what's going on.

"She said you have a new office?"

He nods, looking over at me as we walk side by side away from the main office, then past what was his. "Yeah, I asked to be moved."

"Why?" I can't fathom why he would possibly want to move his office. That seems silly. Even though the place was sparsely decorated it was still his.

He shrugs, rubbing a hand over his stubbled jaw. The watch on his left wrist reflects in the light. "Needed a change."

We turn down a hall I've never been to before. There are a few doors we pass, most marked as a storage or supply closet. We pass a community room the school uses to rent out before making another turn and stopping in front of the final door.

"This place is way out of the way," I comment as he stuffs his hand in his pocket, pulling out his key. "I don't understand why you had to move all the way over here."

He looks over at me, sliding the key into the lock. "That room was a little small. Kind of dark. I thought something different would be good and Mr. Gordon agreed."

He opens the door, motioning for me to go inside first.

My breath catches and I nearly burst into tears taken off guard like I am.

His body heat presses behind me since I'm blocking his entry into the room.

But I can't move. I'm frozen.

My right hand drifts up to my mouth, my fingers shaking.

"Dani?" He's concerned, worried he's done something wrong or perhaps even triggered something.

If he's triggered anything it's gratitude.

It's only my fifth day of school, our fifth time meeting, and he's gone out of his way to accommodate me already. This is the last thing I would expect him to do. He owes me nothing but he's given me everything.

I stare out the window. At the sunlight. At the freedom he's unknowingly handed to me. The blinds are open, bathing the room in a warm yellow hue. There are boxes of books and things sitting around, he's not fully moved in, but his desk is here and instead of the chairs there's a comfy looking loveseat.

I turn around and surprise us both by wrapping my arms around his middle and hugging him. I bury my face in his hard chest, damming back my tears, but they come anyway. I hate crying, but as they come I embrace them. I'm sure I'm ruining his shirt, but he doesn't tell me to stop or push me away. A moment passes before he hesitantly wraps his arms around me and hugs me back.

Human touch—such a seemingly normal thing, but absolutely vital to our survival.

He doesn't rush me, just lets me embrace my emotions.

I finally let him go, embarrassed, wiping my tear-stained eyes on the backs of my hands. Black smears them from the little bit of mascara I put on this morning and his shirt ... yep, I ruined it.

"I'm a mess." I laugh, trying to lighten the heavy cloud that's settled. "I'm sorry about your shirt."

He looks down at it and then at me. "It's only a shirt."

I take a step away from him so he can enter his office. He passes me a tissue from a box I didn't notice on his desk and bends down, rummaging through a duffel bag. I sniffle, drying the last of my tears. I feel ridiculous, losing my cool over something so simple, but I wasn't prepared for his kind gesture.

I mean, he asked the principal to give him a new office because he knew how much it would mean to me to not feel singled out by having to go to the conference room. I throw the tissue away in a small wastebasket by the door and squeak when I turn around to find his bare, muscled back right in front of me.

He turns at the sound, slipping the black cotton shirt down over his abs.

I swallow thickly, wishing the racing in my heart wasn't because I find my counselor attractive.

"Sorry about that." He grabs the chair from behind his desk, pulling it around in front of it. Waving his hand, he indicates the loveseat to my left. "Have a seat."

"Oh, yeah, right." I shake my head. I'm flustered from this whole situation.

"What's on your arm?" he asks, leaning forward and wrapping his hand around my wrist, turning my arm over so the black numbers glare up at him. He raises a brow, giving me a half-smile. He releases my arm and sits back.

"A phone number," I answer, even though he already knows that.

"Making friends?"

"Making … something," I finish with a small shrug. His brow arches again and I explain, "I don't know what Ansel is."

"A boy?"

"Well, I know that, but I don't know what I want him to be." His brows rise farther up his forehead. "Not like *that*," I protest, blushing. "I just…" I look out the window, allowing myself a moment to take a deep breath and regroup. Mr. Taylor waits patiently, not trying to force any words from me. "I don't know if I want … *friends*."

He leans forward, resting his elbows on his knees. "Why wouldn't you want friends, Dani?"

I close my eyes.

I hear the laughter cut off by shouts, then screaming, then the horror of the minutes that followed.

I open my eyes, staring into the cool blue-green ocean of his. "Because it hurts too much."

CHAPTER NINE

THE SHOWER WATER CASCADES OVER MY ARM, BUT THE black numbers don't smear. I rub vigorously at them with a washcloth. They fade, but don't disappear. My arm starts to turn red and I let the cloth drop onto the shower floor with a plop.

Tilting my head up, I let the water pelt my face.

It pings against my skin and I shove my fingers through my wet hair.

Opening my mouth, I scream.

I scream because I have to do something. I have to let out the emotions inside me in some way. If I don't they're going to suffocate me, snuff out my life from the inside out.

I don't want to be broken, but I don't know how to be whole. How can I embrace new people into my life when I'm a shattered vase with shards threatening to stab anyone who tries to get close?

Climbing out of the shower I dry my body, clip my hair up, and dress in a pair of cotton pajama bottoms with bananas and one of Sage's old college shirts I swiped years ago. The number on my arm is now a muddy gray color. I stare at it unblinking.

After I told Mr. Taylor I didn't want friends because it hurts too much, he said to me, "Sometimes we have to hurt to be reminded that the best things in life bring us joy and pain."

I don't really understand what that means, but maybe it'll make sense one day.

I swipe my phone from the counter and put Ansel's number into it before I change my mind.

Just because I saved his number doesn't mean I have to text him.

———

I'M SITTING at the kitchen counter painting my nails Chop Sticking To My Story orange when Sage finally gets home. My eyes flick to the clock on the microwave, flashing in blue the fact he's late.

He drops his work bag by the door, unbuttons the collar of his shirt, and swipes a beer from the fridge.

Turning around, he rests his elbows on the lower counter, taking a swig of the amber liquid. He runs the fingers of his left hand roughly through his hair, mussing it, before exhaling a weighted sigh.

"Please tell me your day at school was better than mine."

I press my lips together.

"Fuck," he groans, gulping down more.

"It wasn't too bad." I have to give my brother some hope. If there's anything in this world we all deserve it's hope.

He lets out a gruff, disbelieving grunt.

"Why don't you quit?"

"We have to have money, D." Turning around, he opens the fridge and begins to rummage through the meager contents.

The stool squeaks on the tile floor as I scoot forward. "You have money from the house, the life insurance—"

His shoulders stiffen, drawing up until his neck disappears.

"I'm not touching that fucking money unless I have to."

"Sage—"

He whips around, smacking his hand against the black granite counter. "I shouldn't even have that money. I'll use that money to take care of you, Dani. But I won't touch that fucking money to live off of because I hate my job. That's blood money that sits in an account because our mom was *murdered*." I wince, but he keeps going. I let him, because clearly this is weighing on him. "Her death won't be my gain."

"She wouldn't want you to be miserable."

He drops his head in his hands then lowers them slowly, looking at me with tear-filled hazel eyes. "I'm not … I'm not *miserable*, Dani. You wouldn't understand how nasty and cutthroat this world can be."

I feel like I've been stabbed. I screw my nail polish cap on tight and slide off the stool. His brows furrow as he watches me pick up my stuff.

Holding my things in my hands I look across the counter at him. "Yeah, Sage, me of all people knows absolutely nothing about this cold, cruel world."

He straightens, horror contorting his face.

"Dani, I—"

I turn away, heading to my bedroom. Over my shoulder I say, "I ordered Indian."

I hear his footsteps behind me but as soon as I reach my room I close and lock the door.

He stops on the other side.

He doesn't knock.

He doesn't say anything.

Because he can't.

He can't make this better.

He can't take back his words.

He can't bring Mom back.

I stare at the door and I realize this is what my entire existence is going to be like from now on.

There's always going to be a wall separating me from everyone else, because they'll never understand the true horror of what I survived.

The sad thing is how often these things are happening, the number of deaths mounting, the survivors living with guilt, but we're being forgotten, because at the end of the day we're nothing.

———

THE FOOD ARRIVES and Sage knocks on my door.

"D? The food is here. Please ... fuck, please come out."

Clutching my pillow to my chest, I close my eyes. I don't like fighting with Sage. He's my brother, my best friend, the last of my family.

I wait for the sound of his footsteps retreating before I slide off my bed, dropping the pillow onto the rumpled surface.

Easing the door open I walk down the hall and find Sage spreading the white to-go boxes on the coffee table.

He straightens when I enter the room, hands on his hips. He exhales a heavy sigh. "I'm sorry, Dani. I shouldn't have said that. Work has been rough and I'm a little testy. Snapping at you was wrong."

"I'm sorry, too."

He wraps me in his arms, hugging me tight. He rests the side of his cheek against the top of my head.

"You're all I have left in this world, D. We have to stick together."

I hold on tighter to him.

He releases me from the hug, but keeps a hold on my shoulders. He doesn't say anything, only stares at me like he's trying to memorize my features.

Finally, he lets go and takes a step back, clearing his throat.

"Let's uh eat then."

He grabs waters from the fridge and we sit on the floor in front of the coffee table.

"Want to put a movie on?" I ask him, opening the tops on the to-go boxes.

"Sure. Pick whatever you want."

He hands me the remote and I scroll through the options On Demand.

"Twilight!" He cries indignantly. "You're still pissed aren't you?"

I drop the remote in my lap. "I happen to love these movies even if I've never read the books."

He blows out a breath and pulls one of the boxes closer to him, digging into the steaming contents. "The whole first movie is *blue* he grumbles."

"It's supposed to look dreary and rainy," I defend, taking a bite of food.

I feel his eyes on me as the movie begins with Bella's opening monologue.

"I can't believe I already had to sit through these years ago when you were like twelve, but now? I'm wounded."

"You said I could choose." I point my fork at him in reminder.

He frowns. "Yeah, you're right. I'll be quiet."

I doubt he will, but I appreciate the gesture. I wanted to put a comfort movie on and this franchise reminds me of better, happier times.

When the movie is halfway finished Sage packs up the leftover food and puts it away. I move onto the couch, curling under a blanket, and I'm more than a little surprised when Sage joins me, sitting down on the opposite end.

I sit up, fighting a grin. "Wait, are you *willingly* watching the rest of Twilight with me?"

He rolls his eyes and huffs out a breath before crossing his arms defensively. "I'm invested now."

"But you've seen it before."

"Shut up," he grumbles good-naturedly.

I lay back down, burrowing under the blanket.

When the movie is over I start the next one and Sage doesn't make any move to leave.

We watch all of the second one before deciding to head to bed. It's after midnight, but I'm not all that sleepy. I pretend I am anyway.

We head to our separate bedrooms but Sage stops me before I can go in mine.

"Yeah?" I blink up at him.

He presses his lips together and swallows. "We have to stick together, Weed."

I squeeze his hand. "Always, Herb."

He smiles back and I go into my room, closing the door behind me.

Herb and Weed.

They're ridiculous nicknames we used to call each other years ago when we were little and constantly pestering each other. Sage said I was an annoying weed, always getting in his way, and I said if I was Weed then he was Herb. It's been a long time since either of us have used those nicknames, but tonight it's good to hear them.

CHAPTER TEN

SITTING AT THE KITCHEN COUNTER I STUFF A SPOONFUL of Captain Crunch in my mouth. Sage is already dressed, whereas I'm still chilling in my PJs, and rinses off a glass in the sink, scrubbing it so no residue of sticky orange juice clings to it.

"I have to run some errands today. You wanna go?"

"No." I always try to pass on the weekends. Sage makes it a point to ask me, but I want him to be able to leave the condo and do things with friends or whatever without me tagging along.

"You sure? I'm going to get some groceries, so write down whatever you want on the list."

"What list?"

He passes me his phone, open to the notepad. I have to laugh. Of course Sage would keep the list in his phone and not on an actual piece of paper.

I add a couple of items, only because I know it makes him feel better to have things in the house that I like.

"Have any plans with friends?"

He shakes his head. "Nope."

"Sage," I sigh, passing his phone back to him. He tucks it in his front pocket. "I know you have friends here. Go do something with them. Don't let me stop you."

"It's fine."

He truly doesn't seem bothered but *I'm* bothered by it. Sage built a whole life before he got stuck with me. That shouldn't stop because I'm here.

"You should date. Surely you were dating before I moved in."

He blows out a breath. "You don't need to worry about that, Dani."

"All I'm saying is you're a guy … you have needs, go forth and conquer."

His mouth parts and he chokes. "No, no, *no*. Take that back. I don't want you to ever talk about my needs or conquering anything ever again. You're my little sister. No." His whole body shakes like he's having a seizure, but really he's trying to rid himself of the icky feeling.

"Don't be such a baby," I pester, getting up to clean my empty bowl. "I'm eighteen. I know things."

He bumps into me and I nearly drop the bowl on the floor. Some milk tips over the lip, splattering onto it instead.

"You should know absolutely nothing. You're too young."

I snort. "Oh, Sage. That's adorable."

Stepping around him I set down the bowl in the sink and grab a paper towel to wipe up the mess from the floor.

"I want to pretend this whole conversation never happened," he grumbles, walking back to his room.

I laugh to myself. "Boys."

A minute later, he leaves his room, car keys in hand.

"Hang out with your friends, please." He pauses at the door, looking over at me. I hop up on the kitchen counter, crossing my arms over my middle. "I know you're worried about me, and don't want me to be alone, but it makes me feel horrible that I'm keeping you from your life." He opens his mouth to protest. "I know you're fine being here with me, but it bothers *me* because I know you would normally be doing other things." I can tell he's still not convinced. He's doing what he thinks is right, and I get that, but I don't want to feel like this constant burden that he always has to be concerned with. "Besides," I hop down, "I've made a couple of friends at school. I was thinking about seeing if one of them could hang out."

He exhales a weighted breath. "I'll see if any of my friends are free."

"Thank you."

He points a finger at me in warning. "If you go out, I need to know what time, who you're with, what you're doing, and what time you'll be back."

"Of course." I won't even argue with him on all those details, because I know it stems from fear. I'd be the same way.

"Okay. I'll see you later."

He heads out and I hop in the shower. I hadn't planned to actually use Ansel's number, but now I feel guilty not to.

Once I'm dressed I send him a text.

Me: Hey, it's Dani. Are you free today?

Ansel: Holy shit. You used my number. Are pigs flying? Let me go look out the window.

Me: Ha. Ha. Ha. You're not funny.

Ansel: Bet you're smiling.

Me: I'm not.

I am.

Ansel: I'm free. What do you want to do?

Me: I don't know. I'm not from here.

Ansel: What? How did I not know that? I thought you were from here. The school's huge so I never thought to ask. Where are you from?

Me: Oregon.

Ansel: Shit. That's cool. Anyway, there's plenty to do around here. Can I pick you up?

Me: Yeah, that'd be great.

I send him my address and he tells me he'll be by to pick me up in thirty minutes.

I blow-dry my damp hair the rest of the way. I don't bother styling it, instead leaving it in its natural beachy wave. Grabbing what I need, I head down to the lobby to wait.

The lobby of the building has shiny tile floors and black and chrome accents. It's modern and cold in my opinion, but I suppose beautiful in its own way.

Stuffing my hands in the pockets of my jacket I walk with my head bowed to wait outside for Ansel. There's an area for him to pull up, like at a hotel.

Before I reach the double doors to exit, something makes me look up.

Call it a sixth sense, or a coincidence, it doesn't matter.

"Mr. Taylor," I blurt out in surprise.

He looks up from his phone, rearing back when he sees me.

"Dani?" He fumbles with his phone, finally stuffing it in his pocket.

We stand maybe two feet apart, both confused and unsure what to say.

I speak first. "You live here?"

"Yeah. I take it you do, too?"

I nod. "I live here with my brother."

"Is he around?"

"No, he left to run some errands. I'm actually hoping

he'll hang out with his friends." Mr. Taylor arches a brow and I explain, "He's neglected his social life since, you know, he got saddled with me. I don't want to stop him from living his life."

"I'm sure you don't keep him from anything."

"Believe me, I do." I look down at my yellow vans. Bright against the black tile. "Have you met him yet?" I force my eyes up to meet his gaze. "He said you asked for a meeting."

He shakes his head. "We haven't scheduled anything yet."

"Oh, okay."

"Do you not want us to meet?" He doesn't sound accusatory, only curious.

I tell him the same thing I told Sage. "You said I could trust you. I want to know I can."

"I won't tell your brother anything we talk about. That's ... I would never do that to you or any student."

"Right. Thank you." He adjusts a pair of glasses on his nose and because I hate awkward situations, I blurt, "I didn't know you wear glasses."

He's totally Clark Kent now.

"Oh, yeah," he touches the side of them, "I try to give my eyes a break from contacts on the weekend."

"You look nice." I wince. "I meant they look nice."

He chuckles, but I want to crawl under the nearest table and hide.

Behind him I see the green car pull up that Ansel told me to watch for. "My friend is here. I better go."

He steps to the side, out of my way. I take a few steps before he says my name.

"Yeah?" I turn around.

"I'm happy to see you're making friends. It's good for you."

"I'm trying."

"I know."

It feels impossible to break contact from his intense stare, but somehow I manage to do it.

Climbing inside Ansel's car, he gives me a quizzical look. "Who was that?"

"No one." I pull the seatbelt across my body as he slides the gear into drive. "It was no one."

———

"OKAY, THIS PLACE IS COOL." I spin in a circle, looking around the coffee shop Ansel brought me to.

Watchtower Coffee & Comics is a simple place. The walls are a light gray, except for part of one that's a chalkboard. Up top it says Watchtower and below it is the menu. The floors are concrete and there are plenty of tables to sit at and some comfy chairs if you want to grab one of the comics to curl up and read.

"Glad you like it." Ansel gets in line behind three other people and I join him.

"You don't strike me as the comic book kind of guy."

His dark brow arches. "What kind of guy do you think I am?"

I shrug. "The tortured artsy type who smokes behind the school and has a trashcan full of unfinished poems."

He busts out laughing, causing a few people working on their computers to turn and look at us. "That was very specific."

"I have a vivid imagination." I look at the menu. "What's good here?"

"Everything."

"That's not helpful."

"It's true." We move up in line.

"We're only stopping here, though. Now that I know you're not from here, it's time to open your eyes to what the city has to offer. Oh, and I only smoke on occasion. Don't tell my mom."

"I don't know your mom."

"Yeah, but you will."

I shake my head at his cockiness.

It's finally our turn to place our order. Ansel insists on paying mine even though I refuse. I'm learning he's even more stubborn than I am.

We don't have to wait long for our order. I take a sip of the BB-8 boba tea I ordered and exclaim, "This is the best thing ever!" A couple of laughs echo through the shop.

Ansel shakes his head, trying not to smile at my antics.

"Come on, Meadows. Much to see, much to do."

He grabs his Tatoonie Sunrise—a frozen coffee—and leads me onto the street.

"Where are we going now?"

"Well," he sips his coffee, "that's my favorite coffee shop. Now we're going to my favorite place in the city."

"Which is?"

He wags a finger. "This is a show game, not tell."

"Any hint?"

"It involves something you already know about me."

My forehead wrinkles as I try to think about everything I know about him so far. "It doesn't involve smoking does it?" I think back to his comment in the coffee shop. "My brother will kill me if I come home smelling like smoke." I flinch at my own words. It's such a simple phrase of words, one I would normally use without second-thought. But now it feels crass.

"I'm wounded that you think so little of me." Considering he's grinning, I think his ego is hardly bruised at all. "No, it does not involve smoking. You're such a hater."

"Hey," I bump his shoulder with mine, "someone has to keep you humble."

"I have no idea what you mean," he plays coy.

"Mhmm, Mr. Popular."

He guffaws, throwing his head back. "I'm not popular."

"Okay, so maybe you're not in the jock, cheerleader crowd but you *are* popular. People like you. I see people stop you in the halls to talk."

He busts out laughing, lowering his head to my ear as we walk. "That's because I'm their dealer, Meadows."

"What?" I stumble, nearly face planting on the ground. His warm hand wraps around my elbow and prevents me from eating the pavement. "You're a drug dealer?" I hiss, yanking my arm from his hold.

He doesn't seem at all bothered by my proclamation. "Say it a little louder for the people in the back." He winks, lifting his coffee cup in toast. "It's only pot. It's harmless."

"Wait, I thought it was legal here?"

He shakes his head. "Not for recreational use."

"So … that's why people are always stopping you?"

"Yup." He pops the p and pouts his lips.

"You could get in trouble." As if he doesn't already know this.

"I could get in trouble for a lot of things, but rules were meant for breaking."

"This isn't a rule, Ansel. This is a *law*."

"Worried about me?" We stop at a crosswalk and he pushes the button for the pedestrian lights.

"Yeah, I am."

"Don't be. But don't tell anyone." He narrows his eyes on me. "Snitches get stitches."

I can't tell if he's kidding or not.

I shake my head, my hair swaying around my bare shoulders. I opted to wear a tank top because I know the cold weather is going to be rolling in soon. "I wouldn't do that."

"Cool beans."

"I don't know if anyone's ever told you this, but you're a weird guy."

He winks again. "Thanks."

We cross the street and walk a couple more blocks—I have no idea why he didn't drive, but it *is* a nice day so I can't complain—and end up in front of a modern looking brick building. There's a sign on the left side of the front that says UMFA.

"UMFA? What's that?"

We start across the street. "Utah Museum of Fine Arts."

"This is your favorite place in the whole city?"

He tosses his empty coffee in a recycling can in front of the building. "Yeah." He shoves his hands in his pockets. "I love drawing, painting, pottery, all of it. I think it's about working with my hands, being able to create something from nothing except a vision in my brain."

"Wow," I murmur, leaning my head back to stare up at the building. I squint against the harsh sunlight.

"And here you thought I was taking you somewhere to smoke." He shakes his head but grins at me.

I finish my boba tea and toss the empty cup in the recycling bin. "What's that over there?" I point to a driftwood looking figure to our right, a ways over, but clearly a part of the large building.

"I'll show you."

I follow him over and gasp. "It's a horse! Is it made of sticks?"

"Among other things."

I study the sculpture, amazed by the amount of work and craftsmanship that had to go into this.

"Its name is Rex. An artist named Deborah Butterfield made him. Her pieces are awe-inspiring. I'm not much of a sculptor myself, I do better with drawing, but her pieces make me want to get better at it."

"I don't have words." I truly don't.

"There's more." He points over his shoulder to the building.

I grin at him, actually feeling excited and more than a little happy that I texted him today. "Show me."

He takes my hand. "Come on, Meadows. If this doesn't make you want to be an artist nothing will."

———

IT TAKES us three hours to explore the whole building. Ansel, no doubt, has been numerous times and knows every detail but he never encourages me to hurry up. Instead, it's like he's seeing it for the first time too.

Sage starts blowing up my phone once he's home, despite me texting him numerous times to let him know I'm okay, so I ask Ansel to take me home instead of grabbing a bite to eat like we planned.

"I'm sorry about my brother," I apologize, undoing my seatbelt when he parks in front of the condo building.

"It's fine." He seems to truly mean it. "You live with your brother, then?"

I didn't think about this part, about what potentially gaining friends might mean. Yeah, sure, the school shooting got plenty of media coverage but it's the killer's name that was always on their lips as well as those who died that day. The survivors, we didn't matter, we still don't. We exist out here and no one knows who we are or understands what we lived through.

"Um, yeah."

"That's cool. What about your parents?"

It's a normal enough question, but it spears through me like a physical lancing. "They're gone."

His lips downturn. "Like on vacation?"

I laugh humorlessly, leaning my head against the headrest I let my head drop to the left to meet his confused stare. "A permanent one."

His confusion deepens before bleeding into horror. "Fuck, I'm the worst. I'm sorry, Meadows."

"It is what it is." That's what I keep telling myself anyway. As if I repeat those five words enough the reality will hurt less. "Thank you for today." I mean it, too. His eyes soften and I know he can tell I'm being honest.

"You're welcome."

"I better go before my brother loses his shit even more."

Sure enough, my phone vibrates with another text. I wave the device around.

"I'll text you later."

"Okay. Thanks again." I hop out and close the door behind me. He pulls away as I head inside.

I cross the lobby and get in the elevator.

Me: I'm heading up. Cool your jets big bro.

The elevator dings when I reach the floor and I hop off, heading down the long hall. Before I can pull my key out the door swings open.

"I'm not good at this whole parenting thing," Sage blurts. "I thought I'd be fine to do my thing and know you were out with a friend. But no. I'm a disgruntled mother hen." He throws his arms in the air, stepping aside so I can come in. "Next time, I'm meeting this friend first. What's her name again?"

"Uh…" I bite my lip, because Ansel is definitely not a *her*. I didn't purposely keep that information from Sage, it didn't even cross my mind that it might matter. "Ansel."

"Is that a girl's name?"

"I'm sure it can be," I hedge, opening the refrigerator to grab a bottle of water. Unscrewing the cap I take a sip.

"Can be? Meaning in this instance it's not?"

He pinches his brow. "Fuck I am a failure at being a guardian. I let you spend the day with a *boy*, a teenage boy, and didn't even think until now to ask about it."

"Ansel is … Ansel. He's harmless."

And a drug dealer, but Sage doesn't need to know that.

"Dani." His hazel eyes narrow in disbelief. "When I was his age I was constantly having to whack one off. Flirting with girls was basically a full time job and believe me we did a lot more than *flirt*." He uses air quotations and I roll my eyes. Watching my brother have a meltdown over this is mildly hilarious.

"You're blowing this out of proportion."

He scrubs his hands down his face. "How did Mom handle this shit with you? Boys and stuff?"

"Well, I had friends that were both girls and guys. It was never a big deal."

He tugs on his hair and then points at me. "No dating for you. Friends, fine, I'll have to get used to it. But absolutely no dating."

I want to laugh at him but I know it would be the complete wrong reaction in this scenario.

"All right, whatever you say." I pat his chest mockingly as I pass him. "I'm going to my room."

"Why do I feel like you're secretly laughing at me?" he calls after me.

"Because I am."

Closing my bedroom door I lean against it, biting my lip to stifle my smile.

I know not all days are going to be perfect. Happiness is fleeting for everyone. But I allow myself this one small victory.

CHAPTER ELEVEN

"Hey, Neighbor." I drop onto the loveseat cushion in Mr. Taylor's office. He looks up from a piece of paper, laying it aside.

"I suppose we are."

"Bleh." I stick my tongue out like I've tasted something sour. "Don't say *suppose* it makes you sound like a stuffy old man. You're not old."

"I'm not?" He leans back in his chair, fighting a smile.

I don't think he'll ever admit it, but he's amused by me. And I'll never admit it, but what I thought would be a torturous fifty minutes every day is quickly becoming my favorite part of the day. He doesn't push me to talk about what happened. If I don't want to talk that's okay. If I want to have a simple conversation he's cool with that. And if I give him a breadcrumb of information I know he feels like it's a win.

I pull out a sketchpad I bought yesterday, using a basic #2 pencil to scribble some lines on the page. I'm definitely not an artist like Ansel is, but the museum he took me to inspired me to try things out on my own. Art is, after all, experimental and subjective.

"How old do you think I am?" he questions when I don't reply.

I look up from the piece of paper and the lines that look like nothing but to me form a close up image of the trunk of a tree. The ridges and whorls.

"I don't know, but you're not old. I doubt you're thirty yet."

"Twenty-nine," he surprises me by giving me a definitive answer.

I point the eraser end of my pencil at him. "See? Not thirty and not old."

"What is old to you?"

I pause, pouting my lips as I ponder his words. "I don't know. I guess it's more of your being than an actual number. Someone fifty might act older than someone eighty, you know? There are some crazy old ladies out there."

"But I'm not allowed to say suppose?" He cocks his head to the right, waiting for my answer.

"Hey, that was a piece of advice not a judgment. Do you want to sound like a stuffy old fart?"

"You're on a roll today."

"Eh." I shrug. "My real personality was bound to show through at some point." I set the sketchpad aside and crisscross my legs under me. "I guess I'm acclimating."

"Do you think being around kids your age is helping?"

Mr. Taylor is asking more questions today, but it doesn't feel like he's trying to split apart my mind and see inside. It feels like I'm talking to anyone who might ask such a thing, like my brother.

"Maybe. It's not like I got a lot of socialization in the

hospital or rehabilitation center. I was more focused on being able to walk again."

He rubs his jaw, his blue eyes darkening to a navy. "I can't even imagine."

"Yeah," I blow out a breath, melancholy settling on my shoulders as I look out the window. "They told me I'd never walk again, let alone run, but I wanted to prove them wrong. It's a miracle I can stand, but I put everything I had into making it happen. I still have numbness radiating down my left side. It's why I walk funny."

Mr. Taylor stares at me like a complicated math problem, something he's both equally fascinated by and desperate to solve.

I hate to tell him, but there's no mathematical answer when it comes to me.

I'm scarred. Physically. Emotionally. Mentally.

Every way you look at it, I'm broken.

My leg is probably the least broken part of me even if sometimes I hate it so much I'm afraid the anger will choke me from the inside.

Running was my life. I was passionate about it. It was my freedom. Now, I'll live the rest of my life never doing it again.

But, at the end of the day, I have a life where others lost theirs.

Several moments pass before he says to me, "You don't think you're strong, do you?"

I shrug, looking down at my half-painted nails I never bothered to finish. "I'm not. I was put into that situation and I did what I had to do."

"You could've given up," he points out.

"I think I would have," I admit, the words like sandpaper on my throat. "But I couldn't. Not for my brother's sake. He needed to see me whole, well as whole as I can be." He doesn't say anything and I pick up my sketchpad again. "I don't want to talk about this anymore."

"What do you want to talk about?"

Nothing.

"What's your favorite color?"

"Blue," he answers easily, not at all bothered by me shutting down the previous conversation. "What's yours?"

"Yellow."

"Like a dandelion?" Some people have asked that question mockingly. Not Mr. Taylor. I can tell he's genuinely wondering.

"Mhmm," I hum, "dandelion yellow. I used to braid them in my hair during the summer."

Back when things were simpler and easy.

Brushing some eraser shavings off my sketchpad I ask, "What made you want to be a school counselor?"

He leans back in his chair, spinning slightly. He might think he looks unbothered, but I can tell my question has him a tiny bit on edge.

"I wanted to help people."

"Sure, yeah, but why a school counselor?"

He looks me in the eye and I feel a shiver course down my spine.

He doesn't get a chance to answer because the bell rings and I'm forced to go to class.

But the look in his eyes? It stays with me.

———

"We're doing vocabulary words," Sasha hisses beside me under her breath. "What is this? Second grade?"

She looks down at the paper with a list of vocabulary words that we need to draw a line to the correct definition for. Sociology is definitely worth every agonizing minute spent in this class before we can go home.

"It could be worse."

"I'm bored," she whines.

Someone hushes her. Across the room the teacher lifts her eyes from her desk, shooting daggers at us.

Mrs. Kauffman is mildly terrifying. She's probably in her late forties, with a blunt bob past her ears, and thick bangs. She has these beady eyes that seem to stare right through you and there's a permanent scowl glued to her face—unless her son, who also works at the school, pops in. Then she's all smiles.

"Keep your voice down," I hiss under my breath.

I might've walked out of our history class last week, but this is not one I'm willing to rock the boat in. I'm pretty sure Mrs. Kauffman has a dungeon somewhere and gets her shit and giggles out of torturing her students.

I finish the worksheet and turn it in, moving on to the next assignment. I spend the rest of the period looking up the same definitions we matched in an actual dictionary instead of Googling it and write them all down.

It's time consuming and tedious.

I'm beginning to wish I'd fought harder to get my GED. Sage had insisted I finish school and I'd wanted to make him happy.

Regardless, I'm here now and I have to make the best of it.

I manage to get everything done before the bell rings, dismissing us for the day. Several people groan, because they're not as lucky and will have to do it as homework.

Sasha and I walk down the long hall together, descending the stairs to the main floor.

"I thought senior year was going to be great," she whines, the sound of lockers slamming closed echoing around us. "Parties. Football games. Basketball games. More parties. And no school work. So far, it's none of that. It's only week two. I won't survive this."

I laugh lightly. To my ears it sounds forced and fake but Sasha doesn't seem to notice.

"Somehow I think you'll manage."

Her curly blonde hair sways as she jumps the last two stairs, landing solidly on the floor.

I descend the last two like a normal person.

"Well, I guess I'll see you tomorrow in Statistics." She sticks out her tongue playfully, crossing her eyes at the same time.

"Bye." I wave as she heads in the opposite direction to the student parking lot while I walk straight ahead for the bus loop.

I only make it a couple of feet when I hear, "Meadows! Wait up!"

I stop, tightening my hold on my backpack straps.

Ansel strolls leisurely through the crowd of students. They part around him. He doesn't even have to fight against them. It's kind of incredible.

He slings his arm over my shoulders when he reaches me.

"Are you riding the bus?"

"Well, I don't drive, so ... yes."

His arm falls from around me. "A senior riding the bus?" Nuh-uh. Can't have that. You're coming with me."

Before I can protest he grabs my hand. Not to hold my hand, but to pull me along. People begin to stare as he drags me from the direction of the bus loop to the opposite end where the parking lot is.

"I don't mind riding the bus, Ansel."

"Yeah, well, can you stop and get coffee on the bus? No, I don't think you can."

He doesn't let me go until we're at his car, and at this point I don't feel like running to try to catch my bus to make a point.

He unlocks the car and I get inside, setting my backpack between my feet.

Horns honk and tires squeal as students race to get out of the parking lot before they let the buses through.

Ansel turns the car on and I promptly roll the window down as he backs out. "You don't mind, right?"

He shakes his head and lowers his. "Nope, prefer it actually."

It's a fairly warm day, but there's a crispness to the air and I know it means chillier days are around the corner.

Leaning back against the headrest, I let the air whip my hair around my shoulders. It'll be a tangled mess but I don't care.

I look over at Ansel, his strong arm gripping the wheel in one hand. The slender column of his throat. He's a pale skinned work of art and I'm the damaged new girl. He doesn't know that, though, and I can't help wondering why he's taken me under his wing.

His gaze darts to me before returning to the road. "What?"

"Nothing," I answer looking out the window at the mountains in the distance.

Salt Lake City isn't short on the stunning views.

"You were looking at me."

"Am I not allowed to look?"

He chuckles. The sound rumbles in his chest. "Yeah, look all you want, I don't care. I was wondering why."

"I was thinking." I look away from the window. He's haloed by the yellow sun. The golden glow seems at odds with the white, black, and gray aesthetic of him. Ansel has the moody artist vibe down, even if he's the complete opposite of moody.

"About what?"

Getting answers from me is like pulling teeth, but he seems undeterred.

"I still don't understand why you want to be friends with me?"

The blinker comes on and he turns onto the main road leading into the city.

"I don't know." He shrugs, loosening his grip on the wheel. "You seem like someone I'm meant to know."

"That makes no sense." My nose crinkles.

His eyes pierce me for a second. "It does to me."

CHAPTER TWELVE

The condo door opens and Sage enters, dropping his bag on the floor. His tie is askew and his hair mussed like he's been shoving his fingers through it all day.

"You're home early," I remark, closing my laptop lid on my homework. I decided to work at the kitchen bar today, instead of holing up in my room like I normally do.

"Yeah," he blows out a breath, unbuttoning the first couple buttons on his shirt, "I had a meeting today, so they let us go early."

"Well, that's nice."

He laughs humorlessly, grabbing a banana off the counter and ripping the peel off. "Only because it was too late in the day for us to get any work done."

He devours the banana like he's starved. "Have you eaten today?"

He shakes his head. "Let me order a pizza or something." I grab my cellphone to look up places.

"That'd be amazing." He leans on the counter, resting his head in his hands. "I think we should take a cooking class."

I look up from my phone. "Sage, we can't cook."

"We have to learn."

I shake my head. "How have we switched roles? We had this conversation and you shut me down because we're likely to burn the whole building to the ground."

"Well, I'm not expecting either of us to become the next Top Chef but we should be able to cook at least eggs. I can't even do that right."

I gag thinking about the gelatinous blob Sage tried to feed me this summer and called it scrambled eggs.

"How come you were against this before?"

He laughs. "Because we're truly awful cooks. But I feel terrible that we're living off takeout." He straightens, crossing his arms over his chest. "I know I'm not your parent, but I *am* your guardian and I feel like I'm doing a piss poor job of it."

"Sage," I breathe. "You're doing a great job."

My heart breaks that my brother might think he's not doing a proper job of providing for me. I know he's doing the best he can and I appreciate everything he does. He didn't *have* to take care of me, but he has.

His frown deepens. Sliding off the stool I walk around the counter and hug him.

His arms wrap around me and he exhales a shaky breath that stirs my hair. "I don't want to fail you."

"You couldn't. Not ever. But don't expect to be perfect. No one and nothing is."

He releases me and I hop back onto the stool, taking a sip of the boba tea I got before Ansel dropped me off.

"Oh, you've been to Watchtower?" Sage asks, rolling up his sleeves.

"Yeah, Ansel took me this weekend and we stopped there before he brought me home."

Sage stiffens, eyes narrowing.

"Ansel drove you home?"

I wipe condensation off the plastic cup. "He kind of insisted."

"Mhmm." His lips narrow.

"Sage," I laugh, "seriously, you have nothing to worry about."

"You've only known him a week and he's already driving you home," he grumbles turning to the fridge. He pulls out a can of Diet Coke and pops the top.

"He's becoming my friend. Isn't that what you want? For me to go to school? To make friends and be normal?"

He sighs, pinching the bridge of his nose. "Can I at least meet this guy? If you're going to be hanging out with him and he's driving you home I'd like to know him."

"I'm sure I can make that happen."

Ansel doesn't strike me as the type to care if he has to meet my brother.

"You couldn't have made a friend that's a girl?"

"Well, there's Sasha," I admit, picking up my phone. "I think we might be becoming friends too."

"Thank God."

"Can I order pizza now?"

He wiggles his fingers at me. "Yeah, get anything else you want too. I'm going to shower."

He passes behind me and I call a random pizza place a couple blocks away that delivers. I wonder if Sage is actually serious about learning to cook. Maybe when I brought it up before it got him thinking. In my class at school we haven't cooked yet, apparently we only do that once a quarter, and it's mostly been bookwork.

Sage and I are both such horrible cooks I can't imagine us actually being able to learn to make anything. But it could be worth a shot.

I finish my homework and when the pizza arrives I sign the receipt and take it. I also bought—well, technically Sage bought it—breadsticks and an order of chicken tenders.

I lay everything out and start making my plate. My stomach rumbles from the delicious aroma.

"I smell food!" Sage calls out from his room and I laugh to myself, because his words echo my thoughts. He might be seven years older than me, but we're eerily similar despite the age difference. "Ooh, you got chicken tenders." He rubs his hands together and grabs the plate I set out for him.

Sitting down on the couch, I curl my legs under me and dig into the pizza. It has arugula, prosciutto, and parmesan cheese layered on top.

"You pick the weirdest pizzas, D." Sage eyes mine as he sits down with three slices of his meat lovers.

"You're missing out. This is amazing."

He looks doubtful. "Looks more like a salad than a pizza to me."

He picks up the remote and turns the TV on, flipping through the channels before stopping on a rerun of Bones.

We don't say anything as we eat, which allows my thoughts to drift.

That's usually a dangerous thing, and tonight is no different.

I think about the fact that our mom isn't here. I think we've both come to terms with our dad's death since it's been so many years and he was sick, but our mom? She was killed in a horrendous way, taken by force from this world, and it's *wrong*. She should still be here, laughing. I should be back home with her in Oregon. But that's not the reality we have to live with.

The bites of pizza I've eaten sit heavy in my stomach.

I get up and set my half-eaten plate of food on the counter.

"D?" Sage asks, concern clouding his voice. "What's wrong?"

"I need to go for a walk."

"Dani—"

He starts to stand and I look over my shoulder at him. "Eat your dinner. I'm … I'll be fine. I need some fresh air."

"It's dark out, let me go with you."

"I'll only go around the block. Promise."

He opens his mouth to protest more, but I slip out the door.

He could follow me easily enough, but thankfully he doesn't. Pushing the button for the elevators, I wait. It dings merrily when it reaches the floor and I get in, pushing the button for the lobby.

Honestly, living in a condo, feels a lot like living in a hotel.

I hope one day, when I'm married and have kids, that we live on a farm. With chickens, goats, cows, all the animals and wide-open space. City living, while convenient, isn't for me.

I walk outside into the darkness. Thankfully, my phone is in my pocket if something should happen.

Inhaling the cold air into my lungs, I force myself to slow my steps. My thoughts are erratic and I need to calm them down along with the beating of my heart.

I should open up to Sage when my feelings overwhelm me, but I already feel like a big enough burden on him without adding more onto his shoulders.

The streets are bustling with activity, but no one pays me much attention. I turn the corner at the end of the long block, head bowed.

All I want, more than anything, is to feel normal but I know that's a reality I'll never live again. I have to learn to live this new existence. One where my mom is gone, my friends died, and evil people destroyed my feeling of safety. Nothing can give that back to me.

"Dani?"

My head shoots up so quickly I nearly get whiplash. "Mr. Taylor—oh my God is that a bear?!" I jump back in surprise.

Logically, my school counselor walking a bear on a leash makes no sense, but the dog is massive. The biggest I've ever seen. He doesn't seem real.

The giant brown bear—*dog*—sniffs at my body.

"No," Mr. Taylor chuckles, "he's a Newfoundland." He smiles down at the beast. "Zeppelin, say hi to Dani."

The dog's long pink tongue flicks out to lick my fingers.

"Zeppelin? Like Led Zeppelin?"

He laughs and starts walking back the way I came, so I'm forced to join him. "I've always had a thing for English bands."

"Interesting." I tuck that tidbit of information in the back of my mind. Learning about him makes it easier to open up. It feels as if we're on equal footing. I don't want anyone to know more about me than I know about them.

"What are you doing out here walking in the dark?" He pauses, letting the dog smell the sidewalk.

"I … uh … needed air."

"Air." He presses his lips together fighting a smile. "There wasn't enough oxygen inside?"

I shake my head, exhaling a breath. "No."

He frowns. "Wanna talk about it?"

This is why I've decided I like Mr. Taylor. He doesn't press me to talk.

I bend down to his massive dog, rubbing his head. I laugh when Zeppelin gives me a wet sloppy kiss on my cheek.

This is why dogs are wonderful. They don't judge. They give love easily. If only everyone was so kind to each other.

"I was thinking about my mom," I admit, my throat thick. I stare into the warm brown eyes of his dog. It's easier to speak to him than to look at Mr. Taylor.

"She should be here. I should be back home in Oregon having dinner with her. She should be scolding me for something I did or said, or begging me to stay home instead of going out."

I laugh humorlessly, and finally look up at him. "I regret that so much—that I didn't spend time with her. I took everything for granted, naively—no, selfishly— believing there would always be more time."

I stand up, my left side tingling all over as I do. I look Mr. Taylor in the eyes, putting my thoughts out there.

"She'll never tell me goodnight again. She'll never ask if I finished my homework. She won't see me graduate. She won't drop me off for my first day of college. She won't tell me to think twice about my decisions. She won't see me meet my future husband, or get married, or have kids. She won't see me build a life. And Sage…"

My throat closes up, tears spilling down my cheeks.

"He's twenty-five and he's stuck taking care of his little sister instead of living his life. I'm a burden to him. I know he says I'm not, but I am. I have to be."

I swallow thickly, wiping my tears away on the back of my hands. I feel Zeppelin nudge my legs.

"This shouldn't be my reality, but it fucking is. Some- times I think I should've died that day, the cafeteria ceiling my last vision of this goddamned world, but then I realize that day should've never happened at all and *no one* should've died. It makes me so sad and angry," I blubber, probably making no sense at this point, "and the feelings … they're going to choke me."

Mr. Taylor's blue eyes are soft, tender. "I don't have words to take all that away from you. I wish I did, but that isn't how it works. But you letting this out, letting yourself feel, *this* is what you need. Let yourself embrace the pain. It might not make much sense, but pain can heal you."

"I don't think there's healing from something like this."

He studies me, not like I'm broken, but as if I'm merely fascinating to him. "I promise there is."

I sniffle from my dreadful tears. "Pinky promise?"

He cracks the tiniest smile. "Pinky promise."

Holding out my pinky, I wait for him to twine his larger one around it, sealing the promise like a signature on a contract. Our fingers release, and for the second time ever, I hug Mr. Taylor.

I don't know what it is about him that makes me feel safe, comfortable, but it's something I haven't felt in a very long time.

I let him go and laugh a little. "God, I'm always snotting all over you. Why don't you tell me to take a hike?"

He smiles softly. "Somehow, I imagine that wouldn't work on you. You do what you want."

He sees so much about me without me ever saying a word.

"Let me walk you back."

I don't argue with him.

Instead, I let my school counselor walk me back to the building.

We get on the same elevator together.

I press 11.

He pushes 12.

I don't tell him, that one year ago, that was the day my whole life changed forever.

A coincidence, I tell myself, but in the back of my mind I think it's more.

CHAPTER THIRTEEN

"I DON'T UNDERSTAND WHY YOU EAT IN THE LIBRARY."

Sasha drops into the chair beside Ansel.

I stare across at her. It's been a full month at Aspen Lake High and my short-lived quiet lunch has grown to include not only Ansel, but his friend Seth, and Sasha.

I know Sasha plays tennis on the school team and has plenty of friends from that, but like Ansel, she's taken me under her wing.

Neither of them treats me like some sort of charity project considering they don't know what happened to me, but it still makes no sense why they're friends with me.

I've finally accepted that that's what they are to me.

Friends.

Although, I'm closer to Ansel than Sasha.

Sasha is a bit loud and obnoxious at times whereas Ansel is more easy-going. Honestly, I don't know what I'd do without them.

"You don't have to eat lunch in here," I remind her, munching on a chip.

She rolls her eyes, setting down her lunch. "Like I would make you eat with these losers." She nods her head at Ansel beside her and Seth at the end of the table between Ansel and me.

"Losers, huh?" Ansel raises a brow.

"Oh, shut up." She opens a ketchup packet and squirts some on her burger from the cafeteria. I wrinkle my nose in distaste. I hate ketchup. "We should do something this weekend."

Seth looks up and around at all of us before his eyes dart back down to his lunch. I don't know much about the guy beyond the fact that he's extremely shy and an artist like Ansel.

"Like what?" I ask when no one else says anything.

I'm not the queen of socialization by far, but it might be nice to do something as a group. For the most part, if I do spend time with someone outside of school it's Ansel.

"I don't know." She chews and swallows a bite of her food. "See a movie or something? Surely there's a Marvel movie we could see. Doesn't a new one come out every week?"

Ansel leans back in his chair, pointing at her with a pencil. "I wouldn't have pegged you for the superhero movie lover."

"I'm not. But there are plenty of hot guys in them."

Ansel rolls his eyes and looks at me while Seth lets out a quiet chuckle that turns into a cough like he didn't mean to find Sasha funny.

"What do you think, Meadows? Should we go see a mainstream superhero movie or do something else?"

I bite my lip, thinking of the dark, closed off room I'd be trapped in to see a movie and I know it would send me straight into a panic attack.

None of them know that side of me and I like it that

way. As long as they don't know it means I can pretend I'm normal for a short amount of time.

"No." I shake my head. "Let's do something else."

"What about a hike?" Ansel suggests. To Sasha he adds, "Meadows hasn't seen some of the fucking incredible views around here. She has no idea what she's missing out on."

Sasha purses her lips as she thinks. "Hmm, yeah, that could be fun. It'll be getting too cold for hiking soon enough."

Ansel grins. "The cold means skiing, which is even better."

Sasha nods in agreement. "Can't argue with you there."

"Wow, what a surprise."

She starts to retort but I snap my fingers, getting both of their attention.

"Why are we even talking about skiing? I thought we were going on a hike?"

"Have you ever skied?" Ansel tilts his head, appraising me.

Beside me Seth sinks down in his seat like he's trying to hide.

"No."

"Seriously?" His brows rise. "It's like a religion around here. I'm getting you on some skis soon, Meadows."

I'm sure soon isn't an exaggeration. We're a little less than a week away from October and already the weather has significantly cooled. Most days start in the 40s and might creep up to 65 degrees at the warmest. I'm used to this kind of weather, so I don't mind it. But it does mean snow is around the corner.

"So, hiking this weekend then?"

Ansel and Sasha both nod while Seth shakes his head.

He mumbles something about homework.

"Is Sunday okay?" Sasha asks, looking from Ansel to me. "I have a family dinner Saturday."

"That's good for me." It's not like I ever have plans. Sage and I do occasionally do something together, but he's finally spending more time with his friends, which I'm grateful for.

"Sunday works for me." Ansel puts a piece of chocolate in his mouth from his packed lunch. "I'll pick you up, Meadows."

"What about me?" Sasha jokes, batting her lashes at him.

"You can walk."

"So rude." She sticks her tongue out at him.

"Hey, if you need me to I can."

"Nah." She waves a hand dismissively. "I'll meet you guys there—Bell Canyon?"

"Yeah, that trail is nice."

"How far is it from here?" I ask, wadding up my trash since the bell is going to ring any second.

"About twenty-five minutes." Ansel stands up, slipping his messenger bag over his shoulders.

"It's gorgeous," Sasha gushes, her cheeks flushed. "The views are incredible. Plus, there's a picnic area and a waterfall. Ooh, I'll pack us a lunch." She claps her hands. "This is going to be fun."

The bell rings and we part ways.

I make my way through the halls, the crowd of students thinning when I start down the corridor that leads to Mr. Taylor's new office. It empties entirely before I round the corner down the final hall.

The door is ajar so I walk right in and drop my bag on the floor before sinking my body into the couch.

Mr. Taylor looks up from his computer. "Been a long

day?" He raises a dark brow at my slouched posture.

"A long day, month, year, take your pick."

He clicks around on the computer. "Time seems to stretch and slow when you're dealing with trauma and change."

I exhale. "It fucking sucks."

He looks across the desk at me.

"Sorry, I probably shouldn't cuss in front of a teacher."

He chuckles. "I'm not your teacher, and remember, everything we say in here is confidential. Besides, a cuss word is hardly something for me to get irritated over. That would be hypocritical."

"Have you ever dealt with trauma or change?"

He slides away from his desk, using the heels of his feet to drag the chair with him until he's in front of me.

"Yes, not to your extent, but there are different levels of everything."

"What kind of trauma?"

"When I was in my junior year of college I tore my ACL during a basketball game. Had to have surgery and physical therapy." He rolls up his pants leg, his calf firm and muscular, to reveal the long scar running down his knee. After I get a look at it he lowers the fabric back over his leg. "It ended my dreams of being a professional athlete. At the time it was devastating and I was pissed off at everything and everyone. But I realized that wasn't my path in life. I was meant to do other things."

"Like this?" I gesture around the room.

A high school guidance counselor seems pathetic next to dreams of the NBA.

"Yeah." He studies me, probably seeing the doubt in my eyes. "I know this seems like such a little dream compared to what I'd hoped to do before, but I'm happy."

I nod at his words, unable to wrap my head around it.

"What do you want to do when you graduate?"

I don't know why his question catches me off guard. It's something anyone should be asking someone my age, it's an answer I should have readily on the tip of my tongue, but I don't have one because...

"I don't know."

"What about college?"

"I'm applying." I pick a piece of lint off my black jeans and hold it between my fingers. "But I'm not sure I'll actually go."

Sage expects me to go—not that he'd ever force me, but it's what he did, it's what we always spoke of as a family. But things are different now, and the future I thought I'd have a year ago was ripped away, now the rest of it feels rocky too.

He leans back in his chair, like he's thinking carefully about what he's going to say.

"If you could do anything, be anything, what would you choose?"

I look away from him, out the window, to the light and freedom beyond.

"I don't know," I whisper, voice shaking.

My stomach churns and I hate how unhinged I feel. There's nothing tethering me to a future anymore. I'm lost, floating and adrift at sea with no one to pull me back to reality.

"Did you have plans before?" I can tell he's hesitant to ask, but it also has to be voiced.

Reluctantly I bring my gaze back to him.

"I was definitely going to college. I wanted to be a lawyer."

"Why don't you want that anymore?"

I swallow thickly past the giant lump lodged in my throat. "Because I can't fight for a system that's broken.

One that fails innocent people every fucking day. I refuse to be a part of that."

His blue eyes deepen and I swear he looks at me with something like respect.

"Now, I don't know what I want to be."

I can't even add *when I grow up* onto the end of that because I am grown up now. These decisions are upon me and I'm going to have to make some difficult choices soon.

"What's something that makes you happy?"

"Talking to you," I admit and his shoulders straighten.

"Really?" He seems so surprised.

"You don't pressure me to talk and you listen but don't judge. You don't try to force opinions on me like other people. When I was in the hospital most of the therapists they had me see wanted to tell me what they thought I should do. I know that's not what they're supposed to do, but it was happening. Maybe it was because I was a kid to them, but it always bothered me."

"What's something else that makes you happy?"

"My friends." I can't believe I'm admitting that, or even classifying them as my friends, but that's what they are. "Sage, my brother."

"So, people make you happy?"

"Yeah, seems that way. I miss running, though." I whisper the last part like a confession. "I hate myself for missing it as much as I do. I'll never run again and I wish I could forget about it."

He frowns slightly and I wonder if he's thinking about basketball, what it meant to him. He found something else he's passionate about so maybe the same can happen for me.

Like always, I can't talk about the deep stuff for long.

"How's Zeppelin?" I ask. I haven't run into his giant bear of a dog again, but I have bumped into him a few times going in or out of the building. It's such a huge place that it surprises me that I see him there as often as I do, but I guess it's not so crazy considering we have the same schedule.

His eyes narrow on me. He knows what I'm doing, moving the topic to something safer, but he always lets me. I've already told him far more than I've told anyone in the last almost year. I still haven't figured out why, but since talking to him makes me feel better I haven't pondered too much on it.

He rubs a hand over his thickly stubbled jaw. I bet he's the kind of guy who shaves and still has five o' clock shadow.

"Zeppelin is good. I feel bad for him though. A condo isn't exactly the best place for a dog his size. Hopefully one day I'll have more room for him."

"I want to live on land, own lots of acres," I admit, a wistful smile gracing my lips as I allow my mind to drift and envision a future that has the things I want. I suppose it's ironic how I know I want certain things but I still haven't figured out what I want to be. "Wide open space seems nice. It's crowded here."

"Yeah, it is," he agrees.

"Where'd you grow up?"

He pushes his dark hair from his eyes, leaning forward with his elbows on his knees. "Arkansas."

"And you ended up here?"

"Mhmm," he hums. "Moved here for college and fell in love with this place. The views are spectacular, and the mountains," he muses, tapping his index finger to his lips. "But one day I'll move outside the city."

"Sage moved here for college. He stayed too. Obviously." My eyes look around the room, at all the books. "You read a lot?"

He looks behind him at the shelves filled with rows of books of varying length and size. Most of them are work related I'm sure, but I notice some novels interspersed throughout.

He lets out a husky laugh and stands up, walking over to the shelves. "Yeah, a lot can be learned or enjoyed in the pages of a book." He looks over his shoulder at me. "Come here."

I listen to his command, standing at his side. Warmth radiates from his body and I try to ignore the zap of energy I feel in the air.

Can he feel it too?

Tilting my head back, he angles his down to look at me. His eyes trace my face before he looks me in the eye.

Yeah, he feels it too.

He clears his throat, pulling his eyes from me and back to the shelf.

I shouldn't be feeling this connection, this draw to be near him.

He's the *school* counselor.

He's practically a teacher.

He's almost eleven years older than me.

I repeat those sentences in my head in rapid-fire succession, but they don't calm my racing heart or lessen the heat growing in the room.

Mr. Taylor reaches for a book on the top shelf. He's so tall, probably six-three, which means he doesn't have to stretch far.

"Read this."

He places the book in my hands, careful not to touch my skin with any part of his.

I look down at the white cover with the blue eye.

"*1984* by George Orwell," I read, running my finger along the cover. I can tell its been read many times. The pages yellowed and the corners of the cover curling upwards. "Why this one?"

I know of the book, but never read it. I'm not a big reader as it is, and I can't imagine ever enjoying something like this.

"Because it's my favorite. I'm loaning it to you for you to read."

I try to hand it back to him. "No, I couldn't. I can go buy it."

He does touch me then.

His hands close around my flailing ones, holding them against the surface of the book. Those blue eyes of his, so similar to the one on the cover, render me frozen.

"I know you'll take care of it, Dani."

"Are you sure?" I blink up at him.

"If I wasn't sure I wouldn't have offered it in the first place."

"Well," I clear my throat, suddenly overcome with some kind of emotion I can't place, "thank you."

He releases my hands and I instantly miss the feel of his rough palms pressed against them, strong and sure.

I open the front cover and find his name scrawled in the corner in scratchy handwriting that's kind of sloppy but still legible.

Lachlan Matthew Taylor.

"Lachlan is a unique name." I close the cover of the book. I've seen his first name on his badge, but never asked him about it before. "Family name?"

He nods, straightening a model car on his shelf. I notice he's made this office space much more his own compared to the generic, no window, office I first stepped into.

"Named after my great-grandfather who immigrated from Scotland."

"It's a cool name."

He chuckles. "I guess that's a compliment coming from a girl named Dandelion Meadows."

He grins at me, his eyes crinkling in the corners.

Do not think about how handsome he is. Don't do it.

"Dandelion is not cool," I scoff, scanning more of the books on his shelves.

The heat in the room grows. "I think it is."

I close my eyes, trying not to think about the fact that I want him to touch me. To ghost his fingers along my shoulder. Cup my neck.

Stop!

Having a crush on him is one thing, he's one of the best looking guys—*men*—I've ever seen and I'm only human. But picturing him touching me? Kissing me? That's taking it too far.

"We'll agree to disagree on that one." I move away from the bookshelf and back behind his desk.

Space, I have to put space between us.

His eyes narrow on my shuffle as my left side decides now is the perfect time to give me a fit. The bell rings and I grab my backpack.

Holding the book up in one hand I say, "T-Thank you for the book. I'll bring it back after I read it."

"You're welcome. Dani—"

But he can't finish his thought as I scurry from the room, closing the door behind me. My leg is stiff and unyielding as I limp down the hall, holding my breath to see if he comes after me, to ask what's wrong, why I'm freaking out.

But he doesn't.

I'm thankful for it, but I also know he doesn't because he already knows the answer.

CHAPTER FOURTEEN

"WHERE ARE YOU GOING AGAIN?" SAGE ASKS AT MY back as I dig through the fridge for orange juice.

"Bell Canyon." I wrap my hand around the bottle and pull it out, pouring a glass for myself and Sage.

"Oh, yeah, I know that place. Been a few times. You'll like it." He sits down on one of the barstools. "Do you need a ride?"

I take a sip of juice and bite my lip. "Uh, actually Ansel will be picking me up in about fifteen minutes. We're going to grab breakfast first." His eyes narrow. "Sage," I groan, because I know he's about to go on a tangent.

His fingers tighten around his glass. "Tell that kid to park in the garage and come up here. I want to meet him."

"Sage, seriously? He's my friend. It's not like he's a serial killer."

His hazel eyes pierce me and he looks like he wishes he could knock some sense into me. "I have a right to meet who you're hanging out with, Dandelion."

I know he's pissed when he calls me by my first name.

"I'm sorry." I mean it too. "Balancing the fact that you're my brother but also my guardian isn't easy."

He exhales a weighted breath, shoving his fingers through his wavy golden brown tresses. "It's weird for me too, D." His hands flex into fists before he flattens them on the granite. "I don't want to fail you or mom and dad."

I've never stopped to think about what it must be like to be in his shoes, to be responsible for his younger sister now that there's no one else.

Sure, we have extended family, but our normal family unit is obliterated. I imagine this would be even more difficult if I were younger.

"I'll be more respectful," I whisper quietly.

He groans. "You're respectful, Dani. I think for you I'm your annoying, overprotective older brother, which is fine — I still am in a way, but I'm also basically your — " He stops, pressing his lips together.

His sorrow filled eyes meet mine.

We both know the word he kept himself from uttering.

Parent.

Sage is basically my *parent.*

But if that's true, then who does he have to look out for him?

"I'll text Ansel."

"Thank you."

"I better finish getting ready."

I can tell he's turning inward and I don't know how to pull him out of it.

I talk to Mr. Taylor, but who does Sage have to talk to?

Shooting a quick text to Ansel I slip my feet into a pair of tennis shoes I haven't worn in forever. I know a hike might be too much for my leg, but I want to try. I'm tired of being crippled, not by my leg but my fears.

It isn't long until Ansel tells me he's parking.

Walking down the hall, I find Sage in the spot I left him, sitting forlornly at the kitchen counter.

"Ansel is here, I told him I'd meet him in the lobby."

"Okay." His voice is deeper, gruff, and I know he's lost in things he can't say.

I close the door softly behind me so the click of the door is barely audible.

Down the elevator I go until I find Ansel waiting in the lobby, gaze on the ceiling. I can't blame him for staring. The blown glass chandeliers are pretty amazing. His dark hair is parted, brushed back from his forehead and he's dressed in basketball shorts and a plain tee. He almost doesn't look like himself. I'm used to seeing him in tight jeans, a white v-neck, and some sort of jacket even if it's above seventy degrees.

"Ansel," I call, and he drops his eyes from the ceiling.

A large smile softens the angles of his face when he sees me. "Your brother is giving you a hard time, huh?"

"Yeah," I admit as he closes the distance, "but I understand where he's coming from. You don't mind, do you?"

He shakes his head. "Does this place have room service?"

I laugh, pushing the elevator button. "Actually they do."

"Fuck, you're living the dream, Meadows. If I get hungry my mom tells me to figure it out. This would be convenient."

"But expensive. Still, my brother and I order out for the most part anyway."

"Right, you mentioned you can't cook. He can't either?"

"Nope."

We step onto the elevator when the doors finally slide open. "That's rough. My mom's a great cook."

"My mom was, too."

"Fuck, Meadows, I'm the worst."

I push the button for the eleventh floor.

Ansel leans his body against the side of the elevator, giving me a sympathetic look. "Forgive me?"

"There's nothing to forgive. I'm not going to be mad about a comment like that. You're allowed to talk about your mom."

His eyes soften and he looks at me fondly. I'm sure he's curious about what took my parents away from this earth, but he hasn't asked. Maybe he assumes since they're both gone it was a car accident or something. For now, I'll let him believe that if it is what he thinks. One day, hopefully I'll have the strength to tell him the truth, but I can't right now.

When the doors slide open I lead him silently down the hall.

"Your brother doesn't own a gun does he?" Ansel now looks a tiny bit afraid as he realizes my big brother waits for him beyond a door.

"No, no guns," I whisper, trying to block out the memories that are creeping from the recesses of my brain.

Swinging open the door I laugh when we find Sage leaning not-so-casually against the kitchen counter, glaring at the door.

I walk in first, letting Ansel use me as a shield.

"Sage, this is Ansel. Ansel, my brother Sage."

Ansel clears his throat and takes a step around me. "It's nice to meet you." He holds out a hand to my brother.

Sage looks at his hand like it's some exotic animal who could possibly bite him. His eyes drift up, taking in Ansel's appearance before staring daggers into him. "You don't touch my sister with that hand do you?"

I mentally slap my forehead.

"Uh…" Ansel looks back at me and then my brother. "N-No?"

"Why was that a question?" Sage's eyes narrow dangerously and I hold my breath, unsure whether I should laugh, or grab the back of Ansel's shirt and drag him out of here.

"I-I don't know? It shouldn't have been." Ansel straightens his shoulders, deciding not to cower beneath my brother's deadly look.

My brother makes some sort of disbelieving growl.

"Where exactly are you taking my sister?"

Ansel's expression silently asks me, *"Didn't you tell your brother?"*

I did, but my psycho brother wants to make sure our 'stories' match up.

"We're going to Bell Canyon. It's over near the Wasatch Boulevard neighborhood," Ansel replies, his throat bobbing from nerves.

Poor guy.

"I know where it is. Dani mentioned you were stopping for breakfast."

"Uh, yeah. I was going to take her to Penny Ann's Café."

Sage looks over Ansel's shoulder and points a finger at me. "Get the sour cream pancakes." His stare returns to Ansel and poor Ansel inhales a shaky breath. "You paying?"

"Yeah, I was planning on it."

Sage smiles and I hide behind my fingers. "D?" My hands drop. "Order the peanut butter pie, too."

"YOUR BROTHER IS INTENSE." Ansel pours half a bottle of syrup on his pancakes. He passes me the bottle when he's finished and I add a little to my own stack of hotcakes. They smell like heaven.

"He didn't use to be so bad," I admit, spearing the side of my fork into my breakfast. "But he's my guardian now, so he's extra cautious." Wrapping my lips around the fork I stifle a moan. "Oh my God, these are fantastic."

I let the pancake sit on my tongue, savoring the flavor. They're light and fluffy, like what I imagine eating a cloud would be like.

"Who knew bringing you to Penny Ann's would earn your brother's approval. I'm surprised he hasn't brought you here."

"He's busy."

"Works a lot?"

I chew and swallow another bite, certain I'll be coming back here soon because I've never had a breakfast this good before.

"He works for a tech company and kind of keeps everything running, so he leaves early and works pretty late."

"That's a bummer."

"It's okay. I like being by myself."

"Don't you get lonely?" He pauses, a piece of pancake dangling from his fork.

"Sometimes."

He frowns, shoveling the food into his mouth. Around the mouthful he says, "Well, you've always got me, Meadows."

"Thanks."

"I'm serious. Call me, beep me, if you wanna reach me."

"Okay, Kim Possible."

"You got the reference." He claps. My eyes narrow when he forms his hands around his mouth. "Yo, she got the reference," he shouts into the café, causing pretty much everyone to look at us.

"Shut up," I plead, hating the feel of so many eyes on me.

He chuckles, brushing his hair away from his forehead since it stubbornly falls in his eyes.

"Just trying to make you laugh, Meadows."

"Do I look like I'm laughing?" I point to my stoic face.

His smile falls. "Uh … no. Sorry."

"I don't like people looking at me."

His brows furrow in confusion. "Why?"

Because I'm afraid they'll see the pain. The hurt. The sadness. The fact that I'm broken.

"I don't like it. Shy, I guess."

He snorts, wiping his hands on a napkin. "You're not shy, Meadows."

He's right, I'm not, but it seemed like an easier explanation.

We finish our breakfast and order a pie to share.

"I'm going to the bathroom. I'll be right back."

He slides out of the booth and I send Sasha a text, making sure she's going to be at the trail on time. She sends me a selfie of her in gym clothes outside of her car.

Sasha: Leaving my house now! See you losers soon!

The waitress leaves the piece of pie on the table with two forks. "Here you go, sweetie. Enjoy."

Ansel comes around the corner from the bathroom, rubbing his hands together when he spots the pie. "Prepare to have your mind blown. If you thought the hot cakes were good, you haven't seen anything yet." He slides into the booth in his spot across from me. Picking up his fork, he holds it out. "Cheers, Meadows."

I clink my fork against his and dig in.

"Oh." I cover my mouth as I chew. "This is great."

Ansel chuckles. "I'm glad you like this. I'm a total foodie and Salt Lake has some great fucking cafés and restaurants."

"It definitely does. I guess that's a bonus of living in the city, there are a ton of unique eatery places."

"This isn't even the tip of the iceberg."

We finish every bite of the pie, and despite my protests Ansel pays the whole bill. He doesn't say it, but I'm pretty sure he's paranoid my brother is going to pop out from behind a booth or potted plant and yell at him if he doesn't.

We drive to the hiking trail, finding Sasha already waiting. She leans against her white hatchback in a black sports bra and black leggings. Her curly hair is braided down each side and a pair of small black sunglass sit on the end of her nose.

"Took you guys long enough," she remarks as we hop out.

"How long is this trail?" I ask, squinting from the sun. I raise my hand to shield my eyes.

"Two miles to the waterfall," Ansel replies, coming around the front of his car with a backpack strapped to his back.

"And another three from there to the reservoir, but I don't think we'll do that. Four miles total is enough for today." Sasha grabs the backpack at her feet and straps it on.

I suddenly feel unprepared now that I realize I'm the only one that doesn't have one.

"I packed sandwiches and water for when we get to the waterfall."

"I've got water too." Ansel points behind himself at his bag.

Sasha rolls her eyes behind her sunglasses. "Suck up."

"How does bringing water make me a suck up?" he grumbles as the three of us start up the trail.

I haven't tried anything like this since I was released from the rehabilitation clinic I was in after the hospital and I pray my leg holds up to the two mile trek up and back.

I gulp at the four-mile total distance, but decide to mentally tackle one portion at a time.

A year ago four miles would've been nothing. I could've run it without being winded. Now the idea of *walking* it threatens to give me a panic attack.

I do my best to silence my thoughts and focus on Ansel and Sasha's bickering.

"You knew I was bringing lunch. It should be implied I would cover the drink portion."

"You can never have too much water."

"True, but now you're carrying a backpack for no reason."

Ansel tries not to laugh as I lag behind the two of them, my limp slowing me down. "Would you like me to turn around and put my backpack in the car?" He comes to a complete stop and I stumble, trying not to bump into him. "Whoa, sorry, Meadows." His hand closes around my arm and he keeps me from falling on my face. "I should've looked behind me before I stopped."

"S'okay," I mutter, my cheeks heating. Not because he's touching me, but because he shouldn't have had to stop me from falling. When he came to a stop in front of me, I couldn't move in time because of my stupid leg.

I look down at my leg, feeling the anger bubble inside me. I allow myself to feel that emotion for only a moment before I shut it down and focus on gratefulness instead, because I'm lucky to even walk. My leg and foot might cause me trouble, but being able to stand and take one single step is a blessing I'm thankful for.

The two of them cease their bickering and we follow the trail up.

I find my breath constantly lodged in my throat at the stunning views. It's more beautiful than I expected. It's becoming obvious to me why my brother fell in love with Salt Lake and never left.

Eventually we reach the waterfall. I try not to think about the fact that it takes us nearly an hour because of me, both of them slowing down until we all walked side by side, me in the middle.

The waterfall is larger than I expected, surrounded by trees beginning to turn shades of red, orange, and yellow. There's a large rocky outcropping and that's where we set up our picnic, careful to avoid the slippery moss in some areas.

"This is peanut butter and jelly," Ansel accuses, unwrapping his sandwich.

Sasha rolls her eyes, blowing a piece of loose hair from her eyes. "What did you expect? Steak and potatoes? You're lucky you got that."

She passes me a wrapped sandwich. "Ignore Ansel," I tell her, glaring at him, "he eats peanut butter and jelly three times a week."

Ansel grins at me. "Paying attention to what I eat, Meadows?"

"Only because you annoy me."

He laughs, knowing he doesn't annoy me, at least not anymore.

"You guys should date," Sasha announces, chewing a bite of her sandwich. Ansel and I look at her stone-faced. "What?" She blinks innocently. "You two bicker like an old married couple already. Just make it official."

I feel Ansel's eyes drift to me, but I ignore his look. "We're friends. I'm not interested in a relationship."

Ansel clears his throat. "Why ruin a good thing?"

Sasha looks at us like we're dumb. "Whatever you say." I swear there's relief in her eyes, though.

"This is beautiful." I look around at all the trees and waterfall. I'm not sure our exact elevation, but it doesn't matter because the views are incredible.

"There are a lot of places like this around here. I kind of get lost in my own world and forget they exist." Ansel picks a piece of his crust off and Sasha glares at him.

"Stop ruining my masterpiece. I worked hard on that."

Ansel looks up when he realizes she's talking to him. "Uh...?"

"Boys," she mutters to me. "So, incredibly dumb."

"I'm dumb for picking crust off?" He looks genuinely offended.

"No, your species as a whole is dumb."

"We're from the same species, Sasha. Just different genders."

"You sure about that?" she argues, her eyes narrowed and deadly.

If she thinks Ansel and I argue like an old married couple, I don't know what she calls what they do.

We finish our lunch, pack everything up, and make the descent.

I hug Sasha goodbye and hop in Ansel's car so he can drive me home.

After a thirty-minute drive, he pulls up in front of the

108

building. For some reason I find myself reluctant to leave him, which is completely irrational and silly.

"Je te verrai demain, Meadows."

I'll see you tomorrow.

"Thanks for the ride."

I slip out of his car and walk into the building toward the elevator.

Pushing the button I stand there and wait, trying to ignore the pain radiating from my left hip down my leg. I overdid it today and I'm going to pay for it. But I enjoyed myself too much to care.

The doors slide open and I'm promptly pushed to the ground by a giant brown floof. A large wet pink tongue licks my face all the way from the bottom of my chin to the top of my forehead.

"Zeppelin! Down, boy. You can't run over strangers." The giant dog is pulled off me and I giggle, wiping my face free of drool. "Oh, Dani, it's you." An easy smile transforms his face, softening his features.

"Hey, Lachlan."

I wince.

Lachlan — you're calling him Lachlan now?

"Sorry about Zeppelin." I'm surprised he doesn't correct me and tell me to call him Mr. Taylor. I breathe a sigh of relief at that. "Here, let me help you up."

He extends his hand and I take it. Normally I would refuse, but with my left side practically numb I do need the help. Behind him the elevator has closed and the arrows lit up above it show that it's going back up and I'll have to wait for another.

"Don't worry about him. I like this guy." I pet the dog on top of his head. I still can't get over his size. I'm five-foot-five and when he sits on his hind legs he's nearly as tall as me.

"Still, he shouldn't be knocking people over." He wraps the leash around his right hand a few times. "Having a good weekend?"

"Not too bad."

"Good." He swallows, pressing his lips together. "Have you started the book?"

I shake my head, crossing my arms over my chest. The gesture pushes my boobs together and his eyes, unbidden, drop to the swells and then away. I don't miss the subtle tick in his jaw. I let my arms drop.

"I'm planning to start it tonight."

"I'll be curious to hear what you think of it."

I smile. A book discussion with Lachlan sounds nice, despite the fact I'll probably hate his favorite book.

Leaning around him I push the button for another elevator. "Don't get too excited. I'll probably rip it apart."

His smile grows and he takes a couple of steps backward, toward the exit. "Disagreements can be healthy. Opinions are vital."

The elevator dings and I point at the open doors. "I'll … uh … see you."

His blue eyes are bright, so bright they twinkle like the stars in the sky. I think I could get lost in them forever and it wouldn't bother me.

"See you later, Dani."

I step onto the elevator and let out a shaky breath the second they close.

Ansel told me he'd see me tomorrow and I felt nothing. No excitement, no fluttering in my belly, not a thing.

But when Lachlan said it?

I felt it all.

CHAPTER FIFTEEN

IT'S THE MIDDLE OF THE NIGHT AND THE LIGHTS IN MY bedroom are dimmed. I lay curled on my side under the covers holding onto the pages of the book like a life preserver. I can't believe what I'm reading. My mouth is open in horror as I turn page after page, shuddering at how scarily realistic this book is to today.

I only meant to read a few chapters before attempting to go to sleep, but I know that won't be happening. I have to know how it ends.

If I knew exactly where Lachlan lived in the building, I'd be banging on his door right about now demanding answers. But since knocking on every door on floor twelve isn't possible I continue reading.

An hour later it's three in the morning and I lay wide-eyed staring at the ceiling. The finished book lays on my chest, my fingers clasped overtop of it.

I feel angry, infuriated, and if I didn't know this book was so special to him I would throw it at the wall and punch it for good measure.

There's little to no chance I'll get any sleep tonight,

which isn't all that unusual. I throw the covers off my body and place the book on my dresser before tiptoeing from my bedroom into the kitchen. I make myself a bowl of cereal and sit down on the couch, turning the TV on. It's a bunch of infomercials, and since I'm not interested in buying a vacuum cleaner or a thingamajig, I end up putting a movie on.

Spooning the cereal in my mouth, I can't seem to get rid of the ache in my chest from the novel. I've never read anything that's made me feel so much. True, I'm mostly pissed off, but I know this is a book that I'll think of for years to come.

Finishing my cereal, I clean the bowl before I lay back down on the couch, pulling the blanket over me. I keep the volume on the TV low enough that it shouldn't wake up Sage.

By some miracle, I manage to drift off to sleep and wake up around six. I get ready for school, eat a quick breakfast of a muffin from the grocery store, and say goodbye to Sage when he leaves for work.

I place Lachlan's copy of *1984* carefully into my backpack. It's in rough shape so it's not like a bent page would be my fault, but for some reason I find it necessary to treat it with reverence.

Heading downstairs, I wait for the school bus. When it arrives I hop on and walk all the way to the back, sitting down and putting my earphones in. Fire and the Flood plays by Vance Joy and I lean my head against the glass as the bus starts moving.

I probably should get a car. I got the all clear to drive after I was released from the rehabilitation center, but I've been too scared. It's one of those things I can't seem to explain, the fear. It's completely irrational, but that doesn't mean it isn't a real thing.

After a couple more stops, the bus heads for the school.

I wait for it to clear off before I stand up, walking down the narrow aisle.

"Have a nice day," I say to the bus driver before stepping off.

My morning passes in mind-numbing slowness. All I can think about is my everyday period with Lachlan. I itch to talk to him about the story. I can't decide whether I enjoyed it or hated it, but I guess it doesn't matter since it's affected me so deeply.

"You seem distracted," Ansel remarks, wadding up his trash from lunch and tossing it in the can a few feet away. His hands are stained with pencil from his latest project of an intricate and twisting abstract collection of shapes.

"I have a lot on my mind." My own sketchpad is tucked into my bag, untouched today since my brain is focused elsewhere. I haven't been using it much during lunch anyway since we're now joined by Sasha and Seth.

"Wanna talk about it?" He holds the door open for me out into the busy hall. Sasha and Seth left out the opposite end of the library.

"No, I'm good."

"Where are you headed? I can walk you there." He angles his head down, waiting for my answer.

My fingers tighten around my backpack straps. "Uh … no that's okay."

He smiles. "I have time."

"No, really." I tuck my hair behind my ear. "It's way out of the way. I better hurry."

I push through the bodies of students, leaving a confused Ansel behind.

I don't want him and Sasha to know where I have to go every day. They'll ask questions, questions I won't answer, and if they happen to Google my name then they'll find the truth staring them in the face. A truth I don't want them, or anyone else here to know. I'm not ashamed of what happened. It was a horrible reality I've had to face, still have to every single day, but that doesn't mean I want to be confronted with stares or difficult questions I don't want to answer.

My feet pound on the stairs and I tamp down the rising panic inside me.

Ansel and Sasha have become my friends and they're going to want to know more about me. It's inevitable, friends typically know everything about you.

The halls begin to empty as most people reach their classes. Turning down the hall that leads to Lachlan's office I do my best to force my worrisome thoughts away. For a moment, I want to be normal again. I want to talk about this book, and not about how I feel or my memories or how fucked up I am.

The door is cracked when I reach his office and I push it open.

"Dani." His smile transforms his face and my stomach flip-flops.

I have a crush on my school counselor. If that doesn't say trouble I don't know what does.

"Hey," I breathe, trying to mask my relief at being near him.

Something about his presence calms my insides in a way nothing or no one else can. It doesn't make sense and I can't explain it, but I guess that's how feelings work.

"Did you start the book?" His eyes are lit up with excitement.

"Actually, I finished it." I dig into my backpack, placing the worn and well-loved copy on his desk.

He picks it up and looks from it to me in surprise. "You finished it."

"Yep." I plop onto the loveseat, my backpack at my feet.

"What'd you think?" He sounds hesitant but hopeful.

"It made me mad."

Laughter explodes out of him. "It makes you think, huh?"

"He's tortured and in the end he loves Big Brother! It was all for nothing! What was the purpose of it?"

His long fingers wrap around the book and he picks it up, looking it over like he's never seen it before. "It's a message warning against the dangers of totalitarianism. I find it enlightening. So, you hated it then?"

"I don't know how I feel about it, I don't love it but I'm not quite sure I hated it. I'll never forget it, though."

He runs his finger along the cover reverently. "That's what makes it my favorite. It's the kind of story that turns in my mind long after I've finished it."

"How many times have you read it?"

He looks down at the weathered pages. "I don't know. Five, maybe six, times."

"Wow." My eyes widen in surprise. "I've never read a book more than once."

"Would you like to read another?" He stands, walking over to the far right of his bookshelf unit. He puts *1984* away and waits for me to join him.

"I don't know." I slip my hands into the back pockets of my jeans, rocking on my heels. "Is everything you have to recommend so depressing?"

His lips turn down in thought, his eyes scanning his shelves. "Do you think you'd like a thriller? Something psychologically twisty?"

I shrug, picking up a picture frame from his shelf.

"Maybe. I'm not exactly a hearts and flowers kind of a girl so a mind-fuck sounds right up my alley."

His lips quirk into a smile.

I study the picture inside the frame. It's a younger Lachlan, maybe nineteen or so dressed for a game of golf, the club held in his hand. He stands beside a man that could be his twin if it weren't for his more auburn hair compared to Lachlan's jet black. But the facial structure, shape of the lips, and eye color are all the same.

"Your dad?"

He looks down at the image with a fond smile. "Yeah." I put the frame back where I found it, scanning more of the knick-knacks there. "Dani?" Lachlan prompts me and I force my gaze from the shelves. "I have a book I think you'd like, but it's at home. You can drop by and get it if you want?"

I know he's not inviting me over, but my body warms anyway, humming with some sort of electricity.

"That'd be great."

His arm brushes mine as he moves, picking up a frame higher up and handing it to me. "My mom, sister, dad, and grandpa." He points out each individual surrounding him at his college graduation. My heart pangs because I'll never have a picture like this. His mom has raven black hair that hangs down in long waves and an olive complexion. His sister is a perfect mix between both parents. Her hair is dark, but not as dark as Lachlan's, with hints of red.

"Your mom and sister are beautiful. You're close with your family?"

"Very. I have a ton of cousins too that all feel like siblings."

"What are their names?" I point to his family in the picture.

"My mom is Catriona, my sister is Isla, my dad is Niall, and my grandpa is Leith."

"Wow," I hand the frame back to him, "that's a lot of unique names."

"My Scottish roots run deep."

He stretches up to put the picture back on the top shelf, his shirt stretched taut over his muscular form. I bite down on my lip to keep from making some sort of noise.

"Do you own a kilt?" I blurt.

He straightens, lips twitching with laughter. "I do actually."

I thought picturing Lachlan in a kilt would help calm my racing heart but it's having the complete opposite effect.

Not cool, heart. Not fucking cool.

"It's the family tartan pattern and everything." The way his eyes sparkle I'm not sure if he's being serious or having fun with me.

"Have you ever been to Scotland?"

Only inches separate our figures. Neither of us has made any move to return to a seated position. I wonder if he notices the way our bodies seem to gravitate toward one another without any thought, at least on my part. Yes, I'm attracted to him, I think any sane female would be, but I wouldn't purposely cross a line. My body, his too, doesn't seem to know there is one.

He shakes his head. "No, not yet. It's on my bucket list."

"I've never given much thought to things I'd like to do before I die," I murmur softly, finding looking at him suddenly difficult. I swallow stiffly. "I guess I should now, you know, after everything." My heavy sigh echoes through the room, hanging there in weighted suspension.

"Can you think of one thing you might want to do?"

"Traveling would be nice, I guess. Mostly I want…"

He turns, his body angling downward toward mine in an almost protective gesture. "You want?" I don't know if he realizes it, but his voice is husky. It makes my center clench and ache in a way it never has before. I had a few brief relationships before the shooting, one that lasted nearly a year. So, it's not like I'm totally inexperienced. But none of those guys ever made my body react like this. "Dani?" His tongue slides out the smallest bit, wetting his lips.

I don't want to admit what I have to say, because I don't want him to think it's about him, but he's giving me no choice.

"I want to fall in love." His eyes darken in color, but I don't miss the small step he takes away from me. "When I was lying on that floor, wet from my own blood, screams echoing everywhere, I knew I was going to die. The only thing I regretted in those brief moments before I lost consciousness was the fact that I was never going to know real, soul-crushing, forever love. I wasn't going to walk down the aisle to the man of my dreams. I wasn't going to hold my child in my arms. I wasn't going to grow old with someone." I have to pause and catch my breath, also allowing myself to take a moment to keep the tears at bay. "It was the simple, ordinary things I was going to miss out on that hurt the most. At the end of the day, those things might seem mundane or unnecessary to some, but to me it was *all* I wanted. So, I guess if I was going to put anything on my bucket list, falling in love would be at the top."

His stare deepens and I feel it all the way down to the tips of my toes.

A shiver starts at the base of my spine, working its way up my body.

"Are you cold?" He sounds concerned.

I shake my head. "No, not cold."

The bell rings.

I hate that Godforsaken bell. I want to stay here, in this little cocoon a bit longer.

Lachlan steps around me, back to his desk. "Let me write down my apartment number." He scrawls a couple numbers down and passes me the blue sticky note. "For the book." He clears his throat. I feel like he's trying to remind me, or perhaps himself, that this isn't a social call.

"Thanks."

I take the note from him and grab my backpack.

"I'll see you after school," I say, heading for the door.

He doesn't reply and I don't look back, because something tells me I don't want to see the expression on his face.

CHAPTER SIXTEEN

I PACE THE LENGTH OF SAGE'S CONDO. THE BLUE POST-it note is pressed into a crinkled ball in the palm of my right hand.

1206.

Lachlan is a floor above me in 1206. It's silly for me to be freaking out over this. He's going to give me a book. That's it. Nothing more. But my heart doesn't seem to realize that and keeps leaping every time I think of him.

"This is ridiculous!"

If anyone could see me right now I look like an insane person.

I stomp to the door, closing it roughly behind me. The sound of it echoes down the hall.

I'm starting to sweat and that's not an attractive look at all.

I push the button for the elevator and cross my arms over my chest. I rock back and forth unsteadily, trying to expunge the adrenaline from my body in some small way.

It's a book," I remind myself. *You're picking up a book from him. That's all.*

Stepping into the elevator I continue to give myself an internal pep talk.

When the doors open I walk down the hall to Lachlan's apartment, pausing outside to take a moment to center myself.

Once I'm confident that I'm as okay as I'm going to get, I raise my fist and knock.

I don't have to wait long before the door opens and he stands on the other side looking way too hot to be the equivalent of a teacher. He wears a shirt with the sleeves cut off and loose gym shorts. His skin is still slick with sweat, his hair damp with it too.

"Hey," he grins, my stomach flipping, "come on in, I'll grab the book."

He steps aside and waves me in when I keep standing there. The door closes and I stand there looking at what's basically the twin of my brother's place, only reversed with the kitchen and bedrooms on my left instead of right.

My eyes flicker over him trying and failing to find anything unattractive about him. He picks up a bottle of water and takes a long swallow, his throat muscles constricting.

Me being here is bound to be breaking some sort of school rule, but Lachlan doesn't seem to have thought of that. Probably because to him I'm a kid. An eighteen-year-old kid who whines to him about her problems five days a week. He doesn't have the thoughts that I'm having—like his bedroom is only a few feet away. He surely doesn't wonder what my skin would feel like against his.

He's the only person that I've felt comfortable *really* speaking to about what happened and that's formed some sort of connection that's making me have those kinds of thoughts. I don't even understand why out of everyone I've spoken to since the tragedy that it's him I open up to.

There's some unexplainable gut feeling inside me when it comes to Lachlan. Maybe if I were older, more experienced, I would have words for it.

"You don't mind if I let Zeppelin out, do you? He's in my room."

My heart ticks faster when he mentions his room.

"I don't mind." I try to inconspicuously stuff the wadded up post-it into my back pocket, suddenly afraid I might drop it. I want to keep it.

"Give me a sec."

He finishes slurping down all sixteen-point-nine ounces of water, wiping his mouth with the back of his tanned hand.

His steps resonate softly down the hall, a plain gray rug softening his steps.

Seconds later there's a bark and Zeppelin races down the hall, crashing into me.

I wrap my arms around him and hug the mammoth dog back.

"Zep, man! Be careful with her!" Lachlan calls from his bedroom.

"You're a good boy, aren't you?" I scratch Zeppelin behind his ears. He gives me a kiss, covering me in doggy drool. I frown because it's kind of gross, but the dog is too sweet to let it bother me for long.

We never had a dog growing up. I always wanted one, but my mom said we didn't have time, which I understood with her working and all my extra-curricular activities. But maybe Sage would let me get a dog?

I stand up when I hear Lachlan's feet padding down the hall. Zeppelin rubs his head against my leg, begging for more attention.

"Here's that book."

He offers the hardback to me and I take it, studying

the cover—dark colors, eyes peeking through, very creepy vibes.

"It's not horror, right? I don't like to be scared."

He chuckles, grabbing the back of one of the stools at his breakfast bar. "No. It'll keep you guessing, but it's not scary."

I arch a brow at him. "Pinky promise?"

He chuckles. "Pinky promise."

He shakes his head, wrapping his pinky around mine when I offer it.

Stepping away, I lift the book in the air, using it to point at him. "Thanks. I'll uh ... thanks." *Why the hell am I so awkward?* I tuck a piece of hair behind my ear. "I'm going to go now."

He chuckles, letting go of the chair to open the door for me. "I'll see you tomorrow, Dani."

I back out the door facing him. I force myself to turn around and go to the elevator. Before I reach the end of the hall I glance over my shoulder.

He's still watching me, his eyes narrowed, his face troubled. When he catches me looking he schools his features and closes the door.

———

"That smells amazing. I'm starving." The door clicks closed behind Sage and I look up from the couch where I'm curled up with the book. It was slow to start, but now it has me guessing.

"I totally forgot I ordered food."

When it arrived twenty minutes ago I went back to reading, too consumed by the story to even eat. Besides, I always try to wait for Sage.

Laying the book on the coffee table, I shove the blanket off and stand.

"You're reading?" Sage asks, his normally deep tone spiking a little high in surprise.

"Um, yeah."

"Where'd you get the book?" The question is muffled from a fry he's pulled from one of the takeout boxes.

I panic for a brief second. "A friend loaned it to me."

"That's cool." He rolls up his sleeves. "God, I'm fucking starving. I'm going to eat before I shower."

He pulls out plates and starts piling food on them. I ordered us each fries and a BLT. He passes one to me, already stuffing a bite of sandwich in his mouth.

"Did you have lunch?"

He shakes his head. "No, didn't have time. There was a mishap and some computers stopped working. It was chaos."

"That sounds rough."

"It was." He plops on the couch with a tired groan.

I join him, pushing the book out of his reach in case he picks it up. I'm not sure if he'll know Lachlan's name if he opens it, but I don't want to risk it. I'll have to ask him why he writes his name in his books, because I don't get it.

"I'm sorry you have so many hours by yourself before I come home."

"S'okay." I cover my mouth as I chew. "It gives me a chance to do my homework and relax."

Actually, I mostly sit around bored out of my mind. My homework is usually finished at school so when I get home there's nothing to do but watch TV or sketch. But I don't love drawing like Ansel does and I can only do it for a little while before I get frustrated with my pathetic lines that barely form a shape. Today, the book has helped occupy my time. I might have to give more books a chance.

"That's true." Sage sounds relieved, and I'm glad I can alleviate the burden from his shoulders even if it's a white lie. "This is really good. Where'd you order it from?"

"It was some sandwich shop a couple miles away. I had Uber Eats deliver it."

"Hmm," he hums, most of his meal devoured while mine is barely touched.

"I think I'm going to go eat in my room if that's okay?" He looks over at me in surprise since I never ask to leave. "I kind of want to read."

"That's fine, D."

I get up with my plate of food and the book. I pause at the edge of the hallway before I disappear completely from his sight. "Sage?" He looks up. "I love you."

He smiles, his hazel eyes softening with something like gratitude. It's such a simple thing to tell someone you love them, but those three little words can mean so much.

"I love you too, sis."

CHAPTER SEVENTEEN

"You have strange taste in books."

I drop the heavy, five-hundred-plus page, book onto Lachlan's desk. He jumps, not having heard me come in since he was so absorbed in something on the computer. I'm sure he has a ton to do with seniors gearing up for college applications to go out.

"You didn't like it?" He closes the browser and takes the book. He flips through the pages before closing it with a snap.

"I loved it. But that doesn't mean it isn't strange. I mean, I know multiple personalities are a real thing and all but this was intense."

He leans back in his chair, his easy smile making my stomach flip-flop.

"What'd you think of the end?"

"I thought she should go to jail." I forgo the couch and perch my butt on the end of his desk. He scoots back so he can see me better. "She knew what her personalities were doing, but she didn't stop Jackie when *she* killed that elderly gentleman. She let her. Going to a psych ward and not facing prison felt like she got off too easy."

"But she couldn't control her personalities when they were in possession," he argues.

"That's true," I oblige, giving in on that point. "But Jackie's personality was still there, like Loretta and Mae. Jackie will come back. Shouldn't she be punished?"

"Isn't she still punished though? She's trapped in a psych ward for the rest of her existence, and Keeley, the real person and main personality, *isn't* insane and isn't *technically* a murder."

"Ugh," I groan, standing to pace the length of his office. "It hurts my brain."

He laughs and the chair squeaks as he gets up. "I think a good healthy debate is fun."

"That's what old people say."

Something flickers in his eyes and he looks away, clasping his hands behind his back. "Want something else to read?"

"Might as well." I shrug, stopping beside him. His cologne fills my nose. It's something fresh, like bergamot, with a hint of something light like water and oak. "It distracts me," I admit softly. My head bows with shame. I don't know why I feel ashamed of that fact, but I do. "It's an escape."

"Reading is a good escape," he agrees, looking down at me. His blue eyes hold me in my spot, unable to move or even breathe for a second. "It's nice to be lost in another world for a little while. But we can't forget reality forever."

His tone holds a warning, reminding me that I have to choose to face that day head on, the months that followed of pain and rehabilitation.

When I don't respond he clears his throat. "You'll have

to come by my place again this afternoon. I'll set some aside this weekend to bring here."

"Actually, can I pick it up tomorrow morning?" I hedge, biting my lip.

His head tilts questioningly. "Plans tonight?"

It's the first Friday in forever that I've actually had plans. "Yeah, I'm going out with my friends." First to the football game and then the after party where I'm sure there will be copious amounts of alcohol and other illegal and illicit behavior.

"Mhmm." He nods, licking his lips as he fights a grin. He's not stupid, I'm sure he knows what's going on tonight. There have been plenty of whispers in the hallway. "Enjoy yourself. Stop by around nine. I try to sleep in on the weekend, if that's too early I'll be home around four."

"That's sleeping in?"

He chuckles, crossing the room and looking out the window. "I'm normally up at five-thirty every morning, so if I can sleep in until seven or eight it's a miracle."

"What are you doing tomorrow? You said you wouldn't be back until four." I wince as soon as the words leave my lips. I sound nosy as fuck and it's none of my business. He's an adult, the school guidance counselor, someone in charge of me and I have no right to expect an answer but I still want one. I don't know why, he probably has a girlfriend, it'd be crazy if he didn't. He's hot, nice, smart. He probably has plans with her tomorrow, some woman beautiful enough to be a Victoria's Secret model. "Don't answer that," I say suddenly. "That was ... not my business. I shouldn't have asked."

He laughs, clearly amused at my unease. His eyes crinkle at the corners. "I'm going out with friends. We're going to the batting cages."

"That sounds fun." I exhale a breath I didn't know I was holding, all because he didn't mention a girlfriend.

I'm insane.

The bell rings. It always cuts my time with him short. Fifty minutes five days a week is all I get and I'm beginning to treasure every second of it. In these precious minutes I feel like myself again, the girl I was before I was struck by tragedy and unimaginable pain. Sure, that part of me is still there, and he's the one person I feel like I can confide in, but even when I do he never pities me.

I'm just ... Dani.

CHAPTER EIGHTEEN

"Does your brother know where you're going?" Ansel asks with amusement when I slide into the passenger seat of his car.

"He knows I'm going to the football game and I'll be home late. I'm sure he suspects, but he won't be too mad. I mean, he partied all through high school. It's not like he can judge."

"Whatever you say, I don't want to be murdered."

"He's not going to kill you." I roll my eyes, pulling the seatbelt over my body. "Maim you, possibly."

Ansel looks at me wide-eyed and I laugh.

"Not funny, Meadows," he grumbles, pulling away from the building.

"A little funny." I hold my thumb and forefinger up a tiny bit apart.

The drive to school isn't too long, but the lot is already full. We end up parking a block or so over in a grocery store parking lot and walking. People pass by with golf carts to pick up people and take them to the football field, so we hop on.

Sasha: Where are you guys? Waiting at the ticket booth.

Me: Almost there.

Sasha: Hurrrrrry.

The golf cart drops us off and we meet Sasha at the ticket booth, paying our five dollars so we can get in.

The dull roar of the growing crowd sends a shiver of fear through me.

Closing my eyes I take a moment to center myself. I can't spend the rest of my existence hiding in Sage's condo. I have to get out here and *live*. If I don't face my fears they'll drown me.

I follow them through an archway and around the track to the stands. The end of the field nearest the scoreboard is painted red with white letters spelling ALH for Aspen Lake High.

We make our way up through the stands, scooting past students and parents until we get to a spot where all three of us can sit somewhat comfortably.

I shiver, tucking my hands into the front pouch of my hoodie.

"Cold?" Sasha asks. "I brought hot apple cider." I open my mouth to ask where the heck she has it, when she pulls out a thermos from her bag and plastic cups. "Want some, Ansel?"

"Sure."

She fills up a cup and I pass it to him before taking one for myself.

I take a sip, and it's surprisingly good with the smallest hint of alcohol.

"Do you normally carry around hot apple cider?"

She shrugs, pulling a red beanie out with the school's mascot, a jaguar, on it. She puts it on, tugging it over her ears.

"Only to football games. It gets cold. Gotta have something to heat you up."

"Do you make it?"

"My mom does. But I add a little somethin'-somethin' if you know what I mean." She winks, taking a sip of her own cup.

"Yep, I do." I finish mine and she fills it up again. "How much do you have in there?"

"Two thermoses. Games can get long," she reasons, lifting her shoulders and letting them drop.

Ansel holds his cup out so she'll top him off.

The game starts, but I don't pay much attention. I'm more entertained by Sasha and Ansel's commentary and cheers.

After Ansel's second drink he stops, since he's driving Sasha and me to the party.

The game ends, our team winning, and the atmosphere is buzzing with life. My body flushes from the excitement, or maybe it's from whatever Sasha put in the apple cider.

We ride a golf cart back over to the parking lot and get in Ansel's car. Sasha piles in the back. "Do you have anything on you I can smoke?"

"Always. You have any money?" Ansel asks her, looking in the rearview mirror before pulling his seatbelt over his body.

She passes her hand up through the middle console and hands him some cash. He pockets the money and pulls something from his pocket.

She takes it and soon the vehicle is filled with something that smells vaguely of grass and it grows foggy inside when she exhales some smoke.

"Where's this party exactly?"

"It's this old abandoned farm out on Todd Hilton's family's property," Ansel explains, turning into the street.

The red of the stoplight reflects into the car, bathing him in an eerie glow.

"You do realize I have no idea who that is, right?"

Ansel chuckles, turning left when the light changes. "He's on the football team. Don't ask me what position he plays. I don't pay attention to that shit."

I laugh, looking out the window at the passing buildings. "Wasn't going to. I don't care."

Fifteen or so minutes later he turns onto a dirt road. Five more after that and he parks in a field with a bunch of other cars. We get out and walk toward the barn. There are lights strung through the inside that reflect out here and there's a bonfire and keg to the right of it. As we walk toward the bigger crowd people continually stop Ansel to score a deal. It's amusing, but still surprises me because Ansel doesn't strike me as the drug dealer type. Sure, he's not selling the hard stuff like cocaine or meth, but that doesn't change the facts of what he is.

Sasha shrieks and runs off to mingle with some of her tennis buddies. I stay by Ansel's side and he pours me some beer from the keg, passing me the red Solo cup. So typical.

Ansel bumps fists with some guys and I hang back, not quite comfortable. I went to a couple parties back ... well, *before*, but they've never really been my thing.

I suppose I've only gone, even now, in an effort to fit in. I feel even less a part of things now. All of this, it's so simple and what's expected, but I've seen the hard facts of life and now this seems dumb and a waste of time.

Ansel introduces me to people as we move along. I promptly forget all their names. Not on purpose, but because the minute I'm hearing it from one, another person is greeting me.

"Do all these people go to our school?" I hiss to Ansel

under my breath. I know our school is big, but this seems like an awful lot of people to be at a party for it to only be our school.

He laughs, pocketing more cash. He's bound to have made at least a grand in the short time we've been here. "Nah, a lot of the other nearby schools show up here too."

"I'm sorry for just hanging around you." I take a sip of warm, stale beer.

Ansel's pale blue eyes sear into me and I stop walking. "You don't have to apologize for wanting to be near me, Meadows." He cracks a grin and I laugh. "I'm fucking awesome." He sobers and clears his throat. "Seriously, you're my friend, so don't say you're sorry. Friends hang out together."

"I ... I feel like I'm in your way." I duck my head when I admit it out loud. It sounds silly once the words are out there.

"Definitely not." He tosses an arm around my shoulders. "Come on, Meadows, let's have some fun."

———

IT's a couple hours before we load up and leave the party. Sasha catches a ride with some of her other friends, so it's only Ansel and me.

"Did you have fun?" he asks, maneuvering his car out around all the other parked vehicles.

"Actually, I did." Ansel ended up pulling me onto the makeshift dance floor inside the barn. Perspiration still clings to my skin from the sweat I worked up.

"Good." He grins, driving down the dark dirt road.

"I'm tired, though," I admit. "I might actually sleep tonight." I barely utter the last part.

"Don't sleep much?"

I shake my head before I realize he can't see me. "No, not usually. Too much on my mind."

"Want to talk about it?"

"No."

"That's okay."

The rest of the drive is quiet and I thank him for the ride as I head inside the building and up to the eleventh floor. Sage is wide-awake, sitting on the couch. A cooking show hums in the background, which makes me laugh.

"You didn't have to wait up." I close and lock the door behind me.

"It's kind of late."

"I know."

It's well after one.

He exhales a heavy sigh. "Next time, come home sooner."

"Are you giving me a curfew?" I stifle a laugh. I'm entirely amused, not angry.

"Yes. Midnight on Fridays and Saturdays and if you go out on the other days you have to be home by ten."

"Okay."

He looks surprised. "You're not going to fight me on this?"

"No. Should I?"

"I would have," he admits reluctantly. I sit on the couch beside him and he sniffs the air. "Have you been smoking pot?" he accuses, looking murderous.

"Not me, but other people were."

I conveniently leave out the part about Ansel supplying most of it.

"Fuck, Dani," he stands up and paces in front of the coffee table, nearly stepping on my toes, "I don't want you hanging out with those kinds of people."

I snort. "Yeah, Sage, because we know you've been the poster boy for good decisions."

He narrows his eyes. "Exactly, don't be like me."

"I didn't do anything wrong," I grumble.

He musses his hair. "I ... fuck, I worry about you, D. You're all I have left. I want to keep you safe."

I stand up, wrapping my arms around his middle. He hugs me back. "I love you, Sage, but I'm trying ... trying to live, to be normal."

"Now I feel like an ass." He lets me go and looks down at me, crossing his arms over his chest. "Be careful and from now on if you go to a party call me to get you. I don't want that kid driving you anymore."

"That kid has a name." My lips twitch with mirth.

Sage rolls his eyes and bites out, "Ansel."

I laugh and hug him one last time before I shower, change into my PJs, and climb in bed. My body is tired and I fall right to sleep, but I dream, good dreams for the first time in nearly a year.

Of blue eyes and clasped hands and tangled sheets.

Of things I cannot have.

CHAPTER NINETEEN

Knocking on Lachlan's door at five minutes until nine I step back and wait for him to answer. I hear barking on the other side of the door and a bang when Zeppelin must catapult his entire body into the door.

"Zep, man, cool it!"

With that exclamation the door swings open and my breath catches as I see a glimpse of tan, smooth, muscled stomach a second before he pulls his shirt down over his body. My eyes travel his body, from the gray sleep shorts, to his bare feet, back up to the dimple in his chin, thick scruff, shimmering blue eyes, and sleep mussed hair.

Zeppelin pokes his head around Lachlan's leg, tongue hanging out of his mouth.

"I've got that book for you," he says, waving me inside. I inhale the smell of freshly cooked bacon and my stomach growls. Lachlan looks over his shoulder with a tiny boyish grin. "Hungry?"

"Yeah," I admit, looking around his home. I didn't pay too much attention to his décor and personal touches when I stopped by Monday. He's painted it warm white compared to Sage's stark white, and where Sage's place plays off the black, white, and chrome of the kitchen, Lachlan has opted for rich wood accents and leather furniture. There's a rumpled worn patchwork quilt piled on the couch like he was lying there sometime before I knocked.

He notices where I'm looking and says, "My gran made that for me when I was four. It's old and falling apart, but…"

"It's sentimental and you love it," I finish for him, reaching down to pet Zeppelin. The large dog rubs his whole body against me and I swear he hums.

He smiles and nods. "Exactly." He picks up a book from the counter, handing it to me. I study the cover, dark blue with a geometric pattern that has images of a castle peeking through. "It's fantasy, I thought you could try another genre. You're welcome to stay for breakfast if you want." He bites his lip, brows furrowing. Maybe he realizes that it wouldn't be normal for a school counselor to invite his student for breakfast, but he doesn't take it back.

"That's okay, I need to … um … get back."

I kind of do, since I snuck out when Sage went down the street to grab coffee and muffins for our breakfast.

"You can take some with you if you want. There's plenty. I kind of go overboard when I cook."

"You cook a lot?"

"I do. I enjoy it."

"I can't cook," I admit with a quiet laugh. "Neither can my brother. We're supposed to take lessons later today, actually."

Sage finally scheduled us for culinary classes and while I'm looking forward to spending time with my brother that doesn't involve moping around his condo, I'm mildly afraid of the chaos we're about to bring to some unsuspecting chef.

Lachlan laughs. "It's not all that difficult and it's fun to experiment with flavors. See what works together and what doesn't," he muses, pulling a carton of eggs from the refrigerator.

"Tell that to the gelatinous eggs my brother makes and the pasta water I burned."

He stifles a laugh. "You burned water?"

"It's an oxymoron, I know, but it happened."

"Interesting."

I want to keep standing there talking to him.

"So, fantasy, huh?" I find myself saying.

"Yeah," he turns the stove on, adding some olive oil to a skillet, "I mostly read psychological thrillers, but I've been known to dabble in other genres. In my opinion you can learn anything from any book."

"That so?" I open the book, flipping through the pages.

He shrugs, cracking an egg into the hot skillet. "Anyone who says you can't doesn't have an open mind."

"Interesting," I muse, and his lips twitch. I realize it's because he used the same word for me. "I better get going." I bend down and love on Zeppelin.

"I'll bring some more books to school so I'll have them when you finish. That one is a series, and I have the rest if you like it." He points at the book clasped against my chest.

"Okay, I'll let you know. Bye."

I wave and let myself out so he can finish cooking his breakfast.

I take the stairs instead of the elevator down to Sage's floor. I slip inside the apartment and close the door, locking it behind me. I've barely set the book on my bedside table when I hear the door open with Sage's arrival.

Fixing my hair since it's fallen out of the messy bun I put it in when I woke up, I walk out to the kitchen.

"Cinnamon dolce latte." Sage passes me the Starbucks cup. "And a red eye for me." He takes a sip, letting out a low whistle. "That's good, and much needed."

He's not lying. The dark circles under his eyes worry me. I know it's partly my fault and I silently vow to be a better sister to him. I don't like adding to his burdens.

I open the box with four muffins from a local bakery, grabbing a blueberry one for myself. Sage picks the banana one.

I pull a piece off, popping it into my mouth. "Mmm, that's yummy."

Sage chuckles. "It should be, they make them fresh. I had to wait in line for fifteen minutes, and that was a short wait compared to the usual. But that's why it took me so long to get back."

"Where exactly are we taking this cooking class?" I ask, taking another bite. Sage surprised me with the news this morning when I woke up that he'd scheduled it for today but forgot to tell me. He tacked on that he hoped I didn't have plans with Ansel I had to cancel. His dislike for my friend is funny to me since Sage was kind of a player when he was in high school, and Ansel truly is only a friend to me. I wonder what he'd think if I told him I had a crush on my guidance counselor. Something tells me he'd kill Lachlan, even though Lachlan is innocent and probably not aware of my scandalous thoughts.

"It's at the Salt Lake Culinary Education. They offer one-time classes for adults and kids, so that seems like what we need."

"I think we might need more than one." I tear the rest of my muffin apart stuffing some in my mouth. Sage eats his like a cupcake, gulping large bites down.

"We probably will, but I figured we'd start with one. My schedule is about to get even busier and I'll have to work on the weekends a lot." He looks down at the counter, his shoulders tight.

I wish he would quit, figure out something that makes him happy, but he feels like this is what he has to do. Maybe it is. After all, I'm eighteen and still in school, so I can't really relate to being in his position. I know I miss his smile, his real smile. But he probably misses the same thing about me.

"You work too much." I brush the crumbs left on the counter from my muffin into my hand and throw them away.

"I have to." He rests his head in his hand, every bit of his muffin gone. He sips at his coffee, watching me.

"What?" Something tells me he's going to ask me something I don't want to answer.

"Have you thought about where you're applying for college? Applications need to go out in, what, six weeks?"

"Something like that." A heavy sigh wracks my body.

"You didn't answer the question." He raises a brow, but doesn't sound accusatory about it.

"I haven't given it much, thought." Leaning my hip against the side of the counter, I look down, drawing idle designs in the granite top.

"You need to make up your mind. You could ... you could go back to Portland, if you wanted."

My head shoots up. "I'm not going back there, Sage."

My heart speeds up at the very thought of it. I can't go back to that city, that state, and not think of what happened. I know our mom and dad are buried there, but I can't even think of going to visit them. That whole place holds too many bad memories now. I can't look at anything the same way again.

His lips turn down sympathetically and he shoves his right hand roughly through his wavy hair. It's getting a little long and he needs to get it cut.

"I'm sorry, D. I shouldn't have suggested it." He looses a long breath.

"Maybe I won't go to college," I whisper, hopping up on the counter. I twist my fingers together, swinging my legs back and forth.

"Dani, you have to go to college."

I glare at him. "I don't *have* to do anything, Sage. Maybe I want to roam the world, discover who I am, I can't do that in a classroom."

"Is that what you want?"

"I don't know what I want!" I shout, tears pricking my eyes. "Don't you get that? I don't know *anything* anymore. I don't know who I am or how I fit in this world."

Sage's face falls. "Dandelion." It takes him three steps to be in front of me. He wraps his arms around my shaking body, hugging me tight. Resting his chin on top of my head, he says, "I didn't know this was bothering you so much."

"A year ago a track scholarship was in the bag to pretty much any school I wanted to go to," I sniffle, letting him go so I can dry my face. "You know I was set on a path toward law school, but I can't do that anymore. I would *hate* it. Our justice system sucks and I would be miserable. I don't want to spend every single day hating my job and my life. Life's too short for that."

He presses his lips together and I think maybe I've offended him. "I won't pressure you to do something you don't want to do. But please, send out applications, that way when the time comes you can make the choice to go or not."

"You're not mad?" My voice shakes slightly.

"A little," he admits, his eyes softening. "But not for the reasons you think."

"What do you mean?"

"I wish I was as strong as you," is all he says, before grabbing his coffee and walking down the hall to his bedroom.

CHAPTER TWENTY

"WE ARE NOT GOOD AT THIS, LIKE AT ALL." I LOOK
down at the explosion of ingredients everywhere; the
liquid spilled on the counters, flour that somehow ended
up on the ceiling, and a dish that looks edible but not
presentable which was half the goal.

"Let's try it."

I cut a bite of Parmesan chicken and put it in my
mouth hesitantly, doubtful that Sage and I could make
anything taste edible.

"Oh, that's good," I admit, closing my eyes as the
flavor explodes over my tongue.

"We did a good job, D." Sage is all smiles, genuine
smiles, and it makes my heart happy to see him enjoying
something so simple as making a decent meal with me.

I try the garlic-roasted potatoes next and nearly melt
on the floor from the sheer delectableness of them.

"Hey," I begin around a mouthful, "I think this means
we can cook."

Sage chuckles. "Yeah, with instructions and help from
them." He points his fork at our two teachers who are

checking up on some of the other groups of people. It's mostly young couples madly in love or families who are trying to get their kids involved in the kitchen.

"That's true." I feel sad about it, because I could eat this every day.

We eat our dish and box up the leftovers, saying goodbye before we head out.

"Is there anything else you want to do today?" Sage asks, climbing in his Nissan Maxima.

I shake my head. "I kind of want to have a lazy day. Just go home and get in my pajamas and vegetate."

His laughter fills the car and makes me smile. It's good to hear. "That sounds pretty fucking amazing to me. I need all the rest I can get."

I want to talk to him about quitting again, I know he could and be fine temporarily until he gets something else, but he's stubborn and will never listen so I keep my mouth shut for now.

Sage parks in the garage beneath the building and we take the elevator up.

"Want to watch a movie?" He tosses his keys onto the kitchen counter, shrugging out of his lightweight jacket.

"I'm actually going to paint my nails and start a new book."

"Still reading?" He quirks a brow, clearly surprised.

"I'm starting to love it."

"Good for you. There's a library two blocks away if you ever wanted to go."

"Oh, okay, that's good to know." I doubt I'll be using it as long as Lachlan continues to lend me his favorite books, but you never know.

Reaching my room, I kick off my shoes and change into a pair of green lounge pants and a black tank top. I put some music on and pick out a new nail polish color, choosing a minty green called Vintage. I don't really understand how Vintage relates to mint green. Like wouldn't EncourgeMint Green have been better? But the nail polish was a gift, so I can't except everyone to pick them based on names like I do.

Sitting on the floor I paint my nails carefully, making sure I don't get any on my skin. It's the perfectionist in me. I let them dry before standing up. My leg has gone numb by the time I do and I hobble over to my bed.

Stretching out, I curl under the blankets, grabbing the book from beside my bed. Lying on my side, I open it up and begin to read.

———

FINISHING the book in record time, I toss it aside, outraged at the cliffhanger ending. I *need* to know what happens next, whether or not Icarus actually killed Lizzie or not. Picking it back up, I storm out of my room.

"Where are you going?" Sage sits up on the couch looking concerned.

"I need the second book," I grumble, shoving my feet into a pair of my shoes by the door.

"Now? It's like ten o' clock."

"Yes, now." I close the door behind me, letting it shut a little too loudly.

I take the stairs up to Lachlan's floor, too impatient to wait for the elevator. Banging my fist against his door, I wait for him to answer.

Zeppelin barks loudly and incessantly. I hear Lachlan shush him seconds before the door swings open.

"Dani?" He blurts in surprise, not expecting me to show up back at his place so late. I push my way inside and he lets the door close, turning around to face me. "What's wrong? Are you okay?"

His genuine concern surprises me. "I finished it." I hold the five hundred plus page tome out to him. "That ending ... you're cruel. I need the next one. Like, right now."

He laughs, his throat flexing as he does. "You finished already, huh?"

"It's amazing," I gush, clutching the book to my chest. "I couldn't put it down. But seriously, Lachlan, I need to know what happens next." Narrowing my eyes on him, I ignore Zeppelin sniffing at my clothes for the moment.

His grin brightens his face. Slowly coming out of my haze over the unexpected ending, I realize that he's not wearing a shirt, and only a pair of very loose, low hanging cotton shorts, and a navy blue baseball cap turned around backwards.

My throat tightens and I realize I shouldn't be looking at him like ... like I have some sort of crush or find him attractive. He's the last person I should ever be attracted to. He's eleven years older than me, he works for the school, he's my *counselor* for God's sake.

"What's wrong?" His smile slips a tiny bit.

"N-Nothing," I stutter, tucking a piece of hair behind my ear.

"You loved the book then?"

"Way more than the other two," I admit, biting my lip. "Those were kind of serious and this had more action and romance. Who doesn't love a little kissing?"

He chuckles, scratching the dark stubble on his chin. "I love your honesty."

I stand there, rocking awkwardly on my feet. I look down only to realize I've worn Sage's massive slippers.

Zeppelin nudges his nose against my leg, demanding attention.

"So, yeah," I ramble, "could I borrow the next one?"

I crouch down and pet Zeppelin. He showers me with kisses and I can't help but laugh because it tickles.

Lachlan watches us. I try to ignore the way his gaze feels on me, but it's impossible.

I like him looking.

Sure, it's innocent, but my brain doesn't want to accept that.

"I'll get the next two for you." He steps around me and Zeppelin. I watch him disappear down the hall to his bedroom.

The dog nudges me with his nose. "Sorry," I laugh, petting him again.

Lachlan isn't gone a minute before he returns with the next two in the series, setting them on the counter. "It's a seven book series. If you happen to finish both before Monday text me and I can drop them by." My face pales and he chuckles. "Or you can come get them."

"Um, sure. That'd be great." I stand up much to Zeppelin's dismay. He whimpers, pawing at the ground. "I don't have your number, though."

He walks into his kitchen and swipes his phone off the counter. He passes it to me. "Put your number in. I'll send you a text so you have mine."

He looks at ease, like my presence doesn't affect him at all. It makes me question if maybe I imagined the whole thing yesterday where we shared a look. I put my name and phone number in, handing him back his phone.

"Thanks, Lachlan." He passes me the books and I look down at the covers, letting my hair fall forward to hide my face. "I ... you don't know what it has meant to me to be able to get lost in someone else's world for a little while."

The very tip of his finger touches my chin, urging me to lift my head. As soon as I do, he drops his hand. "I'm happy it's been able to help you, Dani."

"I hated reading before." I glide my finger over the raised parts on the hardcover book. "Now it's not so bad." I give Zeppelin one last pat on the head. "I'm sorry for bothering you."

"You're not bothering me, Dani."

I look at him from beneath my lashes. There's a part of me that's confident, who doesn't care to speak her mind, but then there's this other part of me that hesitates.

"I should be."

His brows furrow in confusion at my words. I don't elaborate, though. Lachlan isn't stupid and he'll figure out my meaning on his own.

"Thanks, again." I brush past him, ignoring the shiver that courses up my spine when my arm brushes his.

I return to Sage's with the books clasped in my arms.

"Where did you go?" he demands. "You can't walk out like that with half-answers, Dandelion."

"I went to go borrow more books from my friend." I lock the door and turn around, holding them up so he can see them.

He looks suspicious. "Your friend lives nearby?"

"In the building."

"Who is this friend? It's not Ansel is it?" He looks murderous at the very idea.

"No." I shake my head.

"Who, then? I only hear you talk about Ansel and someone named Sasha. Is it Sasha, then?"

I rack my brain for a name and end up blurting, "Taylor." It's not a total lie. "My friend Taylor lives in the building."

"Oh." His shoulders slack. "A girl. Okay, then."

Yeah. A girl.

Taylor could easily be a boy's name, but I'll let him believe what he wants, it's not like I'm going to tell him it's *Mr.* Taylor.

"I'm going to bed now."

He waves me on.

Closing my bedroom door behind me I set the books beside my bed before climbing under the covers. My phone vibrates and I dig around beneath all the blankets until I finally locate it.

My heart leaps when I see the text on the screen.

Unknown number: It's Lachlan. Goodnight, Dani.

CHAPTER TWENTY-ONE

"DO YOU HAVE ANY PLANS FOR HALLOWEEN?" ANSEL pulls out the chair across from me, sitting down. Sasha and Seth haven't arrived yet.

"It's almost Halloween?" I blurt, looking up from my sketchpad. The rough drawing of an old oak tree looks like something a kindergartener would do.

Ansel frowns, tilting his head. "Um, yeah, Meadows. It's this Friday."

Time has been passing in a blur. I suppose that's a good thing. It means my mind hasn't been on things it shouldn't be.

"Clearly, you don't have plans then. There's a party, you're going."

"I don't want to go."

"Meadows," he says in a low voice, "all you've been doing lately is reading and drawing. It's time for you to get out. I'll drive you home today. We'll pick up some costumes before I drop you off."

"What would I even dress up as?"

Sasha plops into the seat beside Ansel. "Ooh, Halloween party planning? I'm going as a sexy kitten."

Ansel gives her an irritated look. "How predictable."

She flips her curly blonde hair over her shoulder, covertly giving him the finger as she does.

Seth snickers and I jump, looking over at him and wondering when the hell he slipped in. I would think the guy is a ghost if Ansel and Sasha didn't very clearly see him as well.

"What are you going as?" Sasha counters, pursing her lips. "A brooding artist? You already fake that every day, maybe you should pick something a little easier to pull off, like a judgmental prick."

His dark brows narrow. "What crawled up your ass and died?"

"Nothing." She looks at her French-manicured nails.

"La pute," Ansel mutters under his breath, shaking his head.

I press my lips together, trying not to laugh. Something tells me Sasha likes Ansel, but he's completely oblivious.

Lunch is tense after that, and Ansel doesn't mention Halloween or the party again, but I know he hasn't forgotten about it either.

The four of us end up parting ways early and I take the rest of my lunch downstairs with me. I sit beside Lachlan's closed office door. Normally I barge right on in, but since there are still fifteen minutes until the lunch period ends I decide to wait.

Digging out my unfinished lunch I start to eat.

A few minutes pass and I nearly jump out of my skin when the door opens with a whoosh. My bag of chips falls off my lap, a few spilling out onto the white and gray linoleum floor.

"Oh, fu—sorry. Dani? You're early."

I look up, up, up Lachlan's impossibly tall frame. He stands there looking like a Dior model in a pair of black slacks and white button down. There's a small stack of papers in his hands. His Clark Kent glasses start sliding down his nose and he pushes them back up. He's never worn his glasses to school before.

"Yeah, sorry." I pick up the fallen chips from the ground, stuffing them in a Ziplock baggy. "Lunch got kind of awkward so we disbanded early."

His lips turn down. "Want to talk about it?"

I shake my head. "It was dumb."

"Well, you can head on in. I have to go to the office to make copies of these." He flips through the papers in his hands. "I should only be five minutes."

"Okay." I smile up at him, watching as he passes and turns at the end of the hall.

Gathering up my stuff, I move into his office and finish my lunch, disposing of the trash in the bin in the corner.

He returns, leaving a trail of his cologne in his wake, an even larger stack of papers in his hands than before. He lays them on his desk, sticking his stapler on top, and grabs his chair, pulling it out from behind the desk before sitting down. He lets out a deep breath once he does and smiles.

"Other than lunch how has your day been?"

"Uneventful. Dull. Boring. Should I continue?" I joke, rubbing my left hand on the rough fabric covering the loveseat.

"No," he grins, chuckling lightly, "I think I got the gist." His blue eyes sparkle like the stars in the night sky. I'm fascinated by his blue hues. They're the brightest eyes I've ever seen and such a unique color.

"No contacts today."

He looks confused for a second before he reaches up and feels his glasses. "Oh, yeah. My eyes were bothering me." He leans back in his chair, cocking his head to the side as he studies me. Normally when someone looks at me the way he is I feel like some rare specimen being inspected beneath a microscope—something to be studied, probed, figured out like an alien from another world. But I don't feel that way at all this time. There's something slightly different in the way he studies me, a warmth, like there's some part of him that feels the deep-seated ache and pain living inside me and he wants to thaw it. "What would make your day better?"

"Huh?" I'm taken by surprise with his question.

"You said school is dull and boring for you. What would make it better?"

I look out the window like I always do when I need a moment to gather my thoughts. It's like a part of me thinks that all the answers I need are out there and I just have to spot them, take them, and give them to him.

"I don't know." I shiver with fear, a fear that's rooted into the pit of my stomach. "I don't know anything anymore."

When I finally have the courage to draw my eyes back to his, they're soft, looking at me not with pity but understanding.

"It's okay not to know."

"I'm scared about what comes after," I admit, nibbling my bottom lip. "What happens when I leave here? The real world isn't a forgiving place."

"This is the real world too, Dani."

"I know, but school feels like a small isolated space compared to what's out there. I used to think I knew where I fit into things, what my role was, I don't know anything anymore. That's something that was taken from me that day."

He doesn't ask which day. He knows.

He taps his finger against his lips. There's still no pity in his eyes, which I'm thankful for. I don't want to be pitied, I want to be understood.

"I don't know what makes me happy." I tug on the sleeve of my shirt, rubbing the fabric between my thumb and forefinger. "I know we can't be happy all the time, that's impossible, but…"

"But what?" he prompts when I grow quiet for too long.

Exhaling a breath, I lift my shoulders, letting them fall. "I don't want to *exist*, I want to live. That's all I've been doing since it happened. Existing, not living." My throat grows thick and I hold my breath, damming back my tears. I don't want to cry. I want to be strong.

"And you think you have to be happy to be living?"

I angle my head. "Don't you? If you're not happy, aren't you merely wandering through life? You're there, but you're not *there*, if you know what I mean." I pause, rubbing my lips together. "Forget it, I'm probably not making any sense."

"No, I hear what you're saying. Do you…" He clears his throat and leans forward, clasping his hands together. His twin azure blue pools stare deep into my soul, seeing everything. "Do you want to talk about that day, Dani?"

My heart speeds up at his question.

Do I want to talk about that day? Do I want to relive that nightmare?

I feel my body lock up, all the tension freezing my muscles.

"Dani?" His voice seems to echo as if he's down a long hall. "Are you okay?"

I close my eyes, clenching my fists as I try to block out the memories. The eerie silence punctuated by pops and random screams. Fear coating my tongue like some sticky syrup I couldn't swallow.

Too much. It's all too much.

"Dani?"

His hand touches mine and it sends sparks all the way up my arm.

I grab my backpack, pushing past him and out the door.

I run down the hall, his steps echoing after mine. I dash into the first place I can find that I know he won't follow — the girls bathroom.

I push inside and into a stall. My backpack falls off my arm onto the floor and I close the toilet lid. Sitting down I draw my legs up to my chest. Tears burn my eyes and I sniffle.

He knocks on the door, still saying my name.

"Dani."

His voice is near, too near.

I look up and through blurry eyes find him standing in front of the stall since I didn't bother to lock it.

"Dani," he breathes my name with worry. I bite my lip so hard I taste blood. He steps fully into the stall in front of me. His large frame is overwhelming and blocks the view of the restroom. "I've got you."

He crouches down and wraps his big strong arms around my small body.

"I've got you, Dani," he repeats, holding me together.

I sniffle into his shirt.

He holds me tight and I close my eyes.

I silently wish he could hold me like this forever, his arms the glue for all my broken pieces.

CHAPTER TWENTY-TWO

"Meadows! Wait, up!" I glance over my shoulder to find Ansel jogging after me. He comes to a stop beside me, exhaling a soft chuckle. "I told you I would take you home today. We have to get costumes. Did you forget?"

I press a hand to my head. "Y-Yeah, sorry, I did forget. I have a headache."

I don't actually, but I do feel exhausted. All I want to do is go home and crawl into my bed.

"Well, fuck." His shoulders sag. He stuffs his hands in his pockets, canting his head to the side. "I can still take you home. It'll be faster."

"You really don't have to." I look away from him. It hurts to look into his carefree genuine smiling face when I feel the way I do.

"It's not a big deal, Meadows." He takes my hand, tugging me toward the student lot. I know if I said a flat out no, he'd let me catch the bus, but frankly I don't want to be alone. Not that I'd be alone on a bus, per se, but I don't know those people.

Ansel opens the passenger door for me and I set my backpack between my feet.

He gets in the car, the engine rattling to life. He doesn't back out right away. He turns slowly to face me, his face etched with concern.

"Are you okay?"

His question catches me off guard, for some reason I'm not expecting it.

"Of course I'm okay." The words splutter out of me in disbelief, like I can't believe he'd think I'm *not* okay.

"Meadows," he voices my name softly and takes my hand gently in his, "at the risk of being punched in the face, you don't look or sound okay."

It's like his words break me and I burst into tears. They flood out of me, soaking my cheeks, and poor Ansel looks shocked.

"Fuck, do you want to talk about it?"

I shake my head. "No, not here."

"Where?"

"Take me home, *please.*" My voice cracks and I wipe madly at my wet cheeks, trying to dry up the evidence of my pain and suffering. It's like subconsciously I think if I can hide it then it doesn't exist.

Ansel backs out of the parking spot and gets in the line to exit the school lot.

It feels like it takes a whole week before he parks at the condo. We head upstairs in silence as I ponder how I explain this — do I lie or give him the truth?

A lie would be easier, but also messy, and Ansel feels like a true friend. I *shouldn't* lie to him. But the truth is scary.

I unlock the door and step inside, waiting for Ansel to join me. He looks around uneasily.

"Your brother isn't home is he?"

I laugh, shaking my head. "No. He works late. He won't be home for hours. Scared of him?"

He swallows. "No, not at all." His voice squeaks.

Putting off the inevitable, I open the fridge and pull out two water bottles. I toss one at Ansel. He catches it easily.

He unscrews the top and takes a sip before facing me. I still haven't left the kitchen, keeping the bar as a barrier between us. I'm not afraid of Ansel, but I am afraid of myself.

"What is it, Meadows? You're acting funny and you seem really upset."

I squeeze the water bottle a little too tight and the plastic protests, making an ungodly noise.

"You're not pregnant, are you?"

My head shoots up and I let out a disbelieving laugh. "No, not pregnant."

Ansel paces a bit, giving me time to gather my thoughts. I must be taking too long because after a bit he says, "You don't have to tell me. Whatever it is ... I wouldn't force you to share anything with me that you don't want to. Seriously, tell me to go and I will."

His pale blue eyes ring with sincerity. I believe one hundred percent that he'd walk out this door right now if I asked him to.

Leaving the water bottle on the counter, I move into the living room and sit on the couch. I pat the space beside me and Ansel sits down.

Like earlier today, I rub my fingers against the sleeve of my shirt.

"You know I live with my brother..."

"Yeah?" He angles his head, wondering where I'm going with this.

"Our dad passed away from cancer when we were younger—"

"Fuck, I'm sorry, Meadows."

I hold up a hand, shaking my head. "That's not the worst of it."

He quiets, sitting back slightly and squaring his shoulders like he's preparing for some sort of battle. I wish I could use him as a shield, but no one and nothing can protect me from the memories. I have to fight them on my own.

"I moved here from the Portland area to live with Sage, because…" I close my eyes. I need to rip it off like a Band-Aid, put it all out there. "There … there was a shooting at my old school."

His lips part and I see he's racking his brain, probably remembering nearly a year ago when it was all over the news for a few days. He wets his lips with his tongue, his eyes sad and haunted, probably imagining what that day felt like for me.

"My mom worked at the school. She didn't make it. A lot of people didn't make it." I lean against the side of the couch, my body suddenly too heavy to hold up.

He places his hand over mine.

"Dani—" I shake my head, quieting him.

"It was pure evil in its rawest form. I've … I've never known fear like that. I don't want to go into details about that day or how I feel about it, but that's … that's why I do certain things the way I do. It's why sometimes I act funny or get upset for no reason. I hate rooms with no windows and the cafeteria," I swallow thickly, "I don't want to be in there any longer than I have to."

"Why?" As soon as the question leaves him he looks apologetic, but doesn't take it back.

"Because that's where I was when I was shot."

Ansel flinches, his pallor paling a few shades. "Fuck, Meadows. I—"

I hold my hands up, silencing him once more. "Seriously, Ansel, I don't want to hear apologies and I don't want to talk about it any further than this right now. Maybe one day, but not now," I plead quietly with him. I feel the tears beginning to sting my eyes, but I don't want to cry. Crying has gotten me nowhere.

His lips thin like he's holding himself back from saying something. Finally, he nods, his eyes soft and understanding.

"Please, don't tell Sasha. Don't tell anyone," I beg.

If people know I'll have to deal with the stares, the whispers, and I know I'm too fragile to handle it. I'm only so strong.

"I won't, but…"

I glare at him.

"You should tell Sasha."

"Sasha is a blabber mouth." I stare him down, waiting for him to protest.

He doesn't. "Yeah, you're right, but that doesn't mean as your *friend* she doesn't deserve to know."

"Maybe one day." It's the most agreement he'll get from me.

"Thank you for telling me."

I know he means it.

CHAPTER TWENTY-THREE

SOMEHOW, I FIND MYSELF AGREEING TO THE WHOLE Halloween party thing, which means the next day Ansel and I go on the hunt for costumes. I honestly don't see the point in dressing up, but both Ansel and Sasha insist it's a must. Why can't I wear sweatpants and a pizza stained shirt and call myself a college student studying for finals? Seems legit to me, and comfortable.

Ansel parks outside the pop-up Halloween store. I follow him inside, my eyes immediately assaulted with flashing lights, giant inflatables, and purple and orange twinkle lights.

"Costumes are this way."

I follow Ansel to the back of the right side of the store. There are plenty of options, but they all look so basic to me.

I hold out a Sexy Unicorn costume and raise my brow, turning around the plastic bag to show it to Ansel. "Seriously?"

"That's terrible. There's a sexy costume for everything though. Want to be a toaster? There's a sexy version somewhere." He winks at me and I hang the garment bag back up. No chance am I going as a Sexy Unicorn.

The store has plenty of things to choose from, but nothing captures my interest.

Ansel finds a couple options, but nothing he loves. We both end up leaving empty handed.

We make a couple more stops, all without any luck. It makes sense with Halloween only two days away, but I can tell Ansel is irritated.

"I guess we'll have to improvise and make our own costumes." I buckle the seatbelt when we get back in the car from the last Halloween store he wanted to check.

"That's not a bad idea, Meadows," he muses, starting the car. "I can probably make something work."

"I think I can too."

"Sweet." He holds out his fist for me to bump mine against.

We make one last stop at Watchtower for drinks before he drops me off.

"If your brother's home, don't tell him you were with me," are his parting words as I get out, dragging my backpack behind me.

I shake my head at him. "Sage wouldn't hurt a fly."

He points a finger at me. "Lies!"

I close the door and he drives off. Heading inside, I adjust my backpack on my shoulder, crossing the lobby. I wait for the elevator and head up, surprised to find Sage already home.

"You're home early." I kick the door closed, since my hands are full and then set my stuff down so I can lock it.

"Not much."

I look at the clock on the microwave and realize he's right—I'm home later than I thought.

"Where were you?" he asks, his tone accusatory.

"Looking for a Halloween costume."

"Are you going trick-or-treating? Aren't you a little old?"

I roll my eyes and start heading back to my room. "It's for a Halloween party."

"A party?" he repeats like this is some sort of foreign concept.

"Mhmm," I hum.

His eyes hone in on the cup in my hand. "Ansel drove you home."

"Yup." I'm not trying to piss him off, but he's been so funny about Ansel that I don't know what else to say. I'm not going to stop being friends with him because Sage has a problem with it. Especially when that problem is specifically about the fact Ansel has a penis.

He grunts in reply. "Where's this party going to be at?"

"I'm not sure yet." Anger rages in his eyes and I'm sure he's picturing Ansel and I alone somewhere. "Sasha is going too, and a couple other people I know."

That seems to calm him down some. "I don't want you out all night," he warns. "You'll be home by midnight."

"I was actually going to stay the night with Sasha."

His lips twist, trying to gauge whether or not I'm lying.

"Fine." He shoves his fingers through his hair. "But text and let me know when you're at her place after the party."

"I will."

Sasha asked me today at lunch if I would want to sleepover. I don't, not really anyway, but decided it would be a good idea if I end up drinking some.

Sage finally backs away, blowing out a breath. "I'm going to order dinner."

I leave him be and go to my room. I drop my backpack on the floor, kicking off my shoes. Digging through my bag I pull out my homework and sit at the desk near my bed. I usually do homework on my bed, but I feel the need to mix it up today.

In the hallway I hear Sage ordering dinner and can't help but laugh to myself. Our lone cooking class did us a lot of good.

By the time I'm done with my homework our food arrives and we sit down on the couch together to eat.

"You are okay with me going to the Halloween party, right?" I voice when I feel like Sage has been quiet for too long.

He looks over at me, studying my face. He inhales a deep breath and nods. "Yeah, I'm not happy about it, but only because I worry about you. But you're eighteen, this is your senior year, and…" He pauses, pressing his lips together. "After last year, I want to see you live your life. It wouldn't be right for me to prevent you from doing that."

Setting my plate of food on the coffee table, I give him a sideways hug and kiss his cheek.

"I love you."

I really do. I know I'm incredibly lucky to have a brother like him.

"I love you, too, D."

He kisses my forehead and we exchange a look, only one the two of us can have, because as siblings who have been through the hell we have, it's cemented a special bond.

CHAPTER TWENTY-FOUR

"What are you wearing?" Sage regards me with curiosity as I enter the living area.

I look down at my fitted black tank top, leather jacket, and ripped skinny jeans. My exposed collarbone, neck, and face are speckled with droplets of blood. There are more on my arms, but since they're currently covered he can't see that. I hold a cereal box in one hand and a plastic kitchen knife in the other.

"A costume."

"That's not a costume." He snorts, looking me up and down, his brows furrow as he tries to figure out exactly what I am.

"Yes, it is," I defend, feeling a little crestfallen that it isn't obvious. "I'm a cereal killer."

His eyes light with recognition, mouth parting. "Oh, I see now."

I roll my eyes and pull out my phone to see the text that has come in. "It's Ansel. He's here. Should I tell him to come up for an interrogation?" I arch a brow, my tone joking but also serious because I won't put it past Sage to give him the third-degree again.

"No, go on ahead."

He stands up from the couch where he'd been watching a football game and grabs his wallet off the counter. "Here, take this." He slaps a couple of twenties fresh from an ATM into my hand.

"I don't need your money, Sage. It's a party."

"Take it," he insists, closing my hand around it. He senses I'm going to complain so he guilts me into taking it by saying, "It'll give me peace of mind."

"Fine." I put the money in my pocket. Probably not the safest place, but it'll have to do.

"Be careful," he warns, eyes stern. "Don't take a drink from anyone, even someone you know. Okay?"

I nod. "I'll be fine, Sage."

I kind of wish now I hadn't mentioned the party to him.

"If you drink too much and want me to get you, I will. Doesn't matter the time."

"You don't have to worry about me."

The look in his eyes tells me he does and to stop arguing with him. "Let me know when you get to Sasha's."

I hug him. "Stop fretting, Momma Bear." My voice is muffled against the fabric of his green Henley.

He chuckles softly, squeezing tight. "I have to."

He releases me, gives me one last warning, and I'm finally on my way down to the main floor to meet up with Ansel outside.

"What took you so long?" he asks when I slide into the car.

"My brother worries."

Ansel's lips pinch, not in disdain but understanding.

Now that he knows what happened he sees why my brother is insanely overprotective.

"Where's the party at?" I pull the seatbelt across my body and buckle it before he pulls away.

"Chuck's." At my blank look he adds, "His parents are out of town this weekend."

I bob my head up and down like this makes perfect sense to me.

"What exactly are you?" He glances at me briefly, coming to a stop at a red light. The red hue fills up the car, making his white face paint appear to glow.

"How is it not obvious?" I mutter more to myself than him. "I'm a cereal killer."

He grins. "Oh, that's genius."

"What are you?" I counter with. "A skeleton?" Half of his face is painted with white and black paint and his clothes are all black.

"Basically." He shrugs, driving forward when the light changes. "I couldn't think of anything else so I grabbed my paints and had at it."

"It looks good."

And it does. With his sharp cheekbones and bright eyes the look really stands out, where on someone else it might look clownish.

"Merci."

He reaches over and turns the volume up, whatever song he's playing from his phone bumping through the speakers. We converse a little, but for the most part the drive is silent between us.

I know we're at the party before I even see the house, thanks to the cars parked along the gravel and dirt road. Apparently the house sits on a few acres, which makes it excellent for party throwing.

Ansel parks his car and I hop out, the two of us

walking the rest of the distance to the house. I shiver in the cool night air. It makes me thankful I did have the forethought to wear a jacket. Regardless, I do only have a tank top beneath it so I still feel the pinch of cold.

Ansel reaches out, draping his arm around my shoulder. Tugging me against his side he shoots me a playful grin. "Cold, Meadows? I'll warm you right up."

I shake my head, but don't pull away from him.

I swear we walk a mile before we reach the house. It's huge, one of the largest homes I've seen, and looks exactly like something that would be on the cover of Modern Mountain Mansions. I don't think that's a real magazine, but this house convinces me it should be a thing.

The house pulses with music and the closer we get to the front steps, the more I feel the ground shaking with it too. The outside is decorated with gravestones, zombies coming out of the ground, and purple lights strung along the roofline.

Ansel jogs up the front steps, opening the door wide. He nods with his head for me to go in first. The lights are mostly off, except for strategically placed purple and orange lights, along with those projector ones that I think are meant for the outside. On the wall to the left green witches flash along it.

"Let's get a drink and look for Sasha." Ansel grabs my hand, tugging me through the crowd of teens. There must be a lot of people here, considering this house isn't small and it's basically wall to wall with bodies.

He's either been here before, or has a keen sense of direction, because we reach the kitchen in no time. There are a couple of kegs, bottles of liquor, and even some snacks—mostly tortilla chips, salsa, and some weird looking thing that I don't even want to take a guess at.

"Beer?" A brow peeks on his forehead, cracking his face paint a smidge.

"Sure." I watch him grab the red Solo cup and fill it up, passing it to me before getting one for himself.

My body moves slightly to the beat of the thumping music, my eyes scanning the room for anyone I recognize.

"Is Seth coming?" I don't really know Seth, but at least he isn't a total stranger like most of these people.

My anti-socialness is really biting me in the butt right now.

Ansel shrugs. "Said he was, but I never know with him." He tips his cup back, gulping down a few large swallows.

I grab onto Ansel's hand again and the two of us push our way through the crowded kitchen.

"Sexy kitten," Ansel announces, pointing with one finger, the rest wrapped around his cup. "Nope, not Sasha. There's another, still not her."

I can't help snickering, because he was right earlier in the week when he said a sexy kitten was predictable. With my plastic knife in my pocket and cereal box under my arm I'm sure I don't even look like I've tried.

"Spiderman also seems to be a popular choice."

Again, he's not wrong. Most guys seem to be some sort of Marvel character. Spiderman, Thor, and Iron Man seem to be the top choices.

Most everyone is either talking loudly over the music, dancing, or making out. The scent of marijuana lingers in the air, and I'm sure Ansel will be selling plenty tonight. He's mentioned that parties really boost his regular profit.

We check out the upstairs, still no Sasha, before making our way to the basement. We spot her almost immediately at a pool table playing beer pong. Two black cat ears stick out on top of her head amidst all her spiraling blond curls. Her dress is skin tight, black and shiny, and barely covers anything. When she moves a significant part of side-boob is shown and more than a few guys stare blatantly.

Ansel shakes his head and mutters, "She's something."

"You don't like her very much, do you?"

I might be convinced Sasha has a crush on him, but he doesn't seem to return the favor. At all.

His lips are pinched and he watches the scene in front of us with narrowed brows. He hasn't let go of my hand yet, despite the fact my palm is beginning to sweat. "I don't like predictability."

Ignoring his comment, I call out, "Sasha!"

Waving, I finally capture her attention and she grins. Her eyes are already slightly glassy and she stumbles trying to reach us.

"My friends!" she cries, throwing her arms around us. When she steps back she frowns at our joined hands. "Come on." She tugs on my arm that's holding the cereal box and it falls. "Oopsie." She puts a hand to her mouth and giggles.

I resist the urge to roll my eyes. Why did I even bother coming? Drunk people are my least favorite kind of people.

Ansel bends down, grabbing the cereal box. He passes it to me, glaring at Sasha as he does. "Watch it, Sasha. You could've hurt her." I don't miss the way he angles his body slightly in front of me.

"I didn't mean to," she snaps, frowning. "You know I didn't mean it, right, Dani?" She bats her big eyes at me.

"Right."

I try to ignore the huff that comes out of Ansel.

"Let's play." She doesn't grab me this time, but I follow her, Ansel reluctantly trucking along behind us.

I join Sasha's team, which consists of her and two other people—a guy named Henry and a girl named Josie—who are both on the school's tennis team with her.

A few minutes into the game Ansel whispers in my ear that he'll be back in a little bit.

He doesn't say it, but I know more than likely he's off to sell some weed.

I stick with Sasha, drinking more alcohol than I intend to during the game of beer pong.

After the game is over, Sasha drags me over to a makeshift dance floor—basically an empty section of the basement where other kids are dancing.

"My cereal," I cry as it gets left behind at the table.

Sasha is oblivious. She gyrates around me while I struggle to find my rhythm. My leg is protesting already and the night has barely begun. The walk from the parked car to the house in my heeled boots was a bad idea, but it's not like I could have gone barefoot.

"Loosen up, Dani!" Sasha yells above the music.

Grabbing my arms she shimmies around me. I'm not used to this kind of dancing, or even this kind of party. Sure, I went to a few back home, but mostly it was a much smaller group of us hanging around in someone's basement drinking beers and being obnoxious. This is a *party* like the ones I've always seen in movies.

After a few minutes I start to feel more comfortable and dance with her, singing along to the lyrics of the song playing.

"This is amazing!" she shrieks.

I nod in agreement, my body flushed from the beers I've downed.

"Where's Ansel?" I voice, looking around for him. It's been about thirty minutes, maybe longer, since he left us.

"Who cares?" she shouts back. "Have some fun, girl!"

With the alcohol burning through my veins I listen to her words, losing myself in the music and vibes from everyone around me.

Tossing my arms above my head, I let out a whoop swaying my hips.

"Yes, girl! Get it." Sasha moves her body far more gracefully than mine.

Closing my eyes, I let go.

I let go of my worries.

My fears.

Doubts.

For a moment, I allow myself to be a girl, any girl.

Only for a night.

CHAPTER TWENTY-FIVE

Pouring more beer down my throat is probably not the best idea, but logic left my brain an hour ago.

"Yes!" Sasha cheers while others yell, "Chug, chug, chug!"

I shotgun the beer in record time, tossing the empty can on the floor. My hands go in the air the same moment cheers ring around me.

The poor guy beside me is still trying to finish his.

A very unladylike burp leaves me, but I can't find it in myself to be embarrassed.

Ansel's figure pushes through the crowd.

"Annie!" I cry, throwing myself at him.

"Oomph." His arms twine around me, holding the majority of my weight. "Are you drunk?"

"Pssh, no," I slur, my feet going out from under me.

"Whoa." Ansel holds on tighter to my body, picking me up. "Find your sea legs, Meadows, I'm not carrying you out of here."

I slap him playfully on the arm. "You would if you had to."

He rolls his eyes.

"Let's dance."

"Let's not."

He has no choice as I tug him into the crowd.

Now that the alcohol has loosened me up even more, I dance freely, finding a rhythm I didn't know I possessed. I turn my back to Ansel, lifting my hair up and looking at him over my shoulder with a flirty look.

He looks pained for a moment, but the look is gone so quickly I'm convinced I imagined it.

"You can touch me, Ansel."

I don't know if he actually hears me above the music, but his hands grasp my hips from behind.

I sway my body against his, laying my head back against his chest.

"This feels nice," I murmur, closing my eyes. My body feels heavy, tired. I have no idea what time it is, but I probably need to sleep even though I don't want to.

"How much did you drink?" His voice vibrates against me.

"Not too much," I lie.

"Mhmm." I feel him hum it more than I hear it. "You okay, Meadows? This doesn't seem like you."

I spin around in his arms, linking mine around his neck. "I'm *great*. Letting loose. Having fun. Being a normal teenager."

The way he looks at me I know he's completely sober and analyzing everything I say. He brushes the backs of his fingers over my cheek, his teeth digging lightly into his bottom lip.

"Let's get some water in you."

He tries to pull me away from the others dancing, but I hold on tight, digging the heels of my feet into the floor. "No, no, no. I want to dance."

"I'm getting you water." This time he untangles my arms from his body so easily I know he wasn't trying hard enough before.

I frown at his retreating figure.

No longer in the mood to dance now I head upstairs, looking for a bathroom. I spot one at the end of the hall with only a couple of people waiting, thank God, I might pee myself otherwise.

Waiting my turn, I all but cry out in relief when I finally make it to the toilet. I'm in the middle of peeing when I hear a bunch of screaming and cries of, *"Get out! Go!"*

My heart rate accelerates and I stand up, yanking my jeans up.

Feet pound against the floor, bodies racing for an exit.

Oh God, oh God, oh God.

"Cops!" I hear someone else yell.

More screams. It sounds like a stampede. I look at the locked bathroom door, panic setting in. My breaths leave me in short small pants.

I have to get out.

There's a window in the bathroom, not a large one, but I should be able to climb out of it—possibly landing face first on the ground in the process, but it's better than being shot at.

Opening the window, I climb up on the closed toilet seat lid so I can get enough height to climb out the narrow space. Sure enough, I fall on the ground, rolling my body so my right side takes the brunt of it and not my face.

Picking myself up quickly, I walk as fast as I can with my limp. I feel like a sitting duck because I can't run anymore.

All I have on me is my stupid plastic knife that won't do any good for anyone that might want to shoot at me.

So, I keep going. Each step is one away from the house.

Other kids are running to cars, but I head for the woods. I don't have a car and Ansel's is too far. I have to hide.

God, I have to hide.

Adrenaline pumps through my veins and the only thing on my mind is survival. It's pure and simple, I have to put space between me and the house, finding somewhere to hide until...

Until, what?

Don't think about that right now. Get away. You have to get away.

Tears streak my face, the cold air stinging them as I move. I make it into the woods and keep going. My leg is tired, barely moving forward. Sheer willpower is the only thing moving me at this point. I feel completely sober at this point, even though logically I know I'm not.

Through glimpses between the trees I see the reflection of red and blue lights, sirens blaring.

Who's dead?

I push that thought from my brain, because I can't dwell on it now. All that matters is making it to safety.

Safety, what is that anymore?

I hear voices of others sneaking through the woods. They're not being quiet at all.

Don't they know you have to be quiet?

"I think they went in the woods!" A voice shouts somewhere behind me close to the house.

I haven't made it far enough away yet.

Panic grips me once more.

I don't want to die.

More footsteps thunder into the woods. I look around

for anywhere to hide, knowing I have to get down and out of the way.

Moving as quietly as I can I find a spot where a tree has fallen. I tuck my body beneath it. My dark clothing provides a camouflage. I lay as still as I possibly can, holding my breath, playing dead.

The voices get farther away, going in another direction.

But I still don't get up and move. I'm too afraid of them coming back.

My fingers grow numb from the cold. My body wants to shiver, but somehow I keep control of every muscle in my body — too afraid of rustling even a leaf.

An hour passes, maybe longer, before I finally climb out from under the tree. Things have been silent for a while. Fear begins to settle in my bones as I trek through the woods, my leg protesting with every single step. I start crying again. I hate being scared. I don't want to be scared anymore. I never want to have to fear for my life and here I am.

Digging my phone out of my pocket, there's no signal.

No fucking signal and I'm alone in the woods. The sounds of animals scampering through the dark forest are the only thing to keep me company but they're only frightening me more. Are there bears out here?

I wrap my arms around myself, but it does little to help me stay warm.

Where's my jacket?

I didn't realize until now I'm not wearing it, but blearily I recall taking it off when I was playing beer pong with Sasha.

God, I'm so cold.

My teeth start to chatter, but I'm scared the noise might draw attention from anyone who could still be out here, so I bite down on my tongue, immediately tasting blood.

I don't know how far I've walked before I finally exit the woods onto a dark gravel road. I look left and right, but there's no sign of any sort of life.

Digging out my phone I find that I have a signal. I call Ansel first. It rings and rings and rings. I try him again. A third time. Still nothing. My worry escalates.

Is he hurt? Shot? Stabbed? Dead?

I call Sasha next. It goes straight to voicemail.

Fuck!

Text messages begin rolling in now that I have service.

Sasha: Where r u?

Sasha: Cops r coming

Sasha: We r buuuusted

Sasha: I'm leaving WHERE R U?

Sasha: Girl I'm leaving ur ass

Sasha: Dani?

Sasha: R U with Ansel? He's not answering either.

Sasha: R u still coming to my helicopter?

Sasha: Hose.

Sasha: Ducking autocorrect. HOUSE.

Sasha: Dani? Did the police get u? Ur brother is going to kiiiiill u.

Her texts slowly start making sense to my inebriated brain.

There wasn't a shooting. There was no bad guy coming after us.

It was the cops coming to bust up a house party. Yeah, that's scary enough, but it's not what I thought it was. My panic and fear was over what is essentially something normal. All because I'm now hard-wired to expect the worst.

I thought, I really truly believed, it was happening

again. That innocent people were being killed and I had to get away.

All the adrenaline in my body leaves all at once. I collapse on the dirty ground. Gravel digs into my knees from the rips in my jeans.

What is wrong with me? Why do I have to be like this? Why can't I be normal? Why? Why did any of this happen?

My hands shake around my phone, my tears blurring the screen. I can't get ahold of Ansel and I don't want to call Sage. I know he'd come get me, but he'd be mad, rightfully so, and I don't want him to blame himself in any way for this. As it is, Sage is probably losing his shit since I haven't told him I'm at Sasha's.

"Shit, shit, *shit*." My fingers fumble with my phone and I shoot him a text.

Me: SO SORRY. I didn't have service. I'm at Sasha's. I'm safe. Love you.

Sage: It's 3am Dani. I've been worried sick.

Me: I'm so sorry. Really.

Sage: We'll talk tomorrow.

Me: Sage, I'm sorry!

Sage: Tomorrow, Dani.

I bury my face in my hands, knowing he's livid. He has every right to be. He'd be even worse off if he saw where I was right now.

I should bite the bullet and tell him, have him come get me, but I'm too upset to deal with what I'm sure is bound to be a lecture.

Scrolling through my phone I stop on Lachlan's contact. I shouldn't be calling him, ever really, and definitely not at this time of night.

I do it anyway.

It rings quite a few times before a sleepy gruff voice answers.

"Hello?"

"Lachlan," I exhale, my breath fogging the air. "I…"

"Dani?" I hear shuffling in the background like he's pushing his sheets off his body. "It's three in the morning. Are you okay?"

"N-No." My voice shakes and I feel tears coming again.

"Are you hurt?"

All the emotions from before come rushing back.

"No, I'm okay, but … can you come get me?"

"Where are you?"

It sounds like he's grabbing a wallet, keys.

"I … don't know. I'll text you my location."

"You promise you're okay?"

"Okay as I can be."

"Are you somewhere safe?"

I hesitate. "I don't know."

He exhales heavily. "Send me your location. I'll be there as fast as I can."

I hang up and text my GPS location to him. Shivers wrack my body and I wrap my arms around myself, walking back and forth about twenty feet to try to stay warm.

Lachlan: In my car and on my way.

Me: Thank you.

Closing my eyes I tip my head up to the night sky. Tonight didn't go at all how I expected. Exhaustion settles into my bones and after a few more laps back and forth, I sit down to wait.

CHAPTER TWENTY-SIX

HEADLIGHTS FLASH ACROSS MY BODY, THE TIRES ON THE car crunching on loose gravel. The older model black Acura car comes to a stop beside me. Before I can stand up Lachlan rushes out of the driver's side over to me.

"Dani, *fuck*, why aren't you wearing a coat?"

Before I can blink he whips the hoodie off his head, tugging it down my body along with his heavenly scent.

"I lost it."

His blue eyes narrow on me. "What happened? You know what, tell me in the car, you have to be freezing."

He grabs me by the hands and lifts me up. He wraps his warm, strong arm around my body and guides me into the passenger seat. Heat blasts from the vents and a happy sigh escapes me as I settle onto the seat. His car smells like him with a tinge of peppermint.

He climbs in the driver's side, slamming the door closed with more force than necessary.

"What the fuck happened?" He glances over at me, clear worry shining in his eyes. It surprises me that he's cussing. He must be really worked up. Or maybe he has a potty mouth outside of school.

"I was at a party." I wrap his hoodie tighter around my body like it'll somehow keep me safe as the memories resurface.

"Are you hurt?" he asks again like he did on the phone. "God, Dani, please don't tell me someone touched you."

My mouth pops open and I shake my head rapidly. "N-No. Nothing like that. I was drinking. A lot," I add sheepishly, nibbling my lip nervously admitting this to him since he's basically a teacher.

No, he's Lachlan.

"Did someone spike your drink?"

"No." I look out the window. "But the cops showed up and…"

"And what?" he prompts, his voice tight. "You're worrying me, Dani."

I sigh, swiveling my gaze and taking in his profile. His sharp nose, strong jaw bone. He's beyond handsome. There isn't a word that exists in the English language for Lachlan.

"It's dumb."

"Dani," his voice is stern, "there's nothing you could say to me that I would think is dumb in any way."

"The cops came and I was in the bathroom. I heard the screaming to get out and…"

I trail off and his fingers tighten around the steering wheel. A muscle in his jaw ticks. "And you thought someone had been shot."

He doesn't frame it as a question, but I answer anyway. "Yes."

He glances over at me. "What did you do?"

"I climbed out a window." I show him the scrapes on

my legs that are visible through the rips. "And then I took off for the woods. I had to walk as fast as I could since I can't run anymore. God, I miss running. I thought I was going to die again."

"Fuck," he curses again. I jolt in surprise when he grabs my hand, giving it a soft squeeze before letting me go. "I'm so sorry you had to go through that."

"It's okay."

He winces. "Dani, it's *not* okay. Nothing that happened to you was okay. Don't say that. Don't ever say that."

He gets on the freeway, heading into the city. I know we'll be at the condo in a few minutes.

"Can I stay with you tonight?"

His eyes dart to me looking pained. "I ... that's not a good idea."

"Why? I can't let my brother see me like this. I can't go home drunk," I argue desperately. Dropping my head I whisper, "I can't disappoint him."

Lachlan exhales a weary sigh and nods. "Fine, okay."

He parks in the underground garage and we're both silent as we take the elevator up to his place. He unlocks the door and Zeppelin immediately barrels into us. He takes an extra long time smelling me while Lachlan locks up.

When I turn around I find Lachlan standing with his hands on his hips, head bowed slightly. "You were so scared you climbed out of a window, huh?"

I nod, petting Zeppelin. The dog is so big I don't even have to bend down. "I hid in the woods, under a fallen tree. I didn't move for a long time. I ... played dead."

His eyes close and he looks pained. His Adam's apple bobs as he swallows. When he opens his eyes they're twin glacier pools. "I don't have any words to make it better for you. I wish I did, but they don't exist. What happened to you, before, it should've never happened. You shouldn't have to feel like that. Ever. And I'm sorry that a monster ruined that for you."

"It's okay."

It's okay—two words that are a reflex. He flinches.

"No, Dani, it's not okay." I bow my head and he clears his throat. "You should really go home."

My head shoots up. "Please, don't make me. Sage will be upset and I don't … I don't want to have to explain this to him because it'll bother him even more. I know he feels guilty for what happened, even though he shouldn't. He wasn't even there."

Lachlan twists his lips, giving me a jerk of his head that's the only indication he's agreeing. "Let me get you something to change into. You can sleep in my room."

"That's not necessary." My hands come up in protest, waggling back and forth. "The couch is fine."

He shakes his head. "Nice try, but no, you can have the bed."

He crooks his finger, telling me to follow him down the narrow hall. I do, my boots echoing on the hardwood with every step I take.

He pushes open the master bedroom door. My eyes sweep the room, taking in the very personal space that's entirely Lachlan.

The walls are a dark charcoal color. His furniture is all different shades of rich woods. His bed is a mountain of gray and white blankets. It's the coziest looking bed I've ever seen. At the foot of his bed, on the floors, are stacks and stacks of books. There are more stacks through the whole bedroom. In the corner, the only real pop of color is a comfortable looking low teal chair. Beside it is a small table, one book, and his glasses. Above the bed hangs an art piece of the San Francisco skyline. Beside his bed, stretching above it, is a wired light that hangs down. It's probably the most modern looking piece in the whole room.

Lachlan rummages through his dresser, emerging with a t-shirt and a pair of gym shorts.

Clearing his throat, he says, "They'll be a little big for you, but you should be able to make it work. The shorts have drawstrings." He looks over his shoulder at the sleep-mussed bed. "I changed the sheets yesterday, but I can put different ones on if you want."

"It's fine. Thank you." I take the clothes from him and he nods.

"I'm going to go make up the couch. Goodnight, Dani."

"Night."

He grabs a pillow off the bed and a blanket from the end. His arm brushes mine as he passes and despite the warm hoodie and the chill that has long since left me, my body covers in goosebumps.

Before he can close the door again, I say, "Lachlan?" He pauses, looking back at me with his hand on the door. "Thank you. I mean it. This … thank you."

His lips flatten, his eyes dark. He gives me another single nod and closes the door.

I set the clothes down on the bed, reluctantly removing his hoodie I strip out of my clothes, only leaving my bra and panties on. His shorts are way too big for me, like he said, but I'm able to tie them tight enough that they only slide down my hips a little. I pull his shirt on and the hoodie. He'll be lucky if he gets his sweatshirt back. It's a charcoal gray color, clearly well-worn and loved, with a faded Led Zeppelin logo.

The dog paws at the door, letting out a whimper. From

the living area I hear Lachlan scold him with a stern, "Zeppelin, no."

Climbing into bed, I turn off the light. Rolling onto my side, I yank the covers up to my chin burrowing down. Surrounded by Lachlan's scent I've decided this is as close to heaven as I'll ever get. Now that the adrenaline has abated my body feels a hundred pounds heavier than normal. I don't like the feeling at all. I've never felt exhaustion like this before. If I felt it after the shooting I don't remember because I spent most of those days in a deep sleep after multiple surgeries.

I don't know how long I lay in the dark, but the door cracks open. Lachlan tiptoes inside quietly like he doesn't want to wake me.

"Sorry," he murmurs lowly when he spots my cracked eyes, "I need to grab something. I didn't mean to disturb you."

"I wasn't sleeping."

He crouches down beside me, digging in the drawer beside his bed. "Want to talk about it?" I shake my head. He pulls a wrapped peppermint from the drawer. "Want one?" Again, I shake my head. He puts it in his mouth, dropping the wrapper on the table.

He starts to stand up, to leave. I grab onto his forearm. His pulse thrums against my palm as he halts. "Don't leave yet," I plead brokenly.

Zeppelin jumps onto the bed, curling up beside me. He promptly passes out with a loud doggy snore.

"Do you need something? I can bring you water."

I shake my head, biting my lip.

Him. I need him.

It makes no sense. It's illogical. But I do.

Ever since the first day of school there's been something about him that intuitively I trust, that some part of me, maybe my soul, perhaps something else, recognizes that he's the one I can share my secrets with.

But I shouldn't desire him.

I *can't* desire him.

It's wrong.

It's immoral.

For him.

For me.

"Dani?" His eyes widen with concern.

I swallow past the lump in my throat and go against everything inside me that says I shouldn't do this, instead listening to the part that's inexplicably drawn to a man I can't have.

My hand wraps around the back of his neck, feeling the short dark hair at the base of his skull. He freezes. I don't miss the catch in his breath or the war in his eyes.

But I don't let the battle begin, because I know once it does this won't happen, and *God* I need it to happen more than I need my next breath.

I lean over, closing the short distance between us. The peppermint on his tongue permeates the air and I lick my bottom lip before I press my lips to his. My mouth tingles from the taste of him. He doesn't move at first, but then a manly growl echoes in his throat. His long strong fingers tangle in my hair. His hold is tight enough to hurt, but isn't painful. His tongue finds mine and that minty taste is everywhere.

I've never been kissed like this before. It's a ravaging more than a kiss, like he's a knight claiming his bounty. His stubble burns my cheeks, but I don't mind the sting — it's a welcome reminder that this is real, I'm kissing Lachlan, but more importantly he's kissing me back.

Heat tingles up my spine, and I climb to my knees, wrapping both my arms around him, pressing my body into his. His hands move to my waist, bunching in the fabric. He's still kneeling on the ground, and I love the leverage I have above him from my perch on the bed. Like he's mine to take.

I don't think I've ever wanted anything or anyone the way I want Lachlan Taylor.

Mr. Taylor.

My counselor.

My fucking school guidance counselor.

Logic is a fickle beast when it's your heart on the line.

Why him? Why out of every human being on the planet has my heart decided to beat for him? I'm not even sure it's love I feel, that seems too silly. I don't *know* him like that. But the connection can't be denied. It exists and it demands to be felt. He feels it too. He tries not to, but I see the battle raging within him. We're both, whether we want to admit it or not, walking a thin line.

Tonight, it has snapped.

He pulls away suddenly, turning his head to the side. I feel cold all over from the loss of his touch. That muscle in his jaw twitches and his fists fall to his sides, clenched tight, the veins roping up his arm stand out sharply.

I fall back, my butt resting on my feet. "Lachlan, that was—"

He won't look at me, his voice is a taut wire. "That can't happen again, Dani. Ever."

"Lachlan—" I try to reach for him, but he stands up, stumbling a couple of feet back.

He reluctantly meets my gaze for one second before his eyes drop to the ground.

"I'm sorry. That should've never happened. I'm," he bites his lip hard, "I'm your fucking counselor. It can't happen again. Ever." He sounds pissed. At me? Himself? Both of us? I don't know. "You're ... fuck, you're a student. You shouldn't even be here. In my bed." He waves a hand forcefully at me. "Fuck." He scrubs his hands down his face, his palms rasping against his stubble. "You're drunk," he rambles, "and I kissed you. I fucking kissed a student."

"*I* kissed *you*," I whisper softly, suddenly feeling unsure of myself.

His eyes narrow on me. Those normally bright blue hues look black in his dark bedroom. "I'm an adult, Dani. I shouldn't have let it happen." He growls out the last words. Running his fingers through his hair that was previously mussed by me, he drops his hands to his sides. "You're drunk and I should've stopped you." He looks at me brokenly, so completely ashamed of himself.

I want to open my mouth to tell him not to feel that way.

"You're drunk," he repeats. "You probably won't even remember this in the morning, but I will." He storms from the room, anger radiating off his body.

Zeppelin lifts his head, sniffing at the air but doesn't jump down to follow his master. He rests his big head back on his paws and closes his eyes.

I look out the now open door through the darkened hallway, to somewhere beyond where Lachlan is undoubtedly battling with himself.

I won't tell him, because I know it won't make him feel any better.

But after all these hours, I'm perfectly sober.

CHAPTER TWENTY-SEVEN

I DON'T FALL ASLEEP UNTIL SIX IN THE MORNING. Spending a solid hour replaying the kiss over and over in my brain.

He kissed me back.

It's a truth that's undeniable and sends bubbles of excitement exploding in my body.

Eventually, I do sleep, not waking up until one in the afternoon.

Zeppelin is gone from my side, the bed cold. Slipping out from under the covers I take in the now closed door and my clothes, folded neatly on that teal chair, my shoes on the ground beside it.

I get out of bed, using the attached master bath. Padding back into his room I pace for a couple of minutes, not sure how he's going to act after last night. Blowing out a breath, I strip out of Lachlan's clothes, tossing them in the hamper before pulling on my outfit from the night before. I put his sweatshirt back on. I tell myself it's because I'm only wearing a tank top but it's a lie. I want something of him close to me, to linger in the smell of him.

I crack open the door, peeking down the hall. The TV is on some news channel, bits and pieces echoing back to me. I pause, hoping to hear movement, some indication of where Lachlan is, but there's nothing.

Pressing my lips together, I walk as quietly as I can. The back of his head greets me. He lays stretched out on the chaise part of a sectional couch in a pair of black sweatpants and a gray long sleeve shirt. He raises his arm, changing the channel. Zeppelin lies on the floor near a coffee table. He raises his big head, huffing at me, before using his paws as pillows once more.

"You're up." His voice is deep, gruff.

"Yeah."

He glances at me standing there awkwardly, wringing my hands together.

"Hungry?"

I give him a surprised look. I wasn't expecting that question.

I nod.

He gets off the couch, walking straight past me into the kitchen.

"Do you like fish tacos?" His eyes flick to me, waiting for an answer.

"Yeah, that would be great."

He starts pulling ingredients out of his refrigerator and freezer, piling them on the counter. He turns his back to me, starting the oven. I slide my butt onto one of the barstools.

We're both silent for a while as he cuts and chops stuff.

"I can't cook," I admit sheepishly.

He doesn't look up from chopping some green leafy thing. "I know. You told me once."

"Oh."

Silence once more.

I can't get a read on him, to know if he's angry, upset, or trying to find the words to say something.

It takes about fifteen minutes before he slides two tacos in front of me. He didn't make any for himself.

I pick up a taco, taking a bite. It's delicious, the flavors exploding on my tongue. Before I can compliment him, he narrows his eyes on me.

"Last night can never happen again."

I nearly choke on the bite of food as I swallow. I grab the bottle of water he holds out to me.

"It was inappropriate," he continues, leaning his elbows on the counter. He regards me with a serious stare. "If something like that happens again you can't call me." He looks anguished saying the words, like they scrape against the walls of his throat. "I'm not some knight in shining armor. Do you have any idea how much trouble I could be in right now if anyone knew you were here?" He covers his face with his hands, letting out a groan before dropping them. "Let alone that we kissed."

I don't miss the way he phrases it. He doesn't say that I kissed him.

We.

We kissed.

"I-I thought you liked it."

It's clearly the wrong thing to say. His face pales. "After you eat, you need to go."

"Lachlan—"

He flinches, biting out, "Mr. Taylor."

I press my lips together, fighting tears. "Last night—"

"Can't happen again."

I lower my head, giving it a small jerk in understanding.

As much as I want to protest I know what kind of

position this has put him in. It would be immature of me to argue back. I might be young, but I'm not stupid. Looking back up at him, I hold out my pinky finger. "Last night stays between us. We tell no one. Pinky promise?"

He wraps his finger around mine.

"Pinky promise," he murmurs in that deep voice of his. Looking in his eyes I see the pain and turmoil roiling in them. It hurts me because I know I put that there.

We don't drop our fingers right away.

After a couple of seconds too long we break eye contact and finally he pulls his finger back.

He braces his hands on the counter, his shoulders tense. Looking down at the plate, I force myself to take another bite, ignoring the tension in the air. I can't joke with him like I normally would, not right now at least.

My phone starts vibrating and Lachlan uses it as an opportunity to walk out of the kitchen. I hear him settle behind me on the couch, but I don't dare turn around and look at him.

Pulling my phone out of the hoodie pouch I see an unfamiliar number.

"Hello?" I answer hesitantly.

"You're okay," Ansel breathes on the other end.

"Yeah?" It comes out as a question for some reason.

"What happened to you last night? I couldn't find you."

"It's kind of a long story." I feel Lachlan's eyes boring into the back of my skull. "What happened to you? I called you, but you never answered."

"My phone fell out of my pocket and broke. The whole screen shattered. I'm going to have to get a new one. Are you sure you're okay? Are you with Sasha?"

I tuck a piece of hair behind my ear. It's damn near impossible to ignore Lachlan listening in on every word.

"No, Sasha left me."

He groans on the other end. "Of course she did. Did you get a ride with someone?"

"Yeah, I'm home now."

It's not a total lie. I *am* in the building, just not my brother's place.

"That's good. Want to go to Watchtower later?"

I shake my head, then feel stupid since he can't see. "No, I better stay home."

"I'll see you Monday then."

"Yep."

I hang up, putting the phone back in my hoodie.

"Who was that?" Lachlan asks, his voice tight.

"Ansel." I still don't turn around to look at him.

He makes some kind of noise in his throat that I'm not sure if it's supposed to be a response or not.

I only manage to eat one more bite and down the entire bottle of water. There's a slight headache brewing behind my eyes, but it's the least I deserve after the damage I did last night. Luckily between the adrenaline and how long I was in the cold what could've been a potentially killer hangover is very mild.

I empty my plate, rinse it, and stick it in the dishwasher.

I'm stalling.

I know it.

I'm sure he knows it too.

I stand between the kitchen and his living area. He doesn't look away from the TV when he says, "You need to go, Dani."

"I have to say something."

He forces his eyes from the screen, cocking his head at me. One dark brow arches. I can tell he's pissed. At me? Himself? I don't know. "What?"

"I should say I'm sorry, but I'm not." His frown deepens. "I'm not sorry at all for last night. I'm not sorry for trusting you when I don't confide in anyone. I'm not sorry for calling you. And I'm not sorry for kissing you. I think it's a bad habit to apologize for things you're not sorry for and I refuse to."

His eyes narrow to slits. "Do you not see how wrong yesterday was?"

I swallow, rocking back on my heels. "Wrong doesn't always mean bad, *Mr. Taylor.*"

His lips part, but he doesn't say anything more, instead crossing his muscular arms over his chest. His eyes flick over me once more, head to toe, stopping on the sweatshirt I still wear.

Still, he says nothing.

"I'll see you Monday."

It's the same words Ansel said to me, but somehow so very different.

With those parting words, I turn and walk out, unsure if I'll ever be welcome back again.

CHAPTER TWENTY-EIGHT

"I'M GROUNDED FOR THE NEXT DECADE," I ANNOUNCE to Ansel when he plops into his seat beside me in art class.

He winces, pulling his sketchpad and supplies out of his messenger bag. There are things we can use that are provided, but he always chooses his own. "That bad, huh?" He flips it open to a clean page.

I grab my own sketchpad, opening to the current class project. Ansel finished his a week ago and now works on whatever he wants during class time.

My drawing of a hippo, the animal I was assigned for this project, looks more like some animated made up creature than anything real. Ansel's eyes flick over it, but he doesn't say anything.

I wish I had his talent, but I don't.

"Sage reamed me out. I deserved it, though."

I had ended up confessing almost everything to Sage about the party and the cops coming. I conveniently left out the part of me thinking there a shooter and Lachlan coming to my rescue but I felt better for being *mostly* honest. I used to tell him everything, but things changed after last year. He's not just my brother anymore. He's my guardian. It's put a strain on the roles we normally play. I don't blame him for being pissed at me. I would be too if the rolls were reversed, so I'll take my punishment and not complain.

"How long are you grounded?"

"A month. I'm not allowed to go out on Friday nights or the weekend unless he goes with me. So, if you want to do something my brother will be chaperoning."

Ansel snickers. "See you in a month, Meadows." He tosses a wink my way. "I don't have a death wish and something tells me your brother would kill me." It's quiet for a few minutes, the only sounds between us the scratching of charcoal pencils. "Do you guys have any plans for Thanksgiving?"

I shake my head. "No. Normally ... normally Sage would've gone back ho—" I stop myself, "to Portland. We could go visit our grandparents, but he's swamped with work so I doubt he'll want to do that and neither of us cook. So, yeah." I finish with a shrug.

Surprise floods me when Ansel says, "You guys could come to my house? I mean, I'd have to ask my mom first, but I don't think she'd care. Especially once she hears you guys won't be doing anything."

"Halloween was Friday, how are we talking about Thanksgiving already?" I pinch the bridge of my nose, feeling a headache coming on.

"It's the holiday season, Meadows. You're not a Scrooge are you?"

"No," I scoff. "Not usually anyway."

I don't tell him, but I spent last Thanksgiving in and out of it since I was being heavily sedated, Christmas too was spent in the hospital.

The twelfth is fast approaching. It'll be a year since our mom passed. A year since the worst day of my life.

Dread settles upon my shoulders like a heavy blanket.

I've been avoiding thinking about that day. It's been easier to push it to the recesses of my brain. I think to cope with it, in my brain it's been a *someday* but it's practically here. I can't ignore it forever.

"You okay?" Ansel voices, bringing me out of my thoughts. He looks and sounds worried.

I nod, tucking a piece of light brown hair behind my ear. "Fine." I move my hand and curse when I leave a smear on the paper from the side of my hand.

Without missing a beat Ansel passes me one of his round powerful erasers I've seen him use before. I take it with a grateful smile, erasing the mark from the page. I wish I could erase other things so easily.

"You can talk to me you know," he says in a low murmur.

I'm surprised Mrs. Kline hasn't yelled at us yet for our talking, but when I look over at her she's occupied at her desk speaking with a student.

"I know."

"I'm not sure you do."

My head jerks to the right, giving him a funny look. "What's that supposed to mean?"

He narrows his eerie pale blue eyes. His ultra long dark lashes fan against his high cheekbones. He looks around the room to make sure no one is eavesdropping. "You shared about what happened to you because you felt you had to. Not because you trusted me." My lips part, a rebuttal ready, but he shakes his head to silence me. "That's okay, trust is earned and I haven't earned yours yet. We haven't known each other long, but when you're ready you can talk to me about anything. I'm not the judgmental type. I mean, my side gig is as a dealer. It'd be kind of hypocritical to judge, huh?"

I process his words and nod. "It'll be a year on the twelfth."

His face falls. It wasn't the answer he was expecting. "Oh."

I turn away from him, not wanting to stare at the blank look of his.

His fingers tap against the top of the table. I assume he's searching for words to say, but that's the thing, there are none. I angle my body away from him, focusing on my project. From the corner of my eye I see his head drop, a sigh of resignation echoing in his chest as he finally comes to the realization that he can't say anything.

The rest of class is spent in silence between us. I hope he doesn't take it personally, I'm not offended, I just don't have anything more to say.

At lunch I'm not surprised when he tears into Sasha for leaving me. I'm also not surprised when she argues right back that he left me too. He says, "That was different. I was getting her water and *she* vanished on me." Sasha simply replies with a condescending, "Mhmm."

Seth, as per usual, says nothing. "Did you go to the party?" I ask him softly, letting the other two bicker.

"Yeah."

"What were you? I didn't see you there."

"Invisible."

He says it so deadpan that I stare at him, waiting for the punch-line. When I don't get one, I sit back in my chair, scrubbing my palms over my jeans. "Well, then."

When the bell chimes, signaling the change of classes, I make a mad dash for Lachlan's office. I'm unsure of what to expect when I see him after the way we left things

Saturday morning, but I do know he's my safe place and right now I *need* him.

Speed walking down the long tiled hallway I come to a sudden stop when I reach his closed door, a piece of paper taped to the outside.

In typed letters it says:

In a meeting until 3pm. Please see the office.

His signature is a scratchy thing at the bottom.

At first, I want to be mad because I needed to see him. Even if he said nothing to me I needed to be in the same room as him. Then, almost immediately after, I feel fear.

What if he's in a meeting because of me? Could someone know I called him? That I was in his apartment?

It seems illogical, but when you're doing something so immoral logic goes flying out the window.

I don't want to go to the office.

Compelled by something I can't quite understand, I pull a pen out of my bag and a draw a dandelion. It's a pathetic sort of thing, basically the outline of one in bloom with a simple line coming out of it for the stem.

But he'll know.

Capping the pen, I shove it in my pocket.

Since I refuse to go sit in the office for the next fifty minutes, I go back to the library and settle at a table there, working on homework. At least I'll be ahead for the day.

Nervousness prickles at my brain, wondering what the meeting is about. I can't seem to shake the feeling it's about me.

I spend the rest of the day in a fog. I'm not surprised when the day ends and I get a text message from Sage.

Sage: Don't let Ansel give you a ride home.

I can't help but roll my eyes.

Me: Getting on the bus now.

He sends back a thumbs up as I sit down, leaning against one of the cold windows.

I hover over Lachlan's contact, wanting to send him a message but knowing more than likely he won't even answer which will only make me feel worse.

The bus drops me off and I walk down the street and into the building.

Once in the elevator I lean against the back wall of it and let out a pent up breath I feel like I've been holding most of the day. When the doors slide open I lower my head. Down the hall I go, letting myself into Sage's condo.

Locking the door behind me, I go to my room, dropping my backpack on the floor. I kick my shoes off, flopping on my bed. I have no idea what to do with myself. My homework is done, I'm banned from doing anything with Ansel, and I finished the last book I borrowed from Lachlan.

I don't do well with idle time. I never have. Whenever I used to feel this pent up restless energy I'd go for a run, but that's not an option anymore. My legs are still screaming at me for what I put them through Friday night.

Getting up, I scour the refrigerator for anything that looks like it could be tossed together for a meal. Of course, there's nothing. With a resigned sigh, I step back, placing my hands on my hips. It'll be a few hours before Sage gets home.

In that time I might become certifiably insane.

I pull out my phone, sending him a text.

Me: What do you want for dinner?

He doesn't text back right away, so I sit down on the couch, turning on the TV.

Sage: Food.

I roll my eyes.

Me: Smartass.

Sage: Anything is fine.

I exhale a deep sigh, laying the phone on the couch beside me.

When I start to twiddle my thumbs after an episode of NCIS I decide enough is enough.

Me: Since I'm grounded, does that mean I can't leave to go to the library you told me about?

Again, I have to wait for a response since he's busy working.

Sage: That's fine. There's money in the kitchen drawer if you want to get a library card. But DON'T do anything else.

Me: Thanks. I won't.

With a groan, I get off the couch, shrug into a coat and put some shoes on.

I'm not sure where the library is, but with a quick Google search I get directions. A short ten-minute walk later I enter through the massive double doors. My head swings back, my mouth dropping open as I take in the elegant marble tiling and rich wood. It's elegant, but also somehow cozy, but I guess that's largely thanks to the rows and rows of mahogany shelves and leather chairs dotted through the space.

The first thing I do when walking in is sign up for a library card. As much as I would love to keep borrowing Lachlan's books, after our kiss I don't want to push my luck.

The cheery librarian, a woman probably no more than thirty, passes me a freshly laminated card. "Do you need help finding anything in specific?"

I shake my head. "No, thank you. I want to browse."

"That's fine." She flashes yet another smile and I head

off, moving through the shelves, scanning the different sections.

Brushing my fingers over the spines, I can't help but smile to myself because I never would've imagined I'd end up loving to read like I have. I guess it took the right book, or maybe it took Lachlan.

I let out a hollow sigh, hating that my thoughts constantly want to trail to him as of late.

I manage to kill an hour of time, checking out with two books.

Heading back to the condo, the chill sears through my body despite my layers. I hope one day I live somewhere warm. I might like to look at the snow, but the cold is too much for me.

I flash a smile at Denny, the doorman, and hurry inside the warmth of the building. Rushing over to the elevators, I come to a dead stop when I spot Lachlan waiting for them.

As if he can sense my eyes on him, he turns. He starts to look away but does a double take.

I don't miss the way his jaw ticks, eyes narrowed.

He's spotted me, so there's no point trying to hide. I walk over to him, standing beside him as we wait for the elevator. Zeppelin isn't with him and I can't help wondering if he's just got home.

Doors of one the elevators glide open and we wait for a family to get out. Lachlan puts his arm out, keeping the doors from closing, and motions me in first.

I do, standing in the corner holding the books tight against my chest.

"Which floor?" He voices, his back to me. It's impossible to miss the tension in his shoulders.

"Eleven," I whisper, biting my lip.

God, this is awkward.

He pushes the button and stays by the number pad, like he's terrified to get near me.

Clearing my throat I voice, "Your meeting … it wasn't about me, was it?"

He looks over his shoulder slowly, brows drawn. "Why would you think it was about you?"

I give him a *really?* look. "I mean … we kissed."

He shoves his hands in his pockets, almost glaring at me. "Last I checked, the school didn't have cameras installed in my apartment." My lips part. "No, Dani, the meeting had nothing to do with you."

"Oh … okay." I duck my head, hearing him let out a heavy exhale. My cheeks burn like I've been scolded.

The elevator stops on my floor and I step off.

"Dani?"

I turn around, tilting my head to the side. "What?"

He twists his lips back and forth, seeming to be warring about what to say.

Before he can, the doors slide closed.

I drop my head, letting out a sigh.

It's for the best. There's nothing he or I can say.

CHAPTER TWENTY-NINE

"You seem distracted today."

My head shoots up at Ansel's comment. "I'm not." I sound defensive, even to my own ears, but it's only because I *am* distracted. By thoughts of Lachlan. I can't stop replaying yesterday's elevator incident in my brain. It wasn't that he said anything particularly rude or hateful, it was the vibe in the air. It's never been tense between us before, but it was then. A part of me knows I should regret the kiss, but I can't. I can't bring myself to regret something that felt so inconceivably *right*.

"Sure you're not." He blows out a breath, his hand moving over his sketchpad. "Is it some project or something? Or...?" He lets his question hang loosely in the air.

"Or?" It's Sasha who perks up, looking from Ansel to me across from him with narrowed eyes.

Ansel looks up at me apologetically. "It's nothing, Sasha. Mind your own business."

I swear if she could breathe fire he'd be burned to a crisp. "You know what Ansel, you don't always have to be such an asshole to me. It was a question."

He watches in shock as she gathers her stuff, running out of the library.

I glare at him, picking my own stuff up. "Can you be nice to her? She likes you, you idiot."

His face contorts with horror. "She does *not* like me."

"Trust me, she does." I throw my backpack over my shoulders and take off after Sasha, hoping I can find her since she's already disappeared in the halls.

I hear a noise in one of the restrooms and make a beeline for it.

Inside I find her at the sink, her hands gripping the white porcelain. She sniffles wiping her nose on the back of her hand.

"Go away, Dani. *Please.*" She turns the water on, washing her hands and splashing her face. When she sees me still in the mirror behind her she growls, "Go."

"Ansel is an idiot. I know you like him and I'm sorry he doesn't see that."

She lets out an undignified snort, grabbing the paper towels to dry her hands. "All boys are. He's completely oblivious when it comes to me." She shakes her head and looks up at me with a smile that's anything but happy. "He can't see me when he only has eyes for you." She waves a hand at me.

My mouth pops open. "What do you mean?"

"He. Likes. You." She bites out the words like they grate on her throat.

"That's crazy. We're just friends."

She arches a brow. "Now who's the oblivious one?" My lips part again. Her shoulders tightening she lets out a shaky breath. "Go, Dani. Please."

"I'm sorry," I whisper.

Sorry. Such a useless word, but somehow always feels necessary all the same.

"I can't make him like me." She shrugs like it's no big deal. "It's time for me to move on from this ridiculous crush." She pauses, tilting her head. "How did you know I liked him?"

I want to tell her it's been obvious, but I think that might make her mad.

"I pay attention."

She nods, waiting for me to leave.

Reaching over, I squeeze her hand. She gives me a small smile in return.

"You can always talk to me if you need to."

I finally leave her, because I know when I feel the way she does I like being by myself too.

The bell rings and I groan. I didn't finish my lunch since I ran after Sasha and I'm still hungry. But there's nothing I can do about it at the moment.

Reluctantly, I venture through the chaotic chatter filled halls. Reaching the long hallway that leads to Lachlan's office, I skim my fingers against the white painted walls.

My stomach feels leaden at the prospect of seeing him.

I get halfway to his office before my feet won't go any further. I stand there, suspended, unable to move forward. I don't know what it is that holds me back. Fear? Shame?

His words from yesterday pinball back and forth through my skull.

"Why would you think it was about you?"

I turn around, power walking back in the opposite direction. Each step taking me further and further away from him.

I don't know what he'll think when I don't show up. I don't care either. Maybe he's not even there.

The halls are emptying, only a few stragglers like myself remain.

I could go to the library, but I don't. There are some common areas in the school, but I don't stop in any of them either.

Instead, I find myself venturing to the one place I've avoided the most.

The indoor track field.

The lights are dimmed since it's not in use.

I climb the bleachers, sitting in the middle, staring at the track.

For the most part my whole life revolved around running since I was in middle school. I *loved* it. Running was my oxygen and I'm suffocating without it. It's one of those things I try not to acknowledge much, because I'm sure people would think I'm crazy. I should be *grateful*.

I can walk after all.

Feed myself.

Wipe my ass.

But the one thing that was my whole world besides my family was ripped away that day.

So much was stolen from me, and not running has angered me. Losing both parents before I turned eighteen, surviving being shot, seemed punishment enough. For what, I don't know. But to lose running on top of it felt extraordinarily unfair.

I suppose that's life.

Nothing is ever simple. Or easy.

It's all pain and heartache. Worry and fear. Stress and anxiety.

If you have one sliver of happiness you have to hold onto it with everything you have.

For some reason, my mother's words decide now is the best moment to echo through my head.

"My sweet, Dandelion. May you always be as free as the birds, as wild as the flowers, and untamed as the sea."

It's what she always told me. From the time I was little, until it was the last words she breathed to me when she thought I was dying, but she was the one who died instead.

I wonder what she'd think if she saw that I wasn't free anymore, or my wild self, or untamed. I was always the girl who danced to her own beat, who smiled through everything, who *lived*.

I don't know how to do that anymore.

I feel glimpses of it when I'm around Lachlan. It's wrong for me to feel the way I do, but with him I feel seen for who I am, but felt for what I've endured.

I rest my feet on the bleachers below me, my elbows on my knees, with my hands cradling my face in my hands.

I feel exhausted, weary from the weight of the world around me.

Sitting in the quiet, I try to stay grounded in the moment.

Minutes pass in silence. It's only me, my breaths, and the rhythmic hum of the building around me. It's a sound you wouldn't normally hear unless isolated by silence like I am. It's almost like a heartbeat, the steady thrumming of the school.

"There you are."

My head whips downward.

I'm shocked to find Lachlan climbing the bleachers. His gray slacks are taut over his thick thighs with every step he takes. He has the sleeves of his white button down rolled to his elbows. Doesn't he know this look is kryptonite to any female with a pulse?

I look away from him, staring straight forward.

I try to ignore the creaking of the bleachers, but it's

impossible when his warmth envelops me and he sits beside me. His legs presses against mine.

"You didn't show up." It's an accusation.

"I didn't."

"Why?"

With more control than I think I have I slowly angle my head in his direction. "I didn't want to."

He blinks at me. Those bright cerulean blue eyes of his seem to glow.

Looking back at the track I mutter, "Why does it matter anyway?"

"It matters."

I sigh. What a ridiculous non-answer.

"I figured you didn't want to see me," I murmur, tugging on the sleeves of my powder blue sweater.

He watches my movements and I stop, like they're some tick that can give away some inner thoughts I'm not even aware of.

He glides his fingers through his thick black hair. Clasping his hands together he gives me a peculiar look. "I always want to see you."

He pinches his lips together like he's admitted too much, even his tone implies something he's left unsaid.

I always want to see you—but I shouldn't.

Shouldn't might be the worst word in the English language. It implies not to do something, but is also opened ended.

I shouldn't be falling for my guidance counselor, but it doesn't stop it from happening.

I shouldn't have kissed him, but I did it anyway.

"You didn't seem happy to see me yesterday."

He rubs his jaw, brows drawn together.

"You have every right to be mad," I continue, not looking at him. I can't. Maybe that makes me a coward but I don't care. "But I won't take back that kiss for anything."

He stiffens beside me. When he speaks his voice is ice. So unbelievably chilly. "You think I'm mad because of the kiss?"

My head snaps to him. "Aren't you?"

I might be young, but I'm not dumb. He was livid the next morning, cold, distant. Yesterday, too.

He shakes his head, letting out a self-deprecating laugh. He stands, smoothing his hands down the front of his pants. I tilt my head up. "I'm not mad about the kiss. I'm not even mad at you. But I am *livid*," his teeth gnash together, his hands fisted at his side, "at myself for liking it and wanting nothing more than to take you in my arms and kiss you again."

I gasp.

"That's why I'm mad, Dani." The bell rings. "Show up tomorrow. I don't like scouring the school for you."

He turns, his long legs carrying him away and down the bleachers.

The door slams closed behind him.

And still I sit, stunned into silence, frozen in place.

Lachlan wants to kiss me again.

CHAPTER THIRTY

"I THINK WE SHOULD GO OUT. YOU'VE BEEN TOO QUIET lately and..." I look up from my homework at Sage standing in the doorway of my bedroom with his hands on his hips. He blows out a breath. "And tomorrow is going to be rough for both of us." He pinches the bridge of his nose. "It's hard every day." He mutters the last under his breath.

"I'm doing homework."

I don't want to go out, not when all I can think about is tomorrow being a year. I remember every day, but there's something about the marking of a year having passed that seems so final in a way—as if death isn't final already.

Sage wets his lips, narrowing his eyes on me. They flick over me, seeing more than I want them to. "I think you need to go out." His tone brooks no room for argument. I'm sure he sees the dark circles under my eyes from not sleeping.

I close the textbook and uncross my legs. "Going out isn't going to change anything."

His fingers tap against the side of his leg. "You can't hole up in here forever, Dani." His eyes study my room, my cold white room that has hardly any hint of personality.

"I don't. I go to school, remember?" I arch a brow. "Plus, I'm grounded."

He gives me an exasperated look, lips pinched. "You know what, consider yourself officially ungrounded." My eyes lift to his with surprise. "It's killing me seeing you like this," he admits, his voice dropping. "I-I know I don't help things. I'm rarely here and I … I don't like talking about what happened."

"Even if you did I wouldn't want to."

The tension in his shoulders ease a small bit at that.

"Change your clothes, we're going out for dinner."

I sigh, knowing there's no point in arguing with him further. When he sees me moving to get off my bed he gives one single nod and eases the door closed.

I swap out my sweatpants and sweatshirt for jeans and a nice sweater. I even put on my nicest pair of boots. It's silly, but I hope he'll see that I'm putting in effort.

When I come out of my room, he's already by the door shrugging into his coat.

"What do you want to eat?" He adjusts the collar so it lies flat.

"Sushi?" I suggest.

He grins. "Haven't had that in forever. Sounds good to me. I know the best place. We'll walk."

I wrinkle my nose, reaching for my own coat hanging on the hook by the door. "But it's cold."

"It's not far," he promises.

I pull my yellow mittens out of my coat pocket, slipping them on.

We ride down in the elevator and I struggle to keep up

with his long-legged stride as he crosses the lobby. I'm five-five, so not too short, but Sage is six foot and seems to get everywhere with only a few giant steps.

We exit onto the street and I burrow into my coat.

Sage lets out a laugh when he sees me. I probably look like a turtle attempting to hide in its shell.

"Come on." He tosses his arm out, draping it around my shoulders. He tugs me against his side, ruffling my hair. I should've worn a hat.

When he smiles down at me, I see how forced it is.

This is as hard for him as it is me. But he's trying, so I have to try too.

The sushi restaurant is only another block over from the condo. There's a short wait before we get a table. We end up tucked into a back corner near the bathrooms. It's not an ideal spot, but I'm starving so I won't complain.

"How's school going?" Sage asks after giving the waiter our order.

"It's school."

He narrows his hazel eyes. "You can give me a better answer than that."

I pull the sleeves of my sweater further down my hands, wrapping my fingers around the edges to cover my palms. "Just trying to pass and get out."

"Are you still not sure about college?" He tips his head at the waiter when he sets down two glasses of water.

Sage helped me fill out applications and I mailed out a huge stack a couple weeks ago.

"No." The one word answer floats through the air.

He rests his elbows on the table. If mom were here she'd scold him for it.

"I want you to go."

I sigh, pressing my lips together. I don't want to disappoint him. "I know, but I have to make my own choices. I don't know what those are yet."

This time he's the one that sighs.

"Look at you," I continue, "I mean, you went to college and you have a job that makes you miserable. I'm not sure college is the end all be all."

Sage's jaw tightens and I fear I've said the wrong thing. "Fair point," he mutters.

"Maybe I'll go, maybe I won't. Is it so wrong to live without a plan?"

He cracks a small smile. "No, but you can't live your whole life like that."

This time it's him who has a point.

"Life clips our wings," I murmur softly, wiping condensation from the side of the water glass. "Everyone tells you to dream big, but then society does everything it can to keep you grounded."

Sage suppresses a chuckle and tips his cup at me in salute. "Welcome to adulthood. You've already figured it out."

"Are you happy?" I find myself asking him suddenly.

My brother tilts his head, pondering my question. "I'm happy in moments."

"But moments are fleeting."

Moments are all I have with Lachlan. Moments, stolen glances, and nothing but a feeling of rightness.

Sage stares into my eyes. "So is happiness."

I exhale a breath, his words hitting me straight in the chest like a punch. He gives me a sad look, like he's fearful he's let me down in some way with his answer. But I understand it. Happiness is brief and if it wasn't then we wouldn't understand the power of the emotion.

Sage and I finish our dinner and head back to the condo. I still can't bring myself to think of it as home.

We're almost back when I spot a giant brown dog straight ahead. My heart jolts, my steps faltering.

Sage looks over his shoulder when he realizes I'm not beside him. "D?"

I catch up with him and Zeppelin must smell me because before I can blink the big dog is trying to jump on me, Lachlan barely able to hold him at bay.

"Hey, buddy." I scratch the dog behind his ears. His giant tongue lolls out of his mouth. It's like he's giving me a goofy grin.

"You know this dog?" Sage's voice is gruff, accusing, as his eyes flicker from me to the dog's owner.

"Hi, Dani." Lachlan's voice washes over me like a crisp and cool running river. It's melodic, and I shouldn't like it so damn much.

I straighten my shoulders, staring across at my guidance counselor. Before I can say anything I feel Sage wrap his fingers around my wrist. His hold is tight, but not painful. It's like he thinks he might have to grab me and run.

"How do you know my sister?" His tone is accusing and I'm sure his eyes are the same as he stares at Lachlan.

Lachlan holds out a hand. "I'm Lachlan — Mr. Taylor. Dani's guidance counselor."

Sage's lips part with understanding and he grasps Lachlan's hand, giving it a firm shake. "Oh, nice to meet you."

"Yeah, same." Lachlan nods. I think seeing my brother has jolted him in some way. "We never got to have that meeting."

"Right." Sage snaps his fingers. "Sorry about never rescheduling that. Work's been insane."

"Understandable."

"Do you live nearby?" Sage asks him as I die inside.

For some reason I don't want him to know Lachlan lives in his building. I mentioned I had a friend that lived in the building and I don't want him to put two and two together.

As if sensing my thoughts, or probably reading the panic in my eyes, Lachlan clears his throat. "Yeah, not too far from here."

"Cool." Sage nods. "We're on our way home from dinner. It was nice meeting you."

"Mhmm, you too," Lachlan hums, his gaze lingering on my bundled form.

"Come on," Sage urges me forward, "I know you're cold." He tugs me to the building.

I look over my shoulder at Lachlan and Zeppelin. I thought he would've already started walking away by now, but he's staring at me, his eyes narrowed, his expression tortured but thoughtful.

I'm not cold anymore.

CHAPTER THIRTY-ONE

THE PILLOW MUFFLES MY SCREAMS. I WAKE MYSELF UP with them, my face damp with tears. I roll over and sit up, the sheets pooling at my waist. Pushing my hair out of my eyes, I wipe my face with the back of my hands. I can barely catch my breath. I keep waiting to hear Sage's footsteps, fearing I've woken him. It wouldn't be the first time. But a minute passes, then two, and three before I collapse back down. The pillows seem to swallow my small body.

I glance to my side and the clock on my nightstand says it's three in the morning.

I won't go back to sleep.

Shoving the covers off, I climb out of bed, shoving my feet into my fluffy pair of black and gray slippers. Padding down the hall, I grab a bottle of water from the refrigerator. I greedily slurp it down, the plastic crinkling in my hands.

I don't know why I thought I could ignore this day, that maybe it would breeze on by and I wouldn't even notice. But it's like my body has sensed it coming. I rub the back of my neck. It's sticky with sweat.

I'm a mess. I shove the almost empty water bottle back into the refrigerator. I intend to lay down on the couch and put the TV on, but that's not what happens. Instead, my feet carry me out the door, down the hall and up the stairs. I don't even bother with the elevator.

I hesitate for a second outside his door before I knock loudly with the heel of my palm. This is a bad idea all around. Things have been tense between us, but I *need* him. I need Lachlan to make the pain go away. I need him to hold me together, because I'm not strong enough to do it right now.

I don't hear anything, and I begin to worry that maybe he's out. Lachlan isn't even thirty yet. He's bound to have a social life, one that keeps him out, and with women. God, the thought of it alone makes a lump form in my throat which is pathetic. He's my guidance counselor, he's eleven years older than me. I *can't* be having these feelings for him or feel jealous over some imaginary woman he may or may not be with.

Inside the apartment Zeppelin lets out a booming bark.

I keep knocking.

I nearly fall on my butt when the door is jerked open.

"Dani?" Lachlan looks at me through squinted eyes. His black hair sticks up adorably like rumpled feathers I instantly want to reach up and smooth down. My hand even twitches to do it, but I catch myself. "It's early, why are you here?"

"I—"

Clarity enters his eyes behind his glasses, all traces of sleep disappearing. "You can't be here," he hisses.

"Please," I beg, before he can slam the door in my face, not that I think he would, but the visual of it alone amps up my desperation. "I need…"

"You need what?" He doesn't say it hatefully, but I flinch anyway.

I want to be strong enough not to need anything from him or anyone. But the fact is, I'm only one person and I can't deal with all these emotions on my own. Besides, everyone should have *somebody* and for some stupid reason my heart has chosen Lachlan to trust and share my feelings with.

"I need you." I finally push the words out of my mouth.

I stare at the hard planes of his bare chest, slowly skimming up his wide throat, stubbled jaw, and finally landing on those blue eyes that see too much.

He raises one arm to the doorframe, resting his head against it. He lets out a ragged breath. His whole body shudders with it.

"You can't need me, Dani. You … can't."

I grip my hands to keep from reaching out and touching him. "But I do."

He closes his eyes, his jaw snapped shut. He looks like he's in the worst kind of physical pain and I hate that I'm the cause, but still I don't turn to leave.

"You know what day it is, don't you?"

His eyes slowly swing to me, darkening with a sudden clarity.

No, he didn't know. But he does now.

His shoulders fall and I can tell he's lost the fight within himself.

"Come here." His voice is gravelly, low, and I feel it through my entire body.

He reaches for me first, gathering me into his strong arms. We stand in the open doorway of his condo as he hugs me, pressing the right side of his cheek to the top of my head. My arms come up slowly, taken by surprise with this sudden turn of events. When I come to terms with the fact that he isn't going to push me away, I wrap my arms tightly around him. The muscles in his back flex and a small groan rumbles from his throat.

"I should have known," he murmurs, and I swear he kisses the top of my head.

"You forgot," I accuse, my fingertips pressing against his naked back. I dig my nails in a little bit, selfishly wanting him to feel a tiny bit of the pain I live with every day. "Everyone forgets."

After all, the living very rarely like to acknowledge anything to do with death. They're too scared of the finality of it.

"I didn't forget, but you took me by surprise. You shouldn't be here."

"But I am."

He sighs. "But you are." Not releasing me, he tugs me inside and closes the door. "Your brother?"

I crook my head back to stare up at his tall frame. "Sleeping."

"He can't find you gone."

"I know."

"You need to go back."

I tighten my hold on him. "No, not yet," I beg. "Hold me a little while longer. He won't wake up for a couple more hours, I promise." He takes my face and looks down at me. His Adam's apple bobs and he looks so torn. "Don't make me leave."

He lets out a shuddering breath and gives a single nod.

"You can stay," he finally whispers, the words cracking as he says them. "Down, Zeppelin," he scolds. I was so lost in the moment, in him, in my feelings, that I didn't even notice the big dog rubbing against us.

I squeak when my legs go out from under me and I

find myself cradled against his warm chest with his arms around me. My arms automatically twine around his neck as he carries me. "What are you doing?"

He arches a brow. "Carrying you?"

"Why?"

He bumps the door to his room open with his elbow.

"Because you asked me to hold you."

I bite my lip as he lays me gently in bed. He climbs over my body, settling behind me. He pulls my back against his chest. I close my eyes.

If this is a dream, I never want to wake up.

Wrapped in Lachlan's arms like this is the perfect kind of distraction.

I wiggle against him, trying to get comfortable, and he lets out a groan. "Please, don't do that."

"Why?" I ask.

He lets out a chuckle that rumbles through his body. His breath blows gently against the back of my neck. "If I need to tell you why, then it's all the more reason you shouldn't be in my bed right now."

My lips part slowly. "Oh."

"Yeah, oh." He sighs heavily, his arms tightening around me.

A few minutes pass in silence save for our breaths, the whirring of a floor fan, and Zeppelin's soft snores coming from somewhere behind Lachlan.

"Your eyes were red. Were you crying?"

"Huh?" My hair brushes against his arm as I turn my head to look at him over my shoulder.

He sits up the slightest bit so he can look down at me. "When I opened the door, your eyes were red like you'd been crying a lot."

"Oh, y-yeah," I stutter. "I woke up from a night-mare. I have them a lot, but this one was worse, I guess that makes sense considering it's been a year today."

His dark brows draw together into one thick line. "You've never told me you have nightmares."

I wet my lips and give a small shrug, which is awkward lying down with his arms around me. "I tell you more than I tell anyone, but I don't tell you everything."

It surprises me when he glides the large pad of his thumb over my lips, tracing the shape of them. "You can tell me anything, Dani." He looks hurt by my admission that I keep secrets from him, even though he *must* know. I've only given him small tidbits of my inner most thoughts these last few months, like little breadcrumbs — enough to stave off hunger, but not enough to really survive on.

"It's hard to share the most shattered parts of ourselves, don't you think? The thoughts, the memories, the pain … it's all so jagged and cutting. I already have to hurt, I don't want other people to hurt too."

He rolls his body so suddenly he's not holding me at all. Instead, he hovers above my body, his hands on either side of my head like he's doing a push up. He's careful to keep his body from touching mine, but it doesn't change the fact that we're in a very compromising position at the moment. I don't think he's realized it yet, but I have. If I lifted my hips, I could line my center up perfectly with the outline of his dick through his sweatpants. The thought alone dampens my skin with perspiration. If Lachlan could read my mind right now, I have no doubt he'd grab me and shove me outside as far away from him as possible.

"Did you ever think that by sharing more, then someone else could help you carry the burden? You don't have to do it all on your own."

"I'm trying," I whisper, my voice cracking, "with you.

With other people…" I turn my head away, not wanting to look at him right now. "Like my brother … I saw in the hospital how anytime someone mentioned something about what happened, or me, or apologized for the loss of our mother, he … shut down. He already got stuck with me, I don't want to burden him anymore than I already have."

With one hand, he brushes back my hair, his fingers lingering longer against my skin than necessary. "I'm certain you're not a burden on your brother."

My lower lip trembles and I bite down on it, not wanting to cry. "It doesn't matter. I *feel* like I am. And you," I exhale a breath, my fingers shaking as I reach up to cup his stubbled jaw, "I don't know why I've shared more with you than I have anyone else. It makes no sense."

I don't know if he realizes it or not, but he leans into my touch, his eyes fluttering closed for a second. He opens them again, and even in his dark bedroom they're a blinding blue. "Does it have to make sense?"

I press my finger into the dimple in his chin. "No, I guess not."

Lachlan lowers his body the tiniest bit closer to mine and I hold my breath. It's ridiculous how my eyes instantly go to his lips. I want to kiss him again. I want it more than anything, but I don't dare close the distance between us. He'll have to be the one to kiss me.

With a groan, Lachlan falls back onto the bed beside me, gathering me into his arms so he's holding me like before.

"Do you want to talk about your nightmare?"

I shake my head, inhaling a lungful of his delicious scent that clings to his pillow. "No. But I need to."

Lachlan doesn't press for me to continue. He waits.

He's good at that—never pushing me, instead letting me work things out in my brain.

Minutes pass in his dark bedroom, and his breaths go even behind me. I'm sure he's fallen asleep, which is understandable at this early hour.

"The nightmare always starts the same. I'm walking with my friends on our way to lunch. I see my mom, she's on hall duty during this time. I wave at her and she waves back with a big smile. I get my lunch from the cafeteria and sit down with my friends at our usual spot. We're talking about something dumb, the holiday break probably and what we're going to be doing. That's when we heard the first shot. We all looked around in surprise, the whole cafeteria went eerily silent. I think we all wondered if what we heard was actually a gunshot. That's when it happened again, and this time there was screaming."

I close my eyes, fighting the emotions as I'm transported back to that day. The fear still feels fresh today, settling in my stomach like a heavy knot. My throat constricts, like it did that day so I couldn't even scream.

"The alarms went off, and everyone started screaming and running. I saw my mom come into the cafeteria and I got up to go to her. It put me in a vulnerable position, in a more open area, and that's when I got shot. Just before I reached her. The screaming got louder then. I dropped to my knees and my mom started crying. She rushed to me, grabbed me by the elbows and fell to the ground with me. There were more gunshots. And fear ... I didn't know fear had a taste, but it does. It was heavy in the air and coated my tongue—salty, metallic, it stung every time I swallowed."

I swallow now, squeezing Lachlan's hand.

"I thought I was going to die there as my mom held me. She did too."

My sweet, Dandelion. May you always be as free as the birds, as wild as the flowers, and untamed as the sea.

The lump in my throat grows bigger. "But she died instead."

"It's not a nightmare." I startle at Lachlan's deep voice reverberating against me.

Recovering, I murmur, "No, it was my reality."

He doesn't say he's sorry. There's no point to the word sorry, not in this situation at least. Instead, he squeezes me tighter, nuzzling his face into my neck. My heart jumps when he presses his lips affectionately to the crook where my neck meets my shoulders. "I've got you," he hums.

I hold his hand tighter.

Don't let me fall.

CHAPTER THIRTY-TWO

SOMEHOW, I SNEAK OUT OF LACHLAN'S APARTMENT without waking him. I leave a note on his pillow with a simple *thank you*.

The chances of Sage being awake this early are slim, it's before six, but you never know. I ease the door open, I hadn't locked it behind me, and tiptoe inside. I pause, listening. When I hear nothing I close it gently and lock up.

I grab a water and use the bathroom before slipping back into my bed.

I'm surprised when I fall right to sleep, with no fitful turning, or visions of things I'd rather not relive.

I wake up late, almost noon time, and find Sage sitting on the couch.

He looks up when he hears me and turns down the volume on the TV. He gives me a small, forced smile. His eyes are sad. "I didn't want to wake you."

"Thank you." I cross the room, plopping on the couch beside him. "I think I needed it." I also think the time spent in Lachlan's arms helped me get the best sleep I've had in a very long time that wasn't drug induced from the hospital.

"Hungry?" Sage questions, looking at the smart watch clinging to his wrist. "We can go get brunch. I know a great place—"

I can't help smiling. My brother, the foodie who has no idea how to cook, but knows the best places to eat.

"Brunch sounds good. Maybe we could go somewhere after? A market?"

Sage smiles at me, his eyes a little brighter. "Yeah, we can do that, D."

I think he needs a distraction today as much as I do. It's not about forgetting what happened that day, or our mom, but finding a way to keep our heads above water.

"I'll get ready." I hop up, and go take a shower.

I blow-dry my hair since I don't want to be outside with wet locks. I bundle up in some of my warmest clothes —a pair of dark wash jeans, a black turtle neck with a chunky gray sweater over it, and I top it all off with a beanie. Once I put my coat on I *dare* the cold to try and touch me.

When I come out of my room, Sage chuckles at my attire. "Cold?"

"Nope, I'm nice and toasty. Gonna stay that way too." I stick my tongue out at him.

It's easier to be playful than to give into the painful sadness I know is going to come back. Lachlan helped keep it at bay, but his magical powers can't last forever. So, for now, I keep my brave face. Sometimes we have to wear a mask to get through things, fake it until you make it.

Sage shrugs into his black pea coat, while I do the same. I also tug on my mittens.

We head down to the garage and get into Sage's car.

The drive to wherever he's taking me only lasts fifteen minutes tops. He pulls into the parking lot and tells me to follow him.

We end up at a small café on the bottom level of a high rise. It's the kind of place easily overlooked, but the smells wafting from it are incredible. My tummy rumbles in response.

We're seated at a booth and menus handed to us.

"What should I get?" I ask Sage who has already slid his menu to the edge of the table.

I place mine down, waiting for his answer. "The French toast, for sure—the cinnamon one. It's phenomenal. And get the orange juice. It's freshly squeezed."

I give a small laugh. "How about you order for me?" I suggest, arching a brow.

He rubs his lips, hiding a smile. "Deal."

A waitress appears moments later, as if she senses we already know what we want. Sage rattles the order off to her, which is easy since it's the same for both of us.

When she's gone, Sage stares across the table at me. His eyes are sad and as I look him over, I realize how much my brother has aged in the last year. He's young, sure, but there are slightly visible lines by his eyes and the sides of his mouth that weren't there before. The stress and worry has taken a toll on him.

"How are you today?" He winces and shoves his fingers through his hair. "That sounds generic, but I mean it."

I don't know the best way to answer him. I don't want to lie and make it seem like I'm a-okay, but I don't want to worry him any more than I already do.

I shrug out of my coat to give myself a moment to compose myself and come up with an answer. "Not good, but better than I thought I'd be," I settle on. It's true too. I thought I might end up curled in a ball, thinking of the terror, of my mom, my friends, of the innocence that was robbed that day.

Sage nods, his tongue sliding out to moisten his lips. He only does that when he's nervous or bothered by something. "I keep trying to imagine what that day was like for you, and God, Dani ... it kills me inside to think about what you survived."

I close my eyes, blocking out the images that only hours ago I shared with Lachlan. "Don't think about it, Sage. Please."

He continues, undeterred. "Getting that call..." He pauses, shaking his head. He looks pained, sick to his stomach. "It was the scariest moment of my life." He looks utterly heartbroken relaying this. "I think I blacked out. The next thing I knew I was getting off a plane in Portland, on my way to the hospital. You were still in surgery, but I kept telling myself you'd sense I was there. I needed you to pull through more than I needed anything else."

"Sage." Tears fill my eyes, spilling over. I reach across the table, placing my hand over his. He flips his over, squeezing mine.

"You have no idea how terrified I was. I thought my entire family was gone."

I close my eyes, my whole body shuddering. I hate thinking of anything to do with what happened, but that day and the days immediately following were some of the worst. When I was first told I might never walk again, my first thought was that I'd rather have died. Looking back, I know that was a selfish thing to think, but I thought my life couldn't be fulfilling. I was naïve and angry.

Sage clears his throat, leaning back in the booth. "I'm glad I have you, D."

I don't have words for him, so I simply smile and hope it's enough.

———

THE MARKET he takes me to is indoors, which is ideal considering the cold weather, and huge. It spans thousands of square feet as far as I can see.

We stay together, because even with cell phones if we split up it would be hard to find one another.

"What are you looking for?"

I glance up at him, surprised he's noticed my intense scanning. "I'm not sure." I shrug, my eyes roaming the tables we pass. "But I'll know it when I see it."

He jerks his head in a nod and we keep moving.

There is an overwhelming amount of *stuff* on display, from things that look more like junk, or yard sale items, to nice items like antiques and handmade creations.

We've been looking nearly an hour, and I can sense Sage getting tired since he loathes this kind of thing, when I finally spot what I've been looking for.

Well, I wasn't looking for this item in particular, just something that reminded me of our mom. For the last year I've tried not to think about her, and hidden reminders away, but today I'm *choosing* to remember by getting something I know she'd love.

"Dani, where are you going?" Sage calls after me.

I hadn't even realized I was moving away from him.

I stop at the booth, my fingers gliding over the handmade wind chimes. They're decorated with flowers, yellow and white hand painted blossoms, as well as three-dimensional ones made from wire. It's stunning and someone had to spend a lot of time making it. My mom loved nature. She loved gardening and digging her hands in the dirt. She always said outside was where she belonged, wild and free like the birds and flowers, and that the wind chimes she collected were the music of her soul. She had so many of them, hanging from the back porch, trees, anywhere she could put one.

"This is it," I announce to Sage when he joins me.

He gives me a quizzical look. "A wind chime?"

I wet my lips, suddenly nervous. I don't want to make him mad or upset. "It's for Mom. I want to get something for her today."

Sage's features soften and he gives me a sympathetic look. "Yeah, D, of course."

Sage bargains with the guy and buys the wind chime for me. The guy wraps it up carefully so it doesn't get damaged and hands it to me in a brown paper bag.

I clutch the bag to my chest, like I have to protect it, as we plow our way through the crowd to the parking lot on the opposite end.

Nothing is said, but Sage heads back to his condo.

Once inside I turn to him. "Do you mind if I keep it in my room?"

He shakes his head. "It's yours. You picked it."

I give him a grateful smile and head down the hall to my room. I lay the bag down so I can take my coat and boots off. The apartment is toasty warm and I don't want to sweat to death.

Carefully, I unwrap the chimes. They brush against each other, echoing through my room.

Standing on my tiptoes I lean over my bedside table, hanging it on a nail that was already in perfect place to let the chimes dangle in the corner of the large window.

Stepping back, I clasp my hands and smile.

"Hi, Mom."

CHAPTER THIRTY-THREE

"HEY." ANSEL FALLS INTO STEP BESIDE ME IN THE school hall. "I got the okay from my parents that you and your brother can come to our house for Thanksgiving."

I don't tell him, but I completely forgot about his invite. "Oh, um, yeah—tell them thank you for me. I'll ask Sage if he's cool with that."

"You didn't reply to my texts this weekend," he says in a lower voice. "I wanted to make sure you were okay." When I don't respond right away he gently grabs my elbow and tugs me into an alcove. "Dani, talk to me."

"It sucked. I'm not going to lie, it isn't easy."

He ducks his head, trying to force me to meet his gaze. "I'm here for you, Dani. Or I'm trying to be, at least."

"I know."

He frowns, his eyes narrowing on me. "I'm not sure you do." The warning bell chimes and he grimaces. "I have to get to class. I'll see you later."

He stares at me for a second too long and a shocked breath passes through my lips when he kisses my cheek.

Before I can do anything he's already gone, headed in the opposite direction.

I press a hand to the spot he kissed me.

What the hell?

———

LACHLAN SITS AT HIS DESK, his head bent over some kind of papers or forms he's inspecting closely. His head jerks up in surprise as I flounder inside, closing the door behind me. I'm out of breath, having hurried here as fast as I could, which is a pretty difficult feat.

His confusion quickly melts into worry. "Are you okay? Why are you here? It's not time for you to be here, right? Did I lose track of time?" He mutters the last part to himself.

"N-No," I stutter, my back against the door.

His eyes narrow and he stands slowly, his palms flat on his desk. "You're supposed to be at lunch."

"I-I … I had to come here," I blurt, the confusion and anxiety rattling around inside me.

"Why?" His voice is deep, hesitant. I think he's afraid of my answer.

"I can't have lunch with my friends today," I hiss.

"Why not?" He crosses his arms over his chest. The way he's looking at me I know he's dissecting my words and posture, trying to figure out what has me so rattled.

"*Because*," I hold a hand to my chest, "Ansel kissed me."

Lachlan's lips part. "What?" He looks surprised and I don't know whether I should be offended or if his surprise is for another reason.

"It was my cheek," I admit in a hushed tone, "but I got the feeling he wanted to kiss more than my cheek." I cover my face with my hands. "I am not equipped to handle this."

Lachlan's jaw ticks. "Do you have lunch?"

"N-No." *Great, I'm back to stuttering.* "I came straight here. I couldn't risk running into him or my other friends."

Lachlan rubs his stubbled jaw. "I'm going to go grab us something to eat. You…" He waves a hand at me. "You stay here."

I open my mouth to argue, but he easily moves around me and is out the door.

It clicks closed behind him, leaving me all alone.

I take my backpack off, setting it on the ground. My coat comes off next. I rarely stop to use my locker, unlike a lot of other kids, so I carry what I need with me at all times.

Walking over to the window, I gaze outside at the small snow flurries tumbling down through the sky. There's a light dusting on the ground but I have a feeling it'll be gone by the time we leave today. It doesn't matter, though, a heavy snowfall is around the corner I'm sure.

I walk around, realizing this is the first time I've been alone in his office. I can't help but snoop a little. Stepping around behind his desk, I sit down, taking in everything on his desk—what he thinks is important enough to have within arm's reach.

There are several pens, white and gold in color. I pick one up, turning it over in my fingers. I shouldn't do it, it's completely irrational, but I slip one into the pocket of my jeans.

There are two more family pictures, one of him and his sister at what looks like a concert, and the other is of him with his parents at the Seattle Space Needle.

I study the picture closer. He's a lot younger in it, maybe sixteen.

My finger glides against the glass, my eyes widening at a figure in the background of the photo.

I recognize the bright pink shirt.

There was a melting ice cream cone on the front.

I wore it all the time when I was seven — so often my mom swore she was going to throw it away so I'd be forced to wear something else. She never did.

The image of my face is grainy due to the distance, but I know it's me. My hand is clasped in my mom's, she's turned away from the camera and I remember her yelling at Sage for walking away. But he was fourteen and didn't want to be seen with us. It wasn't cool to have his mom chaperone his school trip and for his little sister to tagalong.

My eyes move back to Lachlan in the photo, the teenage boy version of him, with a crooked smile, and youthful innocence. His face is bare of any trace of stubble and there's mischief in his eyes.

I feel confused, my heart stuttering behind my rib cage, because how is it possible that Lachlan and I crossed paths so many years ago?

My chest grows tight and I realize I'm holding my breath.

I loose it, inhaling a fresh lungful of air.

In another plane of time, Lachlan and I existed, for one fleeting moment, in the same place.

Now, here we are today.

The door to his office opens and I drop the photo. It glances off the desk, dropping to the floor where a crack appears down the middle.

I drop to my knees to grab it.

"S-Sorry," I stutter as he enters with food. I stand back up, the frame clasped in my hands. "I was looking. I didn't mean to break it."

"It's fine." He sets the food down on his desk, not at all bothered by my snooping.

He holds out his hand for the photo but I can't give it back right away.

I look at the girl in the corner, that innocent child who had no idea what was ahead of her or who was standing a mere few feet away from her—the man who would one day consume her heart, body, and soul.

"Dani?" he prompts, angling his head and trying to see what I'm so captivated by in the photo.

I hand it back to him with another mumbled apology. He holds the frame, looking at the picture like he's trying to figure out what had me raptured.

I'm not about to tell him it's me in the photo.

He sets it back down, but from his frown I know he's still trying to puzzle it out.

With a shake of his head, he picks up one of the sand-wiches and passes it to me. "I got a couple bags of chips since I didn't know what you like."

I look at the bags of chips on his desk and swipe the salt n' vinegar ones. I'm not hungry anymore, but I know I need to make an effort to eat something.

I sit down in my usual spot, crossing my legs under me. It's not the most comfortable position, but I make do.

Lachlan's eyes feather over me. "Do you want to talk about it?"

"The picture?" I blurt, my eyes shooting up in surprise.

He glances at the frame and back to me with a bewil-dered expression. "No," he shakes his head, unwrapping the sandwich, "about Ansel. You seemed really upset when you got here."

In my shock over the photo I'd completely forgotten about Ansel and the kiss.

"I overreacted." I open the bag of chips, digging through it to pick out one that's curled. "It was only my cheek."

He frowns. "But you were upset."

"Because I was surprised." My eyes meet his reluctantly. Lachlan is probably the last person on the planet I should be having this conversation with considering we shared an actual kiss. "I ... Ansel is my friend but I think he wants more."

"And you don't?"

I continue to stare at him. "No."

"Why?"

The bag crinkles in my hand. "I like someone else."

He sits back, clasping his hands—his sandwich and unopened chips abandoned on the desk. "Dani—"

I shake my head, not wanting to hear what he has to say. "You don't have to say anything. I know it's wrong. I know..." I swallow past the lump in my throat. "I know nothing can happen ... again, but I won't deny my feelings. Not when I've been numb for way too long."

His blue eyes soften, the raging blue waters suddenly still. He looks like he wants to say more, but he presses his lips together.

We eat in silence.

The bell rings, ending lunch.

And still, we sit in silence.

There's nothing else that can be said.

CHAPTER THIRTY-FOUR

"I can't believe I agreed to this," Sage grumbles, re-tucking his pale blue oxford shirt into his pressed navy pants. "Thanksgiving with *Ansel*." He sneers the name, making a face along with it. "I'd rather have dinner with a pack of hyenas."

Sighing from my perch on the barstool, I say for the thousandth time, "We don't have to go."

He places his hands on his hips, narrowing his eyes on me. "Well, I agreed. Can't exactly back out now."

"You didn't have to say yes," I remind him with a pointed finger.

He scrubs a hand over his stubble. Normally he's freshly shaved since his job requires it, but since he has a few days off he's letting it grow in.

"It was nice for his family to invite us. It would've been rude to decline." He exhales a weighted breath. "Does he know?"

"Know what?" I blink at him, confused.

"About…" He waves his hand at me wildly.

I know what he's asking, but I can't help it when I say, "Does he know magic?" I mimic his hand gesture.

"Dandelion," he warns and I laugh, slipping off the stool.

"Yes, Sage, he knows about what happened."

He nods, hands still on his hips. "I'm surprised you told him."

"Me too." There's no sense in denying it. "Are you ready, then?"

"Yeah." He grabs his coat off the rack, slipping it on.

I begin my process of bundling up in a million layers.

We head down to the garage, and Sage immediately starts the car, letting it heat up. I bring up my texts from Ansel, finding the one with the address to his house.

Twenty minutes later we pull up outside a stone and brick monstrosity of a house. It's massive, with a circular driveway and what I'm sure is a sprawling bright green lawn in the summer.

Sage parks the car, letting out a low whistle. "Is his father related to the President of France? Do they have a president? Prime Minister?" he rambles, his nose crinkled in thought.

"I think they have both." I undo my seatbelt, stepping out.

My breath fogs the air as we walk to the front door.

"We should've brought a dish or something," Sage grumbles under his breath.

I give him an incredulous look. "We can't cook."

He laughs. "Right. Nobody would want anything we brought anyway. Could've bought a pie, though."

"Too late now." I push the doorbell.

We don't have to wait long before the door opens and a woman who has to be Ansel's mom opens it. "Oh, you

must be Sage and Dani. Ansel speaks so highly of you."
She smiles at me.

I stare at her in awe. She's beautiful, with dark brown
hair blown out in loose voluminous curls, fair skin and
amber eyes, her pouted lips are a glossy pink color, and
she's dressed in a fitted white dress I'd be terrified of
staining.

Sage and I step into the massive foyer. There's a grand
staircase and to our left is a formal living room, to the
right is the dining room with an already set table and
chandelier glowing above it.

"Let me take your coats."

I give her a skeptical look, because surely she doesn't
want my dirty coat to ruin her dress. But she waves us on,
her nails painted a soft pink.

I wonder what the color is called. I think I'd name it In
the Pink of Time.

She takes our coats, hanging them in a hall closet.

"Oh," she claps her hands suddenly and I jump from
the noise, "I'm Eliza. Elizabeth—but I prefer Eliza."

She looks like an Eliza.

"It's really nice to meet you."

I elbow Sage when he says nothing, too busy staring at
the beautiful home.

He lowers his eyes from the vaulted ceiling to her.
"Yes, thank you so much for having us, Eliza. I appreciate
it."

"I'm glad you could come. Come on, everyone's in the
den."

She motions for us to follow her.

She takes us downstairs to a finished basement where
a group of people are gathered around a theater type
screen watching a football game.

"Meadows." Ansel stands when he spots me, his eyes

immediately going to my brother. "And, uh, Sage." He walks around the people, careful not to trip over any legs. "Glad you guys could come."

"I'll be finishing things up," Eliza says and heads back up the stairs.

I look around at all the people, strangers except for Mrs. Kline. It's funny how seeing her outside of school feels odd and uncomfortable, but it's never felt that way with Lachlan.

"Thanks for inviting us," I say, elbowing Sage again, but this time for a completely different reason.

"Yeah, thanks."

Ansel introduces us to his family, including his father Gaspard.

Once all the introductions are made, Ansel shoves his hands into the pockets of his brown dress pants. "I wanted to give you a tour." Ansel addresses me and Sage harrumphs, rolling his eyes.

"*Sage,*" I bite out, since he promised he'd be on his best behavior.

"If it's a problem..." Ansel trails off.

Sage narrows his eyes on my friend. "A tour, only a tour, and no fucking bedrooms. I will squash your tiny pea-sized teenage boy nuts if you think about even touching my sister."

Ansel gulps.

"It's Thanksgiving, Sage," I groan, my cheeks coloring at his statement.

Sage sighs. "Go, but if you're gone longer than twenty minutes I'll hunt your ass down."

"Oh my God." I grab Ansel's hand, to get away from Sage, but when my brother's eyes narrow dangerously I quickly release my hold.

Before Sage can protest Ansel and I head upstairs. He

gives me a quick tour of the middle level, then leads me to the second story. "Your brother said no bedrooms, but…" He trails off with a shrug, swinging a door open.

His room is exactly what I'd expect for Ansel. Canvases litter the space, sketches taped to the walls, and art supplies everywhere. His bed is low to the floor with a long black headboard. The two windows, with a dresser in-between, look out onto the front yard. The hardwood floor is covered in a large white rug that's speckled with paint.

I spin in a circle with a smile on my face. "I love it. It's very you."

"It's kind of simple." He rubs the back of his head.

I stop in front of him. "It's perfect."

He gives me a crooked grin. Stepping forward until only a foot of space separates us. "I didn't get a chance to tell you before, but you look beautiful."

I look down at my dress. It's a chestnut color with little blue and white flowers, buttons going down the front, and cinched at the waist. It's a fairly simple dress, but I appreciate the compliment nonetheless.

"Thanks." I smile at him, startling when he closes the short distance between us. He gently places one hand on my hip, his eyes hesitant.

My heartbeat skyrockets.

His lips thin. "Dani?"

Ba-ðum, ba-ðum, ba-ðum.

All I can hear is my heartbeat in my ears.

"W-What?"

His eyes flick to my mouth.

"I really want to kiss you," he whispers, his eyes deepening in color. His hand comes up to cup my cheek, the tips of his fingers tangle in my hair.

"Ansel…" I lower my head, shaking it. My hand presses against his stomach, pushing him lightly away.

He exhales a sigh and his hand falls from my face as he steps back. His eyes are sad, but he forces a smile. "It's okay, Meadows."

I bite my lip, fighting tears. I like Ansel, as my friend, but I don't see him in a romantic way. Not when … not when my thoughts are consumed with someone else.

"I don't want to hurt you."

"I'm a big boy, Meadows. Yeah, I like you. Really *like* you. But," he shrugs, toeing the floor with the tip of his dress shoe, "you don't see me that way. It's okay, but I had to try."

We stare at each other and I can't think of anything else to say. I don't understand why I feel like crying, it's not like he rejected me, but I think there's a part of me that wishes I did like him back. It'd make things so much easier.

"Dandelion Meadows! Where are you?"

I exhale the breath I was holding. "We better get downstairs."

"Yeah," Ansel agrees, his eyes sad.

It kills me hurting his feelings, but I won't lead him on.

He takes me down a back staircase so we're able to appear as if we've been downstairs the whole time.

Sage's eyes narrow when he spots us.

"Where have you been?"

"Getting the tour, remember?" I try to keep the sarcastic bite from my words but I'm not entirely certain I succeed.

"Dinner's almost ready," he replies, looking between Ansel and me.

Finally, he shakes his head and turns, walking away.

Ansel and I pause in the hallway. I feel like something

needs to be said, but I don't know what. I'm at a loss for words.

"Ansel…"

"Don't, Meadows. It's okay."

His mouth is saying one thing, but his eyes are saying another.

I don't feel like arguing with him on the matter, so I nod.

We join the others.

He laughs, but his eyes don't.

He smiles, but his eyes don't.

And I can't help feeling like I broke my best friend's heart.

It's not like I asked him to like me in that way, but I still never want to hurt him.

And maybe, if it weren't for Lachlan I could like him back.

But there is Lachlan. Perhaps not a Lachlan and Dani, but still, I have my feelings like Ansel has his.

When Ansel's eyes meet mine across the table, I can't help wondering what he'd think if he knew I'd kissed our guidance counselor, that my feelings far surpassed those of *innocent*.

The food I've eaten suddenly sits leaden in my stomach.

I'm not so hungry anymore.

CHAPTER THIRTY-FIVE

DECEMBER INVADES WITH BLISTERING COLD.

Slushy snow plagues the streets, piling up into nasty gray mountains.

I climb onto the school bus, shivering inside my coat despite my layers.

Locating an empty seat in the back, I sit down, putting my earphones in.

Say Love by James TW plays in my ears as the bus pulls away from the curb. It's only been a week and a half since Thanksgiving, but things are still awkward between Ansel and me. In his defense, I've been far more skittish about the whole thing than he has. I know it's largely in part to my guilt over my feelings for Lachlan.

The bus arrives and I get off, taking a moment to pause and tilt my head up to the sky. It's a grayish color, a few flurries beginning to fall. They're calling for a snowstorm to start this evening. I doubt it'll be as bad as they're claiming, it never is.

Inhaling a cold lungful of air, I head inside straight to the art room.

Pulling out my sketchpad, I idly work on my latest personal drawing. It's an outline of Sage. Troubled eyes, thick brows, worried lines. Because it's mostly eyes someone else might not recognize it as my brother, but I do.

Students filter in, and it is no surprise Ansel is the last.

He takes his seat beside me.

"Avoiding me, Meadows?" He arches a brow, his tone light but eyes sad.

"No," I hedge, closing my sketchpad and putting it away so I can work on our latest class assignment—a watercolor landscape.

He makes a noise that's somewhere between an indignant scoff and a cough. "Don't lie to me. We're friends. I know you're … fuck, I know *I* messed things up, but please talk to me. I would never forgive myself if I ruined our friendship."

I ignore his comment for the moment, getting up to retrieve my canvas from the rack. He follows, grabbing his own, and we return to the table.

"I don't know what to say." It's a shitty response, but it's all I've got.

He blows out a breath, stirring his shaggy hair. "Can we at least talk about this? If we don't, it's always going to be awkward."

I bite my lip. I know he's right, but my stomach churns at the thought.

"Fine," I agree reluctantly.

"Let me drive you home." I open my mouth to protest, so he quickly adds, "I know Sage told you I couldn't bring you home anymore, but he's not going to know. We'll stop at Watchtower and talk—neutral ground."

I flick my eyes up at him, nodding. "Okay."

He smiles back. "Thank you."

Don't thank me. Not when one day you might hate me if you ever learn who really has my heart.

———

I PULL out the latest book I borrowed from Lachlan and pass it to him behind his desk. He's wearing his glasses again and pushes them up his nose before taking the book. His long fingers wrap around the hardback before he turns around and puts it on the shelf.

I've yet to tell him I got a library card, not when I would much rather borrow books from him. It's silly, I know, but I enjoy sharing his love of books. Watching him light up talking about his favorite reads is some of my favorite moments shared with him.

He doesn't ask if I want to borrow another. Instead, he automatically grabs another and passes it to me.

I don't look at the title, or even the cover, before I put it in my backpack. At this point I trust his choices.

"How's your day going?" he asks, shuffling some papers on his desk.

"Okay, I guess." I shrug, putting my backpack on the floor near my feet.

He has the blinds rolled up, the ground outside dusted with fresh snow. Flurries fall from the sky, twisting and swirling.

"They're saying it's going to be a blizzard."

My head slowly swivels back his way. "I'll believe it when I see it."

Snow might be a fairly regular occurrence here, but a blizzard, not so much.

"I don't know, the sky is getting darker."

"Really? I hadn't noticed, Sherlock."

His eyes widen at my snappy tone. "Something's wrong."

A statement, not a question, because Lachlan sees all and knows all.

I never told him about Ansel wanting to kiss me on Thanksgiving. I haven't told him about how it's strained my relationship with my only true friend. Don't get me wrong, I like Sasha, but she doesn't understand me the way Ansel does.

"Ansel wants to talk to me after school." I tap my foot against the ground, the carpet muffling the sound.

"Oh?" He leans back in his chair, crossing his fingers together as they lie on his chest.

There's no point in trying to keep it a secret anymore. "He asked to kiss me, but I said no, that I don't like him in that way. He's ... he's been fairly normal since, but I don't know how to be, because I feel terrible."

"Why? You shouldn't feel bad—if you don't see him in that way you can't help it."

I hesitantly raise my eyes to meet his baby blues. "Yeah, but how would he feel if he knew what's holding me back?"

Lachlan's lips twist and he swallows thickly. "What's holding you back?"

His eyes tell me he knows.

His expression, too.

"You."

His body softly shudders, it's barely noticeable, but I'm watching him closely so I don't miss the tremor.

He leans forward, hands clasped on the table. He hasn't moved around in front of it today. It's probably good he hasn't.

"Dani ... this ... we..." He exhales a weighted breath looking pained. "Nothing can happen with us."

Lachlan has never verbally said he returns my feelings, but he's never denied anything either. He could tell me I'm crazy, that he's over a decade older than me, but he does none of that because he feels it too. To deny it would be a crime.

"I know," I whisper, tugging on my sleeves, "but when feelings exist they can't be turned off with a switch. I can't force myself to like him the way he wants me to."

Lachlan stares at me, his eyes troubled. When he speaks again, it's with two simple words.

"I'm sorry."

———

THE BELL ABOVE WATCHTOWER COFFEE & Comics chimes merrily, signaling our arrival. The line is longer than normal, probably due to the impending storm and the arctic cold that cuts through all bundled layers.

Ansel and I get in line, waiting our turn.

Instead of my usual Boba tea, I get a latte. Once we both have our orders we take a seat at one of the tables across from each other.

I pick the label adhered to the side of my cup, waiting for him to speak first.

"Look," he finally speaks, leaning forward with his fingers wrapped around his coffee, "I fucked up and made things awkward. You're ... fuck, Meadows, you've become my best friend. I know you might not believe that, but you have. I don't want to screw things up and ruin our friendship because of a silly crush."

"Silly?" My tone is amused, my lips twitching with the threat of a smile.

He cracks a smile of his own, running his fingers through his unkempt hair. "Okay, maybe not silly, but still

—your friendship means more to me. I'm a big boy, Meadows. I can handle rejection. You don't like me in that way, it's cool. I respect your boundaries."

I loosen my fingers from around my cup. "Thank you. I … I'm sorry *I* made things awkward, but…" I bite my lip, not quite having the words. "I didn't want to do anything you might take as me leading you on."

He shakes his head. "Meadows, you said no. I understand what that word means and I would never disrespect you by thinking some innocent thing you do or say might mean more and trying to take advantage."

"Thank you," I whisper, tucking my hands under the table. "I wasn't looking to make friends here, but then I met you and you're my best friend. I didn't want to hurt your feelings." I duck my head, voice soft.

He reaches across the table, tapping his index finger beneath my chin so I'll lift my head. "You're my best friend, that's all that matters."

He smiles at me and I smile back. Something shifts, and the axis of the world feels righted once more.

CHAPTER THIRTY-SIX

STANDING IN FRONT OF THE LARGE WINDOWS IN THE living room of the condo I look out at the snow falling in a thick white curtain. I can't even see the building across the street. Everything is blinded by whiteness.

The news plays in the background, talking about the expected accumulation and the threat of power outages.

I bite my lip with worry since Sage isn't home yet.

Turning from the window, I swipe my phone off the coffee table and call him. No answer.

Me: Are you on your way home?

His reply comes a few minutes later.

Sage: I can't leave yet. Sry.

Me: The weather is getting really bad.

Sage: I know. But the boss won't let us go until this is done.

Me: Be careful.

Sage: Always.

I put my phone away, shaking my head with aggravation. It's ridiculous that we're in the middle of the storm of the century and his work won't let him leave. He needs to quit, and if he doesn't see it after this then my brother is the biggest idiot to ever exist.

My stomach rumbles with hunger. I heat up some leftover takeout, sitting at the bar top to eat on my own.

The lights flicker and I look around in fear.

Please stay on, please stay on, I silently chant to myself.

They flicker again before cutting out completely.

A small scream tears out of my throat. I slap my hand over my mouth, quieting the sound.

The condo is enveloped in complete darkness, save for the pure white out the window. Abandoning my food, I stumble over to where I left my phone.

The screen lights up and I text Sage again.

Me: The power is out.

Sage: It's out here too.

Me: Are you coming home?

Sage: The snow is too deep already. We're stuck here regardless of the power being out.

"You have to be kidding me," I mutter to myself.

Me: Be safe.

Tucking my phone in my back pocket, I take a deep breath, trying to think if there are any candles anywhere.

But I already know there aren't, because Sage claims they give him a headache.

Me: Do we have a flashlight.

Sage: Check the drawer by the sink.

Navigating around the room, I bump my hip on the arm of the couch before I finally make it to the kitchen. I open the drawer and pull out the large flashlight, clicking it on.

Nothing.

Me: The batteries are dead. Do we have batteries?

My panic is rising, threatening to close my throat and suffocate me.

I'm alone, in a dark and empty condo. This is a recipe for disaster.

Sage: Fuck. No. Sorry, D.

I let out a groan of frustration.

Sage: Are you going to be okay?

Me: I have to be.

Sage: I don't think I'm getting out of here tonight. Maybe not even tomorrow.

I stare at his text, biting back anger.

If he'd just come home, or quit this stupid job, I wouldn't be home alone right now in a pitch-black apartment, moments away from losing my ever-loving shit.

As my anger and panic builds, I make a decision that is both reckless and dumb.

Edging out into the pitch-black hallway, I feel my way down and to the door for the stairs.

God, I hope no one was in the elevators.

My hand closes around the door and I pull it open.

I have to move slowly, since I can't really see, and only have the barest glow emanating from my phone.

I climb one flight of stairs, exiting onto the twelfth floor.

Finding myself in front of Lachlan's door, I knock, sending up a silent prayer that he'll be home.

If he's not...

Zeppelin's booming bark echoes and a second later the door opens.

"Dani," he breathes my name, a hushed whisper upon his lips.

He doesn't look surprised at all to see me.

His large hand wraps around my left wrist, tugging me inside. He closes the door behind me.

The room glows with at least a dozen lit candles. It's

fairly easy to make out the shape of furniture and it smells like fresh baked goods.

"I thought you might show up," he murmurs, tipping his head down.

"You did?"

His hands cup my elbows, and I don't know if he realizes it or not, but our bodies are only inches apart. Zeppelin sniffs at me body, but is oddly more subdued than usual.

He nods. "The dark is a windowless space."

I tip my head up at him, moistening my lips with my tongue. Being this close to him is doing things to me.

It doesn't matter that only a handful of hours ago he spoke of how nothing can happen between us.

Releasing me, he turns, "Sit down, do you want some water or something?"

I shake my head, tucking a piece of hair behind my ear. The flames from the candles flicker in his blue eyes.

"All I want is to not be alone."

He glides the back of his fingers over my cheek. "You're not. You have me."

He's never been so bold with me. Maybe it's the dark, or the storm, or something more. It doesn't matter, because all I know is how he's looking at me right now is the way I've always wanted to be viewed in someone else's eyes.

He clears his throat and steps back, maybe realizing he's being more forward than usual. He lets me pass him, my arm skimming his stomach as I do from the tight space.

Zeppelin is right on my heels. As soon as my butt touches the couch he places his massive head on my legs, wanting me to pet him. I rub his head, smiling as I do. His eyes flick over, watching Lachlan as he sits down on the couch too, right beside me despite the other places he could sit.

The left side of his leg is flush to my right, setting me on fire.

Does he have any idea what his presence does to me, let alone his touch?

Silence envelops us, and I don't know how to break it or even if I want to.

In the silence, he's just Lachlan, and I'm Dani. We're not student and counselor.

The dark and quiet have no labels. They judge no one.

Within the darkness you can hide a multitude of sins. The problem is when the light comes again.

Leaning back against the couch cushions, I angle my head toward him.

He does the same, the two of us blinking at each other.

I jolt in surprise when he cups my cheek in his right hand.

Lachlan is touching me. *Willingly* touching me. I nearly hold my breath, but force a soft breath from between my lips.

"Why do I have to be so torn up over you?" he murmurs, his eyes raking over my face. Shadows dance over his handsome face from the flickering candles. "You," his thumb brushes over my lips, "a student. You're turning me into the worst kind of person, desiring something that isn't mine for the taking."

My heart stutters offbeat.

His fingers dip into my hair, lowering to the nape of my neck.

I place my hand over his, not wanting him to let go. I'm so afraid he's suddenly going to snap to his senses, put distance between us, and I need to soak up every second of this.

His eyes lower, his long, thick, black lashes fanning against his cheeks.

"W-What if you didn't have to take me?" I whisper the words, scared to give them voice. "What if I'm offering myself to you?"

"Dani…" He shakes his head back and forth.

I take his face between my hands, his stubble rasping against my palms. Rising up on my knees, I scoot forward. There's only a shadow of space between us. "How can you take something I *want* to give?"

His tongue slides out, moistening his lips. Those vibrant blue eyes of his are nearly navy in the dark with a hint of gold from the candlelight.

"It's wrong."

"It doesn't *feel* wrong," I argue, my forehead pressed gently to his. Our breaths mingle in the air, sharing space like our thoughts and feelings. His eyes close again, his hands opening and closing into fists on his thighs. "You can touch me." My lips brush his cheek. "I'll let you. I won't mind at all."

I want to climb in his lap, press my body against his. I want to feel all my soft curves melt into his hard planes. I want to feel his lips on mine.

But he needs to make the move this time. This can't be one-sided. It's not fair. I don't want to feel like I'm pushing myself on someone who doesn't want me back, even when everything says he does.

The muscle in his jaw ticks, his eyes at war, fighting a battle I can't even begin to understand.

His dark hair tickles my forehead as he moves. "I *can't* do this. Why do I keep letting you in?"

I don't think he's talking about into his apartment.

We're so close together now, barely a breath separating us. I desperately want him to touch me, but I know I can't force this. If I do it'll only push him away.

I know why he hesitates, it's what keeps me from claiming what I want. I might be young, but it doesn't mean I don't understand the ramifications for the two of us if we're found out. But it also feels like the greatest crime of all to deny our feelings. Something that feels this *right* should never be wrong.

But it is.

We are.

And to admit what we want, to give in, is to change the trajectory of both our lives.

His eyes close once more, murmuring my name.

In a blink his hands are on my hips.

I squeak as he pulls me onto his lap. My hips sink down onto him, a soft moan parting my lips at the feel of him pressed to my center.

"Dani," he croons.

His hands fist in my hair.

I roll my hips, eliciting another moan from my throat.

"Dani," a purr this time.

Finally, blissfully, his lips are on mine.

CHAPTER THIRTY-SEVEN

THIS IS WHAT A KISS SHOULD BE. SOMETHING YOU FEEL through your whole body. My skin feels hypersensitive to every touch. My palms land on his solid chest, scrunching the fabric of his shirt between my hands. He kisses me with a desperation I mirror with my movements. I'm eager to get closer to him, to feel every part of him.

Our tongues tangle together with a passion we've kept chained for months. This is the kind of kiss I've seen in movies and read in the books he's let me borrow. It's a kiss that changes things. There's no coming back from this. It doesn't in any way compare to our first kiss. That was a hesitant, fragile thing, while this is a claiming.

I know for a fact, no one will ever be able to kiss me like Lachlan does.

It's not like I have many kisses in my past to compare it to, but I know this is special.

Our lips move together, creating a melody of our own creation. My knees press against his side, and if my weight against him is a bother, he doesn't show it.

Wrapping my arms around his neck, my breasts push

into his chest. His hands skim up my sides, his thumbs resting beneath their swells.

I want him to go higher. I want him to strip me bare. I've never felt this aching kind of need before. My center pulses and I rub myself against him needing some kind of relief. I whimper, but he stifles the sound with a kiss.

My thoughts are a constant loop of *Lachlan* over and over again, his name echoing through my brain like a prayer.

I wonder if his thoughts are similar because he moans my name before diving in for another kiss.

In the back of my mind, my conscience whispers at me that I should stop this. Not because it's wrong, but because he could get in trouble. That's the last thing I want. I wouldn't forgive myself if he ever got in trouble because of me.

Morally, the only thing separating us is his position.

Other than that, the way I see it, we're both adults. I'm eighteen, I'll be nineteen in a few months on April twenty-second. I *know* what I'm doing. I'm not being coerced, but my being a student and his being a school counselor puts us in a precarious situation.

But for right now, I want to forget all that.

I dive into the kiss voraciously, giving him my all. I live every stolen moment like it's the last, and that means leaving no room for regrets. I have to give and take while I can.

Lachlan hardens beneath me, and the feel of him so long and firm against such an intimate place steals my breath, heating my skin. I wonder what it would feel like to reach between us, skim my hand beneath the band of his sweatpants, and wrap my hand around him.

"Fuck," he growls, roughly yanking down the side of my shirt.

He peppers kisses over my bare shoulder and up my neck. My back arches, causing me to rock deeper into him.

"Lachlan." I pull his hair, keeping him close to me. I'm terrified if I loosen my hold he'll come to his senses and stop.

Biting down on my lip, I continue to rock against him, dangerously close to an orgasm. I've never had one like this before, with a guy—a *man*—only on my own. I'm chasing the feeling, even though I'm slightly embarrassed I could come so easily this way.

Lachlan wraps my hair around his fingers, tugging my lips back to his. He's wild, unhinged. It's building a craving inside me for so much more.

Lachlan is a gasoline cocktail and I'm more than willing to go up in flames.

"Why you?" he whispers between kisses. "Why. You."

I don't have an answer for him, not when I keep asking myself the same thing about him. Some things don't have to make sense, I guess, not when they feel so right.

His hands slip down my body, to my hips, rocking me harder against him.

"Lachlan," I gasp, and he bites my bottom lip, tugging it into his mouth.

His blue eyes meet mine in the dark as he releases my lip. "Let go, Dani, I've got you."

I don't want to let go, because once I do, I'm afraid this moment between us will be over too. There's no controlling it once I fall off the ledge into an abyss of pleasure. His hold tightens on my hips, his own rocking against mine.

He pants, letting out a low groan. *"Fuck."*

We fall together.

Spinning.

Twirling.

Stars.

Pleasure.

Wetness seeps through my underwear, probably onto my pants, but I can't bring myself to care.

Lachlan wraps his arms tightly around me, his breaths as uneven as mine as he comes down from his own orgasm.

I expect him to push me off, to be appalled by what has transpired between us, but he hugs me tighter, burying his face into my neck, pressing soft kisses to my sensitive skin.

I twine my fingers into his hair, kissing his lips softly.

He places a tender kiss to the sensitive skin beneath my ear.

Our bodies are plastered together and I hope he has no plans of releasing me, because I don't want to go anywhere. This right here, with him, is where I belong. It's the only thing I'm certain of anymore.

"Are you hungry?" he asks softly after a while.

I nod against his chest. "But I don't want to move."

He chuckles, the sound vibrating against my ear I have pressed to his chest. I place my hand on the column of his throat so I can feel it there too. He grabs my hand, kissing the tips of my fingers.

"You need to eat."

He stands up with me wrapped around his body, carrying me into the kitchen. He sets me on the counter, where behind me even more candles are lit.

I slowly unwind my body from his.

"Why do you have so many candles?"

He shrugs, opening the dark refrigerator. "I like candles."

It's such a simple response, but makes me laugh anyway.

"I can't exactly cook you anything, so is a sandwich good?"

"That'd be great."

He starts pulling out everything he needs and goes about making two sandwiches. I itch to ask him about what happened, but I don't want reality to set in and for him to regret it. It would kill me if he did, when that was one of the greatest moments of my entire life.

Lachlan finishes making the sandwich and adds some chips to the side before passing me a plate. He hops up onto the counter beside me, our legs swaying similarly. Sitting here with him like this, things feel so simple, like I'm a girl, a *woman*, spending time with the man she likes. Things don't feel nearly as complicated as they are.

I take a bite of my sandwich, chewing in silence.

"Is it any good?" he asks for a moment.

"It's great." I pick up a chip, nibbling on it.

"You're awfully quiet," he muses. "You're not regretting things are you?"

My head shoots in his direction. "No, but I'm worried you are."

The breath that leaves him is a mighty gust. Setting his plate to the side, he turns to me. His lips are a thin line as he looks down at his hands, flexing them in and out of fists. I wait for him to say something, biting my own tongue.

"I should be." His voice is barely above a whisper. "But I'm not." He finally looks at me head on, and even though it's dark I can see in his eyes that he means it. "Fuck, it's so wrong." He drops his head, shaking it. "But nothing has ever felt as right as it does when I'm with you. The second you walk into a room, I'm aware. It's like my body *knows* and senses you. I've never experienced anything like it before." He grinds his teeth together. "It makes me angry, because you're young, Dani. So much younger than me. You might think eleven years isn't a lot, but it's more than a decade, and believe me we do a lot of growing and changing in that time. I'm so afraid my feelings for you are going to rob you of something."

I put my plate down, grabbing his hands in mine. It tears me apart how tortured he looks. "You can't force me to feel the things I do. That's all me. You have no idea how crazy I've felt crushing on you. It feels so cliché—the sexy older guy, but feelings aren't a faucet you can turn on and off. They just *are*."

He pulls his hands from my mine. I can't even feel the sting of rejection before he's touching my cheek, stroking his thumb tenderly against the curve.

He leans in slowly, eyes on mine, looking for any hint of hesitation from me, but I give him none. Our eyes close in the same second. In another his lips are on mine. It's dangerously wrong, but undeniably right.

The next thing I know he's sliding off the counter and I'm in his arms once more.

I wrap around him, never breaking the touch of his mouth, as he carries me through the apartment and to his bedroom.

I hear Zeppelin's nails on the hard floor following us, but Lachlan manages to close the door, shutting him out.

He sits down on the bed, and my legs fall on either side of him, pressing into the mattress. I feel him lengthen beneath me again.

He maneuvers me so I'm lying flat on his bed, head pressed to the pillow, with him above me. His body heat swathes me, and it feels like nothing else exists outside of the two of us.

My hands find their way under his shirt, skimming the hard planes of his muscles. He sits up, reaching back to hook his thumbs into the collar and yanks it off. He kisses me again, his tongue twining with mine.

One of his hands touches my hip, hesitantly feathering beneath my shirt. He traces a circle around my belly button before withdrawing. I wiggle my hips, grinding into his pelvis.

"You can take it off," I practically beg.

He rolls off me, but before I can feel the sting of his loss he pulls my body against his large frame so I'm practically sprawled overtop. Our legs twine together and I lay my left arm over his chest where he promptly tangles our fingers together.

"Why did you stop?" I pant, breathless. "I thought —"

He squeezes my hand against the rapidly beating pulse of his heart. "No."

"No?" I repeat, hurt coloring my tone.

He angles his head down, and even though I can't see him clearly in the pitch-black bedroom I feel the weight of his gaze. "Because I'm not about to fuck you like some horny teenage boy that can't control himself. You mean more to me than that." His other hand finds my cheek. He brushes the back of his fingers over my sensitive flesh. "The best things in life are meant to be savored. Treasured." He swallows, clearing his throat. His fingers wiggle slightly in mine from nerves. "The thoughts I have about you break so many fucking rules. If I'm going to hell for this, I want to do it thoroughly. I want to take my time. I want to explore every crevice of your body with my tongue and pluck your thoughts like a guitar string. I want to know the ins and outs of what you love and why you love it. I want to know the most sensitive parts of your body, what makes you moan my name and beg for more. I'm a selfish bastard, Dandelion Meadows, and I want every fucking part of you."

I don't reply, not with words anyway.

Instead, I kiss him.

You already have me.

When he kisses me back, his lips say *I know.*

CHAPTER THIRTY-EIGHT

WAKING UP IN LACHLAN'S ARMS IS THE LAST THING I expect, and for a moment I think it's a dream. I try to stay burrowed in the sweet clasp of sleep, but it won't hold me any longer. I blink my eyes open and as Lachlan's room comes into view in the morning light the night before comes rushing back to me. A slow smile tickles my lips and I bite down, trying to keep it contained. I don't know why, since he's still sound asleep, his soft breaths caressing my exposed neck.

His front is wrapped around my back, our legs twined. One of his arms rests between my breasts. I worry that when he wakes up he'll be ashamed to find himself in this position with me, but I can't bring myself to regret what transpired between us last night. Every touch, kiss, and intimate moment is something I'll cherish forever. As much as I wanted more, I'm glad now he didn't give in, because it'll be all the much sweeter when it happens. And I know, without a doubt, it will.

Lachlan and I are inevitable.

An ocean could separate us and I know deep down we'd still find our way back to each other.

His hand flexes against my stomach and I know he's seconds from waking.

His thumb rubs in a circle around my belly button where my shirt has ridden up. He lets out a sleepy yawn, burrowing his face into the back of my neck. His stubble scratches my skin and I try not to giggle when it tickles.

Slowly, I roll over to face him. His hand finds it's way back to my hip, pulling me closer. He blinks his eyes open, the blue becoming brighter as he fully wakes.

"Dani." My stomach dips at the sensual sound of my name in his deep sleep-thick morning voice.

I brush my finger over one of his dark brows, suddenly shy. "Hi."

He smiles, those straight white teeth blinking into existence. He grabs my hand, playfully nipping at my fingers before circling our hands together.

I wait for the shoe to drop, for him to realize how wrong this is and shove me out of his bed, his apartment, with anger on his face.

But he keeps looking at me, his eyes feathering over my face like he's trying to memorize every detail and feature.

Last night, he kissed me in his bed for a long time before he got up to extinguish the candles from the main room. When he returned, we kissed some more, our hands exploring each other's bodies, but not too much, before we finally fell asleep.

Lachlan cups my cheek and my skin automatically heats from his magnetic touch. My nipples pebble as goosebumps pimple my skin.

"What are you thinking?" I whisper, breaking the silence.

He traces the shape of my lips with the tip of his index finger. "Nothing." I open my mouth to say I doubt that, when he adds, "I want to remember what this moment looks and feels like. I don't want to taint it with reality."

I understand what he means. Placing my hand on the column of his throat, I feel the steady pulse of his heart.

"Can we stay here forever?" I don't mean to say the words aloud, but somehow they slip out.

The lines beside his eyes deepen for a second with thought. "I wish." His hand moves down to my hip, staying there. "I need to let Zeppelin out."

"I don't want to move."

"Me either, but life waits for no one."

I know he's right. Somehow, we manage to finally move from beneath his warm covers. I try the light on the nightstand, but it doesn't come on. "Still no power."

He sighs, tugging on a sweatshirt that was hanging on the doorknob. It's not as worn in as the one I kept of his. He hasn't asked for it back. I think he knows it's mine now.

"I'll be back." He opens the door and Zeppelin immediately barrels inside, running from me to Lachlan and back again.

"I better call my brother."

Lachlan winces at the reminder of my sibling. That truth creeps in as an unwanted stain on the night we spent together. No matter how hard we try, reality is a bitch that won't stay away.

He gives a single nod before escorting Zeppelin from the room. I follow, watching him tug on his winter coat and leash the dog. He gives me a small, hesitant, almost shy smile before leaving.

I grab my phone from where I ended up leaving it on the couch last night and call Sage.

He answers on the first ring.

"Fuck, Dani, I'm so sorry I couldn't get home. I have no idea when I'll be able to leave. The roads are still hell and the power —"

"It's okay, Herb, don't worry." I hope the dorky nickname will help alleviate some of his stress. "I'm fine. Don't stress. Get home when you can."

"I will." A relieved sigh echoes through the phone. "I'll let you know when I finally get out of here."

"I love you."

He's quiet on the other end for a moment before he returns the sentiment.

I end the call and head back to Lachlan's bathroom.

After relieving myself, I wash my hands and steal some of his toothpaste. I swipe it on my finger and brush my teeth as best I can. My hair is a wild mess from Lachlan's fingers. As much as I don't want to brush away the evidence I know if I don't my hair will be impossible to deal with later.

Finally feeling a little more human, I leave the bathroom as Lachlan comes back.

I lean against his bedroom doorway as he pauses in the hallway, the two of us staring at each other through the narrow space.

My heart beats with reckless abandon. With every surge it's saying *I belong to you*.

Zeppelin runs up to me, forcing me to look down and break eye contact with his owner.

"Hey, buddy." I bend down, hugging the lovable bear of a dog.

Lachlan clears his throat. "Did you get ahold of your brother?"

I look up from my crouched position. "Yeah. He's still stuck at his work. The roads aren't safe."

"It's bad out there." He scratches his jaw. "I'll try to figure out something for breakfast."

"I can help." He arches a brow and I laugh. "Well, I mean, there's no power. It's not like I can burn the place down." I give a small shrug as I stand up straight.

He cracks a grin. "I'd love your help."

With one last scratch on Zeppelin's head I follow Lachlan into the kitchen. He starts pulling things out of the refrigerator, piling them on the counter.

"Do you like avocado toast?" He holds up the fruit … vegetable … whatever it is. "I mean, it'll be more like avocado on bread since I can't exactly toast it, but it shouldn't be too bad."

I laugh, stealing the avocado from him. My blue nails are bright against the skin of it. "Tell me what to do."

Lachlan tells me how to cut it and remove the giant seed in the middle. I scoop out the middle of it into a bowl, all while he watches with an amused smile because I'm convinced I'm somehow going to mess up something as simple as this.

We each spread the avocado over the bread, and Lachlan adds some grape tomatoes he cut in half. With a touch of pepper it's done.

I pick up the non-toasted avocado toast and bite into it. "Not bad," I compliment, holding a hand in front of my mouth to hide my chewing.

He smiles back, holding out his "toast" for me to cheers mine against.

"We probably should've done that before we bit into it, but better late than never." His eyes sparkle with humor.

I like seeing this relaxed side of him, where he lets his guard down with me.

"Are you visiting your family this Christmas?"

School will be shutting down in less than two weeks

for break. It would make sense for him to head back to Arkansas for an extended stay.

He shakes his head. "They're coming here, actually."

I look around, like I'm trying to mentally picture his family in his apartment. "That'll be nice."

"Mhmm." He wipes a crumb from his bottom lip.

"You need a tree."

"A tree?" He repeats, arching a black brow.

"Yeah, a Christmas tree. I mean, Sage and I don't have one either, but you should get one. You have the perfect spot." I point to an open area near the windows.

"Why don't you have one yet?" He leans his hip against the counter, angling his head down.

I give a small shrug, pulling off a bite and sticking it in my mouth. "Sage is busy with work. He ends up having to do stuff from home a lot when he is around."

"That must suck."

I arch a brow, licking avocado off my finger. "Don't go all shrink on me, *Mr. Taylor.*"

He lets out a small chuckle, shaking his head. "It was a statement."

"It is what it is." Those five words should be my life motto. "He has to do what they say. I know he hates it, even though he tried to convince me for a while he loved it, but he won't quit."

"Why?" Lachlan looks puzzled, a wrinkle forming in his normally smooth forehead.

"Why won't he quit?" He nods as I exhale a breath. "Because we Meadows are a stubborn bunch."

"No, seriously, what does he do? He probably could find something else fairly easy. It's a big city." He swishes his fingers lazily.

"Stuff with computers. I swear he's a secret genius." I finish my piece of bread and pull off a sheet of paper towel to wipe my fingers on. "And I'm sure a lot of places would love to have him, but I'm not kidding when I say he's stubborn. It's like he thinks he has to tough it out to prove a point."

"To who?"

"Himself?" I let my arms fall to my sides. "I really don't know. I keep begging him to leave, but he won't."

"Hmm." Lachlan presses his lips together.

"What are you thinking?"

"Nothing." He shakes his head and reaches out, placing a hand on my waist. His touch is gentle as he tugs me closer until I stand between the halo of his arms. With his other hand he cups the right side of my cheek. "Why do you feel like a dream?"

"A dream? I'm more like a nightmare."

He tosses his head back, his Adam's apple bobbing with laughter.

When he stops, his teeth dig into his bottom lip while his eyes bore into me. He looks like he wants to say something, but holds the words inside.

Tell me, Lachlan, I silently beg. *Give me all your thoughts, your words, your fears, dreams and ambitions. Give it all to me. I'll cherish it, I promise.*

He swallows and instead takes my hand, tugging me into the living room.

Zeppelin lifts his mighty head, watching us from the floor as Lachlan sinks onto the couch and pulls me down with him, fitting my small frame between his legs so I collapse on top of him with my front to his. The dog settles back down, clearly used to my presence now.

I cross my hands on his chest and rest my chin on them. Blinking up at him I wait for him to do or say something. He stares right back at me. I wonder what he sees when he looks at me.

Do I look as broken as I feel most of the time? Does he see the hopelessness beginning to fade from my eyes? Is it plastered all over my face how fucking enamored I am with him?

"You know," he begins, clearing his throat, "when I figured you'd show up yesterday, I told myself to tell you that you had to go back home, that you couldn't be here with me. But then, I opened the door and saw you. All those words … they no longer existed. When it comes to you, I'm incapable of common sense. I don't understand it, but I think … I think I'm tired of fighting. I think about you when I shouldn't, I have dreams of you that are immoral, I worry about you, I wonder what you're think- ing, and more than anything I want to make everything better for you and I'm so fucking torn up inside because I'm terrified I never can."

He rubs his thumb over my cheek. I'm not even sure he realizes he's doing it.

"You already are."

His blue eyes lighten at the same time he smiles—and that smile?

It's like a brand across my heart, a fiery piercing feeling as he signs his name across it in ownership.

He doesn't even realize it belongs to him.

CHAPTER THIRTY-NINE

LACHLAN RUBS HIS THUMB ABSENTMINDEDLY IN CIRCLES around my calf where my legs are draped across his lap. He looks sinfully sexy with a book clasped in his hands, and his glasses perched on his nose. He gave me a book to read too, since the power is still out, but all I want is to stare at him in the glow of the candlelight. I want to commit the sharp slash of his jawline, the slope of his nose, and angle of his brow to my memory. I might never have this opportunity again to spend this much time alone with him without the worry or threat of everything that exists against us outside these walls.

"I can feel you staring at me."

I giggle, leaning the side of my head against the couch. "I can't help it."

He slowly hinges his gaze from the words on the page to me. "I promise that book is as good as others I've lent you."

I bite my lip slightly, trying to hide my growing smile. "I'm sure, but I'd rather look at you."

"Why?" He sounds truly curious about my answer.

I hesitate, not wanting to sound creepy. "Because, right now, I can look at you however I want, and I don't have to worry about someone seeing something they shouldn't in my eyes." His eyes darken slightly to a stormy blue. "Like the other day, when I passed you in the hall, all I wanted to do was look at you but I was too scared my friends might notice that I don't look at you like the school counselor."

He swallows thickly. "What do you look at me like, Dani?"

"Like you're mine."

His breath catches just the slightest, the small sound amplified by the completely silent apartment. He tosses the book aside and I yelp when I find myself suddenly pinned to the couch with his big body over mine. My hips wiggle of their own accord, and he uses his own body to prevent me from moving any further. His hands are clasped on my wrists, holding them above my body. I feel vulnerable like this, but I have no desire to get away.

"Why do you have to say stuff like that?"

"Like what?" My voice cracks as I stare at him. He's so close I can count every eyelash and freckle dusted across his nose if I want.

"Stuff that makes it feel so fucking impossible to be a good guy."

If I had use of my hands I would touch his stubbled jaw. "You are a good guy."

He shakes his head. "No, Dani, I'm not. A good guy wouldn't be locked in his apartment with his student. A good guy wouldn't have kissed her. And a good guy *definitely* wouldn't be in the fucking position we're in right now." His breath caresses my lips with every word. "A good guy, definitely wouldn't be thinking the things I am right now."

It takes me a moment to find my voice. "What are you thinking?"

His eyes flash and his jaw snaps together like he's trying to jail the words in his throat. He shakes his head back and forth, his eyes falling closed.

"Tell me," I plead, wiggling my fingers and testing his hold.

When his eyes pop open it's like the blue is on fire. "I want to know how you taste." I open my mouth to protest that we've kissed, but he shakes his head. "Not your mouth, sweetheart." My heart stutters at the endearment. "I want to know how you sound, how you feel, I want to know what brings you the most pleasure. That's not what a good guy thinks about his student."

I have no words. They're stuck inside me, all the letters floating and jumbled. I'm unable to grab any of them and form them into sentences.

"Pretend I'm not your student."

"But you are."

"No," I bite out. "I'm Dani. I'm just Dani."

He brushes his nose against mine, his lips close to mine but still so far away. "That's where you're wrong."

He takes me by surprise when he finally kisses me. His lips are warm on mine. He still doesn't release my hands, leaving him entirely in control. He kisses me the way he wants, slow, taking his time, stealing another little piece of me.

His lips were made for mine to kiss. His hands for mine to hold.

Be mine, my lips speak to his with movement, not a sound passed between.

I'm already yours, his say back.

I don't think either one of us can make sense of these feelings between us, but they can no longer be controlled.

They're a wild, chaotic, living and breathing thing. All the reasons that should keep us apart are crumbling around us.

Behind my closed lids there's a flash of light. For a heartbeat, I'm stupid enough to believe it's us, that we're creating some kind of energy, but when I blink my eyes open I find the room flooded with light.

Lachlan's lips break from mine, his grasp loosening, but he still holds his body above mine, slowly blinking down at me.

"The power's back on," he says breathless, stating the obvious.

"Yeah," I breathe, unsure what else to say.

He sits up, scooting back from my body in the process. I instantly miss the feel of him and ease up, my throat closing up when I see the shame slowly leeching onto his face. I want to scrub it away. It's the last thing I want to see. Not after this, not after last night.

He rubs his hands roughly over his face.

When he lets them drop his eyes are watery.

"Don't say it," I plead, begging even more so with my eyes.

"This is so fucking wrong."

"You were kissing me five seconds ago," I protest, my voice cracking. "What changed?"

My hands clench into fists. I want to go back to when the lights were off, where the darkness hid our sins.

Lachlan stands suddenly, beating a fist against his chest. The veins in his neck stand out. I've never seen someone look so purely tortured before.

"I'm killing you and I'm killing me," he chokes up. "Fuck." He inhales a breath, his whole body expanding with it. "Being with you feels so fucking right, but it's —"

I stand too then, pointing at him. "Don't you dare say it's wrong. Don't do it." I shake my head.

"But it is, Dani. Don't you fucking see that?"

"I don't care!" I shout. "I, for once in my life, don't want to question everything and instead follow my gut to what feels right. Is that so wrong?"

His eyes grow bigger. "Yes, Dandelion! It is!" He tugs at his hair, and he looks so tortured I want to wrap my arms around him and make it better, but I know *I'm* the problem so I can't do that. "I'm not going to name off all the reasons this is wrong, because you already know," he swings his arm at me in a wild gesture, "don't you see? I can't be with you in the light, I have to hide like a coward in the darkness and I refuse to do that." His jaw clenches and he shakes his head roughly. "I won't do that to me or you."

I look around at all the glowing lights in the apartment —hatred burning through my veins, because such a simple thing has ruined everything.

"I don't care about the light," I whisper in defeat.

There's no point in fighting with him.

"I shouldn't have allowed myself to give in to my feelings." His words are barely audible, the struggle going out of him too. "You deserve so much more than this back and forth bullshit."

I close my eyes, releasing a pent-up breath. "I understand. I know what … what we feel is technically *wrong*, and I get where you're coming from. I won't lie and say it doesn't hurt, because it does. Five minutes ago I was blissfully happy, sitting with you, watching you, kissing you. Now…" I let my hands fall to my sides. "All because the *stupid* lights are back on it's ruined everything."

We stare at each other, the foot of space between us suddenly feeling insurmountable.

Lachlan swallows, working his jaw back and forth. "I'm sorry."

I know he is. I am too.

"I'll go." My voice cracks.

His eyes track my progress as I move around him, heading for the door. Zeppelin lifts his head, watching me go too. Neither he nor his owner make a move to stop me.

I look over my shoulder and find Lachlan watching me with sad eyes, his expression pained.

Turning back around I leave, letting the door click closed behind me like a period on the end of a sentence.

———

HOURS LATER, the door finally opens and Sage enters, looking utterly exhausted. I can't quite make sense of the utter relief I feel upon seeing him, but I dive off the couch into his body.

"Whoa." He stumbles back from the force, wrapping his arms around me. "I missed you too, Weed."

I hold him tight, not wanting to let go.

"Don't leave me," I beg my brother brokenly. "Everyone leaves, but you can't."

He squeezes me tighter, resting his head on top of mine. "Never."

CHAPTER FORTY

IT TAKES A SOLID WEEK FOR THE SNOW TO CLEAR enough for us to go back to school. The record blizzard was so bad that trucks were brought in from out of state, not just to fix the power, but to clear the snow from the streets. I watched from Sage's window as snow was loaded onto dump trucks to be hauled away. It looked eerily apocalyptic.

Tying the laces on my yellow Vans, I say a grateful prayer that this is the last week of school before winter break. Sure, it means a lot of time spent by myself with Sage working most days, but for the first time since the school year began I'm not looking forward to my fifty minutes spent with Mr. Taylor every day.

I've spent the whole week reminding myself he's Mr. Taylor, not Lachlan.

All my reminders didn't stop me from buying him a Christmas present, though.

Standing up, I brush my hands down the front of my jeans and shrug into my gray sweatshirt with the school's mascot on it. Sasha had gotten it for me, and I forgot about it, burying it in my closet. I'm sure she'll be happy to see me wearing it.

Layering on my coat, gloves, and hat, I finally swing my backpack onto my shoulders, ready to brave the cold and catch the bus.

Calling out a quick goodbye to Sage who would normally already be gone for work, I dash out the door.

I barely manage to catch the bus in time, and I'd be lying if I didn't admit I was tempting fate a bit, hoping I'd miss it and get to go back home.

Climbing the stairs, the door squeaks closed behind me as I find my seat and sit down by the window. The cold from the glass seeps through, chilling the air.

Popping my ear buds in, I search through my playlists. I pick a random one and click shuffle. *Hollow* by Jome begins to play.

Leaning my head back, the bus pulls away from the sidewalk while I pretend I don't see the black Acura driving beside it.

———

"NICE SWEATSHIRT," Sasha comments, flipping her curly blonde hair over her shoulder as she sits down at the library table.

"Thanks, some weird girl got it for me," I joke, plucking at the fabric.

"Rude." She sticks her tongue out. "It's nice to see you sporting some school spirit for a change."

"I'm trying."

"She looks nice in whatever." Ansel winks at me as he pulls out a chair. I know he's not flirting with me, just trying to stick up for me.

"It's okay."

I look over at Seth with an open mouth. "It speaks." It's so rare for him to reply at all that it takes me by surprise. I'm pretty sure this is only the second or third time he's spoken at lunch all year. I don't have any classes with him, but I can't help wondering if he talks in those.

Seth gives a shrug in response, picking at his packed lunch.

I unwrap my sandwich. I didn't get chicken salad today and I'm beginning to regret that decision. My turkey sandwich looks more like regurgitated cat food. But I didn't want to look at the chicken salad sandwich, let alone eat it, because I knew I would only think of Lachlan. I'm dreading enough seeing him today.

I understand where he's coming from, why he keeps pushing me away. I'm not dumb. I see how wrong this is. But that doesn't mean it doesn't break my heart a little being around him, especially when I seem to always give him a little piece of me in each of our sessions. It seems there's always one single truth I leave him with before I go.

"You look distracted," Ansel notes.

"Yeah, I guess it's weird being back after a week."

"You have bags under your eyes." My gaze swings to Sasha. "Are you not sleeping?"

I rarely sleep a full night, but I did when Lachlan held me. Now sleep is even worse than usual. I barely manage an hour at a time before I'm awake worrying about something, or fighting a memory that's clawing its way to the surface.

"Sasha," Ansel groans, shaking his head.

"It's okay." I know Sasha isn't trying to be rude. She sounds worried. "No, I haven't been sleeping much."

"Oh." She frowns, flattening her lips. "What's wrong? You want to talk about it?"

I shake my head. "No, I'm sure it'll straighten out soon enough."

Ansel gives me a sympathetic look. I know I should tell Sasha about my past, but I'm so afraid of letting more people in. I don't want who I am to change in her eyes because of what happened to me.

"What are you guys doing over break?" Sasha asks around a bite of her sandwich.

"Going skiing," Ansel answers, tilting his chair back on two legs. "Meadows?"

"Nothing planned." I give a small shrug. It doesn't bother me much that we won't be doing anything. I'm relieved not to be going back to Portland. I wish Sage wouldn't be working most of the time, but I don't have any say in the matter. "What about you?" I look at Seth, waiting for an answer. He stares steadfastly at the table.

"I'm going to New York City," Sasha speaks up when Seth refuses to answer. "We're spending over a week in Manhattan and celebrating Christmas and New Year's there."

"That'll be fun."

"I'm looking forward to it." She must feel Ansel staring at her, because she turns to him, blinking. "What?"

"Nothing, Princess." He tries to suppress a smile.

Sasha rolls her eyes and looks across at me, giving her head a shake. Even though we haven't talked more about it, I know she still has a crush on him, but she's also growing irritated with his behavior.

"If you have some opinionated crap to spew, say it," she challenges him.

Ansel arches a brow.

"What? Nothing to say?" she counters. "Your family is rich so I don't know why any of this matters to you. Besides, my grandparents live there and we're visiting."

Seth looks up at the ceiling, so I do too, but I don't find anything interesting.

"You know, Ansel, I don't know if anyone's ever told you this, but you're kind of a dick."

He chortles, completely amused. "I'm not kind of a dick, I have a dick. Would you like a description?"

"In-fucking-furiating."

"Guys," I groan, wanting to smack them. When I glance at Seth again, to silently beg him for help, he's gone.

Is this guy even real or is he a figment of my imagination?

Luckily, I'm saved by the bell. I wad up my trash, say goodbye to their bickering forms, and toss it before I exit into the hall. I head downstairs, walking in the direction of Mr. Taylor's office. Before I make it to the long empty hall that will lead me to him, I stop, freezing. It's like my feet won't move any further. It's silly. I have nothing to fear in seeing him. Everything he said to me before I left him was a valid point. But not seeing him for a week has left an awkward knot in my chest.

Before I know it, I'm heading away, and find myself in the last place I should be.

I sit down on the hard bleachers, staring at the indoor track.

Setting my bag down between my feet, I lean back, resting my hands on either side of my legs. If I close my eyes, I can hear the cheers from the stands. Feel the excitement buzzing through my veins and jitteriness in my legs. But when I open them, it's nothing but an empty track again, and silence. A blatant reminder of what I'll never have.

I sniffle and wipe a tear away before it can fall.

I jolt when Mr. Taylor sits down beside me.

"That didn't take you long," I remark, sniffling again.

It's maybe been five minutes since I should've been at his office.

I feel him shrug. "I knew where to look this time." It's impossible not to sense his stare. "Why didn't you come?"

"I don't know." I wrap my arms around myself. "I was going to, but I found myself here instead."

"You're mad at me."

I don't miss how he makes it a statement, not a question.

"No." And I'm not. Finally, I look at him. His eyes are soft today, but his beard is a little thicker like he hasn't felt like shaving. "I understand how complicated this is." I nearly said wrong instead of complicated, but I didn't want to use that word. The way I see it, how we feel about each other isn't this evil ugly thing, but the situation is, his position versus mine.

Mr. Taylor exhales a weighted breath. I have to keep reminding myself that's who he is — Mr. Taylor, not Lachlan. He should never have been Lachlan to me and that tears me up inside.

"I never meant to hurt you, Dani."

I tuck my hair behind my ear, angling my head in his direction. "I don't think either of us meant for things to get to where they are." I clasp my hands together. "It just happened."

His eyes lower. "I'm twenty-nine, almost thirty, I shouldn't have let it happen."

I let out a humorless laugh. "I don't think age, or maturity is the problem here, we have a connection and it's made us make some choices that aren't the best."

He swallows, his Adam's apple bobbing. "And we need to stop making them."

I bite my lip, wanting to keep my words at bay, but of

course, I can't. "Do you really think that's possible? A lot has happened in the heat of the moment."

He scrubs a hand over his jaw. "I'm not … I'm not trying to fight with you, or act like I feel nothing for you." Those Caribbean blue eyes stare into me, *through* me. "I could lose my job if someone found out," he whispers under his breath, and I jolt.

Selfishly, despite understanding that I'm his student, and he's my counselor, that I'm eighteen and he's twenty-nine, I never quite grasped that he could potentially lose his job over this. My stomach coils into a tight knot.

"I…"

"I'm not trying to make you feel bad, Dani. But you need to understand how complicated and fucked up this is."

I lower my head. "I'm sorry."

I don't know what else to say.

He glides his palms over the front of his navy blue slacks. "You have nothing to be sorry for. If anyone should be sorry, it's me."

"But you're not?"

He shakes his head, rubbing his jaw. "No, I guess that makes me a bastard, but I'm not sorry for liking you."

I let out a sigh, clasping my hands as I look down at the track. "I miss it so much. I hate that I can never run again."

Mr. Taylor grows thoughtful. "I think you need to focus less on what you can't do and more on what you can."

His words strike a cord.

"You can walk," he continues, "you can laugh, smile, *breathe*. There are other forms of exercise besides running, you know." He playfully knocks his knee into mine.

I know his words are innocent, but I can't help but

mentally picture exactly how I'd like to exercise with him. I'm a menace.

He stands up, holding his hand out to me. "Come on, there are thirty minutes left, let's go to my office."

I stare at his hand for a few seconds before I take it, letting him haul me up. He releases my hand, and it's just in time because the doors open and one of the janitors enters heading for the trash can to empty it.

It's such a blatant reminder of what he said moments ago about losing his job if someone learned about us.

Both of us watch the janitor, and when his eyes swing back to mine they're immeasurably sad.

It reminds me so much of what he said to me in his apartment, that he can't be with me in the light.

Another little piece of my heart crumbles.

CHAPTER FORTY-ONE

"I HATE THIS CLASS SO MUCH," SASHA WHISPERS UNDER her breath, passing me a worksheet.

I nod my head in agreement. I hate Sociology too. Honestly, I thought this class might be vaguely interesting, but I was wrong. The teacher is a tiny dictator, and the work is annoying.

"At least that one movie was interesting," I remark, passing the papers to the student behind me. "You know, the one based on the play or whatever with the little girl who kills people."

"But it was black and white." She shudders like this is the most blasphemous thing.

"Well, it was an old movie." I suppress the urge to roll my eyes.

"Filling out the page in front of you does not require talking, ladies," Mrs. Kauffman calls out, giving the two of us a withering glare.

I press my lips tightly together and Sasha glowers at Mrs. Kauffman's turned back.

The worksheet takes the majority of the class period to

fill out, which is quite the feat considering it's a ninety-minute class.

When the bell rings, the whole class can't leave fast enough and piles the completed papers on her desk.

Sasha and I walk out together. She clasps her Sociology textbook to her chest. Mrs. Kauffman insists we bring them to each and every class, but we've yet to crack open the spine. We spend more time with the dictionary than anything else.

"This week can't end fast enough." We descend the steps along with the onslaught of other students eager to go home. "I'm so ready for Christmas vacation."

I don't comment. What would I say anyway? I'll be alone the majority of the time, so I'm not particularly looking forward to it, but it will be fun to exchange gifts with Sage on Christmas day.

"I'm sure that'll be nice."

"Mhmm," she hums, and starts rattling on about Manhattan, the other boroughs, and everything she can't wait to do—mostly shopping.

We part outside when she heads to the student lot.

I board my bus, and sit beside a kid I think is a freshman.

I'm a senior, older than a senior, riding the bus.

My hands flex on my lap. I could tell Sage I'm ready for a car, I know he'd be thrilled and get me one in a heartbeat. We sold my first car before I moved here with him. There was no point in keeping it, especially when I wouldn't drive it anyway. But something keeps stopping me from seeking the freedom a car would give me.

It's at least ten minutes before the doors finally close on the bus and we pull away from the school. We bump along and I give my seat partner an apologetic smile when my body knocks his.

When I finally reach my stop, I can't get out fast enough. My boots slosh through the gray snow as I trek up the street to the condominium building. Reaching the warmth of the lobby sends a shiver through my chilled body.

Catching the elevator, I finally make it to Sage's apartment and let myself in.

I hate the empty quiet that surrounds me. I still haven't grown used to it. Dropping my backpack on the floor, I turn the TV on for some background noise.

I have some homework to complete so I pull out what I need from my bag, spreading the books and papers over the coffee table so I can get it done.

Piles of homework are the bane of my existence so I do my best to not let it get out of control. Because we missed a whole week, the teachers overloaded us today, which is especially sucky considering Christmas break is next week.

Sitting on the floor, I sift through the assignments choosing the one I know I can finish the quickest.

Hours later, when Sage finally gets home, my stomach is growling restlessly but I've finished three of the five assignments due by the end of the week.

"Did you order dinner?" Sage unwinds the scarf from around his neck.

"No." I stand, stretching my stiff limbs. "I've been doing homework."

"Damn." He looks at the explosion of papers and my laptop I had to grab from my room to start a paper. "I'll call something in."

"Thanks." I rub my tired eyes, then start organizing my mess so I can move it to the bedroom.

"You can leave that if you want," Sage says with a

wave of his hand, pulling out his phone with the other. "I don't mind."

"Nah, I'm done for the night. I need a break and food." I crack a smile.

Sage chuckles, dialing one of the various delivery places we eat from way too often.

Carrying everything back to my room, I dump it on the desk. I wrinkle my nose at the mess and organize it the best I can. Luckily, I won't have to pack any of this stuff up until Wednesday morning.

Sage's steps echo in the hall, pausing outside my room.

Looking up, I regard him as he leans his shoulder against the doorway. He looks around my room, at the limited decorations and lack of personality. Beyond the wind chime, there's not much of anything that says this is my room.

He gives me a sad smile. "You should paint the walls."

I look at the bare white walls, crinkling my nose. "What's the point?"

His shoulders sag while guilt eats at me, because I'm responsible for that immeasurable weight he bears. "It's home, D." His voice is soft, my initial crackling on his tongue.

I press my lips together before I can tell him this isn't home. I don't want to break his heart.

It's not that I even think of the house we grew up in all that often, but a home holds happiness inside its walls, it has a personality, a beating heart of the people who live there. Sage's condo doesn't have it. It's pretty stark with only a few masculine touches. There's nothing special about it. It's a place to sleep, to eat, and watch TV. That's about it.

I don't tell him any of my thoughts though.

Instead, I say, "Maybe one day."

Padding over to my dresser, I slide open one of the drawers and yank out some pajamas for after my shower.

I still feel Sage watching me. Easing the drawer closed, I hesitate to look in his direction but I make myself do it. His jaw works back and forth, the hazel of his eyes more brown than gold for once.

"Sage?" I prompt, wanting to drag him from wherever the depths of his thoughts sent him.

He meets my stare.

"What?"

He continues to blink at me.

"Sage, come on…"

He rubs a hand over his jaw, letting it fall to his side. "Your room back home was always a mess. It was an explosion of color and things you loved. Your shoes were almost always kicked off on the floor, dangerously close to tripping you or anyone who entered. There were pictures of you with friends, of me and you, mom and dad, there was life and personality. It was *you*. This cold, lifeless space, it isn't you." He tosses a hand at my room.

I look around, at the white walls, white bedspread, white furniture, and even the fluffy white rug. I picked the stuff out and he bought it.

"Your old room was yellow," he continues. "God, it was that awful shade of bright yellow and I hated it so much. I asked mom once why she let you pick that color. You know what she told me?" He doesn't wait for me to answer, he knows I don't know anyway. "She said everyone deserves to express themselves in some way and color is the easiest way to do that. She told me Dandelion was the perfect name for you because dandelion yellow is the color of your soul." I want so desperately to pretend I can't see the tear making a track down his cheek. "White is … it's empty. And it fucking terrifies me to think that this *is* a reflection of you now. What if your new color is white because your soul is empty? What if it's my fault for not trying harder?"

"Sage—"

He thrusts his fingers through his hair and I bite my lip, because I know he needs to get this off his chest. He works day in and day out, in what I'm sure is a cubicle, but who knows. Since he hates his job I assume he hates talking to most of his coworkers. He still rarely goes out with friends. He comes home to *me*, to his broken little sister he's been saddled with, and it kills me that he carries this kind of burden on his shoulders.

"I don't know why mom thought I could do this." His voice cracks as he waves his arm at me. "I'm such a fucking failure."

"You're not a failure, Sage," I murmur, clasping my fingers together in front of me.

He lowers his head, brushing the backs of his hands over his wet cheeks.

"Fuck, I don't know why I'm spilling this all out."

"Because you need to."

He lifts his head. "Dani..."

"White, to me, is a new beginning." I look around the blank slate. "Yeah, it's cold, sometimes clinical, but it's symbolic. It's starting over. It's learning who I am now, who I'm going to be. White is the freedom to choose. But I think you're upset about a lot more than the room." I whisper the last part.

He sniffles, his eyes a little red now. "I'm stressed, worried, my sanity is non-existent," he admits with a forced laugh.

"You know how I have Mr. Taylor to talk to?" I ask quietly, like he's some frail injured bird I might frighten if I speak too loud or move too fast. He gives a single jerky nod of his head. "You need to see someone, Herb." I hope using the nickname will soften the blow.

Surprisingly, he doesn't dismiss my comment. "Yeah, I know," he croaks, his voice raw. Schooling his features he says, "I ... uh ... I'm going to shower. The food is paid for, just the sign the receipt if it comes before I'm out."

"Mhmm," I hum, watching him walk down the rest of the hall.

I plop onto my bed, suddenly exhausted. Letting out a mighty groan that should rattle the walls, I cover my face with my hands. It all feels so overwhelming. The past, Sage, Mr. Taylor, life itself. Nothing is simple anymore.

Getting up, I go in search of my phone, finding it on the floor near the couch. I bend, picking it up, and bring up my texts.

Me: I know things are complicated and I'm sorry for bothering you, but is it okay if I text you?

Barely twenty seconds pass before his response comes.

Lachlan: You can text me anytime.

Me: Are you sure?

Lachlan: Yep.

Me: Pinky promise?

He doesn't respond right away, but when he does it's with a photo of linked fingers.

Lachlan: Pinky promise.

A stupid, silly, treacherous smile curves my lips.

Lachlan: What's up?

I lay down on the couch, crossing my feet.

Me: It's Sage. He's keeping a lot inside.

Lachlan: We all tend to do that.

Me: He needs to talk to someone ... like I talk to you.

Lachlan: I can recommend some counselors he could see.

Me: Could you give me a list to give him?
Lachlan: Yeah, sure I'll give you one tomorrow.
Me: Thanks.
Lachlan: It's not a problem, Dani.

I tuck my phone in my pocket, and decide to set some plates out and two glasses of water. By the time I do there's a knock with the take-out. I grab the two paper bags, sign the slip, and start divvying out the Greek food Sage ordered. If there's one thing that can be said for our take-out habit, it's that we do eat a variety.

Pizza will always be my favorite, though.

Sage emerges from the hall with damp hair and red-rimmed eyes.

"Thanks, D." He presses a kiss to my cheek, giving me an apologetic smile. "I'm sorry about that."

"Don't be sorry. It's a bad habit to apologize for things we have no point in apologizing for."

"Stop being so smart," he jokes, taking one of the plates, ruffling my hair with his free hand. I reach up and smooth it down, giving him some epic side-eye he misses.

We park our butts on the couch with our dinner and glasses of water.

Holding my cup up, I give him a small smile. "Cheers?"

He chuckles, shaking his head. He grabs his glass, clinking it against mine. "Cheers, D."

CHAPTER FORTY-TWO

"I REALLY DON'T UNDERSTAND WHAT WE'RE HAVING AN assembly for," I grumble behind me to Ansel. We arrived at first period only to be sent to the gymnasium for a mandatory assembly. It wasn't planned or we would've known about it. There's a low rumble tumbling through the school from the murmurs of hushed conversation. "Do you know what it's about?"

"No clue." He looks around like there might be some sort of hint on the walls.

I hear whispers of excitement, like maybe there's a surprise guest. I hear someone say something about perhaps a famous alumni visiting.

The dread sitting low in my stomach says it's something more.

"I'm sure it's okay." He reaches for my hand giving it a small squeeze before letting go.

I hyperventilate as we enter the gym and the entire student body fills up the vibrant red bleachers. I freeze, and Ansel waits behind with me. There's no way I can sit in that crowd of people. I'm doing better, but not that much better.

Ansel stays by my side, waiting for the seats to fill in until we can grab a spot in the front row.

The conversations around us are so loud I'm tempted to cover my ears with my hands.

Mr. Gordon enters the gymnasium along with the vice principal and Mr. Taylor. I'm so stressed I can't even take in how good Mr. Taylor looks, with his fitted black slacks and charcoal button down. His badge hangs from the lanyard around his neck, swaying back and forth as he walks. He stops beside Mr. Gordon, so both he and the vice principal flank the man.

What is going on?

He starts speaking and I reach for Ansel's hand squeezing the life out of it.

I hear words like *active shooter.*

No casualties reported.

Minimal injuries.

The police are handling it.

You're safe.

But we're not safe. It's happening again. At a school only a few miles from here. It's happening *all the fucking time and no one is doing anything to stop it.*

Why don't they care?

Why won't they save us?

I feel like I'm going to throw up.

"If anyone would like to speak with Mr. Taylor about this, his office is always available for you to drop by or schedule to see him during the day. In light of these recent events the school board has elected to begin the holiday break early. This will be your last day."

He starts droning on about other things, but my ears are ringing making it impossible to hear him.

I think Ansel says my name, but I feel like I'm going to throw up.

Somehow, I manage to stand.

If I could run, I would, but I limp out of there as fast as I can before I can get sick in front of the entire school.

I burst through the doors into the hall, searching for the nearest bathroom. I know there's one close.

"Meadows, are you okay?" Ansel's voice is right beside me, thick with concern.

Slapping a hand over my mouth, I shake my head.

"Dani."

I close my eyes.

Mr. Taylor.

"I've got this," he says to Ansel, as I move down another hall mercifully spotting a bathroom. "I'll take care of her."

Stumbling into the girl's bathroom, I collapse in the first stall, emptying my stomach.

Mr. Taylor's presence looms behind me as he lowers his body, crouching behind me. His big hand presses to my back.

"Dani," he murmurs, rubbing soothing circles.

"Go away," I cry, my stomach cramping as it searches for anything else it can empty into the toilet.

"I'm not going anywhere." His voice is stern behind me.

I gag, heaving, but nothing else comes up. Shoving hair from my eyes, I tell him again, "Go *away.*"

"No."

"Stubborn ass." I try to shove his arm off me, but can't reach him.

"I wanted to tell you, before Mr. Gordon called for the assembly, but he wouldn't let me."

I flush the toilet and don't have the energy left to

protest when he helps me stand. Washing my hands and face, I nearly crack a smile when he reaches into his pocket, passing me a lone peppermint like the ones he keeps by his bed.

I rip the wrapping off and stick it in my mouth. It's not a toothbrush, but it'll have to do.

The back of his index finger follows the curve of my cheek before he tucks my hair behind my ear. When he blinks at me in surprise I realize he didn't mean to do that.

The door opens and closes to the bathroom. "Oh," a girl jolts at the sight of Mr. Taylor. "Sorry, I'll go some-where else."

"No, it's okay. Ms. Meadows is coming to my office."

"I am?"

He gives me a look.

"I am," I clarify.

We walk side by side to his office and I plop uncere-moniously onto the loveseat. I don't have my bag, since it's back in the art room, but I figure I can get it later.

Mr. Taylor pulls his chair out and around the desk, sitting in front of me. Leaning forward, he clasps his hands, blowing out a breath. Rubbing his hands nervously on his slacks, he watches me, not knowing what to say. I don't know either, and silence reigns.

After a solid five minutes, he pleads, "Say something. I want to help you but I don't know how."

"That's the thing," I whisper, tearing my gaze from the window, "there's nothing you can do to help. You might look like Superman, but you're not him. You can't save the world, you can't save me, you can't stop bad people from doing bad things."

His face screws up with frustration. "There has to be something," he begs. "Talk to me, please."

"What do you want me to say?" I fight back. "That

hearing that was like being shot all over again? That the memory of the screams echoed through my head, that I felt the warm wetness of blood beneath me, that I hate the fucking color red so fucking much and it's everywhere in this Goddamn school?" My voice rises to a shout, thank God his office is on this lonely hallway.

He pales, his fists opening and closing like he's having a hard time not touching me.

"So much evil exists in the world," I continue, my voice lowering to a soft whisper, "but there's good too, I know it, the problem is when the good guys do *nothing* to stop the villains. The shooting at my school changed nothing and this won't either. I'm not trying to be cynical, just realistic. And you know what? It's maddening living in a world where our lives are valued so little and if something brings you even a sliver of happiness it's in some way wrong." He knows I'm talking about him now, I can see it in his eyes. "It becomes selfish to want one thing that's *yours*."

"Dani—"

I sit back, crossing my arms over my chest. "Talk to Mr. Gordon, or whoever is necessary, I want to go home. I want my brother to come get me."

He stares at me for a long moment, his jaw working back and forth. "Okay," he finally says, standing. His chair rocks back and forth in his absence, squeaking slightly.

He rounds his desk, picking up the black-corded phone. I barely listen to his words as he speaks to the office.

When he hangs up the phone he tells me they're calling Sage.

"My backpack is in the art room." I still won't look at him, I don't want him to see the anger simmering inside me, ready to explode. I'm not mad at him, so I don't want him to misinterpret.

I'm so fucking furious at the people who have the power to make a change, but don't give a damn.

We're all a bunch of helpless sheep, whether you realize it or not.

The sigh he exhales is sad, tinged with a little bit of frustration. "I'll go get it for you."

"I can get it myself."

Another sigh, this one even heavier with frustration. I force myself to look at him, the fingers of his left hand sit on his hip and he rubs his brow with his right. "I said I'll get it, Dani. You … sit here."

He motions for me to stay and heads out, the door closing a bit too loudly.

Laying down on the couch, I stare up at the ceiling reliving the fear all over again, what I experienced a year ago is fresh for all those students only a few miles away.

"I never thought anything like this would happen here," I heard so many people say after the shooting.

I think that's part of the problem, the human naivety that wherever you are is safe, but anything can happen to anyone, anywhere. I'm not even trying to be a Negative Nancy, as my mom would say, it's just the damn truth.

Laying my hands on my chest I tap my fingers impatiently, waiting for Mr. Taylor to return. There's more than one art room, but since he didn't ask for details I didn't give them.

The phone in his office rings, and even though I shouldn't, I swing my legs onto the floor and get up to answer it.

"Mr. Taylor's office," I answer.

"Um … is Mr. Taylor there?"

"He stepped out for a moment."

"Oh … okay. Is this Dandelion Meadows?"

"The one and only."

Papers shuffle in the background. "Um, yes, we were able to get ahold of your brother. He said he's leaving work now to get you."

"Thanks."

"Mhmm. Have a good day."

"Yep, you too." I hang up the phone as Mr. Taylor enters the room, with my backpack hanging from his hand. I wonder what he thinks of the patches ironed onto the front. There's a sunflower, a doodled Post Malone, and some other random ones.

"Why were you on the phone?" His eyes narrow as he sets the bag down.

"Office called." I move from behind his desk and since the room isn't the largest, it puts us nearly chest to chest. "My brother will be here soon."

He dips his chin. His eyes are dark swirling pools. "Talk to me."

"I already have."

He shakes his head, jaw taut. His hands go to his hips and I try to ignore the veins roping up his forearms. "Not enough, Dani. You give me bits and pieces before you shut down. I am trying so fucking hard to help you, but I can't if all you give me is crumbs." He raises and lowers his hands.

"Who are you trying to help me as?" I counter.

"Huh?" He blinks at me.

I cock my head to the side. "As Mr. Taylor or as Lachlan?"

"B-Both," he stutters.

I shake my head back and forth, taking one small step away from him. I have to move from the intoxicating scent of his cologne so I can think straight.

"I wish I could give you more, tell you everything, but when I can barely make sense of my thoughts..." I trail off, wrapping my arms around myself. "I'm already giving you all that I have, bit by bit, I am *trying* and that needs to be enough."

His features soften and he reaches for me before letting his arms fall to his sides with a crestfallen expression as he realizes where we are and he can't touch me like that.

Innocent touches shouldn't matter, but when there are real feelings behind them that's when it becomes a problem.

"I'm going to wait at the front." I bend at the waist, picking up my backpack he set down only moments before.

"It's cold."

"I'll wait inside."

He lets out a frustrated breath. "Let me wait with you, then."

"Why?" I counter, my tone snarkier than I intend it to be. "If I was any other student, would you be offering to wait with me?"

He pales slightly, his lips parted. "I-I don't know."

At least it's an honest answer.

Blowing out a breath, I reach for the handle on the door behind me. "I'm a big girl, Mr. Taylor. I'll be fine."

There's a stricken look on his face, and whether or not he realizes it, he reaches for me again.

Turning, I let the door fall closed behind me.

I trek through the empty halls, waiting in front of the massive doors and windows for the sight of Sage's Maxima to show up.

When it does, I run outside, slipping into his warm car, letting my body melt into the heated seats.

Sage looks worried, and when the first words he utters are, "I'm so sorry," I know they told him about the other school, or he saw it on TV.

I look out the window, pretending I don't see the tall form standing outside, hands in pockets, sans coat.

"Me too."

CHAPTER FORTY-THREE

I'M TAKEN BY SURPRISE WHEN SAGE PARKS ACROSS THE street from Watchtower. He puts the car in park, letting the engine run, and looks over at me with a tender expression. "I guess this is your thing with Ansel," he pulls a face at the name, "but I thought we could get coffee before going home."

Giving a slow nod, I reach for the handle.

We walk across the street, placing our order.

"Should we sit?"

Again, I give him a nod.

He lets me choose the table. Despite it being the middle of the day many are already taken.

While he waits for our order, I sit down, tapping my fingers against the lacquered tabletop.

One of the regular workers hands him the drinks and flashes a smile in my direction with a wave.

Sage places the cups down, pulling out the chair across from me.

He rubs a hand over his face, picking up his coffee cup

and taking a sip. Sitting it back down he wraps his long fingers around it. "I don't even know what to say, D."

"You can't change what happened today." I bring the straw to my lips, sipping my boba tea. "Evil exists and we have to deal with it." Running my fingers through my wind-tangled hair, I take a breath. "I ... wasn't expecting it. I should've, but ... I couldn't anticipate it happening again so close."

Sage flinches.

"It could've so easily been my new school. What are the odds?" I let out a humorless laugh. "It's not fair, and I know the saying is *life's not fair*, but some things should be, you know?" Sage's lips pinch, but he sits quietly, letting me speak. "I should be able to walk into school without fear. I shouldn't have to look over my shoulder, wondering if some asshole with a gun is lurking around the next corner. I shouldn't be afraid of tight spaces or rooms without windows. But that fear lives inside me and so many others, and at the end of the day it doesn't matter. *We* don't matter."

"You matter to me," Sage whispers, reaching out with one hand and placing his on mine.

I turn my hand palm up and squeeze his hand. "I know."

Neither of us say it, but when I look in my brother's eyes, so close to the shade of my own, I know we're both thinking the same thing.

If only it were enough.

———

SAGE DROPS me off at the condo. He has to return to work after a call he received on our way back. I could tell he was pissed, but he didn't tell them to shove it. Instead, he fell into place like a good little minion.

I enter the empty space like usual, turning on lights as I go.

Hating the eerie silence more than usual, I put my music on and grab a change of clothes, padding across the hall to the bathroom.

Turning the water on, I wait for it to steam the room before I slip out of my dirty clothes and toss them in the nearly full hamper. Since Sage had to go back to work, I might as well do the laundry once I'm out.

Anything to keep me busy and my mind distracted.

I step into the glass-enclosed shower, letting the spray drench my body and hair. Standing beneath the rain shower head I watch the water swirl down the drain. Flexing my toes, painted a hot pink color called Flusher Blusher, my thoughts drift to Mr. Taylor.

Lachlan.

As hard as I'm trying, he's Lachlan to me.

I pushed him away today out of self-preservation, but I still feel like an asshole. I could've been nicer, he was only trying to help me and get me to talk, but I needed him to hurt as much as I was.

The hot water cascades around me, quickly pruning my fingers. As much as I want to stay in here for an hour, I know that's not the best idea. I reach for my peach scented shampoo, squirting some in my hand before lathering it into my hair. It isn't long before the suds are swirling down the drain and I'm conditioning my hair. While the conditioner is sitting on my hair, I grab my yellow loofah and slather it with my body wash. I thoroughly scrub every inch of my body, trying to wash away the icky feeling of today, but it doesn't take me long to realize nothing is going to do the trick.

Rinsing my hair and body, I step out, wrapping a fluffy towel around me.

My wet skin and hair drips onto the rug in front of the sink, but I'm the only one who uses this bathroom so it won't matter if it gets damp.

Wiping the condensation from the mirror I lean forward, poking at the skin beneath my eyes and my cheeks. I look exhausted and I know the combination of today's news with my already little sleep has done a number on me. If I'm lucky I might doze off before Sage gets home.

I blow my hair dry a little bit so it won't be dripping wet down my back and change into the clothes I brought in here with me. Stifling a yawn, I grab the laundry basket and carry it to the small laundry room offset from the kitchen. I load up my clothes and start the cycle, moving Sage's clothes from the dryer to a basket, setting it in his room.

It's a while later when there's a knock on the door.

I exhale a weighted sigh, wondering who it could be. We never have visitors unless the deliveryman counts, and I didn't order any food.

Standing on my tiptoes, I peer through the peephole, a small gasp emitting from my lips when I see Lachlan on the other side.

Coming down flat on my feet I nibble my bottom lip as he knocks yet again.

Placing my palm flat on the door, I steady myself and open it.

He clears his throat awkwardly. "I … is your brother here?" He points inside. "I wanted to check on you after today."

"He's not, but what if he was? You shouldn't be here,"

I hiss, glancing in the hall like Sage might magically appear.

He runs his fingers through his hair in an agitated gesture. "I wanted to see if you were okay."

"How do you even know this is where I live?" He's never been to my apartment before, so there's no way he'd know.

"I asked downstairs."

"And they told you?" I arch a brow, still standing in between the door and wall, blocking his entry.

"Yeah."

I harrumph. "Security is pretty lax then, huh?"

He blows out a breath. "Dani, please, I'm not here to argue with you or make myself look like an even bigger ass. I wanted to see you and ask how you are. That's all." He looks me over and I shake my head.

Pushing the door open wider, I silently invite him in. "Sage won't be back for a couple more hours I suspect, but you have five minutes. I want to have some popcorn and take a nap."

Crossing my arms over my chest I give him a challenging look while he's busy taking the apartment in.

"Five minutes is enough." He finally lowers his head and blinks at me. My hair is in a messy bun on top of my head, my sweatpants are loose and baggy, an old pair of Sage's when he was my age, and my t-shirt is loose but it's obvious I'm not wearing a bra.

"Do you want popcorn?" I ask, because I might as well try to be polite.

I don't even know why I'm angry at him—no, not even angry, just irritated.

"I'm good."

"Suit yourself."

I open the cabinet, standing on my tiptoes to reach the

red box, but then Lachlan is there suddenly, his body large and warm behind me. He places a hand on my hip, stretching up and grabbing the box easily. He steps away, holding it out to me.

"Thanks." My gratitude is non-existent in my tone as I snatch it from him.

He clears his throat, stepping away awkwardly, to lean against the column that leads into the kitchen. He's probably realizing how close our bodies were and that while Sage might not be here, this definitely isn't the place for us to be testing our limits.

I peel back the cardboard flap, pulling out the plastic wrapped popcorn. While my fingers make quick work of ridding the popcorn pack of plastic, I eye the tall, imposing man taking up space in the kitchen. It was over a week ago when I slept in his arms, and I want nothing more than for him to wrap them around me now, hold me tight, but I've heard what he's said and I might be young but I'm not stupid. While I don't care about our age difference, or our positions, I do care about someone finding out and it hurting him. If he lost his job because of me I would never forgive myself.

"You better start talking. Your five minutes already started." I turn around, opening the microwave to place the pack inside. I push the button on the microwave and it hums to life with power while I turn back around, facing Lachlan.

Mr. Taylor, Mr. Taylor, Mr. Taylor, I chant silently in my head. *He's not Lachlan to you. Not anymore and he never should have been.*

I stand with my hands behind me on the counter, staring straight at him.

He stares back with a stubborn set to his jaw and those dark brows drawn tight.

Canting my head to the side, I decide to wait him out.

After another minute he blows out a gust of air, shoving his fingers through his dark hair. There's a stubborn set to his lips when he looks back at me, but he shakes his head.

"I wanted to see if you were okay, I guess."

"You guess?" I arch a brow, moving my arms to cross them over my chest. "You have my number. You could've texted me."

"*See*, Dani. I wanted to *see* if you were okay. With my own two eyes. I felt so fucking helpless today. I don't know what to do or say to make this better for you."

I wet my lips, glancing away from him. "You can't do any of that, no one can," I admit with a soft breath. "What I need you can't give me." My tone is sad, and if he keeps standing there I'm afraid I'll cry and I really don't want to. I want to eat my popcorn and take a nap—hide away from this hateful world for a little while.

He takes a step forward before he stops himself. His jaw ticks, hands opening and closing at his sides. "Tell me anyway, tell me what you need."

I twist my lips back and forth, but I know I won't be able to keep the words to myself.

"To be held," my voice cracks, "comforted, understood, *loved*. Being there makes all the difference, because words often aren't enough, it's action that I need."

It takes him two more of his massive steps before he's in front of me. One second and his arms are around me. One heartbeat and his lips are kissing the top of my head.

Behind us, I smell the popcorn burning as it over pops but I don't care. I don't want the popcorn anymore, but I do want Lachlan even if I shouldn't.

He tucks my head under his neck. Pressing my ear to his chest, I feel the steady pounding of his heart. So solid, so sure. As strong and powerful as he is. The smell of his cologne and something more that's uniquely him fills my lungs as I breathe him in.

I was irritated when I saw him standing outside the door, but now I'm more than happy he's here.

"I'll hold you," he murmurs against the top of my head, his embrace tightening. "I'll hold you as long as I can."

"Forever." I fist the back of his shirt in my hands, shuddering with the admission of how much I truly want him. "I want you to hold me like this every day for the rest of forever."

"Dani—"

"Shh," I hum. "I know."

But let me dream.

He sways me back and forth slightly. The microwave beeps behind us, reminding me I haven't gotten it.

"Your popcorn." He starts to let me go but I wrap my arms tighter around his torso. God, I could live in this man's arms.

"I don't care about the damn popcorn."

He lets out a small chuckle, hugging me again.

I itch to stand on my tiptoes and kiss him, but I know I can't. It kills me a little inside. But having him hold me eases some of the ache that's filled my body today since I found out the news.

I decide, since he came here and all, to share some of my thoughts. It's a thank you without using those two words.

"Hearing what happened today reminded me so much of that day. How a day can start off so normal and suddenly become something else entirely. It's a shattering of naivety and even though I lived through that, I've become comfortable here." His hands flex at my sides.

"This was a reminder that comfort is an illusion. Any moment can be your last."

"You're allowed to feel comfortable, Dani." His voice rumbles against me.

"Doesn't seem that way." I let out a humorless laugh. "I hate that all those people at that school had their naivety taken from them too. Sometimes it's better to remain in the dark."

I tilt my head, looking up at him. My words remind me of what he said. He must be thinking the same thing because his eyes look sadly down on me.

"You're a strong person, Dani. I hope you know that."

His words mean a lot, but I shake my head. "I'm really not."

"Believe me, you are." He presses his lips tenderly to my forehead. "I need to go," he whispers in a pained voice.

"I know."

But I hold him and he holds me and neither of us lets go.

———

THE OPENING and closing of the door hours later rouses me from a deep nap on the couch. Buried beneath a pile of blankets I sit up, rubbing my tired eyes.

"Hey," I croak in a sleep-filled voice. "What time is it?"

"Eight," he grumbles, his fingers making quick work on the buttons of his pea coat. "The boss forced me to stay later for having to leave."

My jaw drops. "You're joking."

"Wish I was." He rubs his jaw. "What's that smell? Is something on fire?" He starts looking around for the source of the smell.

"I burned popcorn earlier."

He cracks a grin. "Gotta take it out before the microwave finishes, D."

"Yeah, yeah, I know. What's up with your boss? I thought they were cool when you had to take off to come be with me in the hospital?"

"I thought so too." His sigh ripples out of him and he starts unbuttoning his shirt. "Apparently they're giving me hell for it now."

Pushing the blankets off of me, I plead with him again. "Sage, *please* quit. You can find something better than this. You're smart, a valuable asset. Any company would be lucky to have you. You don't have to put up with this shit."

"It's a job," he retorts. "It is what it is."

"Yeah, a job you spend the majority of your time at. One that makes you miserable. How is that fair?"

"I'm not going to keep having this argument with you," he warns, pointing at me. "I'm *fine*."

"Whatever." I blow out a breath, not in the mood to get a headache arguing with him. Besides, I missed him and I'm glad he's home. "I haven't eaten. Should I order something?"

He rubs his lips. "Go for it. I haven't eaten either."

I watch him walk down the hall.

Is he not sick of this monotony? He goes to work, hates it, comes home, showers, orders food, wash, rinse, and fucking repeat.

I love my brother and he deserves more than this.

Placing an order, I hear the shower turn on.

It'll be thirty minutes before the food is delivered, so I lay back down on the couch. Picking up the remote, I flip through the channels, settling on an old Cartoon Network episode of Totally Spies.

Cupping my hands under my head I watch the show until the food arrives. Sage is *still* in the shower, because I swear he's trying to burn his skin off. Or at least rid himself of every trace of work. I wish he'd open up to me, and talk about why he really won't quit. I know it has to be something more, not anything bad, but it's like he's scared to go somewhere else.

Grabbing the food from the delivery guy, who recognizes me at this point, I pull all the to-go boxes from the restaurant down the street, popping open the lid on the nachos I ordered. For some reason I've been craving them. I scoop out a chip, popping it in my mouth.

"Mmm," I moan, it's as good as I hoped it'd be. "So yummy," I speak to myself, doing a little shimmy for good measure.

I fix myself a plate of nachos and carry the to-go box with a cheeseburger over to the couch. I'm starving and not waiting for Sage.

I've only eaten a quarter of my burger when he finally joins me. He grabs his food and sits beside me, kicking his feet up on the coffee table. He doesn't lower his legs this time like he sometimes does, as if he can hear Mom scolding him.

He takes a bite of the burger I ordered him, some barbeque sauce smearing his lip, and wipes it away. After he's swallowed, he says to me in a soft, guilty tone, "I'm really sorry I had to go back to work today."

I give a small shrug. I didn't want to be alone, but I wasn't going to beg him to stay. Lachlan stopping by actually helped some.

"It's okay."

"It's not." He angles his body toward me. "Every time I turn around I'm doing the wrong thing. It's not like you needed to come home for the hell of it. What happened today was fucking awful, D, and I know you probably won't stop thinking about it and I … left you."

"Please, don't feel guilty." Sage already carries too much worry and guilt.

He lowers his feet to the ground and leans forward, placing the Styrofoam container on the table. "I can't help but feel it. As soon as I left here I felt like the biggest piece of shit ever, but I knew if I didn't go I'd probably be fired."

"Not to beat a dead horse or anything, but quit."

He chuckles, but there's not a trace of humor in it. "Maybe I will." My brows shoot up in surprise since he was arguing only a bit ago about it being a job and what he had to deal with. "I was thinking during my shower," he admits, crossing his arms over his chest. "I think I've held on so tightly to this job because I wanted *something* to stay the same when everything else is different, but it's fucking stupid to keep doing this to myself."

"It is." I chew on another nacho.

He works his lips back and forth. "I think I'm going to put in my notice and look for something else. I deserve better than this and so do you. You need a brother who's here for you and I haven't been."

"Sage," I say sadly, "you've done the best you can."

He smiles at me sadly, but there's a twinkle in his eye —an excitement. "But I can do better."

When he cracks a grin, my heart feels the teeny tiniest bit better.

CHAPTER FORTY-FOUR

THE NEXT DAY SAGE ENTERS THE APARTMENT, CURSING under his breath. The door slams closed behind him and I look up from the couch where I was curled up with the last book Lachlan leant me.

"What's wrong?" I shove everything off of me, hurrying to his side, thinking maybe he's hurt or something.

He left for work more than an hour ago and surely if he was hurt he'd go to the hospital, not come home. He could be sick though.

He throws his hands up. "I put in my notice and was fired. Stupid, fucking, pompous, *asshole!*" He rages, shoving mail from the day before off the kitchen counter. Gripping the counter he pants out shallow breaths. "Growing up is a fucking trap. Don't do it, Weed."

"Everything will be okay."

He pinches his lips. "It will be," he says after a moment, "but right now I'm fucking pissed." Placing his hands on his hips, he cocks his head to the side. "I'm gonna change and we're going to go somewhere."

I look out the window at the snow flurries. "But it's cold."

Sage rolls his eyes. "You act like you've never lived through winter." He starts down the hall, calling behind him, "Get changed."

I look down at my sweatpants and sweatshirt, frowning. I don't want to get dressed in 'real' clothes. I want to be comfy and hangout here. But I know Sage isn't going to rest until he gets me out of the house.

Closing myself in my room, I change into jeans, a heavy sweater, and winter boots. Sage is already by the front door, shoving his arms into his coat. I grab mine, doing the same.

"Where are we going?" I question him as we step into the hall.

"No idea." He grins—*grins* completely giddy. "That's the beauty of it."

———

"Isn't it amazing?" I gush, walking out of the art museum into the chilly air.

"It's ... something." Sage's response is expected.

I bump his arm with my elbow. "Come on, it's incredible. I can't believe you've never been."

He cracks a small smile. "I'm not exactly an art connoisseur. How'd you even know about this place?"

"Ansel—"

He holds up a hand. "Say no more."

I laugh, climbing into his car. "You have nothing to be worried about when it comes to Ansel. He's my friend, that's it."

He slides behind the wheel, cranking the engine. "You

can tell me that until you're blue in the face all you want, but he's still a guy, and he still has a penis."

I roll my eyes. "Brothers."

"Sisters."

We exchange twin smiles. As he pulls away, I say, "Have you thought any about seeing a counselor yourself?" I have a list from Lachlan sitting on my phone to suggest to Sage. I've also given up on trying to force myself to think of him only as Mr. Taylor. He's Lachlan to me and nothing can change that. Not even if it would be the smarter thing.

"Not much," he admits with a wince. "Guess I have the time now, being jobless and all. It'd probably be a good idea, huh?" He glances at me for assurance.

"I didn't want to talk to any of mine, but Mr. Taylor has really helped."

Despite my crush on him, and what's developed into more, I do think being forced to see him five days a week has helped me chisel away at the walls I put up to protect myself, my thoughts, and my fears. I've gotten to know him and that makes sharing things easier.

"I think I will," he says softly, like if he doesn't speak loudly then it's not as scary.

"I ... uh ... have a list of counselors Mr. Taylor suggested—for after I graduate," I quickly lie when his eyebrows rise, figuring it'll be an easier pill to swallow if he believes the list is for me.

"Oh, cool. Give it to me later."

"I will."

Looking out the window, I stare at the buildings we pass by. The brick and stone colors blend together, occasionally broken up with graffiti.

"Lost in thought?" he asks after a few minutes.

I shake my head. "Blissfully empty for the moment."

When his eyes move from the traffic to me, I know he figures I'm lying, especially with what happened yesterday.

Sure enough he says, "You sure about that?"

I'm quiet. "Yes," I finally say. It's not a lie either, I'd let myself zone out and nothing had been on my mind, but now there is.

"Should we stop for coffee before we go home?"

"Yeah." I reach in front of me, adjusting the vent. "That'd be good."

After swinging by Watchtower we finally return to the condo.

"I'm going to watch a movie," he announces. "Do you want to join?"

"No." I shake my head. "I have homework."

Even though school has been canceled leading into break, I still had things that were due and I'm sure they'll be expected the day we return.

"I was going to watch Transformers," he sing-songs, naming one of his childhood favorites he got me hooked on one summer when he was tired of watching the Barbie movies I kept requesting.

"Really, I have things to finish."

"Okay." He grabs the remote, flopping onto the couch.

I take my Starbucks cinnamon dolce latte with me back to my room. Digging out my books and assignment pad, I read through what I have left to do. With a sigh, I settle onto my bed and get to work, periodically taking a sip of coffee. The condo is small enough that I hear the movie playing in the background, but I don't feel like putting music on to drown it out.

A couple of hours later, all of my homework is complete and Sage pokes his head in the doorway. "My friends asked me out for a beer. Is it cool with you if I go?"

"I don't care. You hardly need my permission."

"I wanted to ask. It didn't feel right to leave without saying something. You'll be okay?"

"I'm fine, Herb."

He chuckles. "Okay, okay. I'm going to head out."

I pack my school stuff away, stuffing my backpack in the bottom of my closet since I won't need it for two weeks.

"Bye!" Sage calls out a moment before the door closes.

Since he's gone, I dig through the hall closet, looking for the artificial tree he used to have—I know because I've seen pictures of it when he'd send them to Mom.

I locate it lodged in the corner, wrestling it out into the living room. I'm glad it was there, because the only other place I could think to look would be his bedroom closet and I'm *not* going in there. His smelly underwear might be lying around. No thanks.

A part of me worries I should wait for Sage, that this should be something we do together. Guilt nags at me, thinking of the Christmases growing up when the three of us would decorate together while drinking hot chocolate with Christmas songs playing in the background.

My phone vibrates, breaking into my thoughts.

Sasha: They r holding a candlelight ceremony for the students & faculty who were injured yesterday. I'm going. Do u want 2?

I freeze, reading her text over and over. There's nothing wrong with what she says, only it's yet another reminder of everything I'm trying to move past. Ansel would know better than to ask me if I'd want to go, but not Sasha, because I haven't shared that defining part of myself with her.

Me: No.

Sasha: K.

A simple letter 'k' as her only response serves to tick me off for some reason. I can't even pinpoint what it is about it that irks me so much. I guess it's feeling like everything bad that happened yesterday, that's happened at other schools, places of worship, movie theaters, on and on the list goes, is somehow simplified into one insignificant letter.

I toss my phone on the couch, getting it away from me before I get mad enough to chuck it through a wall.

Sage or no Sage, I'm tackling this tree tonight.

———

WITHOUT HOT CHOCOLATE or Christmas music to aid me, I finished the tree, decking it out with colored lights, tinsel, and the hand-me-down ornaments our mom gave him when he first moved into his own place.

A movie plays on the TV now, but I'm barely paying attention.

When the door finally opens it's past eleven at night. It's not *too* late in the grand scheme of things, but for Sage it might as well be five in the morning.

"Hey," I call out as he locks up.

He enters the living room, smiling at the tree. "You put the tree up." He points at it. His eyes fall to the handful of simply wrapped gifts under it of things I've ordered for him.

"Yeah, it needed to be more Christmassy."

He tosses his keys on the counter with a clatter. "I should've put it up at the beginning of the month."

"Well, you didn't." I state simply. "So I did."

"Whatcha watching?" he asks, lightly tapping my feet

so I'll lower them from the coffee table and let him by. It's not like he could go in front of the coffee table or anything.

"Some cheesy TV Christmas movie," I admit. "I haven't been paying much attention, but I bet you anything there's probably a cold-hearted city guy dating a city girl. Then the city girl gets stranded in a remote country town and falls in love with some guy who makes ranch dressing for a living or sells rocking horses. Oh there's probably a dog too. And the city guy loses the girl in the end."

He laughs outright, shaking his head at me. "Oh, Dani. Ranch dressing, huh?"

"I mean, it's likely. Oh, and technically you'd be the cold-hearted city boy, working with computers and all."

He arches a brow. "Do I get bonus points for quitting? Well, getting fired," he amends.

I think for a moment. "Sure, I guess. But let's face it, you're a nerd and will get another job with computers. Just don't forget how to talk to girls. I would like some nieces or nephews someday."

I swear he chokes on his own saliva. "Take that back. I don't even want to think about kids right now. I'm too young."

"You'll be twenty-six soon," I remind him.

He gives me a horrified expression like he's caught me kicking a puppy or something. "Yeah, and that's too fucking young to be thinking about kids, Dandelion." He shudders—actually shudders, where his whole body shakes and he makes some kind of weird noise with his lips.

This is too fun for me now. I grin, feeling lighter than I have since the news yesterday. "I could babysit."

He jumps to a standing position. "Shut up, shut up,

shut up," he chants walking away with his hands held loosely over his ears. "I don't want to hear any of this nonsense." I open my mouth and he actually screams, then shoves his fingers in his ears. "La, la, la. I can't hear you."

He disappears down the hall to his room and I actually pay attention to the movie this time. Turns out the guy doesn't make ranch dressing for a living, but he is a dairy farmer. Close enough.

CHAPTER FORTY-FIVE

BALANCING THE SKETCHPAD ON MY KNEES, I MOVE MY pencil back and forth, letting the simple lines I've been drawing transform into a monarch butterfly.

I know my sketches are nothing compared to the beautiful art Ansel makes, but there's a peace I find in letting my mind wander but my hand guide me. It takes me to some surprising places.

When I think the drawing is as close as it's going to get to perfect, I close the pad, setting it aside on my unmade bed. With school out and Sage home I've spent the majority of my time burrowing beneath the bed covers, getting lost in new stories or creating art.

Tiptoeing out of my room, I peek into the living room and find Sage watching sports.

"Hey," he speaks when he spots me. "Do you want to go somewhere?"

I look at the pile of presents beneath the tree, fuller than the night I put it up, containing things Sage got for me and others our extended family has sent. There's even one wrapped in solid black wrapping paper with a silver bow from Ansel that he gave me when he stopped by for dinner one evening. Sage didn't even grumble … *much*.

"No, I'm okay here."

"Seriously, I could maybe get tickets to a play or something." He wrinkles his nose.

Laughing, I wrap my arms around myself. "Even if you could get something on Christmas Eve Eve you don't even like that sort of thing."

"We could go to a movie?" he suggests, brightening.

I think of the dark, enclosed space. "No, I'm good, seriously. Just gonna grab a soda."

"Suit yourself."

From the fridge I grab a grape Fanta I blame Ansel for getting me addicted to. I had one at Thanksgiving, but the obsession didn't really kick in until he was over the other night and brought an entire case, leaving the box when he left. Now, they're mine and I can't get enough of it.

Bumping my hip against the refrigerator door, it closes. Sage lets out a chuckle when I round the corner, shaking his head. "D, you're going to have to lay off the soda or I'm going to have to run down to the convenience store and get some more."

I brighten. "Could you? I only have one left."

He sighs, narrowing his lips, but ends up breaking into a smile. "Sure, I wouldn't mind getting some snacks and food. We need enough to get us through the next two days with so much closed."

"You have a point," I agree, tipping the can in his direction.

Padding into my room, I hear him stir, mumbling about where his wallet is.

Sitting on my bed once again, I cross my legs beneath my body. My phone lights up from beneath the blanket and I have to dig to locate it.

When I do I'm more than a little surprised to find Lachlan's name staring back at me. We haven't had any communication since the day he showed up here.

Lachlan: What are you doing?
Me: Nothing. Why?
Lachlan: Any chance you can come up?

Nibbling on my bottom lip I hear Sage putting on his coat. "I'll be back in a little while," he calls out, the door closing behind him.

I hesitate for a second more before I respond.

Me: Be there in a few.

Hopping out of my bed, I leave the unopened can of soda on the nightstand. Looking down at my pajamas I know changing is a must. I yank on a pair of jeans and an old Led Zeppelin shirt I got from a thrift store with Lachlan in mind. Running a brush through my tangled tresses, I slip my feet into my sneakers, leave a quick note for Sage about being at Taylor's for a few in case he comes back sooner than I expect, and dash out the door but not before I run back to grab the wrapped gift for him I hid in my desk drawer.

Once again I don't bother waiting for the elevator, choosing to take the stairs instead. I wish I could wipe the stupid giddy look off my face. It shouldn't make me this ridiculously happy to see him. But no matter how hard I try, Lachlan is always more than just my guidance counselor.

Reaching his door, I take a second to catch my breath before I knock.

It swings open barely a second later like he was waiting for me.

The wide white smile on his face makes me think he's as giddy as I am. It's not quite a week apart, but we act as if it has been months since we've seen one another.

I tell myself I shouldn't do it, but it doesn't matter since I'm not good at listening to myself anyway, and the next thing I know my arms are wrapped around his neck and I'm hugging him like my life depends on it.

He buries his face into my neck, inhaling my scent. I would even swear he murmurs, "Finally," softly under his breath, but he's pulling me inside so fast, letting the door swing closed that I can't be sure.

Releasing me, he steps back with a clearing of his throat. "How have you been?"

"Okay," I reply with a smile when Zeppelin runs toward me, his tail wagging so quickly he nearly knocks over a lamp. I bend down, rubbing the monster's cheeks, letting him lick me. "I missed you too, buddy."

Standing back up, Lachlan points at me in surprise. Well, not me specifically, but what I wear. "Nice shirt."

"Yeah, some old ass man seems to like them so I decided to check them out. They're not bad."

Something flashes on his face and I wish I could take my words back. I meant it in a joking way, but I know the last thing he needs is a reminder of the age difference between us.

"Do you want anything to drink?" he asks, rubbing his stubbled jaw.

"Uh…"

"I made cookies too."

"Cookies?" I raise a brow. "I might be tempted by some cookies. What kind?"

"Lemon."

"Sure, I'll try one." I shrug, sliding onto one of the barstools. I put the gift on the counter beside me. He grabs a literal cake display that houses his cookies. "You made these?" I blurt in surprise.

"Yeah." He lifts the glass dome off, allowing me to grab one.

"You cook and bake?" I wiggle the cookie between us. "All right, Martha Stewart."

He shakes his head at me, his lips curling in the tiniest of smiles as he waits for me to take a bite.

I do, only a nibble at first. Humming, I cover my mouth in case crumbs fall. "That's delicious."

He chuckles, bracing his arms on the counter in front of me. "You can have another before you go."

"How about all of them?" I bargain.

He presses his lips together to hide a smile.

Looking around, I notice the tree put up in the corner —far nicer than Sage's hand-me-down everything. A few presents rest beneath and that's when I recall him telling me his family was coming to visit.

"Should I be here?" I whisper-hiss, still holding half a cookie in my hand. "Isn't your family here?" I look around like they're going to jump out from behind the couch or from a closet to yell, "Surprise!"

He comes around the kitchen counter, standing beside me. "No, they come in tomorrow."

Finishing my cookie, I blow out a breath. "Why'd you ask me to come?"

His eyes drift to the present sitting on his granite countertop. "I got you something. Seems we both did." He holds up a hand for me to wait where I am. He hurries over to the tree and grabs two small gift-wrapped packages below. He returns, holding them out to me.

I take them gently, smiling at how neatly wrapped they are. The snowmen smile cheerily up at me and little penguins dance on ice. I would've expected maybe something more manly, like plaid paper, but I like that this reflects his playful side.

Sliding him his present, he grabs it, holding it delicately between his big hands.

I bite my lip nervously, feeling silly now for what I bought. It was a total whim, but when I saw the advertisement for it online I knew it was the most perfect gift ever for him. I wasn't expecting anything in return, but I'm more than a little excited to see what reminded him of me.

"One, two, three," he counts down and we both rip into our presents.

The first of mine reveals a mini green camera that prints photos. "I saw it and it reminded me of you for some reason," he explains with a hesitant shrug.

"I think it's awesome." He stares down at the plain cardboard box in his hands. "Come on, take it out," I encourage, eager to see what he thinks.

With a grin, he does, pulling out the metal device. "Wha—" He starts to ask, then sees the sheet with it and the sticker of what exactly the metal device does.

"It's an embosser," I explain, though it's probably not necessary. "I noticed you always wrote your name in your books. Now, you can use this." I tap it, already eager to see his printed books with the round raised edges and his name neatly inlaid among it.

"This book belongs to Lachlan Matthew Taylor," he reads what I had inscribed on it, so he can use it to press into the title pages of the books he owns. "Dani, this is … I don't think I've ever been given such a thoughtful gift."

I shrug like it's no big deal, but inside I'm giddy that he loves it so much.

"You have one more," he reminds me, flicking his fingers at the still wrapped box in my hands, the other lying on the counter.

"Oh, right."

I remove the paper, revealing a brand new e-reader, also green.

"I wanted to get yellow for both," he explains. "I know it's your favorite color, but I couldn't, so I hope green comes a close second."

"How do you know yellow is my favorite?"

"You always wear it, and even if you can't see it, I can always feel your sunshine."

He doesn't know it, but his words hit me hard.

He's the sunshine, I'm the rain, but we're no rainbow together. There is no happy ending for us. How can there be? I want there to be so badly, and I keep pushing and pushing, because I can't stay away. I crave his nearness, because ... well, he's the sun and I need him. But the truths still remain.

My age.

His position.

This could ruin us both.

He must notice the sadness in my eyes and misinterpret me. "I don't want you to think you can't borrow my books, that's not why I got you this, but I thought it might open your eyes to other books that even I haven't read." He cracks a grin. "You could give me some recommendations sometime."

"Yeah, maybe." I rub my finger over the orange packaging housing my new e-reader. I'm trying to force my melancholy thoughts away. They have no business here, souring this moment with him, because even if my gut tells me there isn't a white picket fence waiting for us in our future it doesn't mean I don't want to enjoy the now and whatever it brings me. "Thank you so much for these, it means a lot."

His smile is crooked, almost playful. It makes him look younger than his nearly thirty years. "And thank you for this." He holds up the embosser. "I guess I have an excuse to go buy more books now, huh?"

I eye the growing pile by his TV stand. "I'm not sure you need one."

His eyes follow my gaze. "Guess you're right."

Silence falls between us and I rock my legs back and forth, not knowing what to do or say.

He twists his lips as if he's thinking the same thing. After our last talk about the complications and implications of what we're doing, I don't want to push him, not even if I want to kiss him.

I'm trying to be a grown up, to be responsible. But it's difficult.

"I-I should go," I finally speak, hopping down.

My movement seems to break him from some kind of trance. "Yeah, thanks for coming by." He says it so easily, like I was stopping by to borrow sugar, not for him to give his student a Christmas present.

I grab my presents, cradling them in my arms and treasuring them more than he can imagine.

He walks me to the door, Zeppelin sniffing at my heels. Swinging it open, he waits for me to pass through. I turn around and look at him.

"Merry Christmas."

"Merry Christmas, Lachlan," I whisper back, my heart clenching.

Another half-smile later he closes the door.

I return to the apartment with my spoils, and when Sage gets back with grape Fanta, junk food, and enough takeout to last us a week, I tell him I'm suddenly not feeling well.

It's not entirely a lie either.

CHAPTER FORTY-SIX

BY LUNCH TIME CHRISTMAS DAY, ALL THE PRESENTS ARE unwrapped, the paper tucked neatly in the trashcan. It leaves the two of us, in the too quiet apartment that's surprisingly lonely despite the two souls residing inside.

Sage flips through channels on the TV, clicking his tongue as he does. Sometimes he'll stop on one for a few seconds before moving on, other times it's a few minutes that pass before the inevitable flip of the switch comes.

"You want to pick something?" he asks me suddenly, holding the remote out to me.

"Sure." I might as well, because he seems incapable of choosing.

I end up putting on *Home Alone.* It's a complete classic.

Grabbing a blanket I climb onto the couch from where I'd been sitting on the floor, fiddling with the artist tablet he got me, playing with the calligraphy aspect of it.

Sage reclines back against the cushions, resting his elbow on the arm of the couch and the side of his face into his open palm.

It seems that even on Christmas we're going to spend

our time doing what we usually do when we're together. Eating and watching TV. It's not as if anything is open, but even if it were I wouldn't want to go.

Technically, this is our second Christmas without Mom. But I was still in the hospital this time last year so I don't think either of us noticed, as awful as that sounds. I remember Sage setting up a mini Christmas tree in my room. I'm not sure it was allowed, but no one told him he had to take it down either.

My phone buzzes with text messages rolling in from my friends and extended family wishing me a Merry Christmas. I'm selfish enough to have ignored all of them. Although, I did send Ansel a thank you for the incredible piece he made me—a flower, a dandelion to be specific, crafted out of pieces of wood like the art I admired so much at the museum when he first brought me.

When the movie ends, neither of us moves to start the next one.

"Sage?" I hesitate to ask.

He turns his head in my direction. "Yeah?" His look is skeptical.

"Why don't you have a girlfriend?"

His brow furrows. "What would make you ask that?"

I flick my fingers lazily. "You dated before, in high school, and college, but not now."

He rubs the back of his head. "Haven't had time, I guess," he admits, almost confused himself. "You know what hell work has been. There hasn't been enough of me to give. Why?" he probes again, wondering why I've gone down this sudden train of thought.

"I was thinking about how quiet it is with the two of us."

"Yeah," he muses, looking around sadly, "it never bothered me before, though, when it was only me, but thinking about you leaving for college ... I don't like the idea of being here alone again."

"Sage," I say his name slowly. "I'm not going to college."

His eyes widen, almost looking horrorstricken. "But you applied. I helped you mail them. I—"

I hold my hand up, silencing his rambling. "I specifically told you I'd send in applications, but I wasn't sure I would go. I still don't want to Sage. That's not going to change by the time I need to accept."

"Dani," he begins, "college ... it's what you should do."

"What I should do and what I want to do are two very different things. I might not know exactly what I do want to do instead, but I know going to college right now isn't an option for me."

His mouth opens and closes, his breaths quickening.

"Don't be mad," I beg. The last thing I want to do is fight with my brother on Christmas. Frankly, I don't want to fight with him any day, but on a holiday feels especially hideous.

"I'm not ... mad." But the way he bites out the last word has me thinking the opposite. "I'm..." He thrusts his fingers through his hair. "Mom wanted you to go to college. That's what she expected and wanted for you. If you don't go ... it's dumb, but I feel like I'm failing her."

I shake my head rapidly back and forth. "Sage, no. Things are different now. That was my plan too at that time, but the shooting, Mom dying ... it set up my life to take a different route. I'm not saying I'll never go to college, but I'm not going *now*. I don't want to be a lawyer anymore and I need time to figure out who I am and where I fit into the world."

"Well," he blows out a breath, "I know one thing for sure."

"What's that?"

"No matter what alternate path you take, or choices you make, you'll always be Dandelion Meadows. I love you, Weed."

I scoot over, laying my head on his shoulder.

"I love you too, Herb."

We interlace our pinkies, a silent promise to stick together through whatever is to come ahead of us.

Lachlan might be the man I make most pinky promises with now, but Sage is the one that taught them to me, and my brother has never broken one.

I hope Lachlan doesn't either.

CHAPTER FORTY-SEVEN

ANSEL AND I WALK ARM IN ARM DOWN THE STREET from the condo, headed to a nearby art store that recently opened. He hinted at wanting to check it out and since it's so close we opted to walk once he got here, despite my absolute hatred of the cold.

"I can't believe I let you talk me into this." I shiver from the temperature, tightening my hold on his arm.

He moves closer to me as well. "It's not that cold, Meadows. Stop being a baby. We're almost there. We're barely two blocks from the condo. It would've been silly to drive."

I give him a look that says I whole-heartedly disagree with that statement.

"Whoa, isn't that Mr. Taylor?"

I look ahead to where he's pointing with his free hand. "Who?" I blurt out, feeling blood rush to my face like I've been caught doing something I shouldn't.

"Mr. Taylor—the guidance counselor," he adds, still pointing.

When I look, I know without a doubt it's Lachlan

walking his pet bear. But I squint anyway. "Oh, yeah, looks like it. He lives in my building," I drop casually, hoping my voice isn't quivering like I think it is.

Ansel's head swings in my direction. "No shit?"

As we get closer to crossing paths, I recognize the three figures walking near him from the photos in his office.

It's one thing seeing his family in photos, it's another to see them in person. I feel my saliva get lodged in my throat, all because I'm probably feeling similar to Lachlan the day he ran into me out with Sage. Seeing him with his family is a reminder of how if we'd be found out for what we've done, it's not just our lives that could be affected. Our family would know and it'd hurt them immeasurably.

I know the moment Lachlan spots me, because the casual conversation he was carrying on with his father is abruptly cut off.

It's really not a surprise, us running into each other.

Ansel and I slow, as does Lachlan, which forces his family to as well.

I still haven't told my friend that I spend my every day period with Mr. Taylor. I might've told him what happened at my old school, but it felt too embarrassing to share this fact with him. Besides, I'm worried if he finds out he might begin to realize that I like the school's guidance counselor a little too much.

Lachlan clears his throat, and I try not to notice how good he looks in his fitted winter coat and a gray beanie. "Hi Ansel, Dani."

"Hi, Mr. Taylor," Ansel is the one to speak back.

I give an awkward wave, hoping none of them notices the familiarity with which Zeppelin rubs against me.

"Mom, Dad, Isla, these are two students at the school I work for."

"Oh," his mom brightens, "nice to meet you two." She holds out a red-gloved hand to each of us. She's beautiful, her dark hair streaked with silver, and smile lines beside her eyes. His dad is equally as handsome, an older version of Lachlan himself with a charming smile and glasses. Isla is gorgeous, and I have to elbow Ansel for nearly drooling at the sight of her. Her mahogany tresses hang past her breasts and her cheeks are tinted pink from the chill in the air. A light dusting of freckles are sprinkled across the tip of her nose.

"Yeah, nice to meet you," I finally find the words to speak back.

There's a moment of hesitation before Lachlan says, "Well, see you guys after break."

"Mhmm, bye Mr. Taylor," Ansel replies.

They seem to be oblivious to the way Lachlan and I hold eye contact for a beat too long. We're tiptoeing a tightrope, waiting for it to snap any second.

I don't loop my arm through Ansel's again as we finish our trek to the art shop.

Once inside, Ansel looks like he won the lottery. His light blue eyes get big and round. With a mumbled, "I'll catch up with you in a bit," he disappears down one of the aisles, and I fear I might never see or hear from him again.

I'm only half-joking.

The store is huge, way bigger than I expected.

There are rows upon rows of different pigments, pastels, and every possible thing under the sun you could possibly need to create something.

I hear a cry of joy from somewhere in the store and something tells me the high-pitched noise is from Ansel.

Fighting a smile, I pick up a tube of oil paint, balking at the cost. I know supplies are expensive, but damn, this must be for the professionals whereas I need the elementary school stuff.

Moving to another aisle, I find shelf after shelf of sketchpads with different paper textures. There are pencils, charcoal, smudging sticks, erasers, and more.

It's safe to say this is definitely Ansel's version of heaven.

I find him eventually with his arms weighted down by supplies.

"You're not getting anything?" he questions and I shake my head in response. "Suit yourself." He heads to checkout and after he pays several hundred dollars—I'm not kidding—we head back home.

Ansel sets his stuff down by the door and I grab us each a grape Fanta from the fridge. Passing him one, I pop the top, smiling at the satisfying hiss of the bubbles.

"Where'd your brother go?" he asks, looking around the empty apartment. My brother was here when he picked me up—it was one of those times Sage was an ass and made him come up here.

"No idea," I shrug, flopping on the couch, "he has the freedom to do whatever he wants now."

Ansel shakes his head and joins me, playfully pushing my legs off to make room. "He's not going to murder me and chop me into pieces when he gets back and finds me here, is he?"

"Possibly." His eyes widen and I push his shoulder. "He's not, I swear. He likes to give you a hard time but he's coming around."

Maybe.

Not really.

But Ansel doesn't need to know that.

Ansel looks at me with narrowed eyes. "I want to believe you, but I don't." He gulps down some soda.

"Are you going to go to college?"

He rears back, my sudden question taking him by surprise. But after the conversation I had with my brother, I've been curious to talk to Ansel about it. Art is his passion, his life, what does he plan to do?

He scratches the back of his head, giving me a sheepish look. "I haven't thought about it much to be honest. I know I should. My parents want me to go, I applied, but…"

"Yeah, that's how I feel."

He seems relieved by that. "It sucks going against the norm and what people want from you, but art is my life. I want to create. I want to move people with something I make. I don't want to be an art teacher, which is what my parents have pushed me toward." He takes another sip of the soda, the liquid sloshing around in the can. "Expectations fucking suck."

"Yeah, they do," I whisper in response. "We put enough pressure on ourselves as it is."

"Fuck, this conversation is making me sad. Put a movie on or something before I get depressed and build a fort."

"A fort?" I raise a brow.

He laughs. "When I was a kid, any time I got sad or in trouble I made a fort. I don't know why."

I give him a look. "Are we too old to build a fort?"

He snorts. "You're never too old to build a fort."

———

TWO HOURS LATER, we've built a decent sized fort surrounding the TV, two large pizzas have been delivered, and we've polished off two more cans of soda each—it's a problem, I know.

343

"Your brother is going to lose his shit when he sees this," Ansel remarks, looking above at all the blankets we've used over top of lamps and chairs to create our hideout.

I laugh, genuinely laugh, and lean against my best friend's side, resting my head on his shoulder. "I don't care what he does, this is the most fun I've had in a while."

Ansel grins, letting his head touch mine. "Meadows, I don't know what magic brought you into my life, but I'm fucking glad for it."

"Yeah, me too." I reach for his hand, lacing our fingers together.

I don't mean it in a romantic way, and I know Ansel understands I don't have those feelings for him now. He squeezes my hand and at the same time we both lie back on all the pillows we commandeered from other rooms in the apartment to pile on the floor. The coffee table is currently shoved in the middle of the kitchen floor.

The movie we put on continues to play, one of the pizza box lids wide open, but neither of us makes a move to close it.

"You know what's crazy, Meadows?"

"What?"

"In a few short months, we're about to be shoved from the nest straight into adulthood without a safety net to catch us. Hope we don't die."

It's his tacked on sentence that has me bursting into laughter. "I guess we better practice our flying techniques."

"How are your wings working right now?" He pinches my arm lightly with his opposite hand that's not holding mine.

Rolling my head toward him, I answer him honestly.

"They weren't working for a while, but they're mending. Hopefully they'll be strong enough to keep me in the air."

He's quiet for a moment, and then he speaks softly. "Well, if they're not, Meadows, I'll have to carry you to where you want to go."

I smile to myself. Somehow, I know he will too.

CHAPTER FORTY-EIGHT

Too soon it's New Year's Eve, with school starting only two days later. Why they're sending us back only to attend Thursday and Friday is beyond me, but whatever.

"Are you sure you don't want to go?" Sage asks me for the thousandth time, coming out of the hall dressed in a nice pair of jeans and an emerald green sweater that makes his eyes more green than gold.

"I'm *positive* I don't want to go hangout with your computer nerd buddies at a steak house for New Year's Eve. I'll be fine here. I'm watching The Hunger Games." I motion to the TV where the movie plays. I read the book on the new reading device Lachlan got me and now I'm obsessed. I already told him it was a must-read.

"Why didn't you want to go out with your friends?" He adjusts the sleeves of his sweater.

Sasha is back and both her and Ansel are going to the same party tonight, but I declined. After last time, I wasn't interested.

"Because I didn't want to," I retort playfully. "Seriously, go, be merry, have drinks, kiss a stranger. I'm fine."

"I might crash at my friend's," he warns. He mentioned earlier that they'd eat and go back to someone named Simon's place. Honestly the information went in one ear and out the other because I was busy reading. Lachlan has created a monster.

"Go," I insist. "I'm fine. Have fun. Text me if you need to check on me, but seriously I'm good here." I stand up and give him a hug. "You worry too much, Herb."

"Can you blame me?"

"No," I reply sadly, forcing a smile. "But you still have to live."

"Yeah, yeah," he agrees, money is on the counter if you want to order anything and leftovers are in the fridge."

"I *know,*" I laugh.

He exhales a breath and starts looping his arms into his coat. "All right, I'm going. I love you."

"Love you, too."

I watch him go, sincerely hoping he has a good time.

Turning off the lights, I settle back down on the couch. Lying on my side, I prop my head up on a throw pillow. The glow from the Christmas tree and TV screen makes the condo seem cozier, though I miss the blanket fort Sage forced Ansel and I to promptly remove when he got home the other day.

The second movie is around twenty minutes in when my phone vibrates from the coffee table.

I dart my arm out from the warm confines of the blanket I'm burrowed in and cradle it close.

Lachlan: Happy (almost) New Year.

Me: Thanks, you too.

I try not to smile to myself, realizing that for him to text me he must have been thinking about me.

Me: Are you doing something special with your family?

Lachlan: No, they left yesterday. I'm here by myself. It's me and Zeppelin like always. Are you doing something fun with your brother?

Me: He's out with his friends. He probably won't even come home tonight. He's being a normal twenty-something guy for a night.

Lachlan: So you're on your own too?

Me: Yuuup.

Reply bubbles appear, then disappear. Shaking my head, I turn the screen off and return my attention to the movie. A few minutes pass before my phone buzzes again.

Lachlan: You could come here if you wanted. Then neither one of us would be alone.

I stare at his message in surprise.

Lachlan: I know I said this couldn't keep happening but I'm a fucking liar because I can't stay away from you and selfishly I want to see you. I'm such an asshole, I know.

Me: Are you sure? I'm fine here, really.

Lachlan: Come. Please.

I swallow thickly, wishing I didn't want to go as bad as I do.

But we both know I'm not going to say no.

Me: I'll come up in a bit.

Diving off the couch I turn the TV off and run to my room, then the bathroom, back and forth I go because I look like a hag and need to make myself presentable. An hour later my hair is curled, my breath is minty fresh, and I even dressed up in a lacy black tank top, black jeans, and some heels. I'm worried it's a bit too sexy, but I hope the jeans will keep it a little more subdued.

Fluffing my curled hair I put some clear gloss on my lips and squirt some perfume on my wrists.

"You're being ridiculous," I mutter to my reflection before switching the light off. Grabbing my phone, I head upstairs — this time taking the elevator due to my heels.

When the doors slide open I step inside with a few other people and push the button for the floor above. If any of them think it's strange, they don't say a word.

A minute later I'm walking down the hall and knocking on his door.

My heart patters against the cage I've tried so hard to erect around it. The one that falls whenever Lachlan is near. It's ridiculous how fickle a heart can be. It's such a treacherous organ.

It's a moment before the door opens and when it does I'm so fucking glad I dressed up. His eyes sweep over me lazily, then again for good measure. He's dressed more casually than I am, but since I see him dressed up every day at school this is welcome. The jeans hug his thick thighs like a second skin and his pale blue t-shirt is well worn, stretched across his broad chest.

"You look beautiful," he whispers, clearing his throat like he didn't mean to give voice to the words.

"Thank you." My cheeks flush slightly. "You're not so bad yourself. Gonna invite me in?"

"Uh, yeah." He steps aside.

"Something smells amazing," I hum, inhaling the heavenly scent emanating from his kitchen. "Where's Zeppelin?"

His bare feet pad into the kitchen and I follow, hopping up on the dark granite top. I swing my legs back and forth.

"I have to put him in his crate when I cook. He won't stay out when I'm in here and after a near miss with some boiling water I learned it was safest to put him away until the food is prepared. Hungry?"

"Starving." I wasn't hungry at all before until I smelt the food. But now my stomach rumbles like a little monster lives there. "What is that?"

"Spinach and cream sauce over pork chops. I also made potatoes and bread is warming." He points around to various pots and dishes.

"You made all this for yourself?"

He gives a sad shrug. "I live alone, so when I make something I want leftovers for when I'm too tired to cook."

"Well, I'm glad you're sharing with me today, because it looks yummy." I tap his jean-clad leg with the toe of my strappy heel.

"It's almost done if you want to sit down." He points to the small dining table near his living area. Sage doesn't have a table because … well, Sage is Sage and why bother when you have a couch and bar top counter.

"I like it better here," I admit, my voice raspier than I intend, but that's what Lachlan does to me. He looks over his shoulder at me with a crooked smile.

Something feels different in the air tonight between us.

Thicker.

Heavier.

I watch Lachlan as he finishes the last few touches to the meal and then starts plating. He has me help with that part, directing me easily to where he houses everything in the cabinets and drawers.

We each take our plate to the table along with two glasses of water.

"Should you let Zeppelin out?"

He shakes his head, pulling out a chair for me to sit down. I blush, and take the chair, letting him push me in.

"If I do, he'll only beg for food. I'd like to enjoy dinner with another person for a change."

"Haven't you had dinner with your family every night while they were in?"

"Yeah," he takes his seat, "but I want to have a nice meal with you."

Oh.

We each cut into the pork chops and I take a small bite, not usually a fan of the meat myself. "Oh my God," I cry in surprise, "this is delicious."

He chuckles, swallowing a bite of food. "You like it?"

"So yummy." I cut another bite and eat it before trying a potato. "God, you're an amazing cook." I can't help but praise him, because it's deserved. "Are you sure you wanted to be a basketball player and guidance counselor was your back up? Because you, sir, should've been a chef."

He laughs at my remark. "I assure you, I'm not that much of a talent in the kitchen. I excel far more at other things." His eyes flash and he clears his throat, shaking his head slightly. "But I'm really glad you like it."

I take a bite of butter bread, chewing and swallowing. "Thank you for asking me over. I was fine staying in and watching movies but this ... this is nice."

He lifts his head from his plate. "Yeah?"

"Yeah," I echo.

We exchange a small smile, one full of all the things between us we're both too scared to give voice to. But they still exist there, in the space between words and glances, thoughts and sounds.

When we've both had our fill, we stand in the kitchen together, him rinsing the dishes while I load them into his dishwasher.

Once the kitchen and table are cleaned, he goes back

to let Zeppelin free, and I stand in front of his window, looking out at his view. It's only one floor above Sage's so it's not that different, but maybe it's the impending new year counting down in a matter of hours that makes things look so different.

"What are you looking at?"

I jolt at the sound of his voice, husky and warm right behind me. Zeppelin's wet nose pokes my hand before his long pink tongue swipes out and licks my fingers. I give a giggle before looking up at his owner.

"Time."

"Time?" he repeats with a furrowed brow. "You're looking at time?"

"Yeah," I whisper, wrapping my arms around myself. His apartment is plenty warm, so it's not like my bare arms are cold, but he must think I am because in a blink he grabs a blanket from a side chair and drops it gently around my shoulders. "See it out there," I whisper, touching his window and leaving behind my fingerprint, proof when I'm gone that I was here and something existed in this space between us, "it's passing us by."

"In here too," he whispers, touching my elbow.

Turning from the window, to him, I'm convinced he's going to kiss me and *God* do I crave the touch of his lips. But he doesn't. Instead he twines our fingers together and tugs me over to his couch, putting the TV on to one of the various countdowns.

Bending down, I take my heels off and curl up on the couch with my body against his.

He doesn't say anything, doesn't try to add distance. His arm rests lazily around my body like this is a daily occurrence—him cooking dinner and the two of us sitting together to watch TV.

"I used to always watch the replay of the countdown in

New York City with my mom," I offer the information. It doesn't even feel like glass shards are poking at my throat. "The one with Ryan Seacrest?"

"I know which one you're talking about." He rubs his thumb in circles against my shoulder. "What else did you do?"

"She'd put out snacks, like cheese and crackers, other finger foods, and she'd let me drink sparkling cider and I thought I was so grown up and sophisticated." I give a soft laugh at the memories, how many times I probably made a fool of myself thinking I was drinking real alcohol. "I miss her."

"I bet she was amazing."

"She was, but how can you be so sure?" I tilt my head back, taking in his strong jaw.

"You're her daughter, and I think you're pretty amazing, so she'd have had to be too. I can put that one on if you want." He reaches for the remote lying on the couch near Zeppelin.

"No, I want to make new memories."

His blue eyes are flames, devouring my soul with one little look.

His throat bobs, tongue sliding out to moisten his lips. "Well," he speaks after a moment, "to new memories then."

CHAPTER FORTY-NINE

"WE'RE FIFTY-NINE MINUTES AWAY FROM MIDNIGHT AND a new year!" The announcer on TV proclaims, a little too snug in his suit. "We'll be back after this commercial break."

Grabbing the remote from Lachlan's lap, I mute the TV.

"What are you doing?" His surprise is evident.

"This is boring. Let's figure out our own way to make the next hour fun." I blush as soon as the words leave my mouth, realizing what it sounds like I'm implying. "Don't you have music? Dance with me, Lachlan."

"I don't dance," he grumbles.

Standing, I grab his hands. "You're going to dance with me."

He sighs and lets me force him off the couch. He towers above me and I feel incredibly small. He's larger than life — my Superman.

"I really suck at dancing."

I hold my pinky out. "I pinky promise I won't tell anyone you suck at dancing."

He shakes his head, laughing, and curls his finger around mine. "You're something."

"I'm everything," I counter playfully.

His eyes deepen in color as he tips his chin down. "Yes, you are."

"Music?"

He points to a speaker in his kitchen I didn't notice earlier and passes me his unlocked phone so I can use his music app. It doesn't take me long to find what I want and soon a slowed down remix of *Unsteady* by the X Ambassadors is playing.

Lachlan's lips quirk and he holds out his hands, fitting one into mine and placing the other on my waist.

I step up and squeak when he pulls me in even closer. Lowering his head to my ear he whispers gruffly, "If we're going to dance, Dandelion, we're going to do it right."

His words send a shiver down my spine.

I've never liked being called my full name, except by my mom, but hearing it on Lachlan's tongue gives me a new appreciation for it.

We sway back and forth in the middle of his apartment, my feet cushioned by the fluffy rug beneath my toes. Zeppelin watches us with an amused look, for a dog anyway. I know it's not as if we're dancing like professionals, but this still feels like everything.

"Why'd you want to dance?" he murmurs gently, our bodies so close I feel the vibration of his vocal cords through my whole body.

"Because I can," I whisper. "I might not be able to run, but I can still do this. I'm taking your advice, and focusing on what I can do." A look crosses his face. "What? Tell me."

He shakes his head, his lips quirking the tiniest bit. "You have no idea how incredible you are."

"I'm average. Boring. Definitely not incredible."

His lips find the shell of my ear again. "That's what the most brilliant and remarkable people always say. Trust me, Dani, you're incredible."

His words fill my body with heat, emboldening me to take what I want.

While we sway, my fingers find the back of his neck, sliding into his hair. His eyes close for a second, but it's all I need.

On my tiptoes now, I kiss him. It feels like it's been forever since I have, but I know that isn't true. It doesn't matter though, because my body still reacts like it's the first time. Bubbles jump and burst in my stomach, my heart fluttering like a butterfly desperate to break free. I expect him to push me away, but he doesn't. He tugs me closer, his hand sliding lower over my hip until his fingers basically splay over my entire ass.

His embrace is tight, like he's holding onto what's his.

I want to be his more than anything.

I'll let him have me, all of me, every sad and happy thought, every emotion, my body, my heart. It's his for the taking.

His hands cup my face, nearly swallow it in his grasp, deepening the kiss. He claims me, his tongue and mine twisting together.

"Why does it have to be you?" he whispers gruffly, moving his lips over my face.

"Kiss me," I beg, not even caring if I sound wanton.

He does, our dance long forgotten but a whole new one beginning to play out.

His hands move down my body, creating a trail that sends fire spreading through my body. "Touch me," I beg. "Please." My voice is achy with need.

"Dani—"

"Please."

His uttered, "Fuck," is a deep rumble.

One of his hands moves from my side, up, up, up, until it rests under the curve of my small breast.

"Lachlan," I beg between kisses. "More."

His thumb rubs against the sensitive nub hidden beneath my bra. His other hand goes to my back, fisting the fabric between his big fingers. It might be permanently wrinkled after his touch, but I don't care. He can ruin my shirt, he can ruin me.

Our kiss becomes more frantic, and heat thickens the air until I swear I feel dampness on my skin. My elbows rest on his shoulders, my hands gripping his hair.

His lips move down my neck, causing me to arch my back in response. My hips push into his and there's no ignoring the hardness straining his jeans. The moan that leaves my lips should embarrass me, but I refuse to be ashamed for feeling pleasure.

"Come here," he growls, gripping the backs of my thighs.

I give a small squeal when he picks me up like I weigh nothing. His lips descend on mine once more, stealing the breath I was barely beginning to catch.

His long legs round the couch, carrying me down the hall. He taps the door to his bedroom with his foot and in a blink my back hits his mattress.

His big body is a blanket over mine. With his grip on my neck, our lips are only separated by millimeters. "You're so fucking beautiful."

"Show me."

His eyes flash in the darkened bedroom, only illuminated by the lights emanating from the outside. "Dani—"

"Show me," I beg, kissing his chin. "Show me." His jaw. "Show me." His cheek. *"Show me."*

His eyes stare deep into mine.

Looking.

Searching.

Finding.

The hand on my neck goes to my face, and he squeezes my cheeks, not hard, but possessively. "We can't come back from this." His hold loosens a bit.

"We already can't."

He blinks once, twice, three times. "Are you sure?"

"Yes."

Before he can think too much, I wrap one leg around his waist, my hand flat on his chest, and use all my body weight to push him over until he's flat on the bed. I sit on top of him, rolling my hips against his. My core tightens, my whole body quivering with what I want—*need*.

"Dani—"

"Shut the fuck up."

I lower my head over his, my hair sweeping forward. Our kiss is searing, tongues tangling with passion and our barely leashed desire.

His hands grip my ass tightly, rolling me against him harder, faster.

"Oh God." He's going to make me come if he doesn't stop. Riding him like this, even through both our jeans, is rubbing my pussy in a way that makes my whole body quiver. "Lachlan," I shudder his name, feeling the orgasm build inside me.

His hands move beneath my loose tank-top. My skin is so heated that his touch feels like ice against me. Goosebumps dot my body from his touch as it climbs higher and higher.

"Lift your arms," he commands in a deeper than normal voice.

Still rolling my hips against his erection, which is somehow even larger than before, I do what he says.

Holding my arms straight above my head, he sits up, lifting the flimsy piece of fabric above my body, revealing the lacy strapless bra I put on, and gently lays the garment on the bed beside us.

"You're gorgeous, Dani."

He looks in my eyes when he says it and I believe it.

His gaze lowers to the small swells of my breasts. For a second I want to be embarrassed about my size B boobs, but the look he gives them has me only feeling powerful instead. His mouth closes around my right breast, his mouth warm and wet against the weak covering. I don't know if he can tell in the dark, but I know if the lights were on he would for sure clearly see the round pink buds.

He leans back and I mewl in protest but the sound is cut off when he gives my other breast the same attention.

"God, Lachlan," I cry out, tugging on his hair as I grind down on him.

With a desperate franticness to my movements I pull and yank at his shirt until he hooks his thumbs in the back of it, yanking it off. He places it beside mine on the bed, leaning back he rests his body on his elbows. A hesitant smile playing on his lips as my eyes trace the contours of his body. Reaching out, I glide my index finger over his collarbone, down his chest to his navel and the wiry black hairs there. Bringing my hands back up, I lay them against his chest, the small smattering of chest hair tickling my palms. I swallow, my heart racing, because right now, in this blip of time, he's mine.

Our eyes are locked, so much exchanged between us with one simple look. My heart fills with something out of this world, the kind of feeling people search their whole life looking for, the kind of feeling wars are fought for.

Love.

Some might think I'm too young to understand the concept of love, but it's not something that can be defined by words, only a feeling, and I know, without a doubt, I love Lachlan Taylor. I don't understand it, why him out of all the other millions of people on the planet, but it doesn't matter because it's him I've chosen.

I can't keep the words to myself. I want him to know this is more to me than some affair with my guidance counselor. This is *real*. It's painful, it's raw, it's *us*.

"I love you," I murmur, pressing a tender kiss to his lips.

His hands flex against my sides, his jaw working back and forth as his eyes fill with turmoil. I fear he's going to shove me away, that common sense is going to overtake our feelings, but he doesn't do that. "I love you, too." The words are barely above a whisper, but they're every-fuck-ing-thing and I feel them all the way down to my toes. Saying them once must make him bolder, because he says them again, this time louder. "I love you." Louder. "I love you." He begins to punctuate each word with a kiss. "I love you. I love you. *I love you Dandelion Meadows. Despite it all, despite myself, I love you.*"

Our kisses deepen, fueled by a love that defies the odds.

When his fingers find their way to my belt I beg, "Please."

He undoes it easily, then the button. Down goes the zipper.

"Stand up, Dani," his voice tickles my ear.

Sliding off his lap, I do. He stands with me, forcing me back a step.

His eyes connect with mine before he drops to his knees. I squeak in surprise, curling my fingers in his thick dark hair.

He kisses the skin beneath my belly button, causing my hips to rock involuntarily. With my pants undone all it takes is one tug from him to pull them down my legs. He grabs one of my ankles, then the other, tossing my jeans aside.

I might be wearing a sexy bra, but that's because it's the only strapless one I own. I didn't come here tonight thinking things would lead to here so I didn't put on one of my nicer underwear.

He gives a quiet chuckle at the navy blue panties with polar bears in spacesuits.

"They're silly, I know."

He looks up, shaking his head. "They're *you*."

"Oh my God," I cry out, when he places his mouth over my panties. I want to be embarrassed with how wet I am, and how he must taste it, but when his eyes find mine in the dark all I feel is sexy and wanted.

He places a kiss to the inside of my thigh, and I bow my body over his, running my hand down his naked back.

His fingers loop into the sides of my panties, slipping them down my hips and legs. He doesn't give me a chance to step out of them before his mouth is on my center, licking, suck, *devouring*.

Lachlan!" I scream, already so close from before. I throw my head back, my hair cascading around me. "Oh, God. Don't stop. Please, don't stop." My body is a sensitive live wire around him, and with him doing what he is I'm about to explode.

His right hand glides up my stomach, landing on my breast. He grabs it, tugging the cup down until it's bare.

His thumb circles my nipple while he sucks my clit into his mouth.

"Oh, fuck."

My orgasm shatters through me, my legs shaking. I think I black out because when I open my eyes I'm on the mattress once more and Lachlan is unbuttoning his jeans. Sitting up, I unclasp my bra in the back, dropping it to the side.

His fingers hesitate on the zipper. "Are you sure about this?"

"More sure than I've ever been about anything." He nods once, a muscle in his jaw twitching.

I watch his fingers on the zipper, lowering it. Black spots float across my vision and I realize I'm holding my breath. His jeans drop and he kicks them behind him.

His erection strains against his black boxer-briefs and my eyes widen. That thing is about to wreck me. He starts to pull them down but I clear my throat, reaching out to stop him.

"Let me." I don't even recognize my voice, it's nervous but also somehow sultry at the same time.

With a boldness I didn't know I possessed I scoot forward, inhaling a breath. He reaches out like he can't help himself, rubbing one of my nipples between his fingers. I pull his boxers down barely a centimeter and the tip of his cock sticks out, a drip of pre-cum clinging to the engorged head.

He glides the back of his fingers over my cheek and I flick my eyes up. "I love you," he whispers.

I swallow thickly. "I love you, too."

When his boxers hit the floor I take a moment to take in the sight of him. His cock juts proudly from his body, the dark hair trimmed neatly. The tip is a purple hue and it's lined with veins. I'm staring at it like I've never seen one, because I haven't.

Unless that one time I tried to watch porn counts, but my mom came home and scared me, which sent me accidentally throwing my laptop into the wall where it broke.

I've had flirtations in the past, even one brief boyfriend that barely lasted a month, but there's never been anyone I've wanted to take this step with. Not until him. And thank God for my new found love of books that I don't feel completely out of the loop on what to do.

Tentatively I wrap my hand around him, biting my lip. "It's so big," I blurt. "Thick too." I might not have any dicks to compare it to but my gut says Lachlan is above average.

I don't know what makes me do it, but my tongue slides out, licking away that droplet of moisture. Lachlan's head drops back and a tortured, *"Fuck,"* leaves his lips.

I suck the tip between my lips, not sure if I'm doing it right, but the way he covers his face and looks like he's having trouble breathing makes me think it's okay.

I suck a little more into my mouth. It's a bit weird and uncomfortable since I'm not used to it, but I don't mind it all that much. Especially not when Lachlan lets out a low moan, murmuring my name over and over.

Sliding my hand up and down, I press my thumb against the largest vein on his cock, watching it in fascination.

"Fuck, Dani, stop. You're going to make me come."

Taking my mouth off his dick a string of saliva clings to my bottom lip. He reaches down, wiping it away with a swipe of his finger.

His strong hands help me up and he angles his head down, rubbing his nose against mine. "Are you sure about this Dani? We can stop. Nothing more has to happen."

"Shut up." I grab the back of his head, bring his lips to mine. My breasts push into his chest, his hands resting below their curve. I swear I feel wetness smear on my thighs from my desire. Lying back down on the bed, I pull him with me. "I want this," I pant between kisses. "I want you."

More than anything.

He pulls away and I whine in protest, reaching for him until I see he's grabbing a condom from his nightstand. My chest pangs for a moment because I *know* he didn't buy those with the intention of using them with me. But he *is* and that's all that matters.

He rips the foil, pulling out the round piece of rubber and laying it beside my head.

"Wha—"

I start to protest, but he grabs my hips, pulling me to the edge of the bed until my ass nearly hangs off.

He strokes his cock once, twice, before dropping to his knees.

I start to sit up, but he places a gentle hand on my stomach, silently urging me to lie back down.

My whole body is shaking all over with a mixture of pleasure and nerves.

He bends to his knees, and with my legs spread slightly he's looking right at my pussy. I start to close my legs with embarrassment, but he shakes his head.

"Leave them open." His voice is deeper than normal, guttural.

If he notices how my legs shake he says nothing. The way his arm moves I know he's still rubbing his hand up and down his cock.

"More," he commands, and I open a little wider. A shudder goes through his body and I cry out when he

364

dives in, sucking on my pussy and the sensitive nub of nerves.

"Oh my God, Lachlan." My fingers grip the longer strands of black hair on top of his head, and I can't help but grind my hips into his face. I shiver when his hands skim up my thighs.

He rubs two fingers against my slit, looking up at me with mused hair and glossy lips. He watches my mouth form a perfect 'O' as he slips one, then the other, into me. He pumps them gently at first, then a little faster with his fingers curled.

"Oh, fuck." I squeeze my eyes closed from the feeling. With only two of his fingers I feel stretched beyond measure. I can't imagine when he puts that *thing* in me. He'll destroy me, rip right through my skin.

"You're tight, Dani. So fucking tight."

My fingers curl into his sheets as I rock back and forth, feeling the orgasm building inside me. I'm beginning to understand why people make such a big fuss over sex. This is amazing.

When his mouth sucks on my clit that's all it takes for my orgasm to crest.

I cry his name over and over again, a prayer, a plea.

He moves up my body, kissing his way there, swirling his tongue around each of my nipples. My pussy clenches with aftershocks. When his mouth reaches mine he kisses me and I hold his cheeks between my hands. I taste myself on his lips and I surprisingly don't mind it. Instead, it turns me on further. There's something erotic about knowing those lips he's kissing me with were somewhere intimate on my body, a place I've shared with no one.

Grabbing the condom beside my head, he stands to put it on while gazing down at me naked in his bed.

"I'm going to ask you this once, Dani," his eyes close

for a brief second and when they one the blue shines with something I can't interpret, "and only once, so be honest. Are you a virgin?"

My cheeks flush, hell my whole body does, and I give him a single chin dip in answer.

"Fuck," he growls but he doesn't sound angry.

He fits the condom around his cock and rolls it down with a sure stroke.

This is happening. It's really happening. I'm going to have sex with Lachlan.

"This is going to hurt, but fuck I promise to be as gentle as I can."

I give him a single nod. I know he will. I trust him. With my life, with my secrets, with my promises.

His big hands wrap around my hips, lining me up with the tip of his cock.

"If you want me to stop, tell me. Any time. You say it. I stop."

I shake my head. "I want this. I want you."

A shudder rakes his body and with one hand on my hip, he takes his other and grips the base of his cock guiding into me. He pushes in barely a centimeter and my body tenses.

"Relax, baby," he murmurs. "If you relax it'll be easier."

Breathing out, I try to calm down. He pushes a little more and I close my eyes. My body protests against the intrusion. It feels uncomfortable and unnatural. My nails rake down his chest, probably cutting his skin, but he doesn't act like it hurts. "Lachlan," I whimper. "Just do it. Please."

"Are you sure?"

I look between us and he's *barely in* and it's burning like a fire ripping through the center of my body.

I nod. "Do it."

"Hold on, baby."

I take a deep breath and he pushes forward, past the barrier that was blocking him.

"That hurts, that hurts, that hurts," I chant over and over again.

"I'm so sorry, baby." He bends over my body, plastering kisses on my face, wiping away the tears dampening my cheeks.

I sniffle, feeling like a wuss, but that shit was painful. I always thought people were being dramatic about it when they spoke about it hurting, people liked to dramatize lots of things so I thought this was no different.

Wrong.

"Breathe, it'll ease up, baby."

I shake my head back and forth. "Too big, you're too big."

He chuckles, pressing his lips to the corner of mine. *"Breathe."*

I do as he says, taking a couple of deep breaths. Some of the pain eases, lessening with each inhale. My body relaxes, adjusting to his size and the new fullness.

"Better?" he whispers, holding his weight above my body. I drop my eyes down, seeing how he's fitted inside me completely.

I give a slow nod. "Yeah, just..." My hands grip his biceps. "Go slow."

He doesn't move for a moment longer, and then he drags out slowly. My fingers tighten around his arms, my nails digging into his skin, but he doesn't flinch.

"Breathe, Dani," he reminds me when I hold my breath again.

I nod, blowing out the air imprisoned in my lungs.

I watch him pull out again a little before pushing in.

He rocks in and out, letting my body continue to adjust to him.

After a few minutes I beg, "More."

"More?"

"More," I confirm.

He pulls out further and it's impossible not to miss the bit of red staining the condom. He looks down, seeing it too and groans out, "Fuck, that's hot."

He rolls his hips back into mine. My back arches and a low moan leaves my throat. It's beginning to feel *good*. Not great, but I'm getting turned on again. My nipples pebble from the growing pleasure and he bends, flicking his tongue over first one, then the other, before sucking the left into his mouth fully.

"Holy fuck," I cry, the sensation sending a pulse straight to my core. When my pussy clenches his cock a sound rumbles in his throat.

I run my hands over the smattering of chest hair on his pecs, down over his abs. I want to see and feel all of him. I want to cherish every moment of this, memorize it so I can play it over and over, the way it feels to have Lachlan inside me.

"You're so fucking gorgeous." He peppers kisses from my neck over my breasts. My body arches up into him. "I love you." He grabs my hands, our fingers linking together beside my head. "I love you," he confesses again, over and over as he makes love to me.

I want to dig my fingers into his back, but I can't, so I squeeze his hands in mine.

"I love you," I whisper back in the dark.

God, the dark. It's always the dark with us isn't it? A place to hide? A place to feel? The darkness is our safe haven where we can let our guard down.

"You feel so good, Dani. Better than I dreamed." His lips brush my ear with every word.

"You've dreamed about this?" I voice softly.

He nods against me, his head buried into my neck. "More than I ever fucking should have."

"Kiss me," I beg, and he does.

His tongue thrusts into my mouth and I moan, because it's like he's making love to my mouth and my pussy at the same time. A little whimper echoes from my throat.

Letting my hands go, he rises up, gripping my hips. "God you feel like heaven and hell wrapped in one. You're my sin and my salvation."

I wrap my legs around his hips, and whisper a quiet, "Harder."

He growls, obliging me. His hold on my hips is tight, I won't be surprised if I bruise, but I can't bring myself to care because it feels so good. The pain from before is completely gone, for now at least. I'm sure I'll feel it later, but right now I'm so full of love, of passion, and something even deeper, that it feels like this is the closest thing I'll get to heaven on Earth.

I feel the tide rising inside me. After two orgasms I didn't think it would happen a third time, especially not with losing my virginity, but leave it to Lachlan to prove me wrong.

Biting down on my lip, I look up at him above me. "You're going to make me come again," I confess.

He reaches down to where our bodies meet and I jolt in surprise when he touches his fingers, now wet with my pleasure, to my clit and begins to rub it in circles.

I grind my hips into his, craving the friction as he pumps in and out, still rubbing that sensitive nub of nerves.

"Fuck, Dani, tell me you're close. I'm going to come

and I want you to come first." His face is pinched and I know he's holding back.

"Almost there," I pant out.

And I am, with one last pump of his cock in and out I go over the edge, the orgasm more powerful than the previous two with him seated deep inside me. He stays there, his moans filling the air as his cock twitches inside me.

Neither of us move for a moment, catching our breath, letting the reality sink in around us.

Lachlan moves first, pulling out of me. His dick is still hard when he takes the condom off, padding over to the bathroom.

I take a breath, forcing myself up. It's when I try to move that I realize how much my body has been through in the time since he carried me back here.

Getting up, I follow Lachlan into the bathroom.

He glances from the sink to me, but doesn't say anything when I shut myself into the water closet to relieve myself. When I wipe the toilet paper is smeared with a little blood. Standing up, I flush the toilet, watching the last evidence of my virginity wash away. When I open the door, Lachlan is still standing by the sink. He holds out a fresh toothbrush. I take it silently and the two of brush our teeth side by side. Surprisingly, I don't feel embarrassed standing beside him naked. I mean, I shouldn't after what we did, but it feels like maybe I should be since no one has ever seen me naked like this before.

We spit into the sink at the same time, exchanging a smile.

He passes me a cup to rinse my mouth out with water and when I'm done he uses it to do the same.

Touching his fingers gingerly to my cheek, he lowers his head to mine. "Do you feel okay?"

If I assess certain parts of my body, no, but...

"I feel amazing," and it isn't a lie.

I feel on top of the world.

"Can you stay the night?" A look crosses his face, like it pains him that he has to ask that, that I'm not free to do what I want.

I nod. Before I asked him to dance I'd gotten a text from Sage saying he was staying at his friends and would be home tomorrow afternoon, or today, I had no idea what time it was.

"Good." Lachlan smiles, taking my hand and tugging me back to his bed.

We fix our bodies under the covers and we both jolt in fright when the noise of the TV comes back on in the other room.

Blowing out a breath, Lachlan shoves his fingers through his hair. "Zeppelin must've rolled onto the remote."

The countdown begins and I smile at him.

"Ten, nine, eight..."

Lachlan tugs me closer to his body, and I throw my leg over his.

"Seven, six, five..."

He rubs his nose against mine.

"Four, three, two, one!"

He kisses me, gripping my chin between his right thumb and forefinger, his left hand draped over my bare hip.

Cheering sounds from the other room and he presses a tender, loving kiss to my nose.

"Happy New Year, Dani."

CHAPTER FIFTY

WHEN I WAKE IN THE MORNING, I'M USING LACHLAN'S bicep as a pillow. My face is nuzzled right against his chest in the little dip there that's like it was made for only me. Neither of us dressed and I feel every inch of his naked body against mine. My core clenches and I stifle a whimper because I'm incredibly sore there. It's expected, but damn I feel like I need to ice myself and that doesn't sound pleasant at all.

I trace my finger around one of the pads of his brownish-pink nipples.

He makes some sort of sleepy noise in his throat.

Cracking his eyes open, he smiles. "Morning, beautiful."

Something in my chest eases at his carefree demeanor.

"Morning," I whisper back.

I know there's still so much between us, things we need to talk about after what transpired last night, but right now I want to enjoy waking up with him.

He wraps an arm around me, his hand curling above the curve of my ass.

I trace his lips with my finger. "What are you thinking?"

He grabs my hand, placing a gentle kiss on the tender flap of skin between my thumb and index finger. "How I wish I could wake up to you in my bed like this every day." His eyes darken steadily. "I want you to know last night was *the best fucking night of my life* but it doesn't change the facts."

"I know." I try to tug my hand back, but he doesn't let go. He kisses it again, this time the meaty part of my palm beneath my pinky.

He locks our fingers together, laying our joined hands on the mattress between us. "I won't feel guilty for loving you like I do, Dani. I won't ... I'm not going to torture myself over it any longer. It fucking kills me I can't love you in the open, like you deserve, but for right now this has to be enough."

"It is," I rush to say. I'll take this over not having him any day. I tighten my hand around his. "Love is enough."

He stares back at me. "I hope so." He looks me over. "You don't regret last night, do you?"

"Lachlan." I give a small laugh. "Are you serious right now?"

His cheeks redden, the color spreading across his nose and making the dusting of freckles there more noticeable. "I'm sorry." He releases my hand, gripping my hip instead. "I need to know you're okay."

I lay my hand against his jaw, staring into his eyes so he hears every word and sees the honesty in my eyes. "I'm more than okay, Lachlan." He opens his mouth and I place my palm against it. "Don't you dare ask me if I'm sure."

I feel him smile beneath my hand before I drop it.

I clasp my hands beneath my head, staring at him. I can't help myself. I get so few opportunities to look at him the way I want. His black lashes curl against his cheeks as he blinks, his lips parted slightly with even breaths. Up this close I see every fleck of color in his blue hues, from dashes of green to sprinkles of gold.

"What are you looking at me like that for?" His voice is husky and he pulls the covers up over our bodies, covering our shoulders from where it'd fallen down.

"Because you're mine," I answer back, reminded of another conversation we had.

He gives me a playful smile. "I'm yours, huh? Does that make you mine?"

"I've been yours, Lachlan, from the moment you moved your entire office for me."

"That long?" He arches a dark brow.

"That's when you collected the first piece of my heart. But with your kindness, and caring, I've given you more and more without even realizing until I'm certain the whole thing is here now." I place my hand on his chest, beneath the steadily beating drum of his heart.

He puts his hand over mine. "If yours is here then mine…" he takes that big hand of his, putting it in the same place on my body where mine is on his. "…is right here." Zeppelin lets out a bark and Lachlan curses. "Fuck, he needs to go out. I'll be back. You stay here."

I hold the sheet against my breasts with my forearm, watching him slide out of bed. A small noise leaves me at the sight of his perfectly shaped ass. Everything about him is perfect. He pulls on his boxers and disappears into his closet, emerging in thick sweatpants, a sweatshirt, and beanie.

"I'll be back."

I give him a nod in answer, listening to him speak to Zeppelin and the sounds of a leash going on and then his coat.

"Stay warm," he calls out to me.

"I will!"

The door clicks closed and I roll over, burying my face into the pillow that smells like him. A huge, ear-splitting smile, takes over my face and I giggle.

Rolling onto my back I cover my face with my hands.

Last night ... that happened. It was real. Every touch, kiss, moan ... all of it.

I spread my arms wide.

I'm in Lachlan Taylor's bed.

I'm *naked* in Lachlan Taylor's bed

I had sex with my guidance counselor.

With the man I've grown to know over the last few months.

The man my heart yearns for.

The man I love.

———

THE SOUND of the shower wakes me and I realize I dozed off while Lachlan was out walking the dog. Stifling a yawn, I sit up, seeing steam across the bathroom mirror. Slipping from the bed, naked as the day I was born, I walk into it. The tiles are cool beneath my feet.

I bite my lip when I look over at the glass walled rain shower.

The glass is fogged over, but I still see the outline of his tall frame. His head is bent forehead, the water cascading over him. One hand on the glass, the other...

Oh, fuck.

I bite my lip, my body flushing because he's stroking his cock. He doesn't know I'm awake or that I've come in here. He makes a noise, a deep groan. It propels me forward and I step around his clothes on the floor to open the door.

He turns his head sharply, his eyes bright with lust. My nipples pebble beneath his stare. My feet pad across the wet tiles, one little step at a time.

"Dani," he groans deeply, still stroking his cock.

"Lachlan." I place my hands on his hips, then move them up over his stomach until they stop on his shoulders. I rest my head against his back, feeling his ragged breaths. I can tell he feels unsure, his hand slowing, but I whisper, "Don't stop, I want to watch."

His eyes flash over his shoulder at me and I let go, taking a step back as he turns around completely.

He keeps moving, forcing me to move until my back is pressed against the glass enclosure. He places one of his massive hands beside my head. I allow my eyes to drop for only a millisecond, taking in the length of his member jutting from his body, so big as his hand moves up and down, twisting around the tip.

His lips graze mine as he says, "You want to watch me stroke myself while I think of you, don't you, Dani?" His voice is a rugged growl that sends pleasure coursing through me.

"Yes."

He gives a husky chuckle. "I like you watching."

I bite my lip as he moves away, still in front of me but with his back against the tiled wall. He leans his head against it, eyes closed. He strokes himself faster, harder. A small whimper leaves me and I cup my small breasts, twisting my nipples. Despite my soreness, I feel my pussy getting wet. I don't think my body could handle his cock right now, but it doesn't mean I can't orgasm.

My hand slides down over my stomach, droplets of water pelting me. My fingers find the sensitive nerves and

I've barely begun to rub my clit when he growls out a forceful, "No."

I blink at him. "No?" I still rub myself, biting my lip to hold in a moan.

"*No.*" I let my hand fall away, looking at him in surprise.

"Why?"

"Because I'm going to touch you, baby. But you wanted to watch me touch myself, so watch."

I can barely swallow, my heart beating so fast it's a roar in my ears.

Lachlan watches me as I watch him. Viewing him fuck himself is a vision to behold. He's so tall, muscular, a thing of beauty—and witnessing pleasure overtake him makes the sight before me all the better.

He rubs his thumb around the tip and I lick my lips, wanting to taste him, but knowing I can't move. I stand against the glass, keeping even my hands against it so I'm not tempted to touch myself.

"You fucking love watching this, don't you?"

"Mhmm," I whimper.

"Oh, fuck," he groans, "I'm almost there, baby."

My pussy clenches, watching his hand tighten around his cock.

"Fuck, I'm going to come."

I watch in awe as cum spurts out of him, landing on the tile floor and getting on his hand. His eyes close of their own accord, head dropped back in ecstasy. The tendons in his neck strain and the sounds he makes as he orgasms send shots of electricity through my body, because it's so fucking hot.

It takes him a moment to come down from his orgasm, and when he does, he looks at me with a spark of danger in his eyes.

I squeal when suddenly he's right in front of me.

"Turn around, baby."

"Wha—"

"Turn. Around." He punctuates the words with a spin of his fingers.

I blink at him for a second before I do as he says.

"Hands on the glass."

I obey his command, keeping my head to the side.

"God, you're fucking gorgeous." I see his reflection in the glass, looking me over. I still can't believe this is happening. It feels like a dream I'm going to wake up from and be disappointed when I realize it's not real.

But it is.

I guess with an attraction like ours it was inevitable that we give in. You can only fight gravity for so long, and the two of us have been falling together from the start.

He places his hands low on my hips, nearly on my butt, and brings them upward, around my front, stopping to cup my breasts. The whole front of his body presses to my back, and the feel of our skin, so soft and slick, is foreign but welcome. He dips his head into the curve of my neck and I let it fall back against his massive shoulder.

"I love you," he whispers into the skin, giving a slight bite to where my neck meets my shoulder. His left hand tightens around my breast as his other descends.

I whimper as his fingers get lower, brushing teasingly against my bare pussy. "Touch me."

"Not yet."

I cry out again when his fingers are *right there* but he still won't touch me.

"Lachlan," I beg.

"Shh." His vocal cords hum against my body.

He brings his hand back up, swirling his fingers around my belly button.

378

"Hands on the glass," he commands.

I didn't realized they'd fallen. In a flash I raise my hands back, placing them flat against the fogged glass. He nips my earlobe and I shiver. His hand dips lower again, barely brushing my clit. My hands threaten to close into fists, my fingers flexing, but somehow I keep them on the glass.

"Oh my God," I cry out, my head lolling to the side when his thick middle finger prods my entrance, swirling through my pleasure. I mewl when it leaves, but within a second he's bringing that wetness against my clit, rubbing it in slow steady circles.

"Does that feel good, baby?"

My lips shake. "Y-Yes. So good."

He hums in satisfaction, kissing my shoulder.

My hips begin to move of their own accord, rubbing my ass into his dick. I feel him growing hard again already.

I've heard tales from past friends, and overheard conversations, of some girls' awkward first times, how it was over in minutes, sometimes even seconds. But my experience with Lachlan isn't like any of those stories at all, but maybe that's because he's a man and those were boys.

"Dani," he growls my name into my ear, turning into a feral sound. "Fuck, you're killing me baby."

He applies a little more pressure to my clit, increasing his speed. My orgasm hits like a rocket shooting into the sky. My whole body shakes and when my hands fall from the glass, my body unable to stay upright, he's there to catch me.

He gathers me into his arms, holding me close, gently now.

He rubs my back as the tremors fade. "That was —"

He silences me with a kiss. Rubbing his thumb over my cheek he stares into my eyes. "Amazing," he finishes for me.

———

THIRTY MINUTES later we're freshly clean and my hair is wet from being washed. Leaning against the counter in his kitchen, the shirt of his I borrowed rides up, showing off my underwear from the night before. They seem so childish but every time his eyes flick over from the skillet of eggs, they flash with desire, so it must not be too bad.

"That smells amazing." I rest my head in my hand, watching him cook.

He sprinkles red and green peppers, scallions, and something my brain can't recognize since I can't cook, into the eggs.

He grins over at me, looking carefree and happy. I don't want to see that look go away. I want to remain here in this blissful bubble forever. It doesn't seem like too much to ask for, but I know it's an impossibility.

"It'll taste even better."

While he continues with the scrambled eggs, my eyes take a shameless perusal of his body. He tossed on a pair of sleep pants, no underwear, and that fact has been killing me from the moment I watched him. I think it should be a rule that he doesn't wear pants. That'd be great.

My eyes drift to his ass and how the fabric molds to the curves of it.

"I can feel you staring at my butt." He chances a glance over his shoulder to confirm it and I give him a naughty grin in return.

"Trying to get my fill."

His eyes fill with sadness before he clears his throat

and the look is gone again.

He deposits the eggs onto two separate plates with the pieces of bread I toasted and buttered—somehow they're a tad charred, which I can tell amuses him, but he doesn't remark on it. He opens a drawer, grabbing two forks, and sets one on each plate.

"Grab the orange juice," he tells me, nodding his head at the two glasses I poured some in earlier. "I've got the plates."

With the juices in hand, I follow him to the table and we sit down to eat together.

My cheeks color thinking about our innocent—well, not quite innocent—dinner last night and how neither of us expected any of what came next to happen.

Lachlan takes a bite of egg. After he's swallowed he asks, "Are you sure you're okay?"

Reaching over, I place my hand on his. "I'm great. Stop worrying."

He nods, his jaw taut, but I feel better when it relaxes and he leans over to kiss my cheek.

This feels like the picture of domestic bliss.

If I allow myself I can pretend that we're a couple, and this is what we do every morning. We sit down to eat together, exchange kisses, touches, and make love like it's the simplest thing in the world.

But Lachlan isn't my boyfriend.

He's not my husband.

He's not even supposed to be my friend.

In the walls of his condo it's so easy to delude myself into thinking the outside world doesn't exist, but it *does*, and our love would never be accepted. Definitely not at the school, or even in public if they knew the sordid details. I wonder what his family would think. My stomach clenches thinking of my brother.

If Sage knew where I was, what I'd done last night with my *guidance counselor*, he'd kill Lachlan. I know it as well as I know the sky is blue. It would send my brother into such a rage he wouldn't consider the ramifications.

Lachlan reaches over, smoothing my brow. "You're worried."

I know it's a statement, but I nod anyway. "Yeah. I guess I'm the one freaking out this time."

"This is ... complicated," he agrees, bringing the glass to his delectable lips. "It worries me too. Stresses me the fuck out, actually." He sets the glass down, running his fingers through his hair in aggravation. "It's so hard not to look at you like I care, like I love you, but the moment we're outside of here that's what I have to do and it fucking kills me." He clasps his hands together, bowing his head. "This is fucked."

I place my hand on his forearm. "Let's not ruin this. Please? The last twelve or so hours have been the best of my life. I don't want to feel ashamed for feeling happy."

He touches his fingers gently to my cheek, making sure I look into his eyes when he says, "Okay, we won't talk about it right now." Sitting back, he lets his hand drop. "Frankly, there's not much more that can be said that we haven't already. And look where that's gotten us. I think right now the best course of action is outside of here you're my student, I'm your counselor. But here..."

"We're *us*."

He gives a single nod. "Exactly."

Those words are easier said than done with this love that continues to grow bigger and bigger every single day.

The stare we hold tells me he's thinking the same thing I am.

I'm not sure it's possible for us to make it out of this unscathed.

CHAPTER FIFTY-ONE

IT FEELS STRANGE TO BE BACK IN SCHOOL. THE TWO-week break was a welcome relief, but I grew too used to being home and doing things on my own time. Getting up at six this morning killed me. It's not like I even slept in that late during my time off, only until eight or so, but two sooner hours felt like no sleep at all.

Stifling a yawn, I head for the school from the bus. My coat helps block some of the wind, and the snow we had before is completely melted from the freak blizzard a month ago. A bunch of news stations claim climate change is responsible for the mountains of snow we were pelted with, but honestly, who knows.

I open the door into the school, warm air smacking me in the face.

Spotting Sasha standing against the wall with some of her tennis buddies I head that way with a smile on my face.

"Hey, Sasha, how was your break."

She moves her curly blonde hair over one shoulder. "It was good, nice to get away for a while. How was yours?"

She waves to her other friends as they say goodbye, heading in the other direction.

"Uneventful." It was anything but, but it's not like I can admit that I'm having sex with Mr. Taylor. Although, knowing Sasha she'd probably high-five me. "It was a nice quiet Christmas with my brother," I elaborate, not wanting to come off as rude with my one-word answer.

"That's cool. Has he found a new job yet?"

I had told Sasha via text message my brother had quit his job one night while we were texting back and forth.

I shake my head. "With the holidays he hasn't started looking. He said he's going to start sending out his applications this week." Biting my lip, I add, "I think he's worried his old boss will block him from getting in somewhere new."

"Oh, I hope not." She frowns, smoothing her hair down. "That'd be completely unfair. Is his old boss really that much of an asshole?"

"Apparently."

She looks around hesitantly. "Did you see Ansel any on break?"

"Yeah?" I arch a brow. "Why?"

She blows out a breath. "No reason."

"Come on, Sasha, you can tell me."

She shakes her head. "It's nothing. I know I wasn't even home, but … he hangs out with you outside of school, but not me. It's dumb." She blows out a breath, giving me a sad smile. "I wish I could get over this stupid crush when he clearly doesn't like me back and never will."

I touch her elbow, trying to give her some sort of comfort. "You'll move on eventually. Or who knows, maybe he'll get the stick out of his ass and give you a chance."

I don't tell her, but I don't think he will. Honestly, I don't know why she likes him. They're total opposites with basically nothing in common.

She snorts, rolling her eyes. "I doubt that. Maybe some hot new guy will transfer before the end of the year. You never know."

The warning bell chimes and we say our goodbyes.

I give myself a short pep talk as I walk through the halls, assuring myself I'll get through today, tomorrow, next week, and all the months after that leading up to graduation. I'm better now than I was at the beginning of the year, and while the last day I was here felt like a major set back, I'm here and that's what matters.

———

LACHLAN TAKES one look at me when I enter his office and senses the rising panic inside of me.

I thought I was okay when I got here, and I was for a little while, but murmurs echoed through the halls all day about the shooting before break. It was a harder pill to swallow than I expected hearing the conversations, names of friends injured passed around. It's a relief that no one died, but it shouldn't have happened in the first place. Principal Gordon even had all the teachers pass around papers with information on new safety measures that had been put in place while we were on break. Like more cameras, and extra security checks on anyone that's not staff trying to enter the building. I'm glad they're taking this seriously, but at the same time it's tragic that it's come to this.

The door closes behind me, snapping me out of my thoughts.

Somehow, without me noticing since I was so lost in

my head, Lachlan has appeared in front of me. In a blink his arms are around me.

"What's wrong, baby?" He stiffens the moment the words are out of his mouth.

"It seems like everyone is talking about the shooting." My words are muffled by his shirt. I step out of his embrace, giving him an apologetic smile. Guilt clings to me, because if someone walked in on us I would know in my gut that there's nothing innocent about us touching.

He steps back, leaning his butt against his desk and crossing his muscular arms over his chest. I try not to think about the fact that only a day ago I saw that delectable bare ass in his shower.

I take a seat on the loveseat, away from him. My backpack falls from my arm to rest on the carpeted floor.

Drawing my legs up, I wrap my arms around them and rest my chin on my knees.

"I feel so stupid for getting upset about it."

"Why do you think it made you feel that way?"

I arch a brow. "Don't go all shrink on me."

A laugh bursts out of him. "Sorry, didn't mean to sound like one. But I think the best way to move forward is to figure out why hearing about it upsets you—is it the way people speak about it? Is it because it happened at all? Is it because it's too close to home?"

"All of it?" The words come out as a question for some reason. He gives me a moment to sort through my thoughts. "I think a lot comes back to the fact that it shouldn't be a conversation that's happening at all."

He nods in agreement. "That makes sense."

"Hearing it over and over again sucks. It makes remember what happened to me, and then I think about kids talking about me, and everyone else who was hurt or died that day. It makes my stomach hurt."

I don't tell Lachlan, but I spent my lunch period in the bathroom dry heaving. Sasha and Ansel blew up my phone, trying to see if I was okay, or where I was, but I didn't have the energy, nor the heart, to text them back.

Lachlan stares at me for a long moment, his face tight. "I wish I could make this all go away for you."

"Yeah, well you can't." I'm not trying to be rude, it's just the reality. Rubbing a hand over my face I say, "I'm doing better, but it's hard. It's only been a year. It's still fresh."

"No one expects you to be over it." His voice is assuring, his eyes sad. "Healing takes time, mental scars are some of the deepest, and to be frank with you, Dani, this will stay with you your whole life. The best course of action is to find ways for you to cope. When something begins to upset you, you need to think of something else." He ponders on his own words. "Maybe you could think of a favorite memory, or a dream of the future, to focus on and drown out the other thoughts."

I pluck at the hair elastic on my wrist. "Do you think I should've died that day?"

His eyes widen in horror, lips falling open. "Why the hell would you say that?"

"I don't know ... my mom died, others too."

Suddenly he's squatted right in front of me. Despite the ramifications he grabs my hand, holding it gently in both of his. "Yeah and others survived that day too, Dani. You're meant to be here for a reason. Never *ever* doubt that. Do you hear me? I never want to hear you say such a thing again. You're right where you're meant to be."

With me, he leaves unsaid, or at least I hear those two silent words hanging there.

I glance at the window, the open blinds where anyone could walk by. Quickly, I touch my free hand to his cheek, and lean in to place a tender kiss on his lips. It's over in a second, but it's much needed. I already feel stronger.

I look out the window again, finding it still empty outside.

Quietly, I admit, "That day is always going to be a dark cloud over me, isn't it?"

He shakes his head. "No, baby. That dark cloud is going to turn gray, then it's going to clear off, but here's the thing—we need the rainy days to appreciate the sunny ones. So when those bad days come around, don't dwell on them. Use them instead to remind yourself of all the *good* you have."

"Why are you so smart?"

He laughs. "Trust me, I'm not that smart. I'm in love with you, aren't I?" Even though the words could be hurtful, he grins as he says them.

I punch him lightly in the arm. "Wrong, that makes you even smarter. I'm a catch."

He chuckles, standing up. He grabs his chair, pulling it around and in front of his desk. He settles into it and we spend the rest of the period talking about books.

When I leave my heart feels a smidge lighter.

CHAPTER FIFTY-TWO

STANDING OUTSIDE THE CONDO'S GYM I QUESTION WHY I'm even here.

I know my hesitation is silly, because I can't run doesn't mean I can't exercise. My doctors mentioned how biking would be good, even the elliptical, but my heart yearns for the mindlessness of running, how I could zone out and feel the pavement pounding beneath my feet.

Sometimes, when I think of those days, all my time spent running, it's like it's an entirely different girl.

Blowing out a breath, I grab the handle and push it.

It swings open, revealing the state of the art gym. It's large, much larger than I expected, with shiny equipment, padded floors, and big screen TVs.

There are two other people inside, both men, over by the weights. They glance over at me when the door closes, announcing my arrival, but return to their gym time without a second look which is a relief.

Putting my headphones in *Takeaway* by The Chainsmokers plays. I hop on the bike that's tucked in the farthest corner.

I start pedaling, trying to ignore the frustration I feel.

But I know if I can start exercising again, it'll be good not only for my physical health, but mental as well.

I pedal faster, feeling a sweat start to break out on my skin. My heart rate increases, and while it still isn't as good as running it does feel better than when I first hopped on.

Movement catches my eye and my head shoots up, worried one of the men might be headed my way. I'm not naïve enough to realize that I'm a young, female, and very much on my own in here if someone wanted to try something. At least there are cameras stationed in different areas.

But when I look I see Lachlan entering the room. Navy active shorts hang low on his hips, down past his knees, hiding the scar there. He wears a fitted white tank that shows off every muscle he's worked his ass off to have.

He doesn't know I'm here, and I watch unabashedly as he says something to the other two guys in greeting. He makes easy conversation with them and I wonder if they're friends or acquaintances from bumping into each other here often.

Lachlan moves away from them and sits down on a bench, retying his sneakers.

He grabs some weights and gets to work. It's a sight to behold, watching him grunt and sweat over the heavy weights. It makes the butterflies in my chest flutter madly. It doesn't seem to matter what he does he looks sexy doing it.

The bike beeps at me. I jolt, realizing I've slowed to nearly a stop thanks to my staring. Even my music stopped and I didn't notice.

I push the button on the bike, telling it I'm not finished with my workout, and pick another playlist.

When I look up Lachlan is staring at me from across the room.

Despite the distance between us I feel his stare everywhere. It's like he sees through me, x-ray vision straight to the things I try to hide most from people.

He really is Superman.

He gives a small, crooked smile, and turns his back to me so he can focus on his workout.

There's still no chance of me focusing on mine. Not when the back of him is as nice of a view as the front.

Get your head out of the gutter. Focus, Dani.

It's easier said than done, but I do my best to pedal the last of the ten miles I set out to do today.

When I finally reach them, I hop off and grab one of the antibacterial wipes to clean the bike.

I do my best to ignore the towering, larger than life, man taking up so much space in the room and in my thoughts.

Heading into the hall outside the gym, I bend over the water fountain since I forgot to bring a bottle with me.

I feel his presence before I see him, before even his shadow darkens the space around us.

"You took my advice."

I turn around, wiping the back of my hand over my mouth where cool water clings to my lips. "It's not running, but I have to start somewhere."

He gives me a jerk of his chin. "I'm glad."

I give him a small smile in return. "Hopefully I'll grow to like it." I don't mean to sound as melancholy as I do, but it's hard not dwell on things that used to be.

"Well," he clears his throat, "I'm proud of you for trying."

"Thanks."

His shirt is damp with sweat, clinging to his skin. I watch as he pulls it away slightly with a playful smile. "I better get back. I wanted to say something before you left."

There's two feet of space between us, we're in public after all, and it's killing me a little inside that I can't touch him. I feel like I can't joke with him either since I'm not supposed to know him that way. Does it bother him like it does me? Standing in front of me smiling, it seems like it doesn't, but you never know what's going on in someone's head.

We say our goodbyes and I stand there as he goes back into the gym before I finally get the courage to move my feet.

Catching the elevator, I lean against the railing inside it, hopping off when I reach Sage's floor.

When I open the door, I find him sitting in front of the couch playing video games — only he didn't own any video games when I left here.

He glances over his shoulder, pushing a button to pause his game.

"Look what the delivery guy brought, D! I had to hook it up right away. I haven't played this shit in years. I forgot how fun it is."

It sends a sting through my chest that my brother has been so busy with work that there was no point in investing in a gaming system because he never had time to play it. I really hope wherever he ends up for a new job appreciates what he brings to the table and doesn't work him to death like his last place.

"Is that Mario Kart?" I ask in surprise, finally realizing what's on the TV screen.

"Yeah, come sit down and play."

I smile, actually excited about it. I used to watch Sage play this and other games all the time when I was little. Sometimes he'd give me a controller so I could pretend I was playing, until I got older and that didn't work anymore. Then our mom forced him to teach me how to do it.

"Let me shower first."

He bounces slightly on the couch, un-pausing the game. "Okay, okay, hurry up."

I stifle a laugh and grab what I need from my room, shutting myself in the bathroom. By the time I'm out, Sage is vibrating with even more energy and acting more like he's sixteen and not twenty-six.

But I have to admit, it's more than a little nice to see this side of him again.

I take a quick shower, toss on my clothes, and brush my teeth before I join him so I'm ready for the night.

Plopping on the couch, I take the other controller.

"Let me finish this race and I'll switch to two player," he promises, his tongue sticking out as he races around the track.

It's a few minutes later when he wins that he switches things over, allowing me to pick my character and race car.

"I'm going to whoop your ass," I tell him with a laugh as the countdown shows on the screen.

He snorts. "That so, Weed?"

"Oh, yeah."

We both know it's a total bluff. I *never* win. For some reason I could never really get the hang of how to play, but winning isn't what matters. It's all about having fun.

We spend the entire evening playing different video games. It's some of the most fun I've had with my brother in a long time. Around one in the morning he forces me to go to bed since I have school. It's pointless since it's not like I usually get a full night of rest anyway, but I don't protest since I know he's only trying to be responsible.

"Night, Herb!" I call out before closing my door.

"Goodnight, Weed," he says back. "I love you."

"Love you too."

When the door closes, I lean my back against it, letting my eyes drift shut.

Fear crawls up my spine, I don't even know what triggers it in this moment, but I know without a doubt if he finds out about Lachlan and me, he'll hate me forever.

CHAPTER FIFTY-THREE

BEFORE I KNOW IT, IT'S FEBRUARY. VALENTINE'S DAY to be exact. The lockers are decorated with sticky notes, some project proposed by the student council to leave positive words for people today. It makes no sense to me, but I guess they don't want single people to feel bad?

"Yo, Meadows!" Ansel calls, catching up to me as I make my way to the art corridor. "God, you walk fast." He blows out a breath, slowing his steps beside me. "This is for you." He holds out a single yellow rose to me. "Don't freak out, okay, Meadows? The florist said yellow roses mean friendship. I even got one for Sasha. I'm not a total ass."

I take the rose from him, stifling a laugh that he knows me so well. I was definitely questioning the meaning of the flower.

"It's beautiful." It's the picture of a perfect rose, the petals large and curved. The yellow is vibrant, like sunshine ... like a dandelion. I sniff it and the scent is heavenly. "Thank you."

He tosses his arm around my shoulder, pulling me close playfully. "Gotta look out for my girl."

"By getting me a flower?" I smile up at him.

He shakes his head. "No, by getting you to smile."

My smile grows and I hug his side. "Thank you."

"You don't have to thank me."

We enter the art room, sitting at our usual table. I lay the rose down gently and go to get my current project, a watercolor of the Eiffel Tower, we were each assigned a landmark to do a watercolor of. Ansel is doing Big Ben.

Mrs. Kline barks out instructions for us to get our paints and get to work. The painting is due by the end of the week. I'm actually pleased with how mine is turning out, the blending of the pastel colors and the purposeful random drops.

"Do you have any plans this weekend?" Ansel asks, returning to the table with glasses of water for each of us to dip our brushes in.

"Not that I know of."

Sage found another job and has only been there the last two weeks. He seems to be enjoying it more than the last, he's home at a decent time, and he isn't ending up working at home either. It's too soon to know for sure, but I think it's a better fit for him.

"We should go do something."

"Like what?" Before he can answer, I get up to grab my paints.

When I return he says, "We could head to the slopes for the day. I'll teach you how to ski. Or snowboard. Whichever you prefer."

"You realize I hate the cold, right? Playing in snow isn't my idea of a good time."

He laughs. "Come on, it's one of the best parts of living here. It's an experience."

I know he has a point. "Fine, let's do it. But ask Sasha and Seth too."

"Already have and they're in."

It makes me feel a little better to know he didn't ask me first.

"Okay, let's do it then."

I'm probably going to regret this, but I remind myself that even if I make a fool of myself the memories will be worth it.

———

"HOW WAS YOUR LUNCH?" Lachlan asks when I enter his office.

"Chatty." Everyone, well all of us except Seth, spend the thirty minutes discussing this weekend and how it's going to go.

Apparently Ansel has permission to borrow his mom's SUV so we'll all meet at his house and go from there. I'm sure Sage won't mind dropping me off.

Okay, he probably will since Ansel is involved but he'll be fine when he realizes Sasha and Seth are going too.

"Chatty, huh?"

"Yep," I reply. "I'm going skiing tomorrow."

He arches a brow. "That so?"

"Ansel is going to teach me."

"Nice flower." He eyes the one in my hand. There's a funny tone to his voice, irritation maybe, but he clears his throat and I pretend I didn't notice.

"It's from Ansel." He makes a sound. "He said yellow is for friendship."

"How has that been going?"

I shrug as I get comfortable. At this point in the year Lachlan's office is practically another home. "He hasn't made any moves if that's what you're asking. Ever since we talked and I was honest about my feelings—or lack thereof—things have been better."

"Hmm," he hums.

"What?" I ask, an edge to my voice that surprises me.

"Most teenage boys don't give up."

"I don't want to talk about him anymore." My tone is final. It's weird talking about Ansel with Lachlan.

Ever since New Year's Eve our relationship has blossomed into more. We try to be on our best behavior at school, but there have been times when we exchange looks that if anyone sees it they'd suspect something. There have been a few brief kisses, and sometimes our touch lingers when it shouldn't. We haven't had sex again, though. God, do I want to. It's like some kind of horny beast awakened inside me, but I think about that night and morning way more than I should, craving it over and over. But we haven't been alone in his apartment either. Not while my brother wasn't working, and lately he's home all weekend and the evenings, so it's impossible to sneak away.

"What do you want to talk about?" he allows, leaning back in his chair. He looks a tad tense, his eyes tired.

"My mom," I blurt, the confession taking both of us by surprise. He's quiet, waiting for me to continue. "I've been missing her more than usual."

"That's natural. Grief comes and goes forever. It's like a wave."

"Prom is soon." I look at him through my lashes, thinking about how much I wish I could go to the monumental dance on his arm, but it's impossible. "Graduation," I continue, "it's breaking my heart that she won't be here for these milestones."

His lips thin. "I'm so sorry, Dani. She should be here and it's senseless that she's not. But remember how strong you are and in a way she *is* there. She lives in your heart now."

I don't mean to, but I touch my fingers to my heart. I know he's right. She might be gone in the literal sense, but she lives on. In me, in Sage, in our memories. It's impossible for her to truly be gone.

"Grief isn't easy," he continues. "It's this twisted, complicated ball of emotions. When you think you're unraveling it, it twists up again. But you have to keep working at it, until you find the right string to pull, when you do, suddenly things start getting better. But remember, it's okay to feel sad. Sadness is not weakness, and weakness is not a failure."

Tears burn my eyes. I've done so well keeping it together the last few weeks, but leave it to me to start crying now.

His words were something I needed to hear, even though I didn't know it.

He allows me to cry, though this time he doesn't touch me.

In the beginning the touches were innocent, he hugged me for comfort, to remind me I'm not alone and it's okay, but now too much has happened between us that even a hug feels like crossing a major line.

When I find my words, I speak a little more about my mom, more tears are shed, and when the bell rings he gets up, grabbing my backpack. He holds onto it as I stand and then gives it to me.

Before I leave the room, he whispers, "You're the strongest person I know."

Those words ... they mean more than he'll ever know.

———

SAGE ISN'T HOME when I arrive, but if the past two weeks are any indication he'll be home in the next thirty minutes to an hour.

I place an order for delivery from a local mom and pop shop that makes some of the best home-cooked food.

Kicking off my shoes when I reach my bedroom, I unzip my backpack, pulling out the contents so I can switch them with what I'll need for Monday.

That's when I find the yellow envelope.

Sitting down on the edge of my bed I open the envelope carefully, not wanting to rip it.

Inside is a thick piece of stationary with Lachlan's initials on top.

To my beautiful Dani,

You have no idea how much it kills me that I have to write this in secret. That I can't openly tell you how I feel on a day dedicated to love. You consume my thoughts, and when you're not near I miss you more than I should. I still struggle with my feelings for you, the guilt, but I can't seem to stop. Love is complicated, but when it's true there's no denying it. While I might not be able to show my love for you openly, it's one of the biggest parts of me. You've become my other half. Happy Valentine's day, baby, I love you.

—Lachlan

Something else falls from the envelope and I bend to grab it from the white rug on my floor. My lips part in surprise as I hold the stem of a dried dandelion between my thumb and forefinger. It brings a smile to my lips.

Pulling my favorite book I've read from the small shelf mostly housing trinkets, I press the flower into the middle of the pages.

Hidden, like our love, but existing nonetheless.

CHAPTER FIFTY-FOUR

SOMEHOW, I END UP IN THE BACK OF ANSEL'S MOM'S SUV with Seth, while Ansel drives and Sasha serves as co-pilot, critiquing everything he does and constantly changing the radio station.

An old rock song plays and she makes a face, changing the station *again*.

"Can you stop?" Ansel complains, rubbing his temple with one hand.

"I'm trying to get some good tunes going. Eyes on the road."

He exhales a heavy breath, glancing at me in the rearview mirror as he shakes his head.

Seth, like always, is silent, looking out at the snow-covered trees as we head further north.

We've been on the road around an hour, which means we're about halfway to the ski resort. Somehow, we got the okay to stay overnight from all our parents, and will head home first thing in the morning. Ansel and Seth will be sharing a room and so will Sasha and I.

"Ooh, here's a good one. This is classic." Sasha bops

her head along to some 90's boy band song. Her feet rest on the dashboard and Ansel glances over several times glaring at them.

"Put your feet down," he snaps at her. "My mom will kill me if this car comes back in less than pristine condition."

She huffs, rolling her eyes at him but does as he requests. She mumbles something under her breath, but I don't know what.

Ansel's jaw ticks. He's probably questioning why he invited her. Sasha isn't a bad person, though. Ansel's more quiet and introspective, where she's more out there.

Sasha, thankfully, grows quiet, though her radio fiddling doesn't let up.

We finally arrive, check in, and we all go to change our clothes into something weather appropriate. Thankfully, Sasha had snow pants I could borrow.

"I feel like the Michelin Man," I turn to her, all puffed up, "look at me."

She bursts into laughter. "But you look cute. Besides, look at me."

She's bundled up similarly.

We meet the guys in the lobby and head out to rent our gear and hit the slopes.

———

WHEN I FALL for the five-thousandth time I throw my hands up in defeat, glaring at Ansel. I haven't seen Sasha or Seth in a few hours because they left Ansel and I at the baby slope to go do more challenging hills.

"Don't give up." Ansel stifles his laughter, holding out a thick-gloved hand to haul me up from the mountain of snow. "You're so close to figuring it out."

"Ansel." I give him a death-glare. "It's been hours and I can't go more than a few feet without falling on my ass."

"Yeah, but I think that last time you made it like an inch further than you've been going," he chortles.

I swat at him but he dodges me easily and I fall down again. "Ugh," I groan. "I'm done with this. I want coffee. Or hot chocolate. Something warm. I'm turning into a popsicle."

"All right," he agrees, helping me up *again*. "I'll get you a warm drink and a snack. Let's go."

I follow him to where we return our gear and waddle my stiff bones back into the lobby of the resort. We end up in a café, sitting beside a roaring stone fireplace that goes all the way up to the next level.

Ansel sits down across from me, passing me the caramel latte I ordered as well as a chocolate chip muffin he tacked on. One for each of us.

"Trying to bribe me with chocolate?" I joke, tearing off a piece and popping it into my mouth.

"Depends. Is it working?"

"Maybe a little," I say around a mouthful, some crumbs spraying onto the table. I brush them away and take a sip of my coffee. It's pretty good.

Ansel wraps his fingers around the cappuccino he ordered, watching me.

"What?" I blink.

"Nothing," he replies amusedly. "You're just really bad at skiing."

My cheeks flame and I toss a packet of sugar on the table at him. He dodges it easily, laughing.

"Maybe you're a bad teacher, did you think about that?"

"Nah," he grins, "pretty sure it's you."

I sigh. "It's hard with my leg," I admit brokenly. "It's not strong enough for things like this."

His smile falls, eyes going wide. "Shit, Meadows, why didn't you say anything?"

I shrug, scooting my chair closer to the warmth of the fire. "I wanted to try."

He shakes his head. "If you'd hurt yourself ... fuck, next time speak up."

"Are you going to try to teach me any more sports?" I raise a brow.

He cracks a small smile. "Probably not. Snow sports are the only ones I excel in."

"There you guys are!" We look over to find Sasha unzipping her bright orange puffy coat. "Seth," she commands, "go order me a mocha and get whatever you want." She shoves some money from her pocket at him and he takes off without a peep of protest.

She reaches our table, pulling out one of the empty chairs and collapsing into it. "I'm exhausted, but this was so much fun. Thanks for inviting me." She shoots a tentative smile in Ansel's direction.

He wiggles his fingers in response, silently replying that it's not a big deal.

"Wanna head up for showers in a few? After, we can all head out for dinner."

"That's good with me," I agree, realizing darkness is creeping in. We promised to be on the road early in the morning, so the sooner we eat and settle in for the night, the better.

Seth returns with Sasha's mocha and a steaming cup of tea for himself. He hands her the change and she puts it back in her pocket for safekeeping.

After our drinks are emptied the four of us head up together to our floor and into our adjoined rooms.

I let Sasha shower first while I peel off all the layers of clothes I stuffed myself into.

With most of my layers off, leaving me in black leggings and a fitted long-sleeve black shirt I wait for Sasha to finish.

Flopping back on the bed I send Sage a text, letting him know what we're doing. I've sent him frequent updates throughout the day to help ease his worries.

Sage: Glad you're having fun.

Me: Thanks. I'll see you tomorrow.

Sage: Text me before you go to bed.

Sage: Text me when you leave in the morning too.

Me: I will. Don't worry.

Sage: Worrying is my job.

I shake my head, laying my phone on the bed.

The door to the bathroom opens, steam billowing out with it.

"All yours," Sasha announces, holding a tiny white towel to her slender frame.

I grab my change of clothes and take my turn showering. The chill is starting to leave my bones and the hot shower helps immensely.

Climbing out, I dry my body thoroughly and gather my damp hair up in a bun so it can't drip on the fresh clothes I yank on.

Stepping back into the room, I find Sasha standing by my bed with her phone in her hand.

No, not her phone.

Mine.

I recognize the peeling *You Go Girl* sticker on the back. Her brows are furrowed and she looks up when she sees me.

"Who's Lachlan? Do you have a boyfriend or something?"

"No," I blurt too fast, darting forward to yank my phone from her.

On the screen the text shows clearly.

Lachlan: I miss you.

She rolls her eyes. "You can tell me. I know how to keep a secret."

I stare at her, trying not to laugh, because there's no way in hell I can tell her I've had sex with our school counselor. I'm shocked she doesn't recognize his first name, or maybe she does but thinks there's another Lachlan in the world I know.

"It's nothing." I tuck my phone in the pocket of my jeans.

Her eyes narrow suspiciously. "Dani—"

I turn around, ignoring her. "I'm going to get the boys."

Before she can respond I'm out the door and knocking on theirs.

She joins me, still shooting me confused and speculative looks.

The door swings open, revealing Seth with narrowed brows. His dark hair is damp, curling on the ends. "Is there a fire?"

"W-What?" I stutter, taken off guard because he spoke.

"You're banging on the door like there's an emergency. Is. There. A. Fire?" He enunciates.

I shake my head. "No."

"Seth, man, don't give her a hard time." Ansel appears, slapping his friend on the shoulder. "Maybe she's really hungry or something." He finishes fitting his belt in place. "Let's go."

I POKE my fork at my overpriced dinner, unable to eat much because there's no room with the sheer panic filling my belly because of Sasha seeing that text. It's a good thing it didn't say more than *I miss you* or I would've been in big trouble.

"Guess she wasn't hungry."

We all look at Seth.

"Huh?" Ansel cocks a brow.

Seth nods his head at my barely touched plate. "You said maybe she was really hungry. She hasn't eaten."

"Something wrong, Meadows?"

I shake my head. "I'm fine."

Sasha narrows her eyes on me. It's obvious to her that I shut down after she saw the text on my phone. I want to be mad at her for snooping, but it's my fault for leaving my phone in the room to begin with.

"Tired from today, I think." I push my food around some more. "I could be coming down with something."

"I'll grab the checks and we can go," Ansel replies. All their plates are already empty.

"I wanted dessert." Sasha pouts.

"Then get it to-go," he tells her.

The two of them head off in search of our waitress.

Seth returns to his normal silence.

It's another twenty or so minutes before all our checks are paid and Sasha has her dessert. The drive back to the hotel is another ten minutes.

Sasha and I enter the room and I quickly grab my pajamas, locking myself in the bathroom before she can start in, but I know I can't avoid her forever.

When I exit the bathroom, she's already waiting her turn.

Climbing into bed, I turn off the lights and roll over.

I haven't responded to Lachlan. I can't. I hope he

doesn't take it personally, but I can't risk Sasha possibly seeing any further exchange.

Sasha leaves the bathroom a little while later and I'm not asleep like I wanted to be. I keep my eyes closed though, my breaths even.

Her steps are light across the carpeted floor. A moment later there's the swoosh of the covers being turned back and the mattress squeaks when she sinks down on it.

A minute passes before she speaks, "I know you're awake, Dani." I stiffen, still facing the wall with my back to her bed. "If you don't want to tell me about your boyfriend or whatever, it's cool. We all have our secrets."

Her last sentence feels like a pickaxe slammed right into my chest.

I feel like I have so many secrets. They're piling up one on top of the other.

It's wrong that Sasha is my friend and there are so many things she doesn't know about me, because I haven't wanted to share them. It's not a reflection of her, but of me, that I want to hold these things so close to myself instead of being open and honest.

I roll over and find that she's on her side facing me. Her blonde hair seems to glow within the dark room.

"I don't want to talk about the text, it's complicated, but … there are things I haven't told you that I should. I've been a really crappy friend to you."

"That's not true—"

I continue like she hasn't spoken. "I should've told you this a long time ago, but I wasn't ready, I probably shouldn't have hidden it at all, but it's complicated."

"You don't have to tell me anything you're not ready to. I mean, I'm nosy as fuck so of course I want to know, but I'm not going to shun you for not sharing things with me."

"No," I shake my head, "it's time."

Sasha waits patiently through the minutes it takes me to find what to say.

When I do, the words pour out of me.

So do the tears.

And when Sasha climbs into my bed, hugging me, I don't stop her. Instead, I hug her back.

CHAPTER FIFTY-FIVE

IT'S DARK OUT WHEN WE CLIMB INTO THE SUV TO HEAD home. Ansel has some sort of family thing he needs to be back for, so his mom told him to be home no later than eight. Ansel, probably not wanting to risk getting in trouble, insisted we all be up by five and on the road no later than six. It's five-forty-five so I think we've done pretty good.

This time, I sit up front with Ansel since Sasha wants to try to get more sleep.

It isn't long until a soft snore emanates from the back seat and I know she's out.

"Did you have a good time, Meadows?"

"Yeah, it was fun. I'm sorry you got stuck trying to teach me and didn't really get to ski yourself."

He flashes me a smile in the dark car. "Doesn't matter, I had fun anyway." Stifling a yawn, I lean my head against the cool window. "Put the radio on whatever you want. Or here, plug your phone in." He grabs it, holding it out to me.

"Whatever you want on is fine."

He sighs, letting the cord fall, and turns up the station that's currently playing.

"Seth, you cool back there?" he asks.

There's a grunt in response and Ansel laughs, shaking his head.

I shoot Sage a text letting him know we're on the road. Almost immediately he sends a thumbs up. I wonder if he's slept at all. He's such a worrywart.

The road leading out of the resort is a long and windy one. It's even worse leaving than arriving since now it's downhill.

The headlights shine across the snowy road and—

"Ansel! Look out!" I scream, but it's too late.

He slams on his brakes, but the car slides, slamming into the deer that ran out from the woods. The airbag explodes in my face and the SUV spins, crashing into the embankment. My head hits the dashboard, wetness seeping from my nose, and then blackness coats my vision like a final curtain call.

———

THE BEEPING of machines is an all too familiar sound, and with my eyes closed, for a moment I think I'm back in the hospital after the shooting and all of the last few months have been a dream. Blinking my eyes open, I let out a groggy moan. My face hurts like hell.

"Where is my sister?" I hear shouted in the hallway, followed by a couple of "Sirs".

A moment later, the door to the room I'm in is shoved open and Sage stands there, pale, and panic stricken.

It takes me by surprise when he drops to his knees, and suddenly several nurses are there, trying to help him up.

When he finds his legs again, he rushes to my side. "What happened? I got a call you were hurt and in the hospital. I came as fast as I could. I barely listened to what they told me."

"I-I don't remember," I stutter.

Sage screams at the nurse, "She has brain damage! She doesn't remember! Do something!"

About that time, bits and pieces come flooding back.

The deer. The car spinning. The slam of metal against rock.

I hold a hand to my head, feeling a throbbing beginning in my skull.

"Sir, she hit her head and has a concussion. Her memory is going to be foggy."

I drown out Sage's next rant as he goes back and forth with the nurse.

From what I pick up from the conversation, other than the concussion, my nose took a massive hit, but didn't break, and my ribs are bruised from the seatbelt.

"My friends," I speak suddenly, my throat parched, "are they okay?"

"They're fine, honey," she assures me with a pat on my hand, shooting daggers at my loud-mouth brother, "a little banged up like you, but they'll be okay."

"Can I have some water?"

"Of course. I'll be back with the doctor like your brother requested." She gives him a pointed look.

As soon as she's gone, he's back at my side, pulling a chair up to the edge of the white bed.

The covers are stiff against my body. Grabbing my right hand, he cradles it in his. There are a few scratches on top of my hand, but I have no idea how they got there.

"I could've lost you *again*," his voice cracks, his eyes filling with tears.

"Sage." My hand wiggles in his. I don't know what to say. Sorry feels weak and pathetic, it's not like this was planned, it just happened. "I'm okay," I go with instead.

He rubs his other hand over his tired face. "I don't know what I'd do if something happened to you. Mom left me in charge of you, and I don't think getting you nearly killed would make her very happy."

"It wasn't your fault," I say, confused.

His face pinches. "I let you go. I should've said no."

I roll my eyes. "It was a freak accident. I could get hit by a car on a crosswalk. You can't control everything, no matter how hard you try."

He winces. "Don't say stuff like that, D."

"It's true," I protest. "You can't hide away because you're scared of what *could* happen. You have to get out there and live. I had fun with my friends. A deer ran out in front of the car. No one could've anticipated that."

His lips quirk the tiniest bit. "Stop being logical." I crack a smile and groan. "What?" His hands flutter around me. "What hurts?"

"My face." I touch my cheek gently.

At that moment the nurse returns with a Styrofoam cup of water with a lid and straw, a doctor in a white coat trailing behind her.

I take the water from her gratefully and slurp it down. I have no idea how long I've been here, a few hours I assume, but my throat feels like it's been days since I've had a drop of water.

The doctor explains the same things the nurse had, but tacks on that they'd like to observe me for a few more hours before letting me go home, and that I'll also be sent home with painkillers.

I wrinkle my nose at that news. I hate taking pain pills.

Most of the time they make me sleep the day away and that annoys me.

Sage nods along to everything the doctor says, asking questions here and there. Finally, after fifteen to twenty minutes of endless questions, my brother lets the man go.

When it's the two of us once more, he looks at me with a slight smile and shake of his head.

"Do you think you could stop almost dying on me?"

I squeeze his hand. "No promises, but I'll try."

He exhales a weighted sigh. "What am I going to do with you?"

"Love me, even when I drive you crazy." I feel tears burn my eyes, thinking of all the fear and turmoil my brother has endured because of me.

"Well, that's easy enough, Weed."

CHAPTER FIFTY-SIX

"WHAT HAPPENED TO YOUR FACE?"

I look at Lachlan, wide-eyed, as I enter his office Wednesday. He stands, hands on his desk as he looks at me in complete shock. I guess since he's a faculty member, he hasn't heard the murmurs echoing through the halls about the accident. Luckily, all our injuries were fairly minor. It could've been a lot worse.

"Oh, I..." I swirl my finger at my face. "I was in an accident."

"What the fuck?" he blurts, still staring at me in shock.

I look like hell, I know. The force to my nose has caused two black eyes and purple *definitely* isn't my color.

He unfreezes and suddenly he's right in front of me, taking my face ever so gently in his massive paws he calls hands.

I see the questions reflecting in his eyes.

"I was with Ansel, Sasha, and Seth," he probably has no idea who all of them are, but his eyes narrow when I mention Ansel, "and we hit a deer. It sent the car spinning and we crashed into an embankment. I'm fine, I promise. Sore, but fine."

"Dani," my name is a plea on his lips. "Why didn't you tell me?"

I think of his unanswered text sitting on my phone. After Sasha discovered the message I was too scared to text back and with the accident Sunday morning ... well, Sage has been a mother hen so it's been impossible to let Lachlan know anything.

"I couldn't."

His face falls, but I know he understands.

"But you're okay?" His thumb rubs a gentle circle over my cheek.

"I'm fine. Just banged up. My ribs are bruised too."

He looks down, like he can see the bruise across my chest from the seatbelt through my black sweater.

"I'm so fucking sorry."

"It was a freak accident," I reply, moving around him to sit down on the couch, my body craving the rest. Sage wanted to keep me home the rest of the week, but I wanted to get back to my regular schedule.

"I thought you were sick when you didn't show up yesterday or Monday." His hands sit low on his hips. "I wanted to text you, but figured I shouldn't."

I blow out a breath, looking at him with sad eyes. "This is so complicated."

"Yeah." He leans against his desk, rubbing his face. His eyes flick over me yet again.

"I know it looks bad, but it could've been worse." He clears his throat, and I can tell he's a bit choked up. "Lachlan, I'm fine, I swear."

He opens his mouth to respond, but at that moment the door flies open.

He jumps away from his desk like he's on fire. Luckily, we were nowhere close.

"Oh, sorry for interrupting," one of the secretaries says, "I was told to run these down to you." She holds out a few files, her other hand still on the doorknob.

Lachlan's smile is tight. "Thank you." He takes them from her, dropping them on his desk.

"No problem. Sorry," she says again, flashing me an apologetic smile, "I didn't mean to interrupt."

"Knock next time," Lachlan's tone is icy and rather rude.

She pales, her eyes shooting to his. "Of course, again, I'm sorry."

She closes the door behind her and we both are silent for several minutes.

Lachlan finally moves, collapsing in his chair.

I don't know what to say, so I continue to keep quiet. What happened is proof of how careful we have to be, because it's all too easy to get caught.

I watch as he opens and closes his fists, his jaw taut, brows drawn. My own heart gallops like a reckless horse fueled with adrenaline now that she's gone.

We weren't doing anything wrong, but we so easily could've been, and in one second of time everything could've gone up in flames.

Lachlan's baby blues drift in my direction and his look of torture is a punch straight to my chest.

"It's okay," I say, but I know it's really not.

He shakes his head back and forth, silent.

Word vomit takes over, and I launch into telling him about the weekend trip, more about the accident, I tell him about the last two days and Sage taking care of me. But all it does is darken his face further and the pit in my stomach grows.

I see him shutting down right in front of me and it's fucking terrifying. We've come too far to backtrack.

When the bell rings, it startles me, and I know I have to go.

Pausing in the doorway, I look over my shoulder, "Don't leave me," I murmur.

His eyes look back at me, the fear vivid.

He does give me a nod, though, and I tell myself that's better than nothing.

CHAPTER FIFTY-SEVEN

A FEW WEEKS LATER THERE'S NO LONGER ANY EVIDENCE of the accident, except for the slight soreness still in my ribs, but it's nothing I can't handle.

Entering the gym, I find it empty.

Situating myself on the bike, I put my earphones in and start my playlist.

Letting the mindlessness take over, I zone out for a while until my thoughts drift to Lachlan.

Things haven't been the same since that secretary barged into the room. It's not like we were even doing anything, but I think the fear of what we *could've* been doing has consumed him. Even if someone saw him touching my cheek, that wouldn't be innocent, not between someone in his position and a student.

It's nearing April, though, and I miss his touch so much my entire body aches for it. It's not that he hasn't touched me at all, we've shared a few brushes of our fingers, stolen kisses, but we haven't lost ourselves in each other like we did New Year's Eve.

I want to feel his bare skin beneath mine. Trace the

contours of his muscles with the tip of my finger. I want to feel him inside me, all around me, taking over everything.

But with the wall he's built back up, that doesn't seem likely.

The only thing that comforts me is that he still tells me he loves me. Sometimes whispered in my ear before I leave his office, other times on the street if I bump into him and Zeppelin, and if he can't speak it he texts it.

It's like he wants me to know, despite his distance, his feelings still remain.

With thoughts of Lachlan filling my head I forget to track my workout, and when I look down at the bike it tells me I've done twenty-five miles, which is way more than I need to be doing my first day back. I'd intended to only do a measly ten at a slow speed.

Hopping off, my body is slightly damp with sweat. Wiping my arm across my brow, I take a sip of my water. This time I remembered to bring a bottle with me.

Gulping down every drop, I head for the exit. Swinging the door open, I immediately bump into someone. My body starts to fall, but a big hand grabs me.

"Whoa, so sorry about that," a gruff voice speaks.

I look up at my rescuer, a tall man with thick brown hair and a big beard threaded with gray.

"Thanks for catching me. That could've been bad." I would've ended up with a massive bruise on my hip for sure.

"Take your hand off her!" I look over to see Lachlan marching down the hall in his gym attire.

"What the fuck, man? She was falling. I grabbed her. End of story." He looks down at me with warm brown eyes. "You okay?"

"I'm fine."

Satisfied, he releases me and shoots a look at Lachlan before he heads into the gym.

"What the hell, Lachlan?" I fume. "I bumped into him and started to fall. He was helping me, that's it."

Anger simmers in my veins, because I hate his furious look.

"You can't stop people from touching me," I continue when he says nothing.

His nostrils flare but then the fight goes out of him. A breath whooshes out of him. Running his fingers through his hair, he turns his eyes to me, looking a bit ashamed, which he should be.

"I'm sorry," he whispers. "I'm an asshole. I think…" he looks away for a moment before centering his gaze on me once more. "I think it pissed me off seeing him touching you so freely, openly when I can't do the same. Not without a guilty conscience." His hand raises like he wants to touch my cheek, but he quickly drops it, clenching his jaw.

Tears sting my eyes. "I-I know this is complicated. But I'm eighteen. I'm an *adult*, Lachlan. I'll be nineteen in a couple of weeks. I'll graduate in June … it'll be fine."

He blinks at me.

"R-Right?" I say in a small voice.

He looks so pained, and it fucking kills me that I'm the source of it. "I don't know, Dani."

"W-What's there not to know?"

His hands come up, caging me against the wall with one on each side of me. "Everything."

"Huh?"

His lips brush dangerously close to my ear and I shiver from the sensation crawling up my spine. "When it comes to you, I don't know anything anymore, and I'm definitely questioning what kind of man I am."

"Lachlan—"

He steps back. "Because from where I'm standing, I'm the worst kind out there. Taking something that shouldn't belong to me."

He walks away, disappearing into the gym, and I stand there lost, having to regain my breath.

I want to tell him he's being crazy. He didn't steal anything. I gave him everything.

My trust.

My heart.

My virginity.

My love.

All of me.

I gave it freely. He's not a thief.

He's not.

CHAPTER FIFTY-EIGHT

MY BIRTHDAY FALLS ON A WEDNESDAY, WHICH MEANS I have to spend it at school.

Ansel hunts me down before first period starts to give me a chocolate cupcake with yellow icing, one candle sticking out of the top.

"Ansel," I take it from him, fighting a smile, "thank you."

He shrugs like it's no big deal and not thoughtful at all. "I'd light the candle but if a teacher sees I might get kicked out," he jokes with a playful wink.

I close my eyes and make a wish anyway. He plucks out the candle so I can eat the cupcake. Taking a bite, I stifle a moan, because the cupcake is pretty dang good.

"Here, have a bite." I hold the cupcake out to him.

"Thanks," he says, chewing.

When I look up, I spot Lachlan watching us and an ache fills my belly. After our run in outside the condo's gym a few weeks ago, he's been avoiding me. It's not like he can hide from me during my period with him, but he's been strictly professional, almost cold at times.

It's killing me inside, and I want to talk to him about it, but he never gives me the chance. The last time I tried to bring it up at school, he looked like he was going to choke and kept staring at the door like we'd be walked in on again.

We pass by Lachlan and I try to hide my disappointment when I don't even get a smile from him.

"So, I was thinking," Ansel begins, drawing my attention back to him and away from the brooding man now somewhere behind us, headed back to his office no doubt, "prom is coming up and we should go. As friends," he adds, "strictly friends."

I laugh at him for wanting to make that very clear. Posters line the halls, reminding juniors and seniors to buy their tickets for the upcoming prom on May second.

"I wasn't planning to go," his shoulders fall, "but it could be fun."

Sasha was asked by someone on the baseball team and I know she's thrilled. She's been telling me I *have* to go for the last two weeks.

"I'll buy the tickets," he says.

I roll my eyes. "I'll buy my ticket."

"No, Meadows. I've got this."

I shake my head. "Whatever you say." Though, I still plan to get my own. It's not fair to him to ask me as friends and then pay for everything.

We reach class and have to cease all talk of prom to get to work on our final major project for art class. We'll have a few smaller things after this, but this will count for the majority of our grade. Mrs. Kline divided us into groups of four and then we were given a painting to divide into fourths. The section of the painting we're assigned to paint will be done on a ceiling tile that will be installed in the front office at the end of the year.

Pulling out the paints I'll need, I get to work on my section. I'm nowhere near the level of artist the other students are, but I'm doing my best, and I don't think my section looks half-bad. It blends fairly seamlessly with the rest.

"Looking good, Meadows." Ansel bumps my elbow playfully on his way back over with his paint palette.

"Thanks."

Mrs. Kline puts on some music and we get to work. It's nice to get lost for a while in the swirls of colors in the classic Picasso painting we're recreating.

It's his painting, Girl Before A Mirror, and somehow it feels fitting that this was the one I was assigned to be a part of. That's how I feel a lot of times, as if I'm standing before a mirror, trying to figure out who I really am, if what I see reflected back at me is true.

My paint brush strokes over the tile, adding a second layer of color to a part I already painted, to help fill in some of the whitish gaps where the paint doesn't want to stick to the tile.

"Looking good," Mrs. Kline tells me as she passes by.

My cheeks heat under her approval. Art class has become one of my favorites. I recently had to buy another sketchbook because I filled the first.

Ansel, overhearing her, looks up from his own tile and smiles at me.

His brown hair flops over his forehead and with his grin he's all boyish charm. My heart pangs with something I can't understand, but once again I find myself wishing it was him I had feelings for. Things would be a hell of a lot less complicated.

———

THE LAST NOTES of the very loud, very off-key version of the happy birthday song that Sasha and Ansel sang, lingers in the air. Seth, of course, did not join into the festive song.

The librarian glares at us with a warning, but doesn't say anything since we're always quiet.

"You guys are embarrassing me." My whole face is no doubt lobster red.

"Us? Embarrassing? Never." Sasha winks at me, digging into the salad she got for lunch. "Oh!" She jumps, bending to dig through her bag. "Here's your present." She slides a purple bag across the table.

I take it with a grateful smile. "You didn't have to get me anything."

She rolls her eyes. "Shut up and open it."

I remove the tissue paper and reveal several small items. I pull out the first one, a teddy bear holding a heart that says *happy birthday*, the next is a lavender scented lotion, and finally a small jewelry box. Opening it, I find half of a friendship necklace. My eyes shooting up to her, she pulls out the other half from beneath her shirt.

"Thank you, Sasha. This is … really thoughtful."

I know it's only a friendship necklace, but it means the world to me to know I've made lasting relationships with these people. I never imagined I'd ever tell anyone at school what happened to me, but I've made friends in Ansel and Sasha. Telling her that night in the hotel was the best decision I could've made. She deserved to know, and I've grown closer to her since. I didn't realize it before, but I was holding back, afraid of her finding out the truth. Telling Ansel early on is what I believe helped forge our friendship so deeply.

I take the necklace out of the box and fix it in place. I

hold the half of the jagged heart against my chest and smile at her.

Words seem to fail me so I tell her thank you again and she nods her head.

This time Ansel passes me a gift bag.

"Ansel —"

"You didn't think I'd only get you a cupcake, did you?"

"Cupcake? I want one," Sasha interjects, looking around like she's failed to notice them.

"It's Meadows's birthday, I got *her* a cupcake. Not you."

She sticks her nose up in the air. "I don't know why anyone would buy *one* cupcake. That's a crime."

He shakes his head. "Go on, open it."

As soon as I peek in the bag I notice the prom ticket. "Ansel, I told you I'd get my ticket!"

"I know. That's why I went ahead and got it."

"Wait a minute, you guys are going to prom together? Why didn't you tell me?"

"We decided this morning," I explain.

"Well, this is great. We can go dress shopping together!" She claps her hands excitedly. "I'm going next weekend with my mom."

"That would be great." The last thing I want to do is drag Sage dress shopping. That sounds like my version of hell. He'd probably insist on putting me in something that covered me head to toe.

"Okay, Meadows, open your gift now. Your prom ticket wasn't it."

Seth watches everything without uttering a word. Surprise, surprise.

From the gift bag I pull out a Lucite case filled with

nail polish. My jaw drops and I look at Ansel in shock. "How did you know I love nail polish?"

He snorts. "You always wear it, and it's all over your room. I sat on a bottle once." I laugh, biting my lip as I open the case, pulling out the various colors and looking at the different names for curiosity's sake. "Let me tell you, when I went to go buy all this stuff I got some strange looks. But don't worry, I endured it all for you, Meadows."

I can't help but laugh at his dramatics.

"Thank you, guys. Seriously, this has been a pretty good birthday."

"Are you doing anything with your brother?" Sasha asks around a mouthful of salad.

"We'll probably go out to eat." Not that that's really any different than any other day, but whatever.

"That sounds fun. Your brother is so hot by the way." She fans herself.

She met him for the first time briefly when he picked me up from the hospital.

"Ew, please tell me you're not crushing on my brother."

She gives a dainty shrug. "He's hot, I have eyes. Sue me."

I cover my face with my hands. "Shut up, I'm losing my appetite."

She giggles in response.

Unwrapping my sandwich I take a tentative bite, seeing how my stomach responds. Luckily, I'm okay despite hearing my friend say my brother is hot.

I only get half of my sandwich eaten before the bell rings, but it's enough.

We all toss our trash and say our goodbyes before heading in opposite directions. My stomach clenches with dread at seeing Lachlan. Though I've grown used to his distance for the past near two months, it doesn't mean I like it, especially not with today being my birthday.

When I reach his office I hesitate outside the closed door.

I take several deep breaths, steadying myself, before I reach for the handle and pull it down.

He looks up when I walk in, wearing his glasses today.

"Hey, Clark," I joke, figuring that might lighten the mood.

"Clark?"

I point to his glasses. "Clark Kent, you know ... Superman?"

"Yeah, I know." He turns his attention to his computer screen. I take my seat on the couch and pull out my homework. "What are you doing?" He arches a brow in my direction.

I arch one right back. "My homework."

"Why?"

I curl my legs under me, swaying my hand. "I don't know, maybe because I don't feel like talking today."

"Why not?"

"Because it's my birthday," I glare, not at him but through him, "today is going to be a good day. I'm not talking about the past. I'm not going to be sad or angry. So I'll sit here and do my homework. Continue on with whatever it is you're doing. I'm sure it's far more important than me anyway."

I wince, realizing how whiny the last sentence sounds. I don't want to be petulant, but it's awful having him act so professional toward me lately. I know that's how things should've always been, but the line was crossed, and he can try as hard as he wants, but it can't be uncrossed.

Nothing can erase my memories of the feel of his

hands on my hips, the way his cock fit inside me, how he sucked my breasts. All of that is permanent. His silence can't remove his actions.

The only sound in the room is the heavy breath he exhales like the weight of the world is on his shoulders.

If he's worried about me, *us*, doesn't he know I'm ready to bear this burden with him? In a few months school will be over, this worry will be behind us.

"Happy birthday, Dani."

"Thank you," my reply is soft as I stare down blankly at the homework in my lap.

At least fifteen minutes pass with him continuing to work and me mostly staring at my homework instead of doing it.

"This is ridiculous." He pushes away from his desk.

"I agree."

He shoves his long fingers through his hair, pacing the short length of the room. My belly aches seeing how torn up he is.

He turns around, facing me, swinging his arm in the air wildly. "There are so many things I want to say to you and I *can't*. It's killing me pushing you away, keeping you at a distance, but I have to do this." He beats his chest with a closed fist. "I'm not doing this to hurt you, or make you angry, or any of the things you might think. I'm trying to protect you more than I am myself. I want to help you, but I'm worried I'm hurting you."

"You're not hurting me—"

"Listen," he begins again, "I'm thirty years old, you are nineteen. The walls of this school are a very strict prison that's supposed to prevent you and me from ever being together. I let my feelings corrupt my sensibilities, and because of how I feel for you, I need to protect you. You sitting there, telling me you don't want to talk because it's your birthday kills me, because I *know* if I hadn't been forcing things to remain professional, you would've never said that."

There are several things from that proclamation I should focus on, but instead I say, "You're thirty now? When was your birthday?"

How do I not know when his birthday is? Why have I never asked?

"Today."

I blink at him, thinking I can't possibly have heard him right. "No, my birthday is today."

"So is mine."

"We have the same birthday?" I don't know why I make it a question when he's already made it clear.

"Yes."

"Why did you never tell me?" It's not like I made an announcement to him about my birthday, but he's looked at my information, so he had to know.

"It's not important."

I roll my eyes. "Of course, a coincidence like that is *definitely* not important."

"It's just a birthday." He ruffles his hair again. It's getting more unkempt, like he doesn't care to have it trimmed lately.

"I would've gotten you something," I mumble, crossing my arms over my chest.

He lowers in front of me. "I know you would have."

"Is that why you didn't tell me?"

He gives a shrug. "It never came up."

I look away from him, not satisfied with that explanation. I give myself a few seconds to be angry, and then I look back at him with nothing but sadness. "Happy birthday, Lachlan."

His eyes roam my face like he's studying every detail. "Happy birthday, Dani," he says again.

It startles me when his fingers brush my knee as he stands. I know he did it on purpose.

He sits back down at his desk, returning to his work, and once again we're pretending to be nothing but strangers.

———

I BLOW out the candle on the salted caramel cheesecake. Sage brought me to some fancy restaurant to celebrate, but I would've been fine eating pizza at home. Though, this cheesecake does look delicious.

Taking the candle out, I take a bite of dessert while Sage watches.

"Mmm," I hum.

After the larger dinner we had, I wasn't sure I could stomach any more, but let's face it, there's always room for dessert.

Sage digs into the brownie sundae he ordered for himself.

"How would you say your birthday has been?"

"It's been a pretty good one." As much as I want things to go back to normal with Lachlan, I refused to let it ruin my day.

"Good." He wipes chocolate sauce from his lip.

When he got home from work he gave me my gifts, some new art supplies, a couple of books he thought I might like, and some money subtly hinting at using it to decorate my room.

We finish up our dessert, pay, and head back home.

We're quiet on the drive home, and after he parks in the garage, I turn to him.

"I'm going to take a walk."

"I can go with you," he insists, undoing his seatbelt.

I shake my head. "No, I want to go alone."

He looks a little hurt at first but then nods. "Okay, don't stay gone long."

"I won't."

While he heads up in the elevator, I take the stairs to the lobby, and exit onto the street. The sun is beginning to set, and everything is awash in hues of gold and orange.

Wrapping my jean jacket tighter around me to stave off the chill coming from the slight wind, I start walking, inhaling the fresh air.

The fading heat from the sun feels good on my face as I tilt my head skywards.

I want to stop feeling so lost. How do I find myself again? Show me the way.

I'm not surprised when my thoughts are granted no answers.

I keep walking, probably too far, and force myself to turn back around for the condominium.

My steps slow when I see the massive brown dog ahead of me, its owner standing tall and broad-shouldered beside him.

Why do I have to ache for him? Why? Why him out of all the other millions of people on the planet?

Again, no answers.

As if he senses my presence, Lachlan glances over his shoulder, startling when he sees me. He gives a shake of his head, his steps slowing too, like he's waiting for me to catch up.

I speed up, passing him.

"Dani!" he calls out, making my stomach roll at the sound of his voice. "Dani, wait!"

His pleas slow me and within seconds a massive head

bumps into my leg. I can't help but smile at the brown dog with the sweet soulful eyes.

"Were you going to ignore me?" Lachlan's voice is low.

I tilt my chin, meeting his intense gaze. "I was thinking about it."

He works his jaw back and forth. "I deserve it."

"Yeah, you do." There's no sense in denying the facts.

"I'm sorry." Again, like earlier today, he shoves his long fingers through his disheveled hair. "It ... it has to be this way."

I resist the urge to roll my eyes. The last thing I want him to think is I'm immature about this whole thing. I love him deeply, and miss being with him, whether he knows it or not he's my happy place, but I *do* grasp the severity of the situation.

"Regardless," he continues without me adding anything to the conversation, "I ... I got you something." His lips thin. "It's in my place. Come up with me and I'll grab it. I want you to have it today, while it's still your birthday."

"It's your birthday too," I remind him, as if he doesn't already know, "aren't you going to do anything?"

He presses his lips together as we continue to walk in sync side by side.

"No."

"Why not?" I'm being nosy, I know, but I can't help it. "Birthdays are meant to be celebrated."

His lips work back and forth and I can visibly see the tension clinging to his body as he fights with himself over whether or not he wants to voice what's on his brain.

Finally he looks down at me, his brows drawn. "If I can't celebrate how I want to, with who I want to, what's the point? I made myself a cake, that's enough."

"You made your own cake?" My voice is small. For

some reason, this breaks my heart. No one should ever have to make their own birthday cake.

"Yeah?" It comes out as a question. "What's wrong with that?"

"It's *your* birthday. Someone should make your cake for you."

"It's not a big deal. I've been doing it since I lived on my own."

"Okay, Betty Crocker."

He actually laughs. We enter the building, taking the elevator up to his floor.

When we reach his door, he looks at me over his shoulder. "Wait here."

I do roll my eyes this time. "What? You think I'm going to jump you or something?"

He shakes his head, his tongue sliding out to wet his lips. "It's not you I'm worried about, Dani."

Before I can respond, he disappears inside, letting the door close.

I stand there, feeling like a pathetic loser, as I wait for him to return.

It's barely a minute later when the door opens and he holds out a tiny package and an envelope.

"I..." He starts, then shakes his head. "Take it."

He thrusts the box and envelope out to me and I'm forced to grab it. I hold it carefully, staring at him. Before he can close the door the whole way I say, "Lachlan?"

"Yeah?" he pauses, his eyes tortured.

"Next year, I'm making your birthday cake."

I leave him standing there before he can give me a denial I don't want to hear, and one I refuse to believe is true.

I take the elevator down a floor and have to knock for Sage to let me inside.

"I was getting worried," he says upon opening it. "What's that?" His eyes drop to the tiny package in my hand and card.

"Oh ... I ... um ... Taylor sent me a text while I was walking and told me to come by and get my birthday present."

I mean, it's not a total lie, right?

"That's nice." He closes and locks the door behind me. "Why haven't I ever met this friend? I mean, I know I haven't really met all of them, but if she lives in this building you could invite her over some time for dinner. I don't want you to think you're not allowed."

"Um ... I'll keep that in mind." I bite my bottom lip. Lying like this to my brother is eating me up inside, but it's not like I can tell him the truth. "I'm going to bed."

It's starting to get late, and it's a school night, so at least that part isn't a lie.

Shutting my bedroom door behind me, I'm careful to lock it. I lay the gift and envelope on the white comforter, staring at them both like they're a snake that might lash out and bite my fingers.

Why, Lachlan? Why do you have to play with my heart like this?

I turn away from my bed, rummaging through the dresser for a pair of pajamas. I yank on a green pair of leggings and an old college shirt of Sage's I snatched years ago. But when I turn back around, of course, the two items still sit on my bed waiting.

I groan, picking up the box first.

I know I don't have it in me to hide either away in a drawer. It'll bug me too much.

I rip off the pale pink wrapping paper, revealing the small cardboard box. I lift the lid off gingerly. On top, is a rectangular business card size note on top with Lachlan's handwriting.

When I saw this, I knew it was you and I had to get it.

—L

Lifting the card off, I reveal the dainty necklace lying beneath.

It's a gold wire dandelion, not the kind you make wishes on that so many others have turned into jewelry and tattoos, no this is designed to look like a true yellow dandelion, like my namesake.

I pick the chain up, looking at the wire flower that's about the size of a dime.

"Beautiful," I whisper to myself. Setting the box down, I fumble to attach the necklace around my neck. Once I do, it sits above the friendship one Sasha gave me. I place my hand over it protectively, closing my eyes.

After a moment, I grab the yellow envelope and open it, removing the letter inside.

Dani,

It seems lately the only way I find to communicate my thoughts and feelings properly to you is to write them down. I hope you know my feelings haven't changed, but keeping my distance is necessary. I won't repeat things here that you already know in regard to why, it's pointless.

Instead, I want to say I love you. That's the only truth in all of this that matters.

Wrong, immoral, it doesn't matter, I can't deny what I feel for you.

I wish we were spending our birthdays together, but we can't. It seems as if the list of things we cannot and should not do is growing longer and longer.

But getting to know you these months, falling in love with you, I can't bring myself to regret that. That would mean I regret you, and you, Dandelion Meadows are no one's regret.

Happy birthday, baby. I love you.
Please, if you believe nothing else, know my love for you is real.
—Lachlan

I hold his letter against my heart, closing my eyes.

For a moment, I can pretend it's him I'm holding.

CHAPTER FIFTY-NINE

AFTER SOME GRUMBLING FROM SAGE, HE ACTUALLY expressed—or faked—enthusiasm over me going to prom with Ansel. It might've been my insistence that we're only going as friends that finally got him to stop shooting dirty looks at every mention of prom. He even forked over some money for a shared limo and my prom dress.

Shopping with Sasha had been more fun than I expected. It was only the two of us and we laughed and joked, expressing opinions on various dresses before we both decided on *the one*.

With my hair and makeup done I slip into my dress, luxuriating over the feel of it. It's far more princess-y than I would've ever thought I'd choose, but somehow, it's perfectly me at the same time.

It dips down, exposing more cleavage than I would normally be comfortable with, but this felt like the night to be a little more daring. Though, my brother will probably blow a gasket when he sees it. It's fitted at my waist, before flaring out into a flowy tulle ball gown skirt. The whole thing is a champagne color, but what made it stand out to me is the pink, white, and blue flowers stitched all over the dress with green stems. The amount of flowers is thicker at the bottom, with not as many as it goes up the skirt. There are some stitched into the top and I rub my fingers over them, marveling at the exquisite detail. I've never owned anything like this, but I love it.

Staring at my reflection in the mirror, I brush an errant hair back into its 'do. Sage insisted I get my hair and make up done. I drew the line at my nails, which I painted myself a nude color.

My hair, which is normally always down or tossed up in a messy bun, has two braids on the left side of my head with the rest of my hair pulled back and fixed low on my neck. A few stray pieces frame my face artfully to soften the look. My makeup, which took a surprisingly long time considering how simple it looks, gives my skin a warm, dewy glow. My eyes are shadowed in different shades of pink, and my lips are a nude-pink color with a bronze gloss on top. I feel beautiful—not that I think I'm an ugly duckling—but when I look in the mirror, I look grown up, more like a woman than the girl I feel like I'm stuck as.

Grabbing my glittery clutch off my dresser I stuff my phone, lip-gloss, and the cash Sage gave me for tonight.

Before I can slip my feet into my heels, Sage yells, "Ansel is here!"

Fixing the shoes, I stand, giving myself one last once over.

I removed the necklace from Sasha, but the dandelion from Lachlan hangs above my breasts.

I can't go to prom with him, but at least he'll be with me in some way.

Not wanting to give my brother a moment longer to contemplate changing his mind about letting me go with Ansel, I meet them by the front door.

"Wow," Ansel blurts, looking me up and down.

Sage smiles. "You look beautiful, D." His eyes narrow at my exposed chest. "I don't remember agreeing to that," he grumbles.

I walk up to Ansel and he extends the corsage he got me. It's a beautiful array of what looks like wildflowers. I offer him my wrist and he slips it on. Grabbing his simple white orchid boutonniere I do the same.

He looks strikingly handsome in his deep green, so green it's nearly black, tux. His dark hair is more tamed than usual and those eerie light blue eyes of his are other-worldly.

"You look good," I tell him, finally finding my voice.

"Not as good as you."

"Stop flirting with my sister and let me get some pictures."

I want to tell Sage if he calls that flirting no wonder he's single, but I don't feel in the mood to tease him and possibly make him mad. I want nothing to ruin tonight.

I step into Ansel's side and he wraps an arm around me carefully, not wanting to touch me in any place Sage might lose his shit over.

Once Sage has his fill of photos, he's seriously a mother hen, we're free to go after a lecture about being safe, and when to be home by, which is thankfully much later than normal since he agreed I could go to the after party.

Ansel blows out a breath as we wait for the elevator. "Your brother still scares me," he whispers under his breath, like Sage is suddenly going to appear behind us.

"He's a softy. I swear."

"Trust me, I think he's hidden a few bodies in his time."

The doors open as I start to laugh.

Ansel takes my hand for us to go inside, my breath catching when I finally look and see Lachlan leaning against the side of the elevator. He's in a pair of jeans, a dark gray t-shirt clinging to him like a second skin.

My throat closes up as I stand beside Ansel, with Lachlan only inches away as the doors close.

"Oh, hey Mr. Taylor," Ansel says with a smile.

Lachlan's eyes are on me, taking in every inch of me in my dress, my skin sparkling with the glittery lotion I rubbed on. He looks pained, like something is lodged in his esophagus.

Clearing his throat he says, "Uh, yes. Hello. You two look … nice." That word sounds forced and when his eyes meet mine, they say something different.

Beautiful.

The doors slide open for the lobby and he motions for us to go out first.

Ansel's hold on my hand tightens when I stumble a bit in my heels, but having Lachlan at my back is messing with my head.

Before we reach the doors, I look back. My eyes connect with his where he stands in the center of the lobby watching. The tortured look on his face rips my stomach to shreds. I yearn to run back, to jump in his arms, but I can't.

I have to go.

———

THE LIMO DROPS ANSEL, Sasha, and her date, Brett, off at the hotel.

The lobby is filled with students decked out in their finest.

"This way, guys," Sasha guides, pointing in the direction we need to go for the ballroom. Her pale blue dress swishes around her legs. In the front is a high slit, and it's off the shoulders at the top. Silver strappy heels are wrapped around her ankles and she didn't bother with any sort of jewelry. She chose to leave her hair down in its natural curl, and I'm glad because her hair is gorgeous. I think she looks like Cinderella and I know Brett has been checking her out appreciatively.

As soon as we enter the ballroom, my jaw drops. The lights are dimmed and twinkle lights hang from the ceiling in hues of white, gold, and purple. Tables off to the side are covered in black tablecloths. There's an area cleared for dancing, a buffet with food and drinks, and a DJ station set up.

"Let's dance!" Sasha cries, grabbing Brett's hand and dragging him onto the dance floor. He doesn't protest and they get lost in the crowd.

Ansel swings his body in front of mine and bows slightly with a crooked grin, holding his hand out to me. "What does the lady say? Can I have this dance?"

I slide my hand into his. "Lead the way."

Ansel flashes me a crooked smile and I let him pull me into the fray.

———

MY BODY GLISTENS with sweat when we finally leave the dance floor. I follow Ansel to the refreshments table, surprised by the happy giggle that keeps coming out of my lips.

I wasn't sure I would have fun tonight, but I'm having a blast. It feels good to be out with my friends.

Ansel passes me a cup filled with crisp ice water. I down it while he pours his own and then I refill mine.

Grabbing a plate with snacks, we find a table to sit at for a breather.

I take a bite of finger food, watching Sasha and Brett still tearing up the dance floor. I can't help but find myself smiling.

When I glance at Ansel, he's watching me with a grin.

"What?"

His smile grows. "You ... you look happy."

"I am happy." For the first time in a very long time I can say that with full confidence. I've come a hell of a long way since school started.

Sasha comes running over to us and grabs my hand. "Get back out here."

Brett drops into one of the empty seats. "I need a break."

I let Sasha drag me back out, the two of us dancing together, laughing, *living*. God, I'm living again.

I feel Ansel's eyes on me. I shoot a smile in his direction, trying to fend off Sasha's wandering hands as she tries to put on a show for the whole senior class.

After a few dances with her, I make my way back to the table, gulping down a fresh water Ansel was kind enough to get for me.

"This is the best night ever," Sasha proclaims, finally taking a seat. Brett pulls out a flask from his pocket and holds it out to her. She takes a swig, wincing in the process. "What the hell is that?"

He shrugs, looking into the flask. "I don't know, I mixed a bunch of shit together so my parents hopefully wouldn't notice."

Sasha sticks her tongue out. "That's nasty. Keep it to yourself." Flipping her hair over her shoulder, she asks, "When are we going to the after party?"

"I don't see why we can't go now. We've been here two hours," Ansel replies. "Should I call for the car?"

Sasha looks for any protest from Brett or me and receives none.

"Cool, call for the limo," she bosses. "Dani and I need to run to the restroom."

"We do?"

She rolls her eyes. "Of course."

She drags me away to the bathroom outside the ballroom. We finish our business and wash up our hands before touching up our makeup.

Fluffing her hair she says, "Brett looks good tonight, huh?"

"I guess," I voice, wondering where she's going with this.

She leans forward, dotting some pink lipstick across her lips. "I think I'm going to have sex with him tonight. I want to lose my virginity before college. Tonight seems as good a night as any."

I blink at her. This does not sound like good logic to me.

"Shouldn't you wait until you love someone? Or at least care about them?"

"Eh, I want to get it over with. Everyone makes it into such a big deal and I don't want to do that. Are you going to have sex with Ansel tonight?"

I choke on my saliva. "No, definitely not. He's my friend, that's it."

"I mean, he's hot. Why not? Are you a virgin?"

Other girls are coming in and out of the bathroom, so it's not like we're alone. I can't believe she wants to have this conversation here and now.

"I ... uh ... no."

She turns to me, smiling. "Was it that Lachlan guy?"

"What?" My eyes widen.

"You know, the one that texted you that he missed you?"

A girl I recognize from my English class pipes up from the sink she stands in front of. "Lachlan?" She eyes me up and down. "The only Lachlan I know is the guidance counselor."

"Ooh, he's so fucking hot," someone else says.

My body flames with heat and before Sasha can open her big fat mouth, I drag her out of the bathroom and around the corner.

"Ow, Dani, that hurts." She extracts her arm from my hold. "What's going on? Ignore them, I don't think you slept with the guidance counselor." She finally looks at my face. "Oh my God you totally fucked the guidance counselor."

"Shut up," I hiss. "You can't tell anyone."

"I…" She blinks, open-mouthed at me. "Wow. Way to go, girl."

Then, she shocks the hell out of me by holding her hand up for a high-five.

"I am not high-fiving you over this."

She lets her hand drop. "So … is this why you've never liked Ansel in that way?"

I know my cheeks are a startling shade of red. "Yes."

She stares at me in bewilderment. "Wow, there's so much I still don't know about you. I never would've thought. You seem too good to go after someone that's practically a teacher." She sounds impressed, which makes me feel sick to my stomach.

"I didn't go after him, and he didn't come after me. It just … happened."

"I need details."

"Not happening." I shake my head adamantly.

"Oh, come on —"

"There you guys are," Brett says, coming out of nowhere, "Ansel's in the car already. Let's go."

Sasha walks over to his side, glancing back at me when I don't move. "Aren't you coming?"

I shake my head. "You guys go on ahead. I'll … I'll meet you there later."

"What about the car?"

"I'll get a taxi or catch a ride with someone else."

"Oh, well, all right."

I watch her and Brett leave. I know Ansel will probably try to find me when he realizes I'm not with them, so I hide in the bathroom. Sure enough, texts start rolling in from him.

Ansel: Where are you?

Ansel: Seriously, this isn't funny.

Ansel: Do you want your brother to murder me?

Ansel: Meadows, where the hell are you?

Ansel: We're leaving.

Ansel: Are you coming later or not?

Ansel: Whatever, Meadows.

Ansel: Duck you.

Ansel: F U C K YOU.

Ansel: I'm so fucking mad at you right now.

I turn my phone off.

I don't want to hurt Ansel, but I need to be alone right now.

Leaving the bathroom, I call for a cab.

CHAPTER SIXTY

IT SHOULDN'T BE ANY SURPRISE TO ME THAT SOMEHOW I end up outside Lachlan's door.

I hesitate, not sure if I want to knock or not.

The smart thing to do would be to go downstairs, tell Sage I didn't feel like going to the party, change into pajamas, and go to bed.

But I know I won't do that.

Doing what I *should* do seems to be an impossibility these days.

Hesitating for a second longer, I knock. It's around midnight, so I expect he might be in bed. I'm about to knock again when it opens.

He leans his hip against the doorway, his left arm stretched wide holding the door open. He's dressed in a t-shirt and sweatpants now, and looks ready to crash.

He doesn't say anything, neither do I. His exhale is the only sound that fills the air when he steps aside, letting me in. I can barely get around him with my poufy dress.

I look around, taking in the cardboard boxes sitting against the wall. "What are those for?"

His eyes swing to me and back to them, looking distant. "Getting rid of a few things." He runs his fingers through his hair, his lips pinched. He crosses his arms, leaning his back against the door.

"Was prom not enjoyable?" His tone is a tad snarky, but when he looks away I have a feeling it's himself he's irritated with and not me.

"It was fun, but it's just a dance."

"You should be out doing things with your friends. Normal things with other teenagers. You shouldn't be here with me."

"But I want to be here with you." I smile at Zeppelin when he cracks a sleepy eye open from his cushion. Apparently it's past his bedtime.

"Why do you do this to me, Dani?" He looks like I've stabbed a knife into his heart.

"Do what?" I ask innocently, completely baffled.

He scrubs his hands over his face. "I'm trying to do the right thing by giving you space, but then you show up here and it's not fair. How can I be expected to stay away from you when you're right here?" The words start pouring out of him and he swings his hand in my direction. "Seeing you in the elevator tonight was a punch to the chest, because you're beautiful and you feel like mine, but you're so young, and I can't take you to your prom because it's fucking wrong. I can't take you on a proper date. I can't ... We can't, be seen together."

"Stop repeating things I already know," I growl like a cornered animal. "I get it, okay. You don't have to keep telling me. I know, believe me. But what about what I feel?" I touch my fingers to my heart. "Huh? Does that matter at all? That I want to be with you, that I want you to hold me? That I want to kiss you? Make love with you?"

A muscle in his jaw ticks.

"What about the letters you left me? You ... you said you love me." My voice grows small as I become unsure of myself.

There's something in his eyes that I can't decipher. Something I'm *missing*.

"Lachlan—"

In a blink he's upon me, his mouth taking mine prisoner. He's rough, demanding. His hold on my cheeks is tight and I find my back pressed against the wall.

He claws at me like a wild animal, bunching the tulle of my skirt in his hands, trying to yank it up.

I kiss him back with fervor, a spark igniting into an entire fire inside me from one touch of his lips. I match his desperation, pulling at his shirt, trying to get it over his head.

He tosses the shirt off like he can't get it far enough away from him.

His eyes are twin sapphires blazing when he looks down at me. His whole body is a taut live wire waiting to go off.

"If you don't tell me how to get you out of this dress, I'll rip it off of you."

The gentle, kind Lachlan of our first time is gone. In his place is this wild beast of a man. I'm a tad frightened, but there's something intriguing seeing this side of him.

I turn around, sweeping my hair away that's fallen loose from its up-do, thanks to his greedy fingers.

Turning around, I place my hands flat on the wall, angling my head to the side so he can see the zipper in the back.

He says nothing as he grabs the tiny zipper between his thumb and index finger, slowly lowering it. The dress loosens around my body and I feel the top begin to fall down my arms. My bare back is exposed to him. He sucks in a breath.

"You're not wearing a bra."

It's a statement, but I respond anyway. "You can't exactly wear one with a dress like this."

"No," his voice is gruff, huskier than normal, "I suppose you can't. Lower your arms."

I do what he says and the top of the dress falls easily from my body. His big body presses in behind me and I stifle a moan when he kisses the back of my neck.

"You're so fucking beautiful."

He rains kisses down my spine, dropping to his knees behind me where he places his hands on my hips, pushing the rest my dress down so it pools at my feet.

He glides his fingers beneath the sides of my lacy white underwear, taking them off as well.

"Turn around."

I find it impossible to ignore his command. There's something in his tone of voice that I can't deny. I also would be lying if I didn't admit it's hot as fuck seeing this side of him, like some part of himself he normally keeps leashed has been let loose.

"Put one of your legs over my shoulder."

"Wha—"

I squeal when he grabs my leg for me, tossing it over his right shoulder. He spreads my other leg wider. I whimper, biting down on my lip. I'm completely exposed to him, vulnerable.

He nips at the inside of my leg before diving straight for my pussy.

"Oh my God!" My right hand squeezes his left shoulder.

He hums against me, his tongue sliding against my folds.

"Oh, holy shit." My head hits the wall. "Don't stop." I squeeze his shoulder, my other hand yanking on his hair, trying to hold him in place even though he's not trying to go anywhere. He sucks on my clit and a string of curse words comes flying out of my mouth as I roll my hips against his mouth.

His right arm is looped around my leg, but with his opposite hand he slides it up my body, grabbing my breast roughly between his fingers and squeezes. When he pinches my nipple the sensation of it goes straight to my core and my orgasm hits me hard. My whole body bows over his, shaking uncontrollably.

"Holy shit," I keep repeating over and over again until he's in front of me again, silencing me with a tongue-dueling kiss.

He grabs the back of my thighs and lifts me up to twine my legs around his waist. I rub myself against his erection straining against his sweatpants. I'm probably leaving a wet spot on the cotton material, but I don't care, and from what I feel I don't think he's wearing underwear, so he's probably very aware of how wet I am.

He walks me down the hall to his bedroom, kicking the door closed behind him. The wall shudders and something falls from his dresser, but neither of us stop kissing to take a look.

He lays me on the bed, standing between my legs with his head canted to the side. His jaw is rigid and he rubs at the heavy lining of scruff there. He stares at me, lying naked on his bed, my breasts aching for his touch, and the skin between my legs raw and red from the coarse brush of his stubble. He reaches down, placing his hand on the curve of my waist, studying the smooth planes of my stomach. He looks at me like I'm a feast spread out for only him, but I guess in a way, I kind of am.

I grab his hand, his eyes following my movements as I bring it to my lips. I kiss his fingers, watching as his eyes dilate. When I release his hand, he takes both, cupping them around my breasts like he's measuring their weight or size in his big grasp.

He dives down, sucking my right nipple into his mouth. My hips roll upwards, searching for friction. He moves to my other breast, giving it the same attention before he lavishes my mouth. He's wild, unhinged, greedy as our tongues battle.

"I need you in me." The person speaking is me, but it doesn't sound like me. The voice is husky, drenched in desire, and sounds far more confident and experienced than I am.

His thumb rubs my cheek tenderly, before he stands. My body feels so cold without his over mine.

Leaning up on my elbows, I watch him kick off his sweats, his cock springing free. He grabs a condom, ripping off the wrapper with his teeth, his eyes on mine the whole time. There's something different in the way he looks at me, like he's scared I'm going to disappear. He rolls the condom on and I can't help but watch the strokes of his fingers securing the latex in place.

"Turn over."

"Wha—"

"Turn over."

I swallow thickly, and roll over to my stomach. He grabs my hips, maneuvering me into the position he wants me. He lowers his body and my back arches when his tongue swipes against my pussy again. I cry out, gripping the sheets between my fingers.

I feel him stand behind me, lining his body up with mine. In one smooth move, he sheathes his cock inside me.

Biting down on my lip to hold any more sounds inside, my grasp on the sheets tighten.

"You feel so good," he murmurs, his voice husky and thick. He wraps one arm around my torso, urging me up until my back is flush to his front. His fingers rest around the column of my throat as he pumps into me. I move my hips back against his, meeting his thrusts.

"Oh God," I cry out when his other hand slides around to rub my clit.

With the hand at my throat he urges my head back more, capturing my lips with his.

"Lachlan," I pant his name. I grab onto his hand near my throat and my nails dig into his skin. "It feels so good. You make me feel so good."

His moans and grunts echo against my ear, along with his breath. It's so sinfully erotic and highlighted even more so by the way the planes of his body feel behind me.

He pumps into me harder then pulls out suddenly. Before I can protest he flips me back around and I'm lying flat on the bed. He climbs onto the bed with me, his body shadowing mine. He thrusts back in and he stifles my sounds with a kiss. He loops our fingers together beside my head, rocking in and out of me. The friction has me gasping and another orgasm is building. It doesn't take long before I go off, my body shaking and clenching around the fullness of him inside me.

He rises up, grabbing my hips between his hands, and pounds into me harder than before.

"Lachlan!" I cry out, my fingers grasping at his stomach, scratching the skin.

Another orgasm hits me and I've barely recovered from the last. He grunts, his moan long and drawn out as he comes too. He finishes, yanking off the condom. He tosses it in the wastebasket near the bed and tugs at his sweat-damp hair before lying beside me. He wraps his arms around me, yanking me against his side where he peppers gentle kisses against my neck.

He keeps whispering something over and over again.

It's a few minutes before I realize he's saying he's sorry.

Only, I don't know what he's sorry for.

When he makes love to me again, this time slower, sweeter, I think I must not have heard those words at all.

CHAPTER SIXTY-ONE

On Monday, the majority of the senior class doesn't seem to have recovered from prom. People seem half asleep or still hungover despite a whole day of recovery in between.

I carry my saran wrapped chicken salad sandwich into the library, surprised to find I'm the last one to arrive.

Ansel looks up at the sound of my feet approaching and I know he's still mad. I called him yesterday, but he ignored all calls and text messages from me.

Please don't be mad at me, my eyes say.

He glares back at me and I know my silent communication is doing no good. I messed up, I know. Ansel was my prom date, as friends or not, I disrespected him by disappearing, and if he knew where I'd gone ... well, I doubt he would ever speak to me again.

"Saturday night was wild," Sasha says, stifling a yawn, "I can't believe you ditched us, where did you go?"

I feel Ansel's eyes on me, waiting for some kind of explanation that could possibly be good enough.

"I ... uh, I went home."

"You went home? God, you're such a party pooper." She tosses a wrapper at me.

Seth, of course, says nothing and Ansel has joined him on the silent train today.

I feel sick to my stomach, because the weight of everything is getting to me suddenly. I hate keeping secrets like this and that's all Lachlan and I are—one giant secret.

Picking at my sandwich, I tear it into chunks, suddenly not hungry at all. My stomach churns with unsettling emotions.

Sasha drones on and on about the party. I'm so tempted to yell at her and tell her I don't care about the party, but since she's the only one speaking it's better than the silence.

When the bell rings I rush after Ansel. I catch up to him in the hall, my hand wrapping around his elbow. He freezes, his whole body taut like he's disgusted by my touch.

If he only knew.

"Please, let me talk Ansel. I'm so sorry." I try to tug him toward a less busy hall, but he won't budge.

He whips his head toward me, blue eyes narrowed and brow angry. "You told Sasha you'd meet us there, but you never did. I went in and looked for you, you know?" He seethes, vibrating with anger from head to toe. "You ignored my texts and I was fucking worried about you. But you didn't care about that. I could've taken you home. We could've gotten a cab or the limo could've dropped you off. What the hell went wrong? I thought you were having fun. You seemed happy." He glares down at me, waiting for my rebuttal.

"I did have fun," my voice is so small.

"Then what the hell went wrong? Was it because of what happened to you at your old school? Did you freak out? You could've told me, if that's the case. I wouldn't have cared."

I blink at him. "Y-Yeah, it was … hard. You know … having fun. I felt guilty."

It's a complete lie. That night, I didn't think about my past at all. I lived in the present. I let my anger, my hate, my fears, all go like flushing them down a drain.

Ansel must see something on my face, because his contorts with disgust and he looks at me like he doesn't know me at all.

"Menteuse."

Liar.

————

LACHLAN'S DOOR is closed when I arrive, which isn't new, but what is new is the fact it's locked.

I knock on the door. "Lachlan? It's me."

Nothing.

I press my ear to the door in case he's in a private meeting to see if I hear the murmuring of voices. If he's busy, I'll wait somewhere else. But I don't hear anything.

Nothing but eerie silence.

There's no note on the door either.

With a sigh, I head to the indoor track to sit and wait.

He'll find me.

But he never shows up.

————

ON TUESDAY, he doesn't show either.

Or Wednesday.

Not even Thursday.

Since I hate dealing with the office people I spend each of those days at the indoor track.

I'm afraid he's sick or something, but all texts go unanswered.

Rumors begin swirling about his absence, my name dangerously tied to his.

On Friday, everything goes to hell.

CHAPTER SIXTY-TWO

GETTING CALLED TO THE OFFICE IS RARELY A GOOD thing, and my gut tells me when I show up to the principal's office that this is bad. The rumors that have been swirling the past few days haven't been good, all kinds of talk about Lachlan being fired for sleeping with a student — *me*.

I blame the stupid conversation in the bathroom during prom with Sasha's big fat mouth.

Most of the rumors are far-fetched, about us having sex all over the school and all kinds of lewd remarks, but at the end of the day it doesn't matter, because we *did* have sex whether or not it happened at school. No one cares if the rumors are even true or not.

I knock on Mr. Gordon's door and it swings open a moment later.

"Sage," I blurt, finding my brother sitting in the same chair he occupied all those months ago when I was enrolled. "Why are you here?"

"I have no idea. What's going on?"

A sweat breaks out over my whole body and I'm sure I'm turning a dangerous shade of red.

Bad, this is bad.

But Lachlan still isn't here and that worries me the most.

Did he actually get fired over rumors? Is that where he's been?

"Have a seat Ms. Meadows." Mr. Gordon swings his hand at the empty chair before smoothing down his tie and going behind the desk to sit in his own chair.

I look between Principal Gordon and my brother, fighting my rising panic.

What is going on?

Mr. Gordon lays his palms on the table, stretching out his fingers.

Clearing his throat, he begins, "I don't know quite the best approach for addressing this delicate situation."

"Delicate situation?" Sage's head shoots back and forth between me and the principal. "Let's get to the point, shall we?"

Mr. Gordon blows out a breath. "Mr. Taylor, our guidance counselor, was offered another job and put in his notice a few weeks ago that he'd be leaving before the school's end."

What the hell? Another job? Did he change jobs to un-complicate things between us? Why not tell me that?

"He's already gone, but in his absence rumors began swirling of an inappropriate relationship between him and a student."

Again, Sage's gaze shoots between Mr. Gordon and me. "I'm confused why we're here then? Is it because she was seeing him every day? Do you need to ask questions or something? I'm sure Dani will tell you whatever you need to know."

I'm going to faint. Or throw up. This is bad.

"Well, you see," Mr. Gordon laces his fingers together, "the rumors concern Dandelion."

"Dani? My sister?" Sage snorts. "How?"

He knows how. He knows what's being hinted. But he doesn't want to accept it.

My hands are tight on the arms of the chair I sit in.

Principal Gordon's eyes shift to me and back to my brother. "Rumors have spread through the school that the relationship between Dandelion and Mr. Taylor was more than professional."

Sage's whole face is bright red, his fists clenched on his lap. "I believe what you're telling me is that the student body is spreading rumors, because a staff member left, that my sister must have slept with them? That's the most bullshit thing I've ever heard."

"Ms. Meadows?" Mr. Gordon looks at me.

"T-They're rumors," I stutter. "Mr. Taylor has helped me a lot, with what happened before, but that's it. M-Maybe people realized that I spent my every day period with him and the rumor started that way."

Mr. Gordon stares at me, looking for any trace that I could be lying.

"Ms. Meadows, if he coerced you in any way to do something you weren't comfortable with I need to know. The school will need to do an investigation, his new place of employment will need to be contacted—"

"That's not necessary," I rush out. "Seriously, it's nothing like that."

"If my sister says nothing happened, I believe her."

Mr. Gordon sighs. "Well ... I ... I guess, you can go then. I apologize for bringing you all the way here."

Sage stands up, shaking hands with the man.

When we leave the office, panic begins to grip me. "C-Can you take me home?"

Sage cocks his head to the side. "Yeah, I don't see why not. You got your stuff with you?"

I nod.

He signs me out and I follow him to the parking lot. He drops me off at the condo and leaves to return to work.

Instead of heading up to his apartment I go to Lachlan's, banging my hand on the door.

"Open up," I beg, tears burning my eyes.

I lied to the principal. It was necessary, I know, but I need to see Lachlan. I need him to take me in his arms, to hold me and tell me it'll all be okay.

But he never comes to the door. Zeppelin doesn't bark.

Someone opens a door down the hall and glances my way.

"Are you trying to get ahold of the young man who lives there?" She smiles with kind brown eyes. She's older, probably late fifties, but she has this calm presence that instantly makes me feel at ease.

"Yeah." I sniffle, wiping at my face to rid my skin of the few tears that slipped free.

"He moved out, sweetie." She looks so forlorn at giving me this information.

"Moved? That's impossible."

Isn't it? He wouldn't move and not tell me.

But then I think of his murmured *I'm sorry's* and Mr. Gordon saying he took another job. I believed in that moment he'd done it for *us* so we wouldn't have to worry about being caught. That we'd finally be able to love in the open.

But that's not what he's done.

He's left me.

"Do you live on floor eleven?"

I startle at the sound of her voice. I forgot she was even there. I give a wooden nod.

"Hold on a second." She holds up a finger for me to wait.

She unlocks her door and goes back in, returning only a moment later.

"I was supposed to slip this under the door, but since you're here..." She trails off, holding an envelope out to me. His familiar script is on the front, writing out the number to Sage's apartment.

"T-Thank you." I wrap my fingers around it, taking it from her.

"No problem." She starts to turn to leave. "Are you going to be okay, sweetie?"

"I'm fine."

I'm not, but what good would telling this lady do?

She nods and heads for the elevator.

I stand there for a few more minutes, staring at his door like I expect it to open any second. When it doesn't, I finally catch the elevator down to Sage's floor. I don't have the energy to take the stairs.

Letting myself in, I head straight for my bedroom, slamming the door closed behind me.

I scream as loud as I possibly can and then I scream some more. His letter gets crinkled in my hands but I don't fucking care.

I don't want to read whatever lame ass excuses he wrote for me.

I start to tear the envelope in two but I barely rip it half an inch before I can't go any further. My whole face is damp with tears and I stuff the letter in the bottom of my underwear drawer.

Covering my face with my hands, I let all my emotions

out. I wail, these soul-crushing cries like I've never heard before.

I didn't even cry like this after the shooting, but I guess by the time I woke up I was numb to everything.

I'm not numb this time, though, and I feel *everything*.

I hate it.

I don't want to feel this.

It would be easier to feel nothing.

I swipe my phone out of my backpack and bring up his contact.

Me: You bastard! You fucking bastard! I hate you!

Me: You left?!

Me: How could you do that and not tell me!

Me: I hate you so Goddamn much. I never want to see your face again.

Me: Rumors are circulating about us, but I bet you don't even care.

Me: Did you EVER care about me or was it all a lie?

Me: ANSWER ME!

Me: I hate you. I hate you. I HATE you.

I throw my phone and it bounces off the wall, leaving a dent, but I can't bring myself to care.

Anguished sounds pour out of me and I fall to the floor, cradling myself in the fetal position.

It hurts. It hurts so much. I want it to stop. Mom, I wish I was with you. I don't want to feel.

I squish my eyes closed, more tears leaking out.

Something echoes in my room and I crack my eyes open, looking for the source of the noise. It happens again and my mouth opens in surprise when I see the wind chimes gently moving, barely grazing each other when they shouldn't be moving at all. It's like it's my mom talking to me in this moment. Reminding me of my strength and capabilities.

"My sweet, Dandelion. May you always be as free as the birds, as wild as the flowers, and untamed as the sea."

"It hurts, Mom," I croak, my voice raw. "Living hurts so much."

My eyes fall closed again and I swear I feel the backs of her fingers graze my cheek, a gentle kiss to my forehead.

I keep crying and at some point I drift off to sleep.

CHAPTER SIXTY-THREE

SAGE COMES HOME TO FIND ME ASLEEP ON THE FLOOR, still in the fetal position, with tears dried on my cheeks.

"Dani!"

At his exclamation I jolt awake. My eyes are sore from so much crying. I have trouble opening them, blinking slowly to clear the haze.

"Why are you on the floor?" he asks, bending down. The concern etched on his face makes my stomach roll.

I jump up and run across the hall to the bathroom, collapsing in front of the toilet before I empty the little food I've eaten today into it. I hold onto the bowl and the next thing I know Sage is there, gently pulling my hair away.

"Are you sick?"

My heart is sick.

I can't answer him because I dry heave again. My stomach cramps, looking for anything else it can empty.

"I can run to the store and get you some medicine."

I close my eyes. I wish medicine could fix this.

I squeeze my eyes closed, rolling away from the toilet.

He lets my hair go as I sit against the wall, drawing my knees up to my chest. I lean my head back, looking for some kind of inner strength to get me through this.

Lachlan is gone. I'm alone. How can I cope without him? He's my happy place. My home.

"Are you upset about the rumors, D? It's high school, it'll pass. Something else will happen and everyone will forget. It's not true, that's all that matters."

I blink my eyes open and stare at my brother.

He rocks back, falling onto his butt. "Tell me it's not true, Dandelion. You told the principal nothing happened."

I look away, beginning to cry again.

"What the fuck!" He screams, jumping up suddenly.

I cover my face, trying to hide … what? My shame? I'm not ashamed of loving Lachlan, but I still feel like I've done something horrible.

Sage shoves everything off the counter. My tooth-brush, toothpaste, brush, perfume that smashes on the floor.

He points at me, speaking through his teeth. "You're going to tell Mr. Gordon the truth. That man never deserves to work again. What the fuck happened, Dani?"

"It's not Lachlan's fault," I sniffle, slowly rising from my position on the floor.

"Lachlan." He shakes his head. "You call him by his first name? He's Mr. Taylor, Dandelion! Mr. Taylor. Say it with me. He's your fucking guidance counselor, not your … your … your fuck buddy or whatever!" He flings his hand through the air and I wince, his words slicing through me. The veins in his forehead stick out and he looks seconds away from combusting. Suddenly, he pales, his eyes narrowing. "There is no friend in this building named Taylor is there? It's him? You've been seeing him all this time and I was too fucking stupid to see!"

My face crumples and he has his answer.

"Fuck!" he shouts, punching the wall. It leaves behind a gaping hole and when he pulls his hand away it's covered in drywall debris and blood. "I'm going to kill that man," he points at me, jaw tight, "I will make him regret *ever* laying a finger on you."

"I'm nineteen! I'm an adult! I can do what I want!"

"No, Dandelion, you're an emotionally stunted child! You were *shot*, your friends were killed, you watched our mom die right in front of you. He took advantage of you and nothing you say can convince me otherwise."

"I love him and he loves me," I try to keep my tone even, but there's a warble to it, because I have no idea where he is.

Sage works his jaw back and forth. "Yeah? Well, where is he?" He spreads his arms wide. "Because I don't see him coming to your rescue." He waits for me to say something and when I don't, he screams, "Where is he?" When I still don't answer, he finishes, "He's nowhere, because you don't fucking matter to him."

He stares at me a moment longer and then storms from the bathroom. Seconds later the door slams behind him.

I fall to the ground crying again.

I gave him everything, but he gave me nothing.

———

I JOLT AWAKE from where I sleep on the couch waiting for Sage.

There's knocking on the door and the sound of voices. Blinking open my eyes I look at the time on my phone and see it's after two in the morning.

Sighing, I push my tired body up and head to the door, peeping out. I see someone I don't recognize, around maybe thirty with blond hair, but Sage is slouched against the guy, so I open the door.

"Hi, you must be Dani?" The guy asks and I nod. "I'm Graham." He holds out a hand but quickly pulls it back in when my brother starts to fall to the floor. "I'm a friend of Sage's. He's drunk off his ass, and I was going to bring him back to my place, but he insisted he had to get home."

I push the door open wider. "What can I do to help you with him?"

"Hold the door. I can handle him."

Sage's alcohol-hazed eyes meet mine. He still looks angry, but also sad.

Graham carries him over to the couch, depositing him on it. "Is he good here?"

"It's fine." I wave a dismissive hand.

"I can stay if you need help with him?" he offers.

I shake my head, still holding the door open. "I can handle him."

Graham walks over to me and whispers under his breath, "I'm not sure what he's upset about, but he was already well on his way to drunk by the time I got to the bar and kept going, even when I told him to stop. Try and get some water in him and some Aspirin."

"Okay, thanks for bringing him home."

Graham tips his head in acknowledgment and heads out.

Turning around, I prepare to face more of Sage's wrath but instead I find him halfway asleep.

I pour him a glass of water, making sure it's not too cold so it'll be easier for him to get down. Once I have two Aspirins from the bathroom, I crouch down beside him and force him to take them, as well as down the whole glass of water. Lying on his side, he blinks his hazel eyes at me.

"I'm so sorry I've failed you."

I gasp. "Sage, you could never fail me."

He rubs a piece of my hair between his fingers. "Why did Mom think I could take care of you? I'm a horrible guardian. You would've been better off with anyone else."

I grab his hand, holding it in mine. "That's not true and you know it. Herb, we have to stick together. It's always been you and me, right? We can't change that now. You're the best brother I could ask for."

"What happened with him? The Taylor guy?"

"Do you really want to know?" Treacherous tears flood my eyes again.

"No, but I need to." He clears his throat and reaches for the glass but it's empty. I quickly refill it and pass it to him, settling back on the floor in front of the couch. "Tell me."

"I don't know," I let out a sigh. "Seeing him every day really helped me and we connected. It was completely innocent for a long time. I mean, I had a crush on him but that was it. It wasn't like I was planning to act on it. But … we kept being drawn together. No one has ever made me feel the way he does and we … fell in love. I might be young, but I know love, and there's no denying that's what we have … or had." I look away, anger hitting me in the chest once again.

Sage rubs his mouth. "You need to tell the principal."

"No," I hiss out. "Regardless of everything I will *not* ruin Lachlan's life that way. He didn't pursue me or pressure me into anything, please believe that. I wouldn't lie to you."

He holds a hand to his head. I'm sure it's pounding.

He reeks of alcohol and cigarettes. "We'll talk in the morning," he mutters. "I have a headache."

"Okay." I kiss his cheek, grab the blanket and drape it over his body.

By the time I turn the light off, he's asleep.

———

I SPREAD out the breakfast I picked up as Sage finally comes out of his room, freshly showered and smelling much better. He still doesn't look the best, but it's progress. He's probably still going to feel it come tomorrow.

Sage sits down at the bar and I pour each of us a glass of orange juice.

Sage takes several gulps of OJ, looking at the avocado toast and eggs I got from the restaurant in the building.

"This looks good." His voice is crackly and he winces, rubbing his eyes.

"It's because I didn't make it," I joke, giving him a soft smile.

My lower lip begins to tremble as I look at him. I knew if he ever found out about Lachlan and me it would hurt him, but I didn't realize how badly it would make me feel. I don't like breaking my brother's heart. I don't want him to look at me any differently.

"Hey," he says softly, pinching my lip lightly. "No crying."

I try to smile but the tears come, spilling over.

He gathers me in his arms, resting his chin on top of my head. He rubs one hand gently on my back, blowing out a breath.

"We can go to the cops today."

I stiffen in his arms, shoving him away. "I'm not going to the cops."

He looks at me horrified. "Dani—this man took advantage of you. He deserves to be in jail."

I shake my head. "Don't do this. You don't know anything about the situation."

He narrows his eyes on me. "Did you have sex with him?" I'm silent. "Then I know all I need to."

Anger surges through my veins. "No, you don't know! I'm a good person, I've always been pretty level-headed, and I'm *nineteen*. You should know me well enough to know I wouldn't be coerced into something I didn't want to do. Lachlan and I..." I close my eyes, breathing out. "We struggled, okay, especially him because of his position, but the feelings happened and I don't regret them or him. Falling in love with him reminded me how good it is to be alive. He *saved* me. Can't you see that?"

My brother looks like I've punched him in the chest.

"I'm supposed to protect you."

"And you do. But love is love. I need you to be on *my* side of this. School's almost over and I promise you Lachlan didn't do anything to me that I didn't want. I..." I look down at my nude colored nails, still painted for prom. "Lachlan is a good man, and even though I'm so fucking angry at him right now, I still love him."

"He's gone, D," he whispers. "He left you to deal with this fallout. Look what the kids at school are saying."

"I know." I wipe tears from my cheeks. "But I'm not vindictive and I won't ruin his life because he's broken my heart."

Sage opens his mouth to say more, but I get up and walk to my room. I need to be by myself right now.

Wrapping my arms around myself, I look out the

window in my bedroom to the street below, all the tiny heads of the people moving from one place to the next.

Somewhere, out there, is Lachlan.

He could be down the street, or a county away, he could also be a state away, or a whole country.

I don't know.

Reaching up, I touch the wind chimes. They brush against each other, making music.

"I wish you were here, Mom."

If I pretend hard enough, I can make out her voice saying, *I wish I was too.*

CHAPTER SIXTY-FOUR

THE PAINTING IN FRONT OF ME IS ABSTRACT. A RANDOM swirl of black, red, and purple on white. But I see nothing. My heart and mind are too empty to see any kind of image in the madness.

A body steps up beside mine. Tall, warm, familiar.

But still not the person I want.

"What are you doing here?" I whisper.

Ansel rocks back on his heels, appraising the painting. "I called your brother, said I needed to see you, but he said you left a couple of hours ago for the library. I checked the one near your apartment but you weren't there. Then I went to Watchtower, and when you weren't there either, I knew this is where you'd been all along. I was right."

I shake my head, biting my lip. I hold my arms around myself, so close to breaking down.

It's been another week since Lachlan left and another whole school week of Ansel ignoring me, which has made it all that much worse not having my best friend. Sasha has tried to get me to talk, but she's a blabbermouth, so I refuse to say anything. The rumors still circulate in the school halls, growing worse instead of lessening. My new favorite is that Lachlan runs an underground sex ring and my job is to lure in unsuspecting teens. God, what a load of shit. Mr. Gordon had to hold an emergency assembly the rumors got so bad. A letter even went home to parents after calls and emails started rolling in over concerns.

I hate this.

It's Sunday and I'm already dreading going back tomorrow.

So close to the end of the year, Mr. Gordon hasn't bothered hiring a new guidance counselor so I spend my every day period either at the outdoor track, now that it's so warm, or in the library.

I've sent a few more angry texts to Lachlan. They show delivered but he never reads them. He probably has me blocked, but I keep sending them because I need to get it off my chest.

"It's true isn't it?" Ansel breaks the silence. "Well, not all of it, I don't think you're smuggling Mr. Taylor's sperm in and out of the country, but ... you ... you had a relationship with him didn't you?"

I tilt my head back as the treacherous sting of tears returns. I give him a single nod and he exhales.

"Fuck." He rubs his jaw.

"I'm sorry," I croak.

"Why are you apologizing to me?" he blurts in surprise.

I look at him at my side. "Because I hurt you. Because I continue to hurt you. You're my best friend and I treat you like shit."

"No, you don't, Meadows."

"I do." I nod, sniffling back the tears I don't want to fall. My eyes hurt so bad every day from all the tears.

He grabs my hand, entwining our fingers together.

"I shouldn't have ditched you at prom." My voice cracks and I wipe at the wetness beneath my eyes.

"Did you ditch me for him?"

My lips shake and I look at the ground, toeing my shoe against the gray tile. "Y-Yeah." I reluctantly meet his gaze again. "See, I told you, I'm horrible. I'm a shitty friend. You should get a new one."

He squeezes my hand. "Nah, I like my Meadows just fine. I'm keeping you."

I laugh, but it cracks with my tears turning into sobs instead.

"Come here, pretty girl." He wraps his arms around me, securing me and protecting me against his chest. His body is warm and he tucks my head under his neck so he can rest his chin on top. It feels good to be held by him. It feels like the hug of a friend, of someone who cares and wants to make it better.

My fingers tighten around him, not wanting to let go. "I love you," I murmur, and I realize how true the words are.

I love Ansel so much. He's the best friend I could ever ask for, and to think when I got here I didn't want any. But I needed him, and I think on a subconscious level I knew that even when I didn't want to believe it.

Ansel rocks me back and forth in his arms. "Love you too, Meadows." His lips press softly against the side of my head. He grabs my cheeks, looking into my eyes. "Don't let this break you."

I smile through my tears. "Never."

———

ANOTHER WEEKEND PASSES, graduation fast approaching.

I'm still mad at Lachlan, madder than I think I've ever been at a person before. He won't reply to me and I refuse to read his letter. But with him gone, it's forcing me to do some soul searching.

"Can you explain what you're doing?" Ansel asks, helping me move my desk out of the way so I have the whole wall to work with.

"Making this place mine."

He eyes the black paint I bought.

"By painting the wall black?"

"I'm not painting the whole wall."

He narrows his eyes. "What are you up to, Meadows?"

"Nothing," I sing-song, reaching for the grape Fanta beside my bed. I take a sip and grab the gallon of paint. I don't think I'll use a whole gallon, but I figure if I have to retouch it at all, at least I won't have to worry about buying more.

I turn my music on, *Fortress* by Lennon Stella filling the space.

Sage pokes his head in as Ansel sits his butt on my bed. Ansel shoots to a standing position like he's been caught stealing. Or in his case more likely selling drugs. Sage's eyes move to him and he shakes his head.

"What do you want?" I ask Sage, pouring out the paint.

"Nothing," he watches the black paint fill the tin, "just glad you're finally making the place yours."

Sage leaves and Ansel hesitantly sits back down on my bed, picking up one of the pillows and looking at it before he puts it back.

I dip the brush into the paint and get to work.

It takes hours and I climb on and off the ladder so many times I get a hell of a workout in, but at the end it's all worth it.

The black lines form a sketchy asymmetrical outline of my face and hair. It's like the sketches I've filled my pad with all school year. Like me, none of them are fully formed; the outline is the potential of what's to come. It's the start. The end isn't here yet.

"I like it," Ansel murmurs, stepping up beside me.

"I do, too."

I didn't want to make myself permanent in this place in any way, but that changes now. I still long to travel, to see the world, be free, but it's also okay to plant roots—to *belong*. I haven't allowed myself to do that. It hurt too much after Portland. Losing people I loved and cared about sent me wandering, I was an unmoored raft drifting through a bleak and lifeless existence.

Lachlan pulled me back to shore, but it's *me* who's choosing to stay.

CHAPTER SIXTY-FIVE

Pushing the food around my plate, I contemplate the best way to approach this with Sage. I don't want to hurt his feelings, but I also have to do what's best for me.

"Sage?" I finally broach.

He looks over at me with my legs crossed under my body. I haven't been paying a bit of attention to the TV screen.

"Yeah?" His brow furrows with worry. "What's going on? You look funny."

I reach for my water glass, taking a few sips. Meeting his steady gaze, I blurt, "I'm leaving."

He snorts. "What do you mean you're leaving?"

"Graduation is in less than two weeks. I'm leaving after."

"Leaving?" he repeats. "For where?"

"I'm not sure where I want to go first, but I know I need to get away. I want to travel, see the world, learn more about myself so I can make a decision on what I want to do with my life."

I'll gain access to the money left to me by my parents

after I graduate high school. I know there's plenty of money for me to travel and live off of, and I'll still have plenty whenever I come back.

Sage looks down at his plate. "I don't want you to go," he says softly, "but I understand."

"I need to do this for me."

He grabs my hand, squeezing it. "I'm not happy about it, but I get it. Call me. Don't forget about me."

"Never. You're my brother."

"You're doing this alone?" I nod. "It's not safe, D." He looks concerned.

"I'll be fine. I'm a big girl. This is what I need to do. I have to get away from here."

"From here or the memory of him?"

I bite my lip, hesitating. "Both."

I know Sage is still livid about my relationship with Lachlan. If Lachlan still lived here I'm not certain he'd be breathing. I guess it's a good thing, for his safety at least, that he moved.

A familiar ache fills my chest at the thought of him. I'm still mad, but I'm mostly hurt now.

Does he think of me as often as I think of him?

He probably doesn't. I'm the young, foolish, naïve girl who fell for her older guidance counselor.

How pathetic.

I brush my hair over my shoulder, setting my plate aside. I don't want to eat.

"When will you leave?"

"A few days after graduation. Once I have access to the money."

"I'll give you money, Weed."

"I don't need your money. Save it."

He makes a noise in his throat.

"You won't hate me for leaving, right?" My voice sounds so small.

He chuckles. "You serious?" He raises a brow, looking surprised. When I nod, he says, "I could never hate you. You're my little sister."

"I've put you through hell."

Not just in the last couple of months, but nearly the last two years.

He sets his plate down on the coffee table, swiveling his body on the couch so he's facing me. "You know, this hasn't been easy. Losing dad, then mom, and being told I'm your guardian ... it was terrifying. Not because I didn't want to take care of you, but because I didn't want to fuck things up. Things have happened this year that I'm not happy about." I wince, looking at my lap. "I feel like I've failed you, our parents, but look, it's happened. We can't change it. And I've acted like an asshole a lot through this because I didn't know what I was doing. I've always been your cool big brother and suddenly..." He pauses, shrugging. "Suddenly I was in charge, making decisions I didn't want to make. But I also found a lot of strength through *you*."

"Me?" I blurt incredulously, pointing a finger into my chest.

"Yes, you. I watched you persevere through physical therapy, how you fought to walk again, how you refused to let what happened rob you of your freedom, happiness, of *life*. You kept going even when you didn't want to. *You* gave me the power to keep going too. I said to myself one day, if Dani can do this, then you can too." He rubs his hand over his mouth. "I couldn't ask for a better sister than you, and I'm so fucking proud of the woman you've become."

"Don't make me cry."

But it's too late, the tears come, coating my cheeks.

"Get over here, Weed." He wraps his arms around me, hugging me against his warm, solid chest. I hold onto him. Sage is my rock, the constant I can always count on. He's the best sibling I could ever ask for. He kisses the top of my head, murmuring, "I want you to be happy."

"I was happy," I croak, my sniffles loud in the otherwise quiet apartment.

"With him?" His body stiffens as he asks the question.

"Yes, but he left. I'm so angry," my voice cracks, "he left me. Like mom and dad left us—only they didn't choose to leave and he did."

"If I ever see him I'm going to kill him," Sage vows. "He should've never touched you. Is he the reason you want to leave so badly?"

I shake my head. "I mean, I guess he's part of it, but not entirely. I've always wanted to travel, you know that, and since I don't want to be a lawyer anymore I haven't really figured out what I *do* want to do with my future. Traveling seems like a good way to figure it out."

Sage lets loose a breath, stirring the hair on top of my head. "I wanted you to go to college, D, but I'm also proud of you for being true to yourself."

"I might go to college one day, but not yet. I need time."

"Okay."

I close my eyes, hugging my brother tighter. "I love you, Herb. Thank you for understanding."

"Love you, too, Weed. Love you, too. Everything's going to be okay. Not today, but one day."

I know.

CHAPTER SIXTY-SIX

ME: I'M GRADUATING TODAY.

Me: Do you even remember?

Me: Do you care at all?

Me: You probably don't even read these, but I keep sending them.

Me: For me, not you.

Me: I'm still mad at you. So fucking mad at you.

Me: But I can't stop loving you, even though I hate you.

Me: I'm leaving in a few days. Will you even notice the absence of my presence?

Me: You might not even be in Utah anymore.

Me: One day, all of this won't hurt so bad, but as long as it hurts I know it was real.

Me: I hate you. But I love you.

I close out of his contact, knowing I have to go. Grabbing the red cap and gown, I head for the door, calling for Sage.

"I'm ready! Let's go!"

He runs down the hall. "Does this look okay?"

"You look fine," I insist, taking in his slacks and shirt combo. "We need to hurry, though. We should've left ten minutes ago."

He swipes his keys off the counter and I grab my purse before we hurry down to the garage and out into the busy traffic.

As we near the school my heart speeds up.

I'm graduating.

Mom, I did it.

After the shooting and all the months in the hospital I didn't want to finish school, or at least only get my GED, but Sage had insisted I complete my senior year and I'm glad he pushed me to do it.

Walking across that stage and getting my diploma will make it worth it.

The school parking lot is packed, so Sage drops me off so he can go park.

After a few texts I meet up with Sasha.

"Ugh, there you are, girl." She throws her arm around my shoulder, swaying back and forth. "Can you believe it? We did it!" A few heads turn at her shrill shriek. "We're like adult-*adults* now. Actual members of society. Shit, does this mean we have to pay taxes now?"

I laugh, shaking my head as I spot Ansel a ways down talking to Seth.

Something inside me stirs when I see him. It's nothing like what I feel for Lachlan, even still, but I do know it means I'm happy to see him.

Sasha and I head over to the boys, Ansel's hair is curling out from under his cap. Stretching up, I kiss his cheek and he grins.

"What was that for?"

"Because I wanted to."

"Bleh," Sasha pretends to gag. "Get a room."

I roll my eyes at her.

Suddenly, three teachers appear, rounding us up into alphabetical order. We practiced yesterday, so I already know the classmates I should be near and go in search of them to speed up the process.

Once we're in line, they go over a few rules and things that have already been mentioned, and then it's time.

They lead us outside onto the football field, the June sun beating down on us, but I revel in the warmth. It's like a blanket, draping over my shoulders and comforting me, reminding me that no matter what it's going to be okay.

Row after row of chairs are filled and once every student is seated, the speeches begin. It takes a solid hour before Mr. Gordon begins calling out names.

When Ansel's name is called, I cheer, along with his family in the stands.

Soon it's my turn, as the row I sit in stands, heading for the stage.

Tears prick my eyes and I do my best to keep my emotions in check.

Looking up at the sky, I say a silent prayer, hoping my mom's watching and smiling down at me. I want her to be proud of me, even if I haven't made some of the best choices this year, though I can't bring myself to regret them.

"Dandelion Meadows."

Sage screams from the stands, standing up and clapping his hands. "That's my sister!"

My cheeks flame with embarrassment. Mr. Gordon hands me my diploma with a proud smile. "Good luck, kiddo."

"Thank you," I whisper to the kind man.

Stepping off the stage, the school board official who is

waiting smiles and says congratulations, moving my tassel to the other side.

Striding to the grass I return to my seat, remaining standing until the row is filled back in and we can sit down once more.

I watch Seth and Sasha get their diplomas, cheering for both even though Seth looks like he couldn't care less. Sasha skips across the stage, a wild ball of energy. I can't help but laugh. She's crazy, but I love that girl.

As soon as everyone's seated, Mr. Gordon says a few more words, and then the next thing I know we're tossing our caps in the air.

I did it. I fucking did it.

At the beginning of the school year I was so unhappy and miserable. I didn't want to be here. I didn't want to exist. But I fucking did it.

I scoop my cap up and rush over to my friends, the four of us falling into a pile in the grass, full of laughter.

No one says anything for a moment and then it's Seth who speaks.

"Shit's about to get real."

He's not wrong.

The real world awaits.

CHAPTER SIXTY-SEVEN

"WE REALLY DIDN'T HAVE TO COME ANYWHERE FANCY," I tell Sage for the hundredth time. "This is silly."

I look around the extremely nice restaurant he chose to bring me to in celebration.

"I know, but I wanted to. You only graduate from high school once."

"Well, thank you, this is thoughtful." I peruse the menu, noting the expense of the dishes and wondering if I could get away with ordering a kids grilled cheese—even that's over twenty dollars and boasts exotic sounding cheeses, sun-dried tomatoes, and something else that doesn't sound at all palatable to a kid.

I end up settling on a ravioli dish and Sage orders a steak.

"I'm really proud of you, D." He crosses his fingers, laying them on the table. "You've worked hard this year."

I look away, his praise making me feel bad because I know with all the other things that went on this year he really shouldn't be proud.

"Don't look away," he coaxes me to face him, "despite

everything else, I am proud of you. I wouldn't lie. You're a smart girl and you're going to do big things. What happened with him doesn't rob you of your achievements."

Something about his words pisses me off, but I bite my tongue because the last thing I want to do is get in a useless fight. There's no point in trying to explain to him that Lachlan didn't steal anything from me, I gave it all freely.

While still waiting for our orders we chat about my upcoming plans to leave.

"I figure I'll buy a plane ticket tonight for somewhere in Europe. I don't really care. I want to see it all."

"Are you sure you want to go globe-trotting all by yourself? It's not exactly safe."

I won't lie, that bit makes me nervous, but if we don't step out of our comfort zone how will we ever live.

"I'll be fine." I dismiss his words, refusing to dwell on them.

"How long do you think you'll be gone?" He tries to sound unbothered, but I know he's hoping I won't stay gone long.

I give a shrug, picking up my water glass and shooting a smile at the waiter when he places our dishes on the table. "I'm not sure. A few months."

He chokes on the wine he ordered, sputtering. "Months?"

"This is a once in a lifetime trip," I argue. "I want to make the most of it. Besides, if I go to college after I don't plan to start until the fall."

"You could enroll in a spring semester."

"I could, but I don't want to. I need time."

He cracks a smile. "Well, I tried."

We eat our meal, changing the topic of conversation.

After a while, the waiter clears our plates from the table, placing a dessert menu before he goes.

"Pick something," Sage encourages. "Tonight is a celebration."

"I'm full." I press a hand to my stomach. "I don't think I could take another bite."

"Come on," he encourages. "I'll get one too."

With a sigh, I reach for the menu, scanning the desserts. Once I pick one I give it to Sage so he can choose too. When the waiter returns we place our orders for a chocolate cake for him and a tiramisu for me.

It isn't long before the desserts are placed in front of us and even though I'm full my mouth waters at the sight.

Before I can take a bite, Sage pulls an envelope out of his pocket, sliding it across the table.

"What's this for?" I pick up the long white envelope, testing the weight in my hands.

"It's your graduation gift." He shrugs like it's no big deal, clearing his throat. "Open it."

I smile, secretly delighted by the prospect of a gift. I open it, my mouth parting when the plane ticket slides out. I read over it, seeing that it departs in two days for London.

I look from the ticket to my brother with shock. "Sage."

He leans over the table. "I might not want you to go, but I understand, and I want you to know I support you. You can start your adventure there and then go wherever you want."

"Thank you." I grasp the ticket tightly, this tiny piece of paper holding all the promise of adventure and discovery.

"Spread your wings, Weed, that way you can come back and lay down some roots."

I get up, moving around the table to hug my brother. I inhale his familiar and comforting scent. The smell of home. Somehow, I know, that everything is going to be okay.

———

PACKING MY BAGS IS SURREAL.

I'm really doing this. I'm leaving for I don't know how long.

I fold my clothes as small as I possibly can, not wanting to take up too much room. My t-shirts slide neatly into one side of the suitcase, all rolled up tightly. Next I add in the three pairs of jeans and two shorts I decided to bring as well as one dress. I stuff three shoe options on the other end, leaving room for underwear and toiletries. I pick up my clear toiletry bag I packed after my shower, setting it inside gently. Turning to my dresser, I go to grab a handful of underwear, my breath catching when I spot the letter I stuffed beneath at the beginning of May when Lachlan left me.

A month, more than a month actually, since he left.

Anger rages through me once more and I grab the letter, throwing it in my waste bin.

As soon as it lands inside though a wave of instant regret hits me.

Heart racing I pick it out, holding it between my hands. I bite my lip, debating on putting it back in my dresser or … or I could read it, but I'm not ready. I'm not ready to read his words of regret over what we did. I don't want to have him tell me he doesn't love me. I hesitate a moment longer and end up stuffing the letter into my luggage, afraid if I leave it behind Sage might find it, but that's an excuse. I know Sage would never go through my drawers.

With the letter tucked away I add my underwear and bras inside before zipping it closed.

I wheel it to the door so it's ready to go when Sage drops me off at the airport. Sage watches from the couch, unable to hide the sadness from his eyes.

I hate leaving him, but I need to do this, and I'm glad he understands that.

"You're really leaving me?"

I push my hair out of my eyes where it's come loose from the braid I put it in earlier. "Yeah, I guess I am." I plop onto the couch beside him. "Gonna miss me, big bro?"

"More than you know."

I reach for his hand, squeezing it. "I'm going to miss you."

"You have to go," he says, tears filling his eyes. "I don't want you to, but I know you have to. You're going to come back so much stronger."

"I hope so."

"I know so."

I laugh, releasing his hand and looking at the TV screen. "Twilight?" I arch a brow.

"It was on TV," he defends. "Besides, it makes me think of you."

I lay my head on his shoulder. "You really do miss me and I'm not even gone."

He lays his head over mine. "Yeah, I do. You're all I have left in this world that matters."

"Maybe you'll meet a girl while I'm gone. Fall in love."

He snorts, watching the TV screen. "I doubt it, Weed."

"Hey, you never know."

He ruffles my hair. "Nice try, but I'm not looking for anyone right now."

"I wasn't looking for Lachlan," I whisper and he flinches at the name. "But I found him anyway. You don't look for love. Love finds you."

He turns his head in my direction, rubbing his lips together. "Please, don't say his name around me. It pisses me off."

"I'm still mad too—but being angry doesn't change the fact that I love him."

"And you still do, don't you?"

"I love him as much as I hate him." I pick at a piece of lint on my cotton shorts.

"He should be in jail," he growls.

"I'm an adult."

"You were his *student*," he hisses. "Do you not understand how morally wrong that is?"

I loosen a breath. "Well, he's gone now."

"Yeah, thank fuck."

When Sage gets up and grabs a beer, I know the conversation is over.

CHAPTER SIXTY-EIGHT

SAGE HAULS MY SUITCASE OUT OF THE TRUNK OF HIS car, pulling up the handle.

"Well, this is it." He stares at me, memorizing my features like he's afraid he'll never see me again.

"I'll be back."

"But when?" I know he wants me to give him a definitive answer, but I can't.

"I don't know." I slip my backpack onto my shoulders. He sighs, shoving his hands in his pockets. "I'm going to miss you, Herb."

"Not as much as I'll miss you, Weed."

"Don't make me cry," I warn, throwing my arms around him.

He pulls his hands from his jeans, hugging me back. "Be safe. Call me when you land in New York for your layover."

"I will. Promise." I hold my pinky out to him, trying to hide my pain because it's not Lachlan I'm making a pinky promise with.

"You better hurry. TSA will be a pain in the ass." He

kisses my cheek and takes a step back. "Seriously, be safe."

"I will." I take my suitcase, heading toward the doors. Looking back, I see him slip in the car.

He lifts his hand in a wave and I wave back before he pulls away. I watch his car join the fray of others leaving the airport.

I look at the building and smile.

This is it.

Heading into the building, I make it through security faster than I expect and head to the terminal to wait for my plane to board in an hour.

I grab a coffee before I take a seat.

"Wow, I thought you were never going to show up."

My head shoots up and my eyes connect with Ansel's light blue ones as he heads my way, wheeling a suitcase.

"What are you doing?" I jump up, coffee sloshing out of the lid of my cup and burning my finger, but I pay it no mind.

"Well, I knew you were leaving, and frankly I'm not ready for college either, and I thought to myself why would I let my best friend fly across the world without me. When I told Sage I wanted to go with you he was a little wary, but I think the fact he didn't want you to go alone won out and he told me where he got your first ticket for." He holds his own plane ticket up. "So, you're stuck with me, Meadows. My parents are cool with it, so they're funding my end. Wherever you go, I go."

"Sage knew about this?" I'm stunned, he seemed so upset that I was going to be by myself.

"Yep." Ansel plops in the empty seat beside the one I had been sitting in. He pats that seat. "Get comfy, Meadows."

"I..." I keep blinking at him, no words coming to mind.

"You're not mad are you? I mean, even if you are I'm still going."

"No, I'm glad you're here."

And now that he is I can't imagine doing this without him. I finally sit down in the chair beside him.

"I've got your back, Meadows. An adventure is what we both need."

"It is, isn't it?"

He nods, picking at a hangnail. "You can't grow without exploration. Seeing the world is what I need to become a better artist. Maybe ... maybe I can make something of my art, of myself. I'm scared to dream big."

"If you dream small you'll never even touch the ceiling." I give him a soft smile. "But if you dream big you might be lucky enough to touch the sky."

He takes my hand, crossing our fingers together. "Let's take over the world then."

"World domination isn't really my thing." I fight a growing smile.

I still can't believe he's here. Going on this trip with Ansel will make it more fun. I'll have someone to not only travel with, but that will make me smile and laugh, remind me that I'm not alone in this world. It might sound dramatic, but so often since the shooting I've felt invisible. Unseen, unheard, unimportant. Lachlan brightened my world, and with him I felt seen, heard, and like the most important person to him. But he left me, tossed me away like I was nothing.

But I am something.

I'm me and it's time I saw myself, heard myself, and realized how important I am. My purpose matters.

"So, Meadows, where are we going after London?"

I grin at my best friend. "It doesn't matter."

And it really doesn't, because it's the journey that matters, not the destination.

———

WE ARRIVE at the flat dead ass tired. It's ten in the morning London time, but I don't even know what time that'd be back in Utah because my brain can't function to calculate it.

"This place is nice. There's only one bed, though," Ansel announces, coming out of the bedroom and putting his backpack on the floor.

Stifling a yawn, I rub my eyes. "I'm too tired to care. Let's get some sleep. I promise I won't paw you."

"Thanks for being concerned for my welfare, Meadows," he chuckles, opening the fridge to see if it's stocked.

I send Sage a text that we've arrived at the flat he booked and we're going to bed. I don't bother to see if he replies. I start rifling through my bag for clean pajamas only to realize I never packed any. I have underwear and regular clothes. That's it.

"Oh my God," I groan in pure frustration. "I forgot pajamas."

"I've got you covered." This time he's the one trying not to yawn. He grabs his backpack and pulls out an oversized t-shirt, tossing it at me. I barely catch it. "That should cover all the important parts."

The shirt smells like him and whatever was once printed on it is faded. "Thanks."

"Go shower. I'll make us a snack."

Grabbing clean underwear I don't protest, shutting myself in the bathroom to shower. I feel cruddy after spending the last nearly twenty-four hours traveling. Our flight from New York to London ended up delayed, which was a real pain in the ass.

The warm water cascades over my body, loosening my tired muscles. I didn't tell Ansel, but I doubt I have the energy to eat a snack.

Scrubbing my scalp with shampoo I watch the swirls disappear down the drain. I'm already starting to feel better even if I'm in desperate need of sleep.

Conditioning my hair, I let it sit on the strands to detangle the mess it knotted itself into when I napped on the flight.

Once I'm squeaky clean I get out and dry off, changing into clean underwear and the shirt Ansel gave me. It comes down over my ass, but barely. It'll do though.

Exiting the bathroom, steam billows out with my departure. Ansel looks over from the tiny kitchen, finishing a sandwich. "My turn." He rubs his hands together. "Eat, Meadows. I know you have to be starving." He points to the other half of a sandwich sitting on a glass plate with little blue flowers on the border.

The bathroom door clicks shut behind him. I eye the sandwich, not hungry after all the travel but knowing I need to eat. Sitting on the little stool, I bite into the sandwich, expecting my stomach to protest at the introduction of food after hours of travel, but I end up devouring it until there are nothing but crumbs left.

I rinse the plate and grab a drink from the fridge. Twisting the cap off a water bottle, the bathroom door opens and Ansel steps out. The scent of his soap fills the air, something woodsy the reminds me of the outdoors. It's the complete opposite of Lachlan's fresh scent.

Ansel yawns, pointing to the couch. "I'll sleep out here. You get the bed."

"I'm fine with the couch," I protest. "I'm shorter than you."

He gives me a pointed look. "I'm being chivalrous here. Take the bed, Meadows."

I sigh, knowing I'm never going to get anywhere with him. "Fine, but only because I'm too tired to argue."

After we find him a pillow and blankets, he gets fixed on the small couch and I take the bedroom. There's no air, and it's stifling so I turn on the window unit to hopefully cool down the space, leaving the door open so Ansel might benefit as well.

Climbing beneath the covers, they're scratchy against my skin. I toss them off, since it's hot anyway.

Curling my hands beneath my head, I pray the jetlag will bring sleep quickly. Thankfully, it does, but it's short-lived. It's not long before I wake with cries, my limbs flailing from the dream.

Ansel comes barreling into the room, his hair mussed from sleep, eyes tired. He runs to my side, grabbing onto my arms and then my chin, forcing me to look at him.

"You're okay. Hey, hey, you're okay. I've got you." My body stops twisting and turning and I focus on him, evening my breaths. "It was a dream."

I cling to him like a lifeline.

The dream was worse than usual. Before Lachlan left it had gotten so days, even weeks, would pass without it, but it's been happening more often, and this was the worst one yet. It was so real, the dream clinging to my mind, forcing me to relive those harrowing moments.

"I want it to go away," I whisper into the skin of his neck.

"Is it about what happened to you?"

I nod.

He maneuvers his body, climbing into bed behind me. He holds me against his body.

"I'm here, Meadows. I've got you. I'm not letting you go. I won't let the dream get you while I have you."

I open my mouth to argue that his presence won't be enough to chase it away, but I opt against it, and then by some miracle when I do fall back asleep to him humming in my ear, the dream doesn't return.

I think Ansel Caron might be my knight in shining armor.

I'm sorry, Lachlan.

CHAPTER SIXTY-NINE

I wake up wrapped in Ansel's arms, his breath blowing softly against the back of my neck. His arms are twined around my body, with his legs fully curled against the back of mine. My left arm rests on the top of his. There's something acutely intimate about it, despite the fact nothing sexual happened.

I start to wiggle out of his hold, needing to pee, but he tightens his grip.

"Five more minutes. I'm not ready to get up."

"I need to use the bathroom."

He pinches my stomach. "Five minutes."

"Ansel," I laugh, "let me go."

He groans, releasing his octopus hold on me. "Fine, Meadows. Go to the bathroom. What time is it anyway?"

I pick up my phone. "Four in the morning."

"Fuck, we slept a long time."

Considering we fell asleep after eleven in the morning the previous day, he's not kidding. Seventeen hours is a hell of a lot of sleep, but we both needed it.

Climbing out of bed, I head to the tiny bathroom in the room next door to relieve myself. Washing my hands, I glance at my reflection in the mirror. I look surprisingly well rested considering I woke up with that horrible reoccurring dream. I think I have Ansel's presence to thank for that.

After I've brushed my teeth, I climb back into bed beside my best friend. He reaches for me, pulling me against his solid chest. I wrap my arms around him and he tucks my head under his neck.

"I'm really glad you're here," I whisper like a confession into the dark bedroom.

He squeezes my arm. "Me too."

"I'm not sure I could have done this by myself like I thought I could."

He's quiet for a few heartbeats. "You would've been fine."

"You think so?" I twist my head, resting my chin on his chest so I can look at him.

He angles his head toward me. "I know so. You're stronger than you give yourself credit for. But," a grin spreads slowly over his face like a rising sun, "you wouldn't have nearly as much fun."

I laugh. "Now that's definitely true."

"What do you want to see today?" he asks, rubbing his fingers lazily against my arm. It feels good and my eyes close, basking in the touch.

"Everything."

"I don't think we can see everything in one day, Meadows."

"I want to experience the city, the life, that's what this whole trip is about for me. Living, not just visiting."

"Well, Meadows," he presses his lips to the side of my head, "let's get out there and live."

———

AFTER SEVERAL HOURS of walking the streets, stopping in shops and checking out the changing of the guard, I find myself drawn into a bookshop. Ansel follows, not saying a thing as I open the door and head inside.

I pause inhaling the scent of the books stacking the shelves all the way to the ceiling. The scent makes me think of Lachlan and all his piles of books. It hurts thinking of him, like a painful stab wound that won't stop throbbing.

Looking up, the ceiling is covered in mirrors, giving it the trippy effect of stretching for miles.

"Lachlan would love this," I whisper to myself, but of course Ansel overhears me.

He places his hand on my waist, giving me a sad look, but he doesn't say anything, which I'm grateful for. I don't know how I would reply if he did.

I walk down the aisles of books, smiling when I find cozy nooks set up to curl up with a book of your choosing.

Despite myself I take a picture and send it to him. I know he won't really get it anyway, he still hasn't read any of my messages. I suppose that's a good thing considering some of them are not so nice. It's not like he doesn't deserve it, though, for leaving without a word.

Our last night together, he made love to me knowing he was going to abandon me. He kissed me, pleasured me, all while knowing I would never see him again.

I still can't believe I brought his letter. I should've left it at home. The last thing I need to do on this trip is travel with the baggage of what it might say. I'm terrified whatever is inside will only break my heart more. It's already been battered enough.

Behind the photo I send another text message.

Me: I could get lost in here. Would you even bother to look for me?

With a sigh, I put my phone away. I know I need to stop texting him, but I'm not ready. It's therapeutic, a diary of sorts.

"Are you okay?" Ansel steps around a shelf, finding me with my arms wrapped around myself.

I nod, but the smile I give him is sad. "I'm fine."

He grips my shoulder, giving it a small squeeze. "You can talk to me."

"I know."

If I ever get to the point where I want to talk about Lachlan, get my thoughts and feelings off my chest, I know I can trust Ansel. Despite the rumors, and me confirming the truth, he stood by my side and hasn't judged me for it. Sasha too, was understanding, and I know I need to keep in contact with her while we're gone. I don't want her to think she means nothing to me. If I've learned anything in the last year it's how important relationships are whether they're familial, friendships, or romantic.

I explore the shelves a bit longer, buying two books before we leave. It's nearing dinnertime so we stop in a pub near the flat to eat. With our bellies full we walk out. Ansel loops a few of his fingers around mine. I flash him a smile.

We enter the flat, locking the door behind us. I send Sage a few texts, letting him know we're going to be heading to bed soon.

I take my shower first and while Ansel is getting his I turn the blankets back on the bed, fixing the pillows. It hasn't been discussed but I want him to sleep in the bed again tonight. With him close I feel safer, and it should keep my nightmares at bay.

The pipes squeal as the shower is turned off. I know it'll be a little bit before he leaves the bathroom, but I still feel nervous. I know it's silly, he's my friend, but I don't want him to think I'm broken, or needy, or maybe even leading him on.

Sitting on the edge of the bed, I hold my breath when I hear the door open. His feet pad across the creaky hardwood floor and then he stands in the doorway, leaning his body against it.

"You okay?" He picks up on my body language instantly.

I nod, but don't meet his eyes.

"What is it, Meadows?"

I stare down at my hands, spreading my fingers before curling them into my palms.

"Can you sleep in here again tonight? With me?"

"Sure—is that what you're nervous about?"

I stand up, brushing my hair off my face. "Yeah." I let out a laugh. "It's dumb, I know. But I felt better last night once you were here. When I fell apart, you held me together."

I close my eyes, thinking of how I was once so sure that Lachlan was the glue to all my broken pieces.

I startle when I feel the gentle press of Ansel's warm hand against my cheek. "You don't need me to hold you together. You're doing that all on your own. But I'll keep you safe."

I open my eyes, staring into his light blue gaze. "I don't think I'm doing a very good job."

"Trust me, Meadows, you've never given yourself enough credit."

Taking my hand, he urges me back to the bed, and lays down beside me. It's not that late, but we're both tired from the day's adventures. As soon as his arms wrap around me I fall right into a peaceful sleep.

CHAPTER SEVENTY

WE SPEND TWO WEEKS EXPLORING LONDON AND THE surrounding cities before moving on.

I send more texts to Lachlan. He never responds.

From there we travel to Italy, visiting Venice, Rome, Florence—but spending most of our time on the Amalfi Coast. It's eight weeks before we can bring ourselves to leave.

Still, Lachlan doesn't reply.

Other cities we stop at are Prague in the Czech Republic, Barcelona and Madrid in Spain.

I should stop texting.

Ansel wanted to go to Scotland when we first left London, but Scotland belongs to Lachlan.

I don't know why I can't betray him.

The plane circles over our next destination. Ansel looks out the window with awe and joy. "Look at it, Meadows." He points like a small child for me to look too.

"Wow."

We hover above Paris, exchanging smiles.

The plane starts its descent, the pilot giving instructions over the speaker.

Ansel grabs my hand, looping our fingers together. With a smile he says, "Paris isn't ready for us."

I smile back. I'm not sure I'm ready for it either.

Goodbye, Lachlan. I'm moving on with my life.

CHAPTER SEVENTY-ONE

THE TAXI SCREECHES TO A STOP IN FRONT OF THE apartment.

Ansel speaks to him in French, passing him some crumpled up euros.

We grab our bags, heading inside to the manager's office to get the keys for the apartment we pre-booked on a month-to-month basis. Both of us agreed we'd like to stay in Paris for a while. I'm not sure how long a while actually is, but we've already been gone from home six months. I know Sage hoped I'd be home for Christmas, but this year I'll be celebrating in the city with Ansel.

We take the antique elevator up to the top floor apartment. We're splitting the costs, but the one-bedroom in the heart of Paris is still beyond pricey—especially with the view of the Eiffel Tower the online portfolio claimed. But you only live once, might as well enjoy it.

Stepping off the elevator, we walk down the hall and Ansel unlocks the door to our apartment.

He lets out a low whistle. "Wow, this is nice."

He's not kidding, either. The interior is painted a

creamy white color, with detailing of the walls harking back to a different era. The crown molding is exquisitely detailed and the furniture is all fairly new in a more contemporary style with bold colors. My eyes can't seem to look away from the cobalt blue velvet couch.

"Meadows! Come look at this!" I didn't realize Ansel had left my line of sight. I leave my bags and follow the sound of his voice, finding him in the bedroom standing at the opened double doors leading to a wrought iron balcony. "Look." He steps aside, making room beside his body for me to join.

My jaw opens. "It's beautiful," I gasp, my fingers coming up to my mouth trying to cover my surprise.

The view of the Eiffel Tower is spectacular. It's a distance away, but the view is completely unobstructed and on the top floor of the building it's perfectly aligned.

"I can't believe we're here." Ansel leans his body against the railing. The veins in his arms stick out and I don't know how he can bear standing out here with no jacket.

"I can't either. This whole trip has been surreal."

I still can't believe December is approaching. We took our time in each country and city we visited, truly immersing ourselves in the culture and lifestyle. It's been an experience I know I'll never forget.

Ansel dips his head in my direction. "I might never leave."

I stare back at him, noting the serious tone to his voice even though his smile suggests he's joking. "I wouldn't blame you."

I leave him on the balcony so I can finish exploring the apartment, it's not like there's too much left to see.

The bed in the room is huge, and I'm sure an apartment like this might be used often with honeymooners.

The canopy above the bed is a soft petal pink and with the white and beige bedding it looks like something out of a fairytale. Gliding my fingers over the covers, I blush as I watch Ansel out on the balcony, the breeze carrying in through the open doors.

I've slept with him every night since our first night in London. I haven't had any more nightmares either. I don't for a second think I'm cured of them because he's there at night, but I do think the comfort of his presence keeps my mind from sinking into a dark place where I'm more susceptible to them.

Leaving the bedroom, I step into the attached bathroom. It's small, but nice. I can't help but smile at the claw-foot bathtub, knowing I'll have to make use of it. I pause, taking in my reflection in the mirror.

I look better than I did when I left the States. I've gained a little weight, my body filling out more into womanly curves. My eyes are a little brighter, not quite happy but not so haunted. There are more changes too, but those are on the inside. My confidence has grown with our travels and my heart … it's still a little broken, but it's beginning to stitch itself together.

Sighing, I turn away from the mirror.

"Let's go somewhere," Ansel announces, closing the balcony doors.

"Where?"

He shrugs. "There's probably a café or something close."

"Okay," I agree, eager to get out on the streets of Paris. Already, the vibe in this city speaks to my soul.

We leave our bags to unpack later, too eager to immerse ourselves in the heart of things.

As soon as we step onto the street I inhale the air. I smell the heavenly scent of various foods stirring in the air and people chatter on the streets, walking at a clipped pace to get wherever they're headed.

Ansel's head swivels back and forth, trying to take everything in. The look of awe glimmering on his face makes my heart flutter. There's something in his eyes I can't explain, but I know it speaks to something in my soul. *I* want to look at something like that. Sadly, I think I might've looked at Lachlan in a similar manner, but he's gone and I have to move on.

Moving on is easier said than done. I've vowed to myself to send him no more texts, but knowing me I'll break my promise eventually.

We're only about two or three minutes from the apartment when we spot a quaint café tucked down an alley. It would be all too easy to miss, but apparently Ansel has an eagle eye for these kinds of things.

He holds the door open and I trudge inside, inhaling the heavenly aroma of espresso. American coffee has nothing on the stuff you can get in Europe. I don't know how I'll survive once I return home.

We snag a table by the window, it doesn't let much light in, being in the alley and all, but it's nice. There are only a handful of other tables and people sit around chatting at them.

Ansel places our order, already knowing what I'll want, since his French is better than mine.

"I don't know how my dad ever left France," he remarks, looking out the window to the street we came from. "He met my mom here. She was on vacation with some girlfriends after college. He convinced her to stay the rest of the summer with him and they fell in love. He moved to the States with her and the rest is history."

"I guess he loved her enough to leave." I flinch as soon as the words leave my lips. Did Lachlan leave because of his love for me? It doesn't seem likely. If he truly loved me he would've waited. I was so close to graduating and we would've been free to be together. I shiver at the memories of the nasty rumors that circulated those final weeks of school. All year I had flown under the radar, no one found out about my past, but at the end I became the subject of gossip and ridicule.

"What is it?"

"Huh?" I shake my mind free of my thoughts, looking across the round wooden table at Ansel.

He flicks a piece of dark hair out of his eyes. "You looked lost. Where'd you go?"

I shoot a smile as the waiter brings us our espressos. To Ansel I say, "I ... uh ... I was thinking about the rumors."

"The rumors," he repeats, his jaw ticking. Even though he's been supportive I know the situation makes him angry. "They weren't really rumors, though, Dani," he reminds me.

It's the use of *Dani* instead of Meadows that tells me how pissed he still is. He'd probably punch Lachlan if he ever saw him again.

"Most of them were." My voice is small. I stare down at the tiny white espresso cup on a matching plate.

"You still slept with him."

I bite my lip, feeling the telltale sting of tears. I rub my finger around the rim of the cup. "I know you can't begin to understand it, but we had a connection that was ... unexplainable. We both fought our feelings for so long and I kept telling myself I had an innocent crush but it was so much more." I finally bring the cup to my lips, taking a small sip.

"You really loved him, didn't you? Not infatuation but true love?"

I give a jerk of my head. "Yeah, I did. I still do. Feelings like these are too strong to just go away. I wish they would but they don't."

He stares across the table at me unblinking. "No one deserves to have their heart broken like that."

"Heartbreak is inevitable." I shrug like it's not a big deal, but it is.

I don't think I'll ever love anyone in this world as much as I love Lachlan. It's not that I don't think I might fall in love again one day, but I know it'll never come up to the power of my emotions for him. Some things are one of a kind.

"Besides," I continue, "I've lived through worse."

I'm beginning to finally accept that there is no way to truly move on from that day and the subsequent months of pain, surgeries, and rehab. It'll always live within me, the haunting memories, but I have to go on and live in spite of it. My suffering doesn't hurt anyone but myself.

Ansel taps his finger against the table. "Want to talk about it?"

I shake my head, looking away from him.

Talking about it hurts too much.

"You can talk to me about it. When you're ready."

I force a smile for his benefit, not mine. "I know."

And I do, but it's scary to talk. Lachlan is the only person I've shared the most intimate details of my mind with. My pain, my fears, the darkest parts of myself that recoil from the light. I gave it all to him and in the end he left me. What's to say Ansel wouldn't do the same?

I finish my espresso and he does the same. We pay the check and he stands, shrugging into his jacket.

Offering his hand to me, he gives a small smile. "Come on, Meadows. We have a city to explore."

CHAPTER SEVENTY-TWO

"IF YOU WON'T COME HERE, MAYBE I SHOULD GO THERE for Christmas."

"Sage, that's really not necessary. It's a long flight and it's one Christmas. We'll spend next Christmas together."

"Anything can happen, D. I was supposed to spend Christmas with you and mom two years ago but that didn't happen."

I rub my hand against my forehead, knowing he has a valid point.

I'm not ready to go home, even for a visit, but I'm worried having Sage here will be like having reality smack me in the face. But I know I can't keep refusing my brother.

"Actually, come, it'll be nice to see you."

It doesn't seem possible that it's been six months since I saw my brother, but it has been. Time's been passing quickly, but I guess it has helped that I've been on the move so much. There's been so much to explore since I left the States and so much is only a train ride away here.

Plus, with the rich histories there's always something to learn.

Lately, Ansel and I have been exploring various art museums in Paris. There's an abundance of them and Ansel eats it up, staring at the paintings and studying the strokes imprinted in the paint from a time long ago.

"Really? You're not going to keep arguing?"

"No."

"Good, because I already got a plane ticket and was coming anyway."

I laugh. Of course he is. "You'll have to stay in a hotel though," I warn. "There's not enough room here."

"What do you mean? I can sleep on the couch."

"There's only one room, so Ansel sleeps on the couch," I lie.

Ansel throws an amused grin my way, from where he sits in the kitchen, looking out the windows and sketching the buildings surrounding ours. I bet it's beautiful here in the spring and summer. Even now, the city is stunning, and the light swirls of snow floating down look like tufts of cotton.

"Fine, I'll book a hotel. Send me your address again so I can get something close by."

I hear a voice in the background. "Who's there?"

"No one," he says a bit too quickly. "I have to go."

"Sage—"

Before I can say anything else the line goes dead. I stare down at the screen of my phone, now showing me my wallpaper—a photo of Ansel and I in front of the Trevi Fountain. We haven't been to the Eiffel Tower yet. I think we've both been saving it, so we can savor the moment we're finally beneath it. That might be silly, but moments deserve to be treasured. In the end, our memories are the things that matter most.

"That was weird," I mumble more to myself than Ansel. I toss my phone on the couch, shaking my head as I pad across the room to where Ansel sits at the tiny kitchen table. I bend over, resting my chin on his shoulder as I study his sketch. "That's beautiful. You're so talented."

He rubs the side of his pinky against the charcoal, blending it more. "You're biased."

"I'm honest," I argue.

"You mean you'd tell me if you thought I sucked?" He turns his head to face me and suddenly he's *right there*. His mouth centimeters from mine. For a second I think about how easy it would be to kiss him. All I would have to do is move the tiniest bit closer. Press our mouths together.

I jolt away from him like I've been electrocuted.

His brows furrow, probably wondering what caused my reaction.

I hastily tuck a piece of hair behind my ear, turning for the refrigerator and grabbing some water, gulping it down like my life depends on it.

"It's okay if you feel something for me, you know," he says from behind me, the sound of papers shuffling as he closes his sketchpad. "He isn't going to own your heart forever."

My throat closes up and I toss the bottle in the waste bin. "I'm going for a walk."

I grab my set of keys from the bowl near the door, stuffing my feet into my boots and shoving my arms into my coat.

"Meadows, wait," he calls, following me.

I pause with my hand on the door. "I'm very confused right now, and I need to take a walk." There's more bite to my voice than I intend.

I open the door, but it doesn't close behind me and I

know he's holding it open, watching me walk away while I refuse to look back.

"I'm sorry."

My steps halt. "Don't be. It's not you."

It's me. It's always me.

I hurry to the elevator, down to the bottom level and out onto the street.

The cold chill hits me like a slap to the face. It's just what I need.

The streets aren't too busy, where we live is a quieter street, and I'm able to walk without worrying about bumping into anyone.

My throat feels tight and my eyes burn.

I almost kissed Ansel, and the worst thing is a part of me wanted to. I wanted to see how his lips would feel against mine, how different his touch would be from Lachlan's. But if I'm going to kiss Ansel then Lachlan shouldn't be a thought in my brain, but he is, because despite everything he's always there.

I walk with my head down, trying not to think of all the walks I took from Sage's condo, subsequently bumping into Lachlan and Zeppelin.

I miss him and I hate myself for missing him.

It's maddening loving someone so much when you wish you could hate them instead.

I've sent him so many texts saying I hate him, but it's never true. I don't hate him at all and it's not fair. He's the one who left. He's no doubt moved on with his life, while I'm still here, this many months later, unable to kiss another guy because all I can think of is *him* and how it feels like a betrayal if I kiss Ansel.

I keep walking and walking, refusing to let my limp slow me down. With all the walking we've done in the various cities we've been to my leg has grown stronger, but there have also been days when it aches deep in the bones and joints.

My phone rings and it's Ansel, but I ignore his call. He's the last person I want to talk to right now. I know he probably wants to make sure I'm okay, but I need this time to myself. I need to walk and breathe and think, even if thinking hurts. It stirs up emotions I keep burying instead of dealing with. I'm masking the problem, not solving it, and I'm never going to be able to truly move on from the shooting, from Lachlan, until I do.

I walk deeper into the city, onto unfamiliar streets. I know there's no way I'll ever find my way back to the apartment, but I'm not planning to. When I'm ready to go back I'll catch a cab.

My thoughts drift as I walk, probably going places they shouldn't at times, but it allows me to sort through some things.

I pass a flower shop, and pause, staring at the flowers inside.

There's not a single dandelion amongst their midst. Of course there's not, I doubt they even exist here, but even if they did you wouldn't find one in a florist shop. That used to bother me, being named after a flower that people view as ugly and unnecessary.

Not anymore.

I see now how perfect the name is for me.

Like a dandelion, I'm resilient. I can be cut down but I keep coming back. I won't let life beat me down into nothing. I will grow, I will become. Become what? I don't know, but that's the beauty of it.

It's another hour before I finally catch a taxi back to the apartment.

When I open the door, Ansel has his phone poised in his hand, no doubt about to ring me again.

"Jesus fucking Christ, Dani, you've been gone almost three hours. I was worried something happened to you."

"I'm fine." I lock the door behind me, trying to head to the bedroom.

"Whoa, whoa, whoa. *Wait*, we need to talk."

"There's nothing to talk about," I disagree, trying to bypass him, he blocks my way, refusing to let me by.

"You almost kissed me, I think there's plenty to talk about."

During my walk, I had done my best to forget things, to dismiss it from my mind, but I should've expected it'd be the first thing on his.

"I-It was a moment of weakness."

He snorts. "A moment of weakness." His hold flexes against my forearm where he grips it. "It's okay to like me as more than a friend. It's okay to want to kiss me. And Meadows?" He leans in closer, his breath fanning against my face. My heart beats rapidly behind my rib cage like the treacherous organ it is. "It's okay to move on from him."

He releases his hold on me, allowing me to disappear into the confines of the bedroom.

The bedroom I share with *him*, not Lachlan.

I bury myself under the thick covers, covering my face.

Why can't I let him go?

CHAPTER SEVENTY-THREE

I RUN MY HANDS DOWN THE FRONT OF MY OUTFIT, A pair of jeans and a cream-colored sweater. For some odd reason I'm outrageously nervous to see my brother. I guess after all this time apart I'm afraid he's not going to recognize me, which is beyond silly.

"I can smell your stress sweat from here." I know Ansel's trying to lighten the mood, but it's not working.

It's been two, nearly three, weeks since the almost-not-really kiss. He hasn't brought it up anymore, but his eyes tell me he wants to. He's continued to sleep with me, wrapping his arms around me like every other night.

His touch is comforting and I like being around him. I keep asking myself why I can't feel something more for him. I want to so badly. I want to replace the memories of Lachlan's hands on my body, the taste of his skin, with someone else's, but if I can't feel those things for Ansel, someone I already love and care about in a different way, I can't imagine it happening with a stranger.

God, it's so fucked up.

"I know. I'm a mess," I finally reply, crossing my arms over my chest.

Ansel sits up from where he was lying back on the couch with an arm tucked behind his head.

"It's okay to be nervous. You haven't seen him in a while, but he *is* your brother so I don't think you have too much to worry about. If anyone should be worried, it's me. If he finds out we sleep in the same bed he will murder me."

I brush my fingers through my wavy hair, blowing out a breath and hopefully the last of my anxiety with it.

Ansel stands, wrapping his arms around me. I relax into his hug as he digs his fingers through my hair, gently massaging my scalp to soothe me.

"You worry too much."

"I'm afraid he's going to make me go home," I admit something that's been plaguing me.

Ansel takes a step back, giving me a look that says he can't believe those words left my mouth. "You're an adult. He can't make you do anything, and I don't think your brother would do that to you. He misses you, but he knows you need this."

My phone chimes then and when I look at the screen it's Sage telling me he's here.

"It's show time." I force a smile and playfully bump Ansel's shoulder.

Leaving Ansel in the apartment I head down to greet Sage.

I spot him immediately, climbing out of a cab. His hair is a tad longer and his scruff is closer to a beard than a few days worth of not shaving.

"Sage!" All my worries go flying out the window and I run toward him. He grins at the sight of me, opening his arms. I slam into him, wrapping my arms tightly around his neck. "I've missed you. So freaking much."

He squeezes me back. "Same. You have no idea, Weed." He releases me, looking me over. "It's been weird not having you at my place."

"Being alone must suck," I joke.

Something passes over his eyes and he clears his throat. "Yeah, it's rough."

My brow furrows, I feel like I'm missing something.

"Have you seen much of the city yet?"

He shakes his head. "Nah, I got off the plane and went to my hotel to drop off my stuff and came straight here."

"Are you jet-lagged?"

"I mean, yeah," he runs his fingers through his hair, the brown strands tinged with red and blond, "but I want to force my body to get on Paris time, so I'm staying up."

"You're ready for some sight-seeing then?" I'm eager to show my brother the city I've been living in for almost a month now.

"I want to see as much as I can while I'm here."

"Let's go up and I'll show you the apartment. Ansel can come with us since he's better with the language and getting around the city."

"Ansel," he grumbles as I start leading him toward the entrance to the building.

"Aw, don't tell me you hate his guts. If you did, you wouldn't have told him I was going to London."

"Don't remind me." He looks around the lobby of the building, taking in the old world architecture. I love how nothing is new here. It's timeless.

"How's work?" I ask as we step onto the elevator.

"I love it," he admits, trying to stifle his growing smile. "Working for a small, independent company is what I needed. I'm appreciated there."

"I'm glad."

The doors slide open and I lead him down the hall to the small but elegant apartment.

Ansel jumps up from the couch as soon as the door opens. "Hey, man." He holds his hand out to my brother. Sage reluctantly takes it, giving it a shake.

"This place is ... quaint," he finally settles on, probably thinking about the fact that Ansel and I are near each other all the time.

If he only knew.

After a short tour, Ansel and I pull on our coats so we can head out into the city to show my brother around.

Sage looks like us on our first day, his mouth parted and his head on a constant swivel trying to take it all in.

I've learned it's impossible. I discover something new every day that I've missed all the other days. That's one of my favorite things about this city. It's full of secrets.

"What did you think of the Eiffel Tower when you went?" Sage asks, staring at it off in the distance between the buildings.

"We actually haven't been yet."

His head swings to me in astonishment. "You've been in Paris for almost a month and you two haven't gone to the Eiffel Tower? That's the craziest thing I've ever heard."

Ansel chuckles. "She's saving it for some reason."

"Why?" Sage's brows draw together.

I give a small shrug, stuffing my hands in my coat pockets. "I don't know, it's dumb."

"Come on, D, tell me."

I bite my lip. "It's ... once we go, it feels kind of like the end."

"The end?" Sage repeats.

524

"I told you it was dumb. I want to savor the experience."

I was the same way in all the other cities we've stopped, saving the more iconic landmarks for one of the last things we did before leaving.

It's worse this time and I think it's because deep down, I know I won't be going anywhere else.

Once I leave Paris I'm going home.

Sage lets it go, letting Ansel show him around the neighborhood. We end up catching a cab, heading into the heart of the city to show him more easily recognizable historic sites like the Notre Dame cathedral, currently undergoing repairs from the horrendous fire that damaged it, and drive by the Arc de Triomphe. The cab takes us by the Eiffel Tower, but Sage doesn't ask to stop which I'm grateful for.

After touring for a few hours Sage admits he's tired and asks to be dropped off at his hotel.

Since his hotel is within walking distance of where we're living, Ansel and I get out too.

"I'll see you later." I hug my brother goodbye, certain he's going to pass out as soon as he reaches his bed. His eyes boast dark shadows. The jetlag has obviously gotten to him.

Ansel and I watch him enter the hotel before we start the trek down the cobblestone streets.

"We should stop and pick up something to make for dinner."

It's good that Ansel can produce food that's semi-edible, otherwise we would be spending a fortune on eating out all day long.

"What do you have in mind?"

"Pasta," he grins, the word lilted with a French accent.

I guess growing up with a French father, and now

being surrounded by other French people day in and day out is making his accent come out.

We enter the tiny market around the corner from our building and Ansel passes me a basket as he peruses the aisles, grabbing the ingredients he needs for whatever pasta dish he plans to concoct.

He drops some fresh lemons, olive oil, Parmesan cheese, spaghetti noodles, a fresh baguette, and even a bottle of wine into the basket. We've taken a tiny bit of advantage of the fact that eighteen is the legal drinking age.

Once our items are purchased, we walk to the apartment.

"I'm going to get started on this." Ansel carries the paper bag into the kitchen area.

"I'll shower then." God knows he doesn't want my help. The first night he cooked for us in London he asked me to toast some bread in the oven. I burned it to a blackened crisp and the burnt smell wouldn't leave the apartment for days.

I grab my pajamas—ones I bought after I realized I didn't pack any like the dummy I am—and close myself in the bathroom.

While the water warms, I wipe my face free of makeup. I've taken to wearing more than I used to, but still not a lot. I find it makes me feel more put together and ready to take on the day when I pat on the concealer and coat my lashes in mascara.

Stripping out of my clothes I step into the steamy shower, letting the heat wash over me and uncoil my tight muscles that have been wound from my nerves over Sage's visit.

Closing my eyes, the water pours over my face, dripping down my naked body. Unbidden, images of Lachlan in his shower flood my mind. His hand wrapped around his shaft, stroking his erection. My pussy clenches at the memory and I can't control myself as my hand drifts down my body to that sensitive nub of nerves. I rub my clit slowly, picturing Lachlan's hand in my place and his eyes staring at me like I'm *everything*. A whimper crawls out of my throat and I bite down on my lip, not wanting Ansel to overhear my noises in the small apartment. I'd never be able to look him in the eyes again.

I push my thoughts of reality out of my mind, instead focusing on the fantasy of Lachlan. I shut my eyes tighter, picturing his wet naked body pressed to the back of mine, his erection rubbing against me. I pretend his hands slide around my body, up my stomach to cup my breasts in his big hands. I moan, leaning my head back against his chest, but in reality I rest it on the tiled shower wall.

"You're so beautiful," he whispers in a rough growl directly into my ear. *"You're beautiful and you're mine."*

"Yours," I tell him.

My body aches for him, the orgasm building as I rub faster.

In my mind, he turns me, taking my face between his hands and claiming my lips. He devours my mouth, filling me with the taste of his lips.

"I love you," I murmur as his lips skim down my neck.

"I love you more," his voice is husky with passion. He swirls his tongue around my nipple, making my back arch as my body begs for him to take more.

I slip my fingers into my pussy, pretending it's Lachlan there claiming me. A moan vibrates in my throat, turning into a small cry as my orgasm builds.

I come apart, hoping the shower drowns out my sounds of pleasure. My legs shake and in my mind Lachlan is there holding me up, making sure I don't fall.

I give myself time to recover from the orgasm, the first one I've had since he last touched me with apologies that still haunt me, and when I open my eyes he's not there. Of course he's not, but it still hurts, because he's nothing but a ghost and I wish he'd stop haunting me.

Washing my hair and body, I get out of the shower as quickly as possible, somehow feeling dirtier than when I got in.

Drying the ends of my hair with a towel I dress in my pajamas before facing my reflection. My cheeks are flushed and I know it's not from the heated water. Wrapping my hands around the sink, I lower my head shaking it.

"Let it go, Dani," I mutter softly to myself. "He's not coming back. You have to forget about him."

It's easier said than done. Love is a feeling you can't turn on and off as you please. It lives inside you as vital to your being as every organ in your body.

I hastily turn away from the mirror, hurrying out into the kitchen.

The scent of the pasta Ansel is making permeates the air. It smells amazing and my stomach rumbles to life.

"Good shower?"

"Huh?" I squeak, freaking out that he heard my moans.

"You were in there a while." He turns his back, stirring the pasta in a pot.

"Oh, yeah."

I hop up on the counter near him, and he tosses a grin my way. "Want to help?"

I give him a look. "Have you forgotten the bread incident?"

"No, but I think you can handle grating cheese, right?"

I eye the grater. "Uh … possibly, but I also might scrape my fingers off."

He shakes his head. "Just try."

I jump down and grab the block of fresh cheese, grating it over the bowl he set out.

"How much do you need?"

"About half."

While I grate the cheese he adds olive oil into a bowl and squeezes fresh lemon juice in as well. After adding a dash of pepper he takes the cheese from me and stirs it all together.

"Grab the bowls. Once I drain this it's ready."

Standing on my tiptoes I reach for the bowls, getting them down and setting them on the counter.

He drains the pasta in the sink and then adds the mixture onto the warm pasta, stirring it around before dishing out a serving for each of us. He grabs the bread from the oven, perfectly toasted and not at all burnt, and cuts us each a slice. He sprinkles some olive oil and salt on top.

"This smells yummy." I inhale the heavenly scent of lemon.

"I hope it's good. I picked some things from the store I thought sounded good and put them together."

We sit down at the table by the window, looking out into the darkened night at the beacon that's the Eiffel Tower lit up in all its glory.

I swirl my pasta around my fork, taking a bite. "Mmm," I hum, flavor exploding across my tongue, "this is delicious."

"Thanks, Meadows." He takes a bite himself. "Damn, I'm good."

I laugh. "Don't get too cocky now—you never know, you could burn something next time."

"I'm not you, Meadows," he jokes with a playful grin.

Feel something for him. Anything. You can do it. It's time to move on.

"I'm so glad you can cook. We'd be screwed."

"Face it, you're lucky to have me."

I sober, my smile suddenly sad. "Yeah, I really am."

He grabs the bottle of wine he'd uncorked before I came out of the bathroom and pours us each a glass.

Lifting his glass toward me, he gets a thoughtful expression. "To friendships that matter, relationships that are meant to last, and a passionate future wherever life might lead us."

I pick up my glass, clinking it against his. The sound rings in the air.

"To what's meant to be."

CHAPTER SEVENTY-FOUR

A FEW DAYS LATER IT'S CHRISTMAS. SAGE ARRIVES AT the apartment early and while Ansel answers the door, I scramble to make the bed and rid the bedroom of any evidence that might tip off Sage to the fact that Ansel is sleeping there. It's not like I can keep him out of the bedroom since he has to go through there to get to the bathroom. I don't think telling my brother he can't use the bathroom would go over well.

I dart out of the bedroom, brushing my hair out of my eyes.

"Sage," I smile, running over to hug him, "I'm so happy you ended up coming."

Truly, the past few days spent showing him the city have been some of the best. Things felt normal for a little while.

He chuckles, hugging me back. "And to think you didn't want your big brother to come."

"Yeah, yeah." I let him go and he sets down the bag he brought with him, pulling out a few gifts. There's a small pile of presents in the corner near the living room balcony of things Ansel and I bought to exchange with each other and Sage, plus the gifts his family sent him.

"Something smells good. You can cook?" Sage addresses Ansel, knowing there's no way the heavenly scent of freshly baked scones is my cause.

"A little bit. I'm learning." Ansel walks behind me into the kitchen to check on them.

Sage arches a brow and gives me a look like maybe he hasn't given Ansel enough credit. I stick my tongue out at him and he loops his arm around my neck, tugging me against his side.

"Did you stick your tongue out at me, Weed?" He messes up my hair.

"Let me go," I laugh in protest, slithering out of his hold.

Ansel sets the blueberry scones out to cool.

Pointing at Sage's bag I say, "So, what'd you get me?"

———

SEVERAL HOURS later we've opened our presents, cleaned up, and gorged ourselves on the delicious scones Ansel made as well as the sandwiches he put together later for lunch.

"I can't believe you're leaving tomorrow." I turn my head to look at my brother beside me where both of us lay on the floor in a food coma.

"You could come with me."

Ansel left a little while ago to give us time alone since Sage will be leaving too early in the morning for me to see him.

"I'm not ready." I stare above me at the detailed ceiling.

"When do you think you will be?"

"Soon. I hope. I'm working on it. I've learned a lot about myself being away, but I still have a lot to deal with and I'm beginning to realize I can't do it on my own and I need someone to guide me through it."

He doesn't comment, knowing how difficult it was for me in the past working with a therapist.

"You have to do what's best for you. I'm proud of you, D."

"Thanks."

It means a lot to hear that coming from my brother, especially when I know he wasn't the happiest with my decision to skip college for a year.

"By the way," I begin hesitantly, "I'm starting college in the fall at the University of Utah."

Sage's lips part, his eyes lighting up. "What?"

"I still don't know what I want to do," I admit reluctantly, "but I'll figure it out. I needed this time, though, after everything."

He stares at me, searching for something in my eyes, but I don't know what. After at least a minute, his voice thick, he says, "Mom would be so proud of the woman you've become."

I feel my throat clog with emotion. "You think?"

"I know."

I let out a shaky breath. "I wish she was here."

"Me too."

But she's not. Life goes on. The world keeps spinning. It's time for me to move with it.

CHAPTER SEVENTY-FIVE

"WE SHOULD GO OUT FOR NEW YEAR'S EVE."

I turn at the sound of Ansel's voice where he sits by the window sketching. The apartment is full of his sketches and paintings. He's actually been able to sell some recently.

"Where are you thinking?"

"Maybe get dinner and visit the Eiffel Tower?"

"That sounds good ... there's something I need to tell you."

At my suddenly serious tone, he sets his sketchpad down, swinging his legs out of the window seat.

"Is something wrong?" His true concern for me warms my heart. He sits down by me on the couch, stretching his arm along the back.

"No." I reach for his fingers, playing with them between mine. "I've been thinking about this since Sage was here..." I trail off, nervous to tell him I've decided to go back to the States.

"You're ready to go home." It's a statement, not a question.

"Yeah." I exhale a heavy breath I didn't realize I was holding in. "It's time. There are things I need to do, more ways I need to better myself, and I have to do that there."

"I understand."

"Are you coming with me?"

A small smile tugs his lips and he looks at our fingers wrapped together. "There's something I've been wanting to talk to you about too, Meadows. This city is where I belong. It feels like home. I'm going to get a job and stay here."

I smile back. "Look at us making grown up decisions."

"I'm going to miss you, Meadows."

My throat closes up. "I'm not even gone yet and I already don't want to leave you. I..." Biting down on my lip, I squeeze his hand. "I can't thank you enough for coming on this journey with me. I was set on doing this on my own, but it was so much better with you by my side. I will never ever forget this time."

"Fuck, Meadows, it sounds like you're saying goodbye forever. We'll see each other again. You can't get rid of me this easily."

"I love you." I throw my arms around him, hugging him tight.

He freezes for a moment, then his arms twine around my body and he hugs me back. "I love you, too."

Ansel is so much more to me than a friend. He's family.

"I'm scared to go home." It seems dumb to admit since this is my decision. "But I know I need to."

He lets me go, giving me a serious look. "You'll be fine. Trust me."

"You're not mad I'm leaving?"

"You're not mad I'm staying?" he counters, arching a brow.

I laugh, realizing how silly I'm being.

"When are you going to leave?"

"I'll look for a ticket tonight." I look around the apartment, a little sad to leave this place behind. "Probably pick one for a week from now."

"You're going to be okay, Meadows."

My eyes drift back to him, my lips tugging into a smile. "I know."

———

PARIS ON NEW Year's Eve is a delight. The city is always vibrant, full of life, but tonight it's even more abuzz with energy and excitement over the impending New Year. Ansel and I run out of the restaurant hand in hand, full of giggles, faces flushed from the wine we had with our dinners. It's dark out, the sky sprinkled with glittering stars.

A short distance away the Eiffel Tower looms above us, beautiful and magnificent. It takes my breath away every time I lay my eyes on it.

Ansel's laughter carries over his shoulder as he runs, dragging me behind him.

"Slow down," I giggle, "your legs are longer than mine."

I feel tipsy and happy, loose in a way where the bad things can't touch me.

Ansel doesn't slow and in no time we're below the Eiffel Tower. We actually stopped by before our dinner, riding the elevator up to the top while it was still light out.

I love it like this, lit up in the dark like a beacon.

"Come here, picture time," Ansel commands, when we're near the landmark but at a good spot to get it in the background.

He swings me around in his arms while I laugh. He holds out one hand with his phone and starts clicking, the flash lighting up our faces as he takes multiple photos. I kiss his cheek and then we're both laughing.

"I think I got enough." He flicks through the fifty or so photos he took by accident.

"Send the best ones to me." He starts looking through them. "I didn't mean now."

"Too bad, Meadows."

My phone dings a few minutes later with the photos and I save them to my phone, staring down at our happy, carefree faces, the Eiffel Tower looming behind us.

I don't know what makes me do it, it's been weeks since I last sent him a message and he doesn't read them anyway, but looking down at the photos of Ansel and me, I want nothing more than to make Lachlan jealous.

I send two of the photos to him, one of us laughing, and the one where I kissed Ansel's cheek.

Me: This is what moving on looks like.

I want to blame the alcohol I had, which even though it wasn't much I'm sure it's a contributing factor in me being reckless like this, but mostly I'm sad, because last year I spent New Year's Eve with him and now he's a ghost.

Ansel and I continue walking up to the tower, hand in hand.

There's nothing romantic between us, not in our touches, not in our glances, but I sent those photos and that text to Lachlan because I want him to think there is. I want him to hurt like I have since he left. He's probably moved on with some beautiful woman who's his age, with long legs, and shiny hair, and she probably works an awesome job, and wears skirts and heels every day and—

My phone buzzes and I yank it out of my pocket. It

can't possibly be him, not after all these months of unanswered texts. It's probably my brother or a wrong number or —

Lachlan: You never read the letter.

It's not a question.

It's a statement.

And he's right, I never did.

My body goes cold, a sweat breaking out over my body like a sticky second skin.

"Are you okay?" Ansel asks, noticing the change in my body language.

I look at him with tear-filled eyes, my hands shaking so much he takes my phone from me. He sees the text and a look of anger comes over his face. He puts my phone in his pocket and slings his arm around my shoulders.

"We're going home, Meadows."

I wrap my arms around his torso, leaning against him because my weight is suddenly too much to bear.

He's right, I never read the letter, but it can't possibly change anything.

Right?

CHAPTER SEVENTY-SIX

I PACK MY CLOTHES INTO MY SUITCASE, TRYING TO FIND a way to fit the items and knickknacks I've picked up along the way. Ansel watches from the doorway. He'll be moving out of this place at the end of January since we already paid for the month. I saw his new place, it's not nearly as nice, but he got a job at a local café and wanted to minimize his spending since he can't live off his parents forever.

I joked that I guess he made more when he was dealing weed.

"Why did you sell weed?" I look up from my suitcase and he startles at my sudden question.

"What made you ask that, Meadows?"

"I was thinking about things." And you know, trying to distract myself from the text Lachlan sent a week ago about the letter. The one I promptly tossed in the trash as soon as we got home.

I don't know what made me do it, but I think getting that text from him after *all* this time infuriated me. He'd clearly been reading everything I sent, and because I said I was moving on he finally decided to give me a response.

I kind of regret throwing it away, but I can't do anything about it now.

It's gone, like whatever we were.

Ansel sighs, rubbing his stubbled jaw. The shadow of hair on his cheeks makes him look older. "I don't know, I guess it gave me control over something. And the money was nice too." He winks at me.

"You're so weird." I laugh, stuffing a t-shirt into my suitcase.

Ansel saunters over, picking up one of my bras. "Nice lace, Meadows."

"Give me that." I snatch the lacy bra back from him, shoving it under some jeans.

He chuckles, stuffing his hands in his pockets. "I'm going to miss you."

I sigh, feeling the burn of tears already stinging my eyes. "I'll miss you too."

"Come here, pretty girl." He grabs me into his arms, holding me tight.

"Stop making me emotional."

"Can't help it. Girls just weep when I speak."

A laugh bubbles out of my throat and I push him away, his stomach hard beneath my hands. "You're so full of it."

"Finish packing, Meadows. We need to leave for the airport in an hour."

"Right." I lower my head, stomach coiling at the reminder of the flight waiting for me to catch.

He squeezes my hand as he passes. "It's all going to work out. Don't stress."

I flash him a smile. "I know."

I finish packing and in what feels like no time at all

we're piling into the taxi to take me to the airport. I told Ansel he didn't have to come, but he insisted. Truth be told, I'm glad. It's going to suck saying goodbye to him, but I know he'll make sure I don't chicken out and stay.

Since it's the afternoon, the drive to the airport takes a little longer than normal, but is still too quick.

Ansel hops out, paying the driver despite my protests, and grabs my suitcase for me, wheeling it inside.

"Is Sage picking you up?"

I shake my head. "He doesn't know I'm coming back. There are some things I need to do first."

Ansel arches a brow. "Do what you have to do, Meadows, just don't forget to call, write, send a carrier pigeon — on second thought, no carrier pigeons, I bet they shit everywhere."

I can count on Ansel to make me laugh. We make it to security and I know it's time to say goodbye.

"I love you." Standing on my tiptoes I hug him tight.

"Love you too, Meadows. Don't forget about me."

"Never." I kiss his cheek and step away, tears coming once more.

Grabbing the handle of my suitcase, I start to walk away.

"Dani! Wait!" His voice stops me when I'm barely twenty feet away.

He jogs the short distance to me, pulling something out of his back pocket.

My eyes rest on the envelope in his hands, my name in Lachlan's writing on the front.

"You ... you should read this." He holds it out to me. I stare at it like I can light it on fire with my brain waves alone. "Meadows, read it, okay?"

I finally get my hand to take it. "You read it?" I squint at him, rubbing my fingers over the edges.

"Yeah." He gives me a sheepish smile. "I know I shouldn't have but when I saw it I knew it had to be from him and I wanted to see what he had to say." He scratches the back of his head. Lowering his head, he whispers in my ear, "You were never going to choose me, not when you have someone who loves you like that."

He grips my hands around the letter before backing away a step at a time.

"Read it, Meadows."

He turns his back to me then and I watch him walk away until he's gone from my sight. I look down at the letter clasped in my hands, tempted to toss it in the trash, but I don't.

I have a plane to catch.

CHAPTER SEVENTY-SEVEN

THE PLANE REACHES THIRTY-TWO-THOUSAND FEET
before I finally open the letter.

Dani,

*I know you probably hate me so much right now. You have
every right to. Leaving seems selfish, I know, but I'm doing this for
you. For us. For a chance that maybe one day we'll have a future
together. One where we're free to love in the light, and we don't have
to hide.*

*Things are getting more than complicated—it's downright
impossible to hide my feelings for you. Someone is going to find out
and I know I could handle the consequences, but I don't want you
to have to bear that burden. I know you'd blame yourself, even
though this is on me. I refuse to say it's my fault, because to me
saying there's any fault in the love we have is like saying the feelings aren't actually real.*

*I love you more than I've ever loved anyone. You're the woman
who was meant to be mine. I don't know why it's you, or me for
you, but it is and I'm so glad. I hate that I have to leave you, and I
realize I'm taking a huge risk, one where you may not ever be able
to forgive me, but because I love you I'm willing to take the chance.*

You need to grow without me. I see that clearly and it kills me because I want to be with you more than anything. You're not dealing with your trauma the way you should and I'm worried you're using me as a Band-Aid. I want you to get better, let go of your past, but I see now that I'm not the person that can help you do that. It's why I have to go. You have your wings, Dani. Use them to soar.

You're brilliant, amazing, beautiful, and strong.

Don't be so hard on yourself.

I feel like I'm not making sense. Frankly, my thoughts are everywhere. I don't want to leave you. The scent of you still clings to my pillow. I want it to stay there forever. I want to wake up to the sight of you in bed beside me. I want to laugh with you in the kitchen. I want to watch movies together. I want to marry you. I want to have babies with you. I want everything with you.

If you think for a minute me leaving is because I don't love you, you'll know that's not true. It's because I love you too much—enough to let you go, to give you the room to grow.

I only hope you'll come back to me.

But if you don't, I understand that too.

I love you, Dandelion Meadows.

You're my sunshine.

—Lachlan

My tears sprinkle the paper, making the ink run in some places.

Beneath his name is a bunch of random numbers I don't understand.

I rub my fingers over the numbers, wondering what they mean.

4.22.21 47.6205 122.3493

Somehow, I know in my gut, they'll lead me back to him.

But Lachlan's right, I need to better myself, and I have to do it on my own.

544

CHAPTER SEVENTY-EIGHT

THE GRASS CRUNCHES WITH MORNING FROST BENEATH my feet, a steady drizzle falling from the sky like it's weeping.

Mud sticks to my sneakers and I'm sure if anyone could see me I look like a complete weirdo trekking through the cemetery at the early morning hour in my jeans and raincoat with the hood pulled up, flowers cradled in my arms.

My plane landed in Portland yesterday and I slept for fifteen hours in the hotel I booked. As soon as I woke up and showered, I headed out, wanting to do what I have to do before I catch my flight to Utah in a few hours.

The taxi idles near the cemetery's entrance, waiting to drop me off at the airport once I finish here. I should stop in and visit my grandparents, perhaps even drive by my childhood home, but I purposely wanted to make this a quick visit so I didn't go into a full-blown panic.

I see the gravestone up ahead. I've only been here once. Sage brought me before we flew to Utah, ironic that I'm visiting now and doing the same thing. I didn't get to go to her funeral, not with being in the hospital at the time, but it doesn't keep the guilt from nagging at me. My limp becomes heavier, my leg throbbing and I don't know whether it's from the rain or the memories.

Stopping in front of it, my lower lip trembles.

Laurel Meadows.

Loving Mother and Wife.

I trace my fingers over her name, tears pouring from my eyes.

"Hi, Mom. I'm sorry it took me so long to visit. The last two years have been rough." I lower my head, swallowing past the lump in my throat. "I haven't handled things the best, but I'm going to try now. I'm going to be better. Sage says you'd be proud of me, but I'm not so sure. I'm going to try my best." I lay the bouquet on her gravestone, holding onto the seven other individual flowers I bought as well. "I fell in love, Mom. With someone I shouldn't have, but it happened anyway. Despite the age difference and ... other things, I know you'd love him. He's wonderful. I ... I don't know if things will work out between us, but I know I'll never regret loving him. I lost myself, but I'm finding my way back and he helped. It's up to me to do the rest, so that's what I'm going to do. I love you, Mom." I kiss my fingers, placing them against the cold wet stone.

Standing up, I search the graveyard for the seven other faculty and students who were victims that day.

We were *all* victims, I know no one who was in the school that day will ever forget it. The pain, the fear, the suffering ... but these seven people, eight including my mom, suffered the greatest loss. A life left unlived because a monster decided he had the right to decide when time was up.

With all my flowers gone, I climb back into the taxi.

That's when the text comes.

Lachlan: The first time I saw you, the sadness radiated out of you. I could feel it in the air. I'd never felt the force of any emotion that powerfully from any human being before. My heart broke for you. Not because I felt sorry for you, but because I knew no one deserved to endure what you had. I vowed then to do everything in my power to help you.

Lachlan: Even if it meant I had to leave you.

CHAPTER SEVENTY-NINE

BACK IN UTAH, I FIND AN APARTMENT TO RENT.

Lachlan sends another text.

Lachlan: Letting you go was the hardest thing I've ever done, even if it was for the best.

———

I TAKE my driver's test since it's been so long since I drove. I pass.

Another text.

Lachlan: It's okay that you hate me. I expected it.

I don't tell him that I don't hate him. I never did. I just wished I did.

———

I GET a job at a hardware store a couple miles from my apartment so I'm forced to drive. I keep pretending to Sage that I'm still in Paris. Ansel is sworn to secrecy on the very off chance my brother would contact him. I'm not trying to hide from my brother, just grow, and I can't do that with him breathing down my neck teetering between sibling and parent.

Lachlan: I wish I could stop thinking about you, but I don't think it's possible not to. Zeppelin misses you. I do too.

———

I START SEEING A THERAPIST. One I choose myself. One who specializes in trauma and PTSD—apparently that's what I have. The dreams started up again as soon as I was alone, but with her help they're getting better. She makes me use breathing techniques and meditation because I refuse to take drugs for my issues. I'm getting better.

Lachlan: I hope wherever you are in the world you're happy.

———

ON APRIL FIRST, I knock on my brother's door.

I have a key, but this isn't my home anymore.

CHAPTER EIGHTY

KNOCKING ON SAGE'S DOOR, I STEP BACK TO WAIT FOR him to answer, holding the carrier from Watchtower with our coffees.

But when the door swings open it's not Sage standing there.

"Sasha!" I blurt, taken by surprise.

Even more surprise when I find that she's only wearing a pair of boy shorts, her bra, and an open button-down shirt that I know belongs to my brother.

"Holy shit!" She slams the door in my face.

I stand there blinking. "What the fuck?" I mutter to myself.

The door opens again slowly and she looks like she hopes I'm some sort of mirage. "I thought you were the delivery person."

"And you came to the door like that?" I try not to laugh, but honestly, Sasha totally would open the door dressed in next to nothing and not care at all.

"Babe, who's at the door?" Comes from somewhere inside the apartment and I cannot stop my smile.

"You and my brother?" Sasha gives me a sheepish look. "I'm not mad."

Amused, but not mad.

Sage rounds the corner, paling when he sees me. "Dani! You're home!"

He looks pleased, but then he realizes Sasha is standing there, and what I've easily deduced.

"'Bout time you got laid, big bro." I saunter past my friend into the condo, setting the carrier down. "Sasha if I'd known you were here I would've brought you something."

"I … um … I'm going to change."

She runs down the hall to my brother's room.

Sage leans against the counter, looking a bit ill.

"You're pale. Drink some coffee." I grab his from the carrier and extend it to him.

Sasha returns dressed in tight fitting ripped jeans and a turtleneck sweater.

"I'll go." She goes to grab her bag.

I shake my head. "Stay, I don't care. Seriously."

Maybe a couple of months ago I would've been livid to walk into something like this, especially with the irony considering how Sage felt about Lachlan and me. But I also understand my situation with Lachlan was way more complicated than just our ages. My therapist is helping me see that.

Sasha looks very uncomfortable, but when she exchanges a look with my brother she puts her bag back down and pulls out one of the stools.

"When did you get home?" Sage asks, running his fingers through his already mussed hair—it's not hard to guess from what.

"Oh, a couple of months ago."

Sage chokes on the coffee he was about to swallow.

"Did you say months?"

"I had things I needed to do."

"Like what? Where have you been staying? Not with that fuck face teacher dude, right?"

I glower. "You're one to talk." I shoot my gaze to Sasha, a tad sorry to drag her into this. "But no, I got my own place."

"Where?"

"Near the university."

He scrubs a hand over his jaw. "This is insane."

"I got a car too," I continue, my amusement growing when his eyes threaten to bug out. "It's a cute little Subaru Crosstrek. It's a hybrid and everything." I try to suppress my smile as my brother flounders for a response. "By the way," I trace my finger along the countertop, "if I do speak to Lachlan, it's not your right to judge. I'm not downplaying that things shouldn't have happened the way they did, but I can't change it."

He sighs. "You're going to be the end of me. You've been back all this time?"

"Since January," I interject. "I've been seeing a therapist. It's been good for me. I'm committed this time, to getting better, and she's been a great help."

Sage stares at me like he doesn't know me. I guess he doesn't, even though it's only been three months since I came back I know I've made great strides.

"Are you going to talk to him?" Sage asks.

"Maybe, I'm not really sure what I want. I still love him," I admit, and I realize it's the first time I've said it aloud in a long time, "but ... I guess I'm scared to see him after all this time."

Sasha reaches across the counter, squeezing my hand. "Don't deny yourself something because of fear or whatever else might hold you back."

"So," I change the subject, "how long have you two been together? Are you dating or is this just sex? How did this even happen?"

Both of them turn bright red. I'd be lying if I didn't say it fills me with some joy to watch them squirm.

Sasha speaks up first. "I came to drop something of yours off a few days after you left, I honestly don't even remember what, and things kind of went from there. I'm sorry we didn't tell you." She bites her lip, her eyes sad.

"I don't blame you for not telling me. It's not like I was honest with anyone about Lachlan." I flick a piece of hair out of my eyes. "You guys are serious then? A real couple?"

Sage nods, smiling at my friend. "It doesn't make sense..."

"But it does," she finishes for him.

"I'm not sure I can handle all this lovey-dovey-ness," I joke, finishing my coffee. "But I'm happy for you guys. Truly."

That doesn't mean it's not weird that my brother is dating my eighteen-year-old friend when he's twenty-seven, but if anyone knows that age doesn't matter it's me. In fact, it's good to see Sage happy. His posture isn't nearly as stiff, he's smiling non-stop, and he can't take his eyes off her.

My chest aches a bit, thinking of Lachlan. I miss him, and his texts don't help. I texted him for months as almost a journal of sorts, now it's his turn to do the same. I know in my heart he's it for me, but I'm scared to see him again. I've changed since I last saw him so it's likely he has too. What if the feelings aren't the same? I don't even know where he is, if he's still in Utah or not. He might not even want to see me, despite his texts, after all, I insinuated I was moving on with Ansel. I've never bothered to correct him on it either. When his texts started rolling in it felt like it was my time to stay quiet and let him speak.

"You're thinking about him, aren't you?" Sasha rests her elbow on the counter, head in her hand as she watches me.

"Yeah."

Sage grinds his jaw but says nothing.

"You shouldn't feel guilty for what you feel for him."

"What are you? A mind reader now?" I joke.

"No, but I've been in your situation." She glances at Sage. "My parents weren't the most approving of us," she adds softly. "I get it. And if your brother gets his head out of his ass, he does too."

He exhales a heavy breath. "I want you to be happy, D. If he does that for you at the end of the day that's all that matters."

"We'll see what happens," I whisper softly.

But deep inside me I feel that familiar tug, the one pulling me toward Lachlan and reminding me that no matter what I do or say, he's forever a part of me.

CHAPTER EIGHTY-ONE

I DROP MY KEYS ON THE SIDE TABLE, SHRUGGING OUT OF my jacket.

"Hey, Tally," I greet the Maine Coon kitten who pokes her head out from under the couch when she hears me. I set down the bag of things I took from my room at Sage's. I have a few more things to pick up, but I got the necessities. Like the wind chime that clangs when the bag touches the floor.

Tally startles and dives back under the couch.

Getting a pet was part of my therapy. To have to take care of something. I wanted to get a dog, that'd been my intention anyway, but when I went to the shelter Tally had just been brought in, abandoned on the side of the road by a supposed breeder because she was missing half her tail. I knew she was mine right away. Broken things tend to cling to broken things.

"Come on, Tally." I lay on the floor, peering under the couch to try and spot her gray colored fur. Big eyes blink owlishly back at me. "I'm sorry. I didn't mean to scare you, baby girl."

She sniffs my fingers, lets out a meow, and slowly crawls toward me until I can scoop her up.

I stand up with her cradled in my arms as I pad across to the small kitchen to grab a grape Fanta—damn you Ansel.

The studio apartment I'm renting is as tiny as they come, but it's clean, in a good area, and cheap enough that I can use what I earn to pay for it and not dig any more into my inheritance. I'm saving what's left for school loans and to buy that house on a farm some day. I know it's a big dream, but I'm going to make it happen.

Tally meows when I pop the tab on the can, glaring at me for the loud noise. "Sorry, girly." I let her onto the floor and she scampers over to the couch, waiting for me to lift her up. For some reason, maybe due to something that might've been done to her, she refuses to jump on anything like a normal cat.

I plunk her onto the couch and she darts over to her favorite blanket where she likes to hide the tiny blue mouse toy I got her.

Picking up the remote, I turn the TV on, flipping through the channels until I settle on a home improvement one.

I've been trying to learn some things so I'm better able to answer questions at the hardware store. I know the older man who owns it, Freddie, appreciates it. He didn't have an employee before me, he's been manning the store on his own all these years, but the day he decided to finally look for help was the day I walked in asking for a job. He must've saw something in me, because despite my lack of any kind of hardware knowledge, he took a chance.

Tally finds her mouse and brings it over to me, expecting praise for her 'kill'.

"You're such a good girl." I scratch behind her ear and she starts to purr. I love the way the fur around her ears sticks up in every direction. It makes her look crazed, like you never quite know what to expect from her.

My phone buzzes from one of the bags and I get up retrieving it.

Lachlan: I know you're it for me, but I understand if I'm not the one for you. You deserve to move on. I want you to be happy. That's all that matters. But I'll still be there. 4.22.21 47.6205 122.3493

I've puzzled out the first part, our birthday. I'll be twenty. Lachlan will be thirty-one. But the rest hasn't made sense to me. Until now.

"Oh my God," I mutter, copy and pasting the set of numbers into my phone. "Coordinates. Of course."

I'm an idiot.

When the browser shows me where the coordinates lead, my jaw drops.

He knew.

I book a plane ticket.

CHAPTER EIGHTY-TWO

I GET OFF THE PLANE WITH ONLY A BACKPACK STRAPPED to my back, filled with enough things for an overnight stay.

Lachlan didn't mention in his letter or his text what time he'd be there, but I think if our paths are meant to cross again the matter of time is irrelevant.

Exiting the airport, I find the Uber I booked waiting for me. Slipping in the car, I give him the address of where I want to go and then he cranks up the music, thankfully eliminating any need for conversation with him.

I watch out the window, at the city passing by. It's an oddly sunny day, with the barest hint of golden rays peeking out from between the gray clouds.

My heart is buzzing inside my chest with barely contained excitement and fear. I might be seeing Lachlan. I don't know what I'm going to do or say. I didn't want to rehearse anything ahead of time. That's inauthentic. Instead, I'm going to let the moment play out.

If you even see him, my mind reminds me.

I don't know why Lachlan didn't give a time, maybe he

didn't think, or maybe he's leaving it up to fate, I don't know. I didn't want to ask. Something made me refrain from texting him.

The Uber driver lets me out, muttering about hoping I enjoy the city, but his tone is far from sincere.

Hopping out, I hold onto my backpack straps. I feel like I might throw up, but I know that's only the nerves and not any actual sickness. Wiping my damp palms on the front of my ripped jeans, I walk across the street to a café. My stomach is grumbling, and even though food is the last thing on my brain I figure I should grab a muffin and coffee.

My shoes splash in a puddle, some of the water sprinkling onto my jeans, as I cross the street.

Opening the door into the café a bell chimes, signaling my arrival.

"Good morning!" A cheery woman behind the counter calls out despite the long line.

I shoot her a smile and get in line behind a tall man in a business suit, cell phone pressed to his ear as he rattles off about some board meeting.

Me: I landed.

Sage: You sure about this?

I bite my lip, hesitating before I text back.

Me: Yeah, I am.

Even if I don't see Lachlan, I have to try. If I didn't get on the plane today I know I would've regretted it.

Putting my phone in my pocket, I dig my wallet out from my backpack, grabbing a twenty. It's finally my turn and I order a cinnamon coffee and chocolate chip muffin. Chocolate makes everything better.

When my order is called out, I grab the coffee and paper bag. There are no empty tables in the café, so I head back across the street and manage to find a bench. Pulling the muffin out of the bag, I break a piece off and stick it in my mouth. It's still warm, the chocolate melting on my tongue.

Somehow, I manage to eat the entire thing—the power of chocolate—then I get up with my coffee clasped in my hand, walking around.

Seattle is beautiful. This is the first time I've been since I was seven, so I don't really remember it. The wind coming off the water whips my hair around my shoulders and I inhale the salty air.

Walking beneath the Space Needle, it looms above me like a behemoth.

Taking a sip of my coffee, I smile, thinking of all the places I've been in the last year.

It's ironic that I end up here, where technically it all began for Lachlan and me. We didn't know it at the time, but our paths crossed long before I stepped into his office. I was a seven-year-old little girl, tagging along with my mom and brother on his school's travel field trip, and there was Lachlan visiting at the same time with his family.

Suddenly, my heart rate doubles in speed and my steps halt. My grip loosens around the coffee cup and I nearly drop it, but thankfully manage to keep a hold on it before hot coffee gets all over my shoes.

It's like every cell in my body is waking up and they're all screaming, *he's here*.

I look around wildly, spinning in a circle.

Then, I see him.

My stomach flips. My breath falters. My heart ... I think it stops completely.

He stands a distance away, beneath the shadow of the Space Needle. A red baseball cap sits on his head, shielding his eyes, and his hands are tucked into his jeans, pulling his long-sleeve Henley tighter across his broad chest. Even though I can't see his eyes, and only half his face, I know it's him.

Lachlan.

Lachlan.

LACHLAN.

This time the coffee cup does fall from my hands, landing on the ground with my faded lipstick stain on the rim. I thought I'd be more dignified when I saw him. Walk up and have a conversation. It's been nearly a year since we've seen each other and I wanted to show him how much I've grown. I'm twenty today, I'm an adult, a woman. One who's traveled the world, who has her own place, a cat, and finally decided to get the help she really needed.

But I can't keep my wits about me. Not when the man I know I still love whole-heartedly, is finally in my line of sight.

He's everything I've ever wanted.

All I'll ever need.

My feet carry me across the space separating us. I run hard and fast, butterflies taking off in my stomach when I see the huge smile overcome his face.

His arms open and I barrel into him. I accidentally knock his hat off and it falls to the ground somewhere behind him. Tears dampen my cheeks and I bury my face into his neck, inhaling his heavenly scent that's uniquely him.

In that moment all my fears disappear about where we stand.

This is too perfect, too right, to ever be questioned.

We might have had to go our separate ways, but we are inevitable.

"Dani," he murmurs, his hands rubbing my back. "You're here."

"Don't ever let me go." I grip the back of his shirt tightly in my fist, scared if I release him this will all end up being a dream.

"Never again."

We cling to each other like our lives depend on it. I didn't realize it, but every day since I got on that plane and left the States has been leading to this. Every city, every adventure, every step forward, was to bring me back to him.

"I love you." I kiss his neck. "I love you." I kiss his cheek. "I love you."

"I need to see you. Please, let me look at you."

I let him set me on my feet. I hadn't even realized I wrapped my legs around his waist. Somehow he managed to keep us from toppling over when I mauled him.

Looking him over I realize that in the last year he's gotten even more muscular. His shoulders are bigger, his arms more muscular. His waist is tapered and from what I felt when he held me his abs are even more defined. His hair has grown a tad longer, more unkempt, but his scruff is the same, darkening his cheeks. The blue of his eyes is more vivid than I remember and it breaks my heart that my memories didn't do them justice. It killed me when I realized we had no pictures together, but when your relationship is a secret there can't be proof of your lies.

Even with the subtle changes he's still my Lachlan.

"You're so beautiful, Dani."

His hands settle on the small of my waist and I rest my hands on his chest, staring up at him.

"Are you really here?"

A deep chuckle rumbles in his throat. "I'm really here."

"You left me," I accuse, lower lip trembling.

He wipes my tears away with his thumbs. "I had to, Dani. I'm so fucking sorry."

I sniffle. "I know, but you could've told me."

He shakes his head, his eyes somehow sad and happy at the same time. "I wouldn't have been able to leave you if you asked me to stay, and you would have."

I look away, more tears forming. "You broke my heart."

"I didn't want to." He cups my cheek in one hand, pressing our foreheads together. "God, Dani, leaving you was the hardest thing I've ever done. But I knew I needed to give you room to grow. I was holding you together, but I wasn't solving the problem. I had to let you do it on your own."

"What if this year hasn't been enough? What if I'm still too broken?"

"I have faith in you, and if you still need time then I'll go away. But I'll be waiting until you're ready. And if you're never ready for me, or if you want someone else, like your friend, then that's okay too. I want what's best for *you*. I can't be selfish, not when your happiness means more to me than anything else." A shadow falls over his face. His thumb rubs in soothing circles against my cheek. "And if you've already moved on—"

"I haven't." I shake my head roughly. "That last text I sent you … it was because I was mad. I didn't even think you were reading them and if you were I wanted to make you jealous. Ansel and I … nothing ever happened."

"It's okay if it did."

"It didn't," I say, more for my benefit than his. "I … I wanted to feel something for him, but you can't force love, and a connection like ours…"

"It's once in a lifetime," he finishes for me, and then, blessedly, his lips are on mine.

My body melts into his, aching for his touch. We kiss like it's the first and last time. It's the kind of kiss everyone dreams of getting but doesn't seem to happen in real life, only the movies.

His fingers tangle in my hair, gripping the back of my neck as he holds me to him. My hands tremble where I grasp his face, kissing him with all the love that was absent from me without him.

His mouth leaves mine, and he stares down at me, his lips now slightly swollen and pinker than normal. "I love you, Dandelion Meadows. I wasn't expecting you. I sure as hell wasn't searching for you. But then there you were, standing in the doorway of my office with your wary eyes, and something about you spoke to me. The more you talked, the more I got to know you, and I found myself saying to myself this girl is mine."

"And you're *mine*," I nearly growl the last part, pulling his face back to mine because I need to feel his lips.

Our mouths move together in sync, anticipating one another with ease.

I should probably be embarrassed that we're making out like two horny teenagers in front of the Seattle Space Needle, but I can't bring myself to care.

I pull away from him suddenly with a gasp.

"W-What is it?" he stutters, blue eyes glazed with lust.

"You're loving me in the light."

He looks around, the sun glowing around us, strangers passing by and grins, his lips pulling up more on one corner.

"Well, would you look at that."

Then, he kisses me again, and I know without a doubt that we'll never have to hide in the dark again.

CHAPTER EIGHTY-THREE

AFTER I FORCE LACHLAN TO TAKE A SELFIE WITH ME, our first photo together as a couple, he leads me to a diner down the block. Inside, we grab a booth. I'm hardly hungry, but I know we need to catch up. There's so much to say, but there are no words on my tongue. I want to stare at him, study the minute details that have changed in our time apart.

A waitress comes over and Lachlan asks for two coffees to start.

He laces his fingers together, looking across at me the same way I can't help but stare at him.

I break the silence first. "When did you figure out about the Space Needle?"

I never told him about discovering myself in the photo in his office, but we wouldn't be here right now if he hadn't noticed it too.

"The same day you did. When I came into my office you were looking at the photo and you seemed as if you'd seen a ghost. Your skin was pale, almost clammy. When I looked at the photo I didn't notice it at first and put it away, but when you left for class, I sat there studying it. It was hard to make out your details, but I could tell it was you. I couldn't believe it, to be honest." He removes his hat from his head, scratching at his scalp. "It's crazy, isn't it? All those years ago and here we are now?"

"It's surreal."

I smile when the waitress sets down our coffees, promptly pouring a mountain of sugar and creamer in mine.

Tapping my fingers against the white ceramic mug, I say, "I think you should know, those texts I sent saying I hated you ... I never actually felt that way."

"It would be okay if you did. You didn't have to turn up today." He flicks his fingers lazily, acting very blasé but I can see through him, that he was terrified of what it would mean if I didn't.

"I threw your letter away," I admit, feeling a bit foolish. "Ansel found it and read it after I tossed it while we were in Paris. He gave it back to me before I got on the plane to return home. It reaffirmed for me the reasons I was coming back." Shaking my head, a small laugh leaves me. "I can't believe I took that letter with me, to all those different countries. I don't know why but I couldn't leave it at Sage's. My therapist would probably say something cheesy about how it was all I had left of you and I needed it close."

"I'm sorry I had to leave you." He places his hand over mine on the table. "You're seeing a therapist, though?"

"Yeah, she's great. It was tough in the beginning but it's been easier to open up to her than I expected. It's helping a lot." I tuck a piece of hair behind my ear, suddenly feeling nervous. I still don't like to talk about my therapy and I hate that I feel some kind of shame for it, because there's nothing to be ashamed of when it comes to getting the help you desperately need. "I'm driving again, got my own place too." He grins at that news. "Oh, and I have a cat. Wanna see?"

Before he can answer I pull my phone out and show him a picture of Tally.

"She's adorable." His smile lights up his whole face.

"Think Zeppelin would get along with her?"

"He'd love her."

"Wait, are you living in Seattle now?"

The thought suddenly occurs to me that he might've moved here.

He shakes his head. "I'm still in Utah, just outside the city. I bought a house there, it's small but it's home. What about you?"

"I'm renting an apartment in the city near the university."

"Are you taking classes?" He arches a brow, looking pleased.

"I start in the fall."

"Have you decided what you want to do?"

I wipe up some drops of coffee with my napkin. "I think I'm going to go into Marketing. I'm not sure if I'll stick with it, but right now it seems like something I'd enjoy." Clearing my throat, I ask, "Where are you working now?"

"At a youth center. I do counseling there and I also coach the basketball team."

A smile bursts free of me. "That's amazing, Lachlan. I'm so happy for you."

The waitress stops by again. "Is there anything else I can get you guys?"

"Do you have any cake?" Lachlan asks.

She smiles. "Yes, we do. It's freshly made. Chocolate cake with fudge icing."

"We'll have two slices, please." She starts to walk away but he calls after her. She pauses, turning around. "You wouldn't happen to have two candles would you?"

"Oh, someone's birthday?" She smiles pleasantly, looking between us.

"Both of ours."

"You have the same birthday? That's neat. I'll see if I can find any." She turns, heading back to the kitchen.

Tapping my fingers on the table, he watches the gesture, no doubt picking up on how nervous I am. It's beyond dumb. This man has had his mouth on my vagina for God's sake.

Although, maybe that is why I'm so nervous. He knows me in the most intimate ways, not just my body, but the inner workings of my mind.

"Thinking about something?" he prompts.

"It's ... where do things go from here with us? What are we? A couple?"

He leans back in the booth, appraising me. "We're whatever you want us to be. We can take things slowly." Leaning forward, he rests his arms on the table. "I've waited this long, I can wait some more for us to figure it out."

"That sounds good to me."

The waitress sets down our pieces of cake, a single candle in each, and lights them. "Happy birthday, guys. I'd sing but you don't want that."

"Make a wish."

I look across at him with a mischievous grin. "Don't tell me what to do, old man."

He groans, closing his eyes. "Don't remind me."

"You're thirty-one, and I think that's hot. Makes you distinguished."

He chuckles. "Whatever you say."

We both close our eyes, blowing out the candles. I don't make a wish, not when I can safely say I'm happy and there's not anything else I could possibly want. I'm healthy, I'm thriving, my brother's in a good place, and the love of my life is sitting across from me.

Opening my eyes, I meet the ones shining across from me. "When we get back to Utah can I take you on a date? A real date?"

My breath catches. "I'd like that."

I try to act cool, but there's a part of me screaming on the inside that Lachlan asked me to go on an actual date with him.

"Will I need to dress up on this date?" I ask, taking a bite of cake. I nearly moan. It's one of the best cakes I've ever tasted.

"Do you want to get dressed up?" I nod. Call it cliché, but I want to spend hours doing my hair and makeup, picking out a dress, the whole shebang. "Then definitely."

"You know," I fight a smile, looking at my slice of cake, "I promised you last year that I'd make you a cake for your birthday. Sorry that plan fell through."

"Well, we always have next year." He says it with such confidence that it fills my whole body with joy at the prospect of all the things to come.

"When are you flying back to Salt Lake?" I wipe some icing from the corner of my mouth and lick it off my finger. Lachlan's eyes dilate as he watches.

"Tomorrow."

"Me too. Where are you staying? I haven't booked anything yet."

"A hotel near the wharf." He finishes his slice of cake, pushing the now empty plate away.

"Can I stay with you?" I hedge. "Or you know, it's

okay if you don't want that. Never mind, I can get my own hotel room. Don't mind me."

"Dani," Lachlan says with a laugh, trying to quiet me, "of course you can stay with me."

I blow out a breath. "Thank you."

With our cake gone, Lachlan pays and takes my hand, leading me out onto the Seattle streets.

"Let me show you the city, beautiful."

I can't stop my smile, my hand tightening around his.

Best. Birthday. Ever.

———

AFTER SPENDING our day cruising around Seattle, seeing as much as we possibly can, we don't get back to the hotel until after dark.

Lachlan insists I shower first, so I shut myself in the bathroom, shrugging off my backpack. Standing in front of the lighted mirror, I smile.

I'm in Seattle.

With Lachlan.

Today was better than I could've imagined. This morning when I got off the plane I wasn't sure what would happen, or even what to expect. Being with Lachlan is easy. It's like we've known each other our whole lives. We laughed, talked, and teased each other. I also stuffed myself with way too many sweets today.

Trying to force myself to stop smiling, I grab the hotel provided shampoo, conditioner, and body wash so I can clean up.

When I've showered I change into the tank top and shorts I packed for sleeping. It's ridiculous how nervous I feel stepping out of the bathroom. It's not like I'm in my underwear, or naked, and Lachlan's seen me both ways anyway.

I find Lachlan sitting on the end of the king size bed, texting on his phone.

He looks up when he hears me, his eyes scanning me from my toes—painted a green shade called Shake Your $ Maker—all the way up until his blue eyes meet my hazel ones.

"Feeling any guilt about being here with me?" I try to make my question sound light, but I need to know his answer. I know there's no hope for us moving forward if he's always going to feel guilty for his feelings.

He shakes his head. "Come here." He crooks a finger.

I do as he says, standing between his spread legs. He places his hands on my hips, fingers splaying until they're on my ass.

"We didn't have appropriate beginnings, but the feelings were real, and despite it all I wouldn't change a thing as long as it means at the end of the day I get to love you."

"Lachlan." Damn him, he's going to make me cry again.

Even though he's sitting, we're nearly the same height and he cups my cheek in one hand.

"I'm yours as long as you'll have me."

I place my hands on his shoulders. "And if I want you forever?"

A slow smile lifts his lips. "Then I'd say that sounds pretty perfect."

I lean in, kissing him. I don't ever want to stop kissing him. I want the world to know this man is mine, that our love is undeniable.

"I love you," I murmur between our pressed lips.

He hums low in his throat. "I love you, too."

Pulling away, I admit with a sigh, "I need to call my brother."

Lachlan groans, biting his lip. "Does he know?"

I nod. "He figured it out after you left."

Lachlan stands, a sigh billowing from his chest. "Bet he wants to kill me."

"He used to." There's no sense in sugarcoating it. "But I think he's coming around." Lachlan gives me a look that says *yeah right.* "We've talked about it a lot the last couple of weeks, and I'm not saying he approves of you but ... he understands. He knows I love you and that I choose you and that's all that matters."

"That simple, huh?" His lips threaten to tug into a crooked grin.

I fiddle with the edge of a pillowcase beside the bed. "Why complicate it when you don't have to?"

"That's smart. You're ... you're different, and I mean that in a good way."

I smile at the love of my life. "I'm trying. One day at a time. One step. One moment. The past doesn't have to be an anchor, it can be your wings."

"Fuck, you're killing me," he growls, crossing the few feet separating us. His fingers dive into my hair and then his lips are on mine once more. He pulls away quickly. "I need to go shower before I do something stupid."

"Something stupid?" I repeat, slightly offended.

He rubs his jaw. "I mean ... I want to do this *right* with you. I want to take my time. I don't want to rush you into anything. Besides, I owe you a real date first."

I laugh softly, shaking my head. "I think it's a bit late for that."

He points a finger at me with a playful smile. "You have a point, but I'm not touching you. Not tonight."

I pout. "You suck."

He backs toward the bathroom. "Again, not tonight."

My jaw drops and I grab one of the pillows, throwing it at him.

His laughter booms in the room as he dodges it.

It's so easy between us, like no time at all has passed, only this time we're able to be free.

"Go shower, you smell like you're full of shit."

He laughs again, closing the bathroom door.

While he's showering I turn back the bed and then call my brother.

"So, are you mooning over the Lach-ness Monster?" he asks as soon as he answers.

"Sage," I admonish, trying not to laugh.

"It's a valid question, Weed."

"I guess, technically yes."

"You're going to marry this guy one day and force me to like him aren't you?"

"Eventually ... yes."

"Fuck."

"Get over it, Herb. You're boinking my eighteen-year-old friend."

He fake gags. "Never, ever, say the word *boink* again."

"Whatever you say."

"When do I get to meet Nessie in person?"

"*Sage.*" I cover my mouth to hold in my laughter. "Um ... I'm not sure, but we'll plan something soon, okay?"

"Mhmm," he hums. "Tell Lach-ness I'll be preparing a list of questions."

"You do that."

"I love you, D. Be careful, okay?"

"I will. I love you, too. I'll let you know when I get on the plane tomorrow."

After a few more words we hang up.

The bathroom door opens, and I look up in time to see

Lachlan step out in only a towel. The white cotton looks like a small puff of air would send it falling from his lean frame.

"Forgot my pants."

"I bet you did," I grumble and he chuckles, grabbing a pair of sleep pants and disappearing into the bathroom again.

I pout to myself, disappointed I'll be missing the strip show.

Plugging my phone in to charge, I climb into bed.

The bathroom door squeaks and Lachlan emerges, his large shoulders nearly touching the doorframe. My mouth waters at the sight of his bare chest. I'm pathetic, I know, but it's been way too long since I had my eyes on him.

Lachlan gets into bed beside me, reaching over to flick off the light.

Rolling onto his side to face me in the now dark room, he says, "Are you going to stay all the way over there?"

I don't have to be told twice.

I scoot across the wide expanse of bed until inches separate us. I press my toes to his leg and he exclaims, "How are your toes freezing?"

"I don't know."

He wraps his arms around me, rolling over so he's on his back and I'm cradled against him with my head on his chest. Not able to control myself I rub my fingers over his light dusting of chest hair.

"I love you," I whisper against his heated skin.

His lips press against the top of my head. "I love you, too."

I close my eyes, a smile on my lips, as I fall into a peaceful sleep.

CHAPTER EIGHTY-FOUR

When we land back in Salt Lake Lachlan insists on driving me home, since he left his car there while I had taken a taxi to the airport.

I don't know why, but I feel nervous about him seeing my space. He never saw my room at Sage's, and it wasn't very *me* anyway. But at the urging of my therapist I've put my mark on my apartment as much as I can with it being a rental. I know my eclectic, bohemian style isn't for everyone and that's fine, but Lachlan isn't just anyone.

I give him directions to my place and where to park.

He takes my backpack from me, even though I'm very capable of carrying it myself, then clutches my hand as I lead him up the winding stairs to my home.

Holding my breath, I unlock the door, stepping aside to let him in.

It's a studio, so my bedroom is open to the rest of the place, but I didn't see the need to have anything bigger with it being Tally and me.

As if conjured by my thoughts the kitten who looks like she stuck her paw in an electric socket the way her fur always sticks up, comes slithering out from beneath the couch with a loud meow. The couch is her safe spot when I'm not home. I had Sasha come by yesterday to check on her and refill her bowls and it looks like Tally barely touched them.

"This is Tally," I say to Lachlan, bending to scoop her up as he closes the door, looking around. "She's not usually too fond of other people." I don't want him to be offended if she hisses or tries to scratch him.

"Hi, Tally." He rubs the top of her head. She leans into his touch, purring. My jaw drops. "Traitor," I mutter at my cat. "But don't worry," I look up at Lachlan, "he has that same effect on me."

I swear Lachlan blushes at that.

"This place is nice." He looks around at the mix of woods, fabrics, colors, and textures that make up everything. It's a hodge-podge but it's *me* and I'm a kaleidoscope.

"Thanks." I try to view the space from his eyes.

He grins as he looks at the immaculate kitchen—so neat and tidy because the only thing I use is the refrigerator and microwave.

"Still can't cook can you?" A grin stretches his lips.

I rock back and forth on my heels, toeing my orange Nikes into the floor—an upgrade from my Vans. "No. I haven't mastered the art of not burning things yet."

He smiles, eyes soft as he looks at me. "I can fix that."

I arch a brow. "You're going to teach me to cook?"

"Why not?" He shrugs, holding his hands out for Tally. I hand her over hesitantly, worried her niceness might disappear, but she goes to him easily, cuddling against his massive chest. She looks tiny in his arms. "We can do that now."

I laugh, tucking a piece of hair behind my ear, a

nervous gesture because I'm still a bit in awe that Lachlan Taylor is standing in my apartment. "I keep forgetting we have all the time in the world."

He reaches out with one arm, using the other to hold Tally in the crook of his elbow, and pulls me against him. "We have a lot to make up for."

I look up at him with my chin against his chest. "Like what?"

"Like that proper date I owe you for starters."

My body heats at the mention of a real date with Lachlan. My last date was years ago when I was a junior in high school, and something tells me a date with Lachlan will be vastly different than going to the movies and having a guy try to stick his hand down my shirt.

He passes Tally back to me, kissing me quickly but sweetly before we can get carried away. "I better go. But I'll text you the details." He heads for the door, pausing with it open. "And Dani?" He looks over his shoulder at me.

"Yeah?" My voice sounds soft and airy. I curse myself for being so affected by him.

"Nice collection."

He tips his head at the collection of books slowly growing on the bookcase beside my TV. With those words, he heads out.

"Tally," I whisper into her soft fur, "I love that man."

Setting her down, I pick up my backpack to unpack and put my dirty clothes in the laundry—thankfully my apartment does have a washer and dryer in a tiny little closet. I've barely loaded the washer with my dirty things when there's a knock on the door.

Grinning like a fool, I run to answer it.

"Did you forget something?"

But it's not Lachlan on the other side. It's Sage.

"Oh, hey." I step back, letting my brother in.

He looks around. "The Lach-ness Monster isn't here?"

"You missed him."

"Hmm," he harrumphs. "Such a shame. Would you think he's as good-looking with a black eye?" He cocks his head to the side, waiting for my response.

"Sage," I groan. "Play nice."

"He's not even here," he grumbles.

"Is that for me?" I eye the package in his hand.

"It's your birthday present, since you know, you ran off to meet that dickwad on your actual birthday."

I take the small box from him, setting it on the coffee table. I know it's going to be one hell of an uphill battle getting Sage to like Lachlan.

Sage sits down on the couch, stretching his legs out. Tally hisses from beneath it.

Hands on my hips, I face my brother. "I love him." He looks up at me with an aggravated look. "I know things between us shouldn't have happened the way they did, I'm not that naïve, but they did. Regardless, he's the man I love, and we're together. I hope we're together for a very long time. I'm not saying you have to love him, or even like him, but please for my benefit, be cordial whenever you do see him."

My brother's jaw twitches. "Can I at least punch him once? One teeny-tiny black eye won't kill the dude."

"No," I say firmly. "I'm twenty, Sage. I'm living on my own. I'm seeing a therapist. I'm going to start college in the fall. I'm *working* on myself and you have to trust that I know what's best for me, and Lachlan…" I can't stop the smile that lifts my lips. "He's the one."

"Fuck." My brother groans, rubbing his hands on the legs of his jeans. "I'll … grudgingly accept the guy the best I can, but don't for a minute think this means I approve of this. I know Sasha is younger than me, but she's nineteen and I'm twenty-seven. That's eight years compared to eleven and she wasn't underage—"

"I wasn't either," I defend.

He narrows his eyes. "You were a *student*. It doesn't matter that you were eighteen. You were still off-limits to him."

I bow my head, because I know he has a point and I don't want to get in a shouting argument with my brother.

"I see your point," I say instead.

He exhales a heavy sigh, looking at me sadly, no doubt thinking of all the things I've been through the last two years. "Because he makes you happy, I'll try my hardest to be on my best behavior."

"Thank you. That's all I ask."

"Now open your present." He picks the package up from the table and extends it to me.

Taking it from him, I sit down beside him, ripping off the paper.

Inside the box, I reveal a wind chime. This one with monuments from different European cities for the chimes. As I study each one, I realize there's something from every country I visited.

"Sage?"

"I had it custom made," he explains. "It seemed pretty perfect for you."

My mouth opens and closes, but no words came out. "I … thank you."

I place it back in the box, closing it, before finally hugging my brother. He holds me tight. "I love you, Weed."

"Love you more, Herb."

"We have to stick together."

I smile at him, nodding. "Always."

CHAPTER EIGHTY-FIVE

SEVERAL DAYS LATER, I'M BUSY GETTING READY FOR MY first date with Lachlan.

Rubbing some product into my hair, I bend over, shaking it out. My heart won't stop racing with a mix of nerves and excitement. He won't tell me where we're going, which has only piqued my curiosity even more.

Standing back up, I make sure my loose natural waves look decent and aren't a frizzball. My makeup is simple, like I normally do—mascara, the barest hint of highlighter on my cheekbones, and a soft pink gloss that makes my lips look fuller.

With my hair done, I spray some perfume on my wrists and pad out of the bathroom to the dress I laid on the bed.

The black velvet dress with deep pink roses isn't what I'd normally wear, but since he said to dress up, I'm going for it. The sleeves are sheer, and it's shorter in the front than the back. Slipping on the black-heeled boots, I look at myself in the floor length mirror. I don't look too bad.

"I'm going to be out for a bit," I tell Tally. She cracks

one eye open where she sleeps on my bed. "Hold down the fort while I'm gone."

There's a knock on the door and when I look at my phone, he's right on time.

I can't stop smiling as I walk across to my front door and swing it open.

"Hey, Superman," I murmur, biting my lip. Lachlan looks delectable in a pair of gray slacks and a white button down shirt. The sleeves are rolled to his elbows, showing the corded veins running up his arms.

"You look beautiful." He leans in, kissing my cheek. "These are for you." He passes me a bouquet of flowers. It's an assortment of types I've never seen and absolutely stunning.

"Oh let me put these in some water. They're gorgeous, Lachlan."

He follows me over to my kitchen where I have to put water in a cup since I don't own any vases.

"Next time, I'll bring you a vase."

I arch a brow. "Are you going to bring flowers every time?"

He grins at me. "Only if you want me to."

"I want you to."

He chuckles, placing his hand on my waist. "We better go. My friend is doing me a favor."

"You have me very curious about this date."

"I had to make it special."

"You could take me to McDonald's and I'd be thrilled. I just want to be with you." I lock the door behind us and we start down the stairs to the parking lot.

"I'm not taking you to McDonald's for our first date. Besides, you said you wanted to get dressed up."

"I did say that. McDonald's for the second, then?" I joke.

"Maybe." He winks.

He opens the passenger door of his Acura for me and I hold onto the skirt of my dress so I don't flash anyone.

We don't say much on the drive through the city. We end up near the art museum, but a couple of streets over. He parallel parks and lets me out before putting change in the meter.

"Where are we going?" I giggle, taking his hand and letting him lead me down the street.

"You'll see soon enough."

He reaches for the door to a bookshop and I tug on his hand. "It's closed."

He grins at me over his shoulder. "Not for us."

Before I can ask him what he means, he swings the door open, tugging me inside with him.

"Donovan, where are you, man?"

We pass rows and rows of bookshelves until we reach a back corner.

My breath catches at the sight of the table set for two, candles and flowers in the center of it, with soft music playing in the background.

"Everything is ready." A guy around Lachlan's age pops around a corner.

"Thanks, man." Lachlan gives him one of those weird handshake guy hugs.

"I'm going to head out." Donovan smiles at me with a little wave before vanishing down one of the rows.

"Who is that guy?"

"Friend from college," he explains, pulling out a chair at the table for me to sit down. "He owns the place." Once I'm seated he says, "Hold on."

He disappears through a door, returning a moment later with two plates of food.

"What is this?" I ask, looking from him to the food and then around the store.

Setting the food down, he waits until he sits to explain. "I wanted to do something special for our first date. Something you wouldn't forget."

"I wouldn't have forgotten McDonald's either, but this is *way* better."

"Books were one of the things that brought us together. It seemed fitting to begin again here."

"Did you make the food?" I look down at my plate of some kind of fancy looking fish, asparagus, potatoes, and even a little salad drizzled with balsamic.

He nods, pouring us each a glass of wine. "I probably shouldn't be serving a minor wine, but we've already broken a lot of rules, what's one more?"

I laugh, taking my half full glass from him to take a sip. "I drank wine with almost every meal in Europe, so I'm used to it and actually enjoy it. Now, if we get raided by cops, then you're screwed."

He chuckles, shaking his head. "God, this is strange. Is it weird for you too?"

"A little," I admit. "I got used to spending all our time in your apartment that it's kind of odd to ... exist like normal people."

His smile falls a little. "You don't think that was part of it, do you? The secrecy?"

"What? That the secrecy made me want to be with you?" He nods. "Definitely not. It was you I wanted, not the thrill."

His body eases at that. "Hopefully you enjoy the meal. I wasn't sure what to make."

"It's not burnt so you already have bonus points." I take a bite of fish, moaning at the flavor. "Oh my God, this is fantastic. You definitely have to teach me to cook."

His eyes crinkle at the corners. "I told you I would."

"This is all so unbelievable." I keep looking around the store, the lights are dimmed, making it even cozier. "Do I get to pick a book to take with me? I need a memento from our first official date."

He wipes his mouth with a napkin, his lips upturned in amusement. "Sure. I can settle it with Donovan later."

"I know my brother is going to want to meet you soon," I hedge, nervous to broach this topic.

Lachlan cocks his head to the side. "Understandable. Do you have any ideas?"

"Well, I think it should take place on neutral ground, so that eliminates meeting at any of our homes." Biting my lip, I think. "What about the art museum? It's one of my favorite places, and since it's a museum he'll have to keep his volume at a lower level."

Lachlan's smile falls. "He's never going to like me, is he?"

"I don't know. He's a softy, but I'm his little sister. The one he was tasked with raising for a year, and I think he feels like he failed."

"Because of me." It's a statement not a question.

"For multiple reasons. He's too hard on himself."

Lachlan takes my hand, our joined fingers resting on top of the table. "I want to meet him and get to know him, but if he never likes me are you okay with that?"

I blink at Lachlan. "He's my brother, not my keeper. He's important to me, and of course I'd like for things to be cordial, but I'm not naïve either. It'll take time."

His lips twitch into a smile once more, his blue eyes twinkling. "And we have a lot of that now, don't we?"

Time is fleeting, there's not an infinite amount. I know that better than most. Any moment can be your last. It's taught me to treasure every minute, every moment, because you never know when it'll end.

"We have what we have. Life's too short to worry about other's people's opinions. Even my brother's."

Lachlan holds up his pinky. "Pinky promise you're okay with it?"

I loop my finger around his, grinning, because this is the first time he's asked me to make a pinky promise. I know he doesn't want to come between my brother and me. It's sweet, but Sage will come around eventually.

"Pinky promise."

Finishing our meal, we clean up together—Lachlan doesn't want me to help, but I refuse to sit still doing nothing.

Once everything is clean, he turns me loose to pick out a book.

He follows behind me as I scan the shelves, looking for the book I want. He doesn't say anything as I search, just lets me do my thing.

I finally find it and pull it out with a flourish, turning the cover so he can see.

George Orwell's 1984 was the start of it all in a way. Why not continue the tradition?

"That's the one you want?"

"Absolutely. Do you have a pen?"

He digs in his pockets but comes up empty. "Donovan probably has one at the register."

Sure enough he finds a black Sharpie. I take it from him and scribble on the front page our names and today's date.

"Are you happy?" Lachlan asks me, his eyes darkening.

"Very." It's not a lie. I haven't been this happy in a long time. There's a weight gone from my chest, a burden I carried ever since the shooting. I know I'll never be the same Dandelion Meadows again, but she's still a version of me, like the broken girl Lachlan first met was another version, and the woman standing in front of him now is another incarnation. It's all me, just different pieces.

He takes my face in his hands, cradling it like he loves to do, and slants his mouth over mine. The kiss is slow and deep. I feel it everywhere, buzzing in my veins.

Even though I can't predict time, and how much of it we have, I hope there are many more moments ahead where I feel this happy and loved.

As Lachlan gazes down at me like he's holding his entire world between his hands, I don't think I have anything to worry about.

CHAPTER EIGHTY-SIX

IT'S A WEEK LATER BEFORE EVERYONE'S SCHEDULES align to meet up at the art museum. Thankfully, Sasha will be coming too and I know she'll be a great buffer for my brother with Lachlan. He won't want to act like too much of an ass in front of his girlfriend.

God, I still can't believe those two are a couple, though in the last month since I showed up at Sage's, and I've been around them more, I see how they work together. He mellows her out and she brings out his silly side that's been missing since the shooting. It's nice seeing a light in his eyes again that I hadn't even noticed had been extinguished. Like me, though, he finally admitted that he started to see a therapist about a month after I left the States. It's really helped him and his progress gives me hope for my own.

I wait outside the apartment complex, too nervous to wait inside. I pace the walkway out front, eyes searching for Lachlan's Acura to pull into the lot.

"I'm literally sweating," I mutter to myself, wrinkling

my nose in disgust at my wet pits. "That's gross. Maybe I should change my shirt."

I know if anyone's watching me I look like a crazy person, or maybe like I'm on drugs, but I can't bring myself to care because my brother is about to meet Lachlan. Lachlan is going to meet my brother. It's like I've stepped into an alternate universe.

I know technically they've met before, but passing by on the street barely counts.

I spot Lachlan's car, and cease my pacing, though I'm sure he's already seen.

He pulls up in front of me and I reach for the door, hurrying inside. The sooner we get this over with the better.

"Nervous?" he asks with a chuckle as I slide the seatbelt across my body.

There's no denying it. "You have no idea."

He heads for the exit, his gaze flickering my way. "It's going to be fine, Dani. I'm not sure about great, or even good, but it'll be fine."

"Fine," I repeat. "I'm okay with fine." Fine would mean no punches are thrown and no threats are made. "Will you pinky promise on it?"

He holds his pinky out, watching the stoplight leading out of my apartment complex. "Pinky promise."

I seal the promise with my finger. "If it doesn't go okay, it's your fault now."

He laughs, placing his hand on my leg. "I understand why you're worried. I'm nervous too, but the sooner we do this the better."

I hope he's right.

The drive to the art museum takes thirty minutes since I now live on the opposite side of the city, but I wish it was longer. I've barely gotten myself under control when Lachlan parks his car.

We get out, heading across the street to where we're supposed to meet out front by my favorite horse sculpture.

Lachlan faces me, rubbing my arms to try to soothe me. "Stop worrying, baby." My body warms at the endearment. He tips my chin up with a finger. "I made a pinky promise, remember?"

"Yeah." The single word is so low it's barely audible, but he smiles so I know he heard me.

His lips press softly to my forehead and I inhale a shaky breath, trying to steady myself for the storm named Sage.

Sure, enough, my brother chooses now to show up.

"Hands off my sister, Lach-ness."

"Lach-ness?" Lachlan mouths to me.

"I'll explain later."

Despite Sage's barking orders, Lachlan doesn't let me go. He holds my hand so we face my brother and Sasha head on.

"It's nice to meet you." Lachlan holds out his hand.

Sage glares at it and then up at Lachlan. "I'm not shaking your hand. You touched my sister with that hand when she was your fucking student."

"Sage," I hiss.

"He's right," Lachlan says, squeezing the hand of mine he holds, letting his other drop back to his side. "Look," he addresses my brother, "I know I've done wrong, I won't deny that, but I love your sister and I'll do whatever it is you need me to do in order to prove I'm sincere."

Sage makes a noise in the back of his throat and turns sharply on his heel, heading for the museum entrance. "A fucking art museum," he grumbles like we can't hear him, "only my sister would force me to meet her old man lover at an *art museum*. I miss the French douchebag."

Sasha presses her lips together, trying not to laugh as the three of us follow after Sage.

Sage holds the door open for Sasha, but heads in behind her, blocking us from going.

"I'm going to kill him," I seethe, glaring at his retreating figure. "I'm going to bury him six feet under somewhere no one will find him."

Lachlan grins down at me. "You'd never."

He's right, I wouldn't hurt a fly, but right now I wouldn't mind kicking my brother in the ass.

Lachlan opens the door for me, letting me in first.

Sage and Sasha are already in the first gallery when we catch up to them.

"So what are you doing for work now since you quit before you could get fired like a total pussy."

"Sage!" I cry, my fists clenching at my sides. "I'm going to throat punch you."

Lachlan squeezes my hand, silently telling me it's okay, but it's not. I know we're fighting an uphill battle with my brother, but he doesn't have to be such a dick.

"I'm working at a local youth center. Still counseling and I'm coaching basketball there."

Sage sneers, looking my boyfriend up and down. "Still around kids then, I see."

"Hey, cut it out," Sasha scolds him.

The tightness in his face relaxes some, but not a whole lot. "Just trying to get to know Lach-ness."

"Sage!" Sasha and I both scream at him this time.

We're probably so close to being kicked out and we only got here.

"Oh, I get it now." Lachlan's lips twitch. "Like the Loch Ness Monster."

"Exactly." Sage grins.

"That's funny."

"None of this is funny." I look up at Lachlan, offended he's amused by my brother's antics.

Lachlan gives my hand another squeeze before letting go. "Why don't you ladies go look around and leave Sage and I to have a chat?"

My eyes go wide. "Are you crazy?" I hiss.

Lachlan has a death wish.

"It'll be fine."

Sage looks shocked by this turn of events. "Uh…"

"That sounds like a great idea." Sasha reaches out for my arm, dragging me away from the two men. "We'll be … somewhere."

I reluctantly allow her to pull me away and up the stairs to the second level of the gallery. She finds a corner with a bench, sitting down.

"Are you crazy? Sage is going to kill him."

She waves a dismissive hand. "You know your brother wouldn't *actually* hurt him even if he wants to. But I think it's important for your brother to get some things off his chest."

"You're right." I hate admitting it, but she has a point. I know there are bound to be things Sage needs to say without me breathing down both their necks. "I still can't believe you're dating my brother."

She laughs, her cheeks flushed. "Me either, to be honest. It just kind of happened."

"I know how that goes," I sigh.

"Still can't believe you banged the guidance counselor."

"Oh, ew, please don't say it like that. That's gross."

"Did you guys ever have sex at school?"

"No!" I blurt out. "God, no. That's … *no*."

She smiles at me, her eyes bright and happy. "Sorry, I was curious so I had to ask."

"Are things good with you and Sage?"

Even though I've been around them since I made my announcement that I was home, I haven't had any opportunities to speak to Sasha one on one.

"They're really good. He gets me, that sounds so cliché but it's true."

"I like seeing him happy—both of you happy."

"You're not mad about it, right? I'm so sorry you found out like you did. I know we aren't as close as you and Ansel, but we're still friends. I hated keeping it a secret from you, but Sage wanted to be the one to tell you and he kept putting it off."

"I mean, it's a little weird." I feel the need to be honest. "But no, I'm not mad. Sage deserves to be happy and you do too. I'm glad you found each other like..."

"Like you and Lachlan?" She finishes for me with a kind smile.

Sasha is a lot calmer now than she used to be, almost motherly in some ways.

"Yeah." I rub my hands on my jeans. "I love him so much sometimes it scares me."

"Love is scary. I think that's why so many people are afraid of it. But it's worth it."

We hear a commotion then and turn to see the two men climbing the stairs, talking like old buddies. Sage still has some tension around his eyes and mouth, and I can tell from the set of Lachlan's shoulders that he's not totally relaxed, but it's better than them pushing and screaming at each other. Not that I would expect Lachlan to do that sort of thing, but Sage? Most definitely.

Sasha stands up, almost gliding over to my brother's side. Over her shoulder she tosses me a wink before taking his hand and pulling him to a painting down the way she tells him he has to see, despite the fact she's never seen it herself as far as I know.

Lachlan walks over to me, sitting down on the bench and stretching his long legs out.

"How'd it go?" I hate that I'm scared to ask, but I have to know.

Lachlan angles his head down to me, his eyes void of any joking light but he doesn't seem pissed either. "Not bad. We had a good chat."

"A good chat?" I repeat, wrinkling my nose. "What does that mean?"

"It means I let him talk and I listened and then I talked and he listened."

I narrow my eyes. "You're not going to give me any details, are you?"

"Nope." He stands up, holding his hand out. I take it, but when he tries to lead me away, I hold my ground.

"I need more than that, Lachlan."

He runs his fingers through his hair before rubbing his jaw. "It wasn't bad, okay, but I'm never going to be your brother's first choice for you. Are you okay with that?"

I look from Lachlan down to the end of the room where Sage stands with Sasha looking at another painting. "I am." My answer is sure. I don't have any doubts. "But are you okay with that?" I counter, because I know it has to bother him.

"You're what matters to me most, Dani."

Stretching up on my toes, I kiss him. I don't care who sees or if it pisses my brother off.

"I love you."

"Love you, too," he murmurs, holding me close.

Within the warmth of his body, I feel safe, like I'm home, and I know everything is going to be okay.

I know I'll never forget that day.

I'll never forget the loss of my mom. Of the other lives lost that day.

I won't forget the recovery, the tears, the pain.

But I *will* move on. I *am* moving on.

With every smile, every laugh, I'm not letting that day hold me prisoner anymore. I know I'll always have my moments where dark clouds might block my sunny day, but it's okay. Life is meant to be lived, and I'm finally doing that again.

I once thought that Lachlan was the sun and I was the rain. That there was no happy ending for us.

I was wrong.

There's always a chance for a happy ending, but you have to choose it.

And I do.

I choose this life.

I choose him.

I choose *us*.

And that's a pinky promise.

EPILOGUE

THREE YEARS LATER

I DIDN'T WANT TO DO THE BIG WEDDING THING, WITH the poufy dress, the guests, all the hoopla. But Lachlan insisted that we were doing this right. He said that being able to love in the light meant he wanted to watch me walk down the aisle in a dress to him. I couldn't argue with that — I did have one stipulation though. Well, two.

The first was I wanted to get married in Scotland, it was the root of his heritage, a place he'd never been, and neither had I, because even when I started on my trip across Europe almost four years ago I'd known then that Scotland belonged to him. Now, it would belong to the both of us.

The second was, I wanted him to wear a kilt.

He thought I was kidding.

I wasn't.

"You sure you want to do this?" I roll my eyes at the sound of my brother's voice. He steps up beside me in the little home we rented at the venue for everyone to get ready. "There's a loch nearby, maybe Lach-ness can join his girl Nessie."

"Sage," I groan, punching him lightly in the arm, "that's my soon-to-be-husband you're talking about."

Husband. My stomach dips with excitement at that one word.

"Still can't believe you guys are getting married on your birthdays. You already have the same birthdays, now it's going to be your anniversary? It's weird as hell."

"It's what we wanted."

It already seemed ironic enough that we share the same birthday, it only seemed fitting to get married today too. I definitely never thought I'd be getting married at twenty-three, but here we are. Life is defined by the unexpected.

Walking away from Sage, I look at myself in the mirror one last time.

I knew the white tulle dress was the one as soon as I saw it. With flowers appliqued to the bottom, hip area, and top I was enamored from the start. It reminded me of my prom dress in some ways, but this was simpler, the skirt not quite as full, and I knew my brother wasn't a fan of the plunging neckline, but Lachlan was going to die.

My hair is curled, a few pieces pulled back with fresh flowers woven through the strands. My makeup is barely noticeable, soft and natural. I wanted to look like *me* today. Not some glammed up version of me I'd probably never see again.

"Hey, it's time." Sasha pokes her head in the door, her skin glowing. She looks happy, and I'm glad the two of them seem to be figuring things out. They've broken up twice in the last three years, but honestly they're perfect for each other and too stubborn to take the next step.

Sage holds his elbow out to me. "Let's do this thing, Weed."

I loop my hand around his arm. "You gonna be okay letting me go, Herb?"

The lines by his eyes deepen, a frown forming on his lips. "No." He wets his lips, staring down at me in a way I know he's thinking of how much I've grown. "You're my little sister, it's hard to watch you live your own life. But I am happy for you."

"Are you really?" I have to ask, because I know he's never been a big fan of Lachlan.

"It's obvious he loves you. I might still hold a grudge against him, but I can't deny that. At the end of the day, that's all that matters. I know he's going to love you and take care of you."

"Don't make me cry." I feel my throat closing up.

"Never." Sage smiles at me. "Let's get this thing going."

I let him guide me out of the little cottage, down the rolling green hill, to where Lachlan waits at the end with the pastor from a nearby church. Behind him are the outlines of more green hills, the water below. It looks like something from an enchanted fairytale. The arbor he stands under, adorned with flowers and greenery, adds even more to the fairytale of it all.

Lachlan's eyes take me in and I lose my breath as he looks at me like I'm *everything*.

I start tugging Sage along and he hisses, "Slow down."

Finally, I'm in front of my fiancé.

Sage hands me over and when I kiss his cheek I don't miss the tear falling from the corner of his eye.

I can't help but look over Lachlan, in his black button down dress shirt tucked into a green, brown, and blue kilt.

So glad I made him wear a kilt.

We exchange our vows, our friends and family watching.

I slide the silver band over his thick knuckle until it comes to rest where it will sit for the rest of our lives.

He takes my hand, doing the same. I stare down at the thin silver band with tiny diamonds going all the way around it. It's simple, but stunning.

"You may now kiss your bride."

Lachlan's hands go straight to my face, like always, and he kisses me slow and deep, signing the contract on the years ahead of us.

We turn, hands clasped, and I can't stop smiling as my eyes glide over his parents and sister, my brother, Sasha, and even Ansel and his family. Ansel claps, smiling back at me. I miss him like crazy since he still lives in Paris, doing his own thing, but we talk all the time.

"I present to you, Mr. and Mrs. Lachlan Taylor."

I turn my smile to my husband. "I'm Mrs. Taylor now."

"It's about damn time." He lowers his head, kissing me again. I lean into his touch, still not able to stop smiling even as I kiss him back. "I love you Dandelion Taylor."

"Not as much as I love you, *Mr. Taylor*."

He chuckles against me as we walk down the aisle, away from everyone else, into the start of our forever.

EPILOGUE #2

ANOTHER THREE YEARS LATER

LOOKING OUT THE WINDOW ABOVE THE SINK, I TRY TO hold in my laughter, watching Lachlan spin our honeymoon souvenir around in the air. Lyla's giggles are music to my ears as it carries in through the screen door, the sound of wind chimes tinkling along with it. That little girl is our entire world. Before we got married, we decided to start trying for a baby during our honeymoon. For some reason both of us were convinced that it would take months, maybe even a year or more, but we lucked out and ended up pregnant our wedding night.

There's a kick against my stomach, and I place my hand against the round swell, now watching Lachlan show Lyla how to feed the chickens.

I had wanted to space our children out a little more, but the baby boy growing inside of me had other plans for us. Brodie will be joining us in less than four weeks. I'm excited, but terrified too, worried I won't love him as much as I love Lyla. I know in my gut I'll love him the same, but that doesn't ease my fears.

"Mommy!" Lyla calls from outside. "I feed chickens! Come see!"

I let the dishes I was cleaning rest in the soapy water as I walk out, padding across the yard to join my family.

Lachlan ... God, Lachlan.

He's thirty-seven now, and I swear my Superman is even better looking than the first time I laid eyes on him. The graying at his temples makes him look more distinguished and I love kissing the laugh lines beside his mouth, because those mean I've made him happy.

"Look, Momma." Lyla holds her chubby hand out, tossing the feed onto the ground.

We chose to stay near Salt Lake City, but moved about an hour away. Lachlan still commutes forty minutes to work at the same place he took a job after leaving Aspen Lake High. I got my degree, and work from home doing marketing for an organic health food store. It's nice because I still get to work, but also be home with Lyla.

The house we bought sits on a few acres, which meant I got my chickens, two goats, and one cow. It's a work in progress, but I know this is where we're meant to watch our children grow.

"Wow," I say to Lyla. "You're so good. They love you."

And they really do. I think Lyla thinks the chickens are dogs, which I can't possibly fathom—though Zeppelin is more the size of a bear than a dog, so I guess her confusion makes sense.

Lachlan scoops Lyla into his arms and stands, putting an arm around my waist.

"How are you feeling, baby?"

"Tired." I rub my round stomach. "He's kicking a lot. I think he bruised my ribs."

He laughs like I'm kidding. I'm not.

"Dadda, put me down." Lyla kicks and squirms to get

down. He places her on the grass and her tiny feet take off running, letting the chickens chase her.

"I didn't know it was possible to be this happy," Lachlan murmurs, placing his hand on my belly over top of mine.

"Me either." I lean my head against his side, both of us watching Lyla run and squeal.

She's the perfect mix of both of us, his dark hair, my hazel eyes, my lips, but his nose. She's full of excitement and spunk. She reminds me of myself when I was young, before life happened. But thanks to her daddy, I found joy again.

Lyla runs up to us again, holding out a dandelion ripe with seeds.

"Make wish, Mommy."

I bend down as best I can at eight months pregnant and take the dandelion from her, smiling wistfully.

"Wish," she repeats, touching her small warm hand to my cheek.

"Together?" I wrap her hand around the stem so we're both holding it.

"Otay." I smile, loving how she can never say *okay* even though she talks up a storm already at such a young age.

"Okay, baby girl, let's make a wish."

I feel Lachlan's hand squeeze my shoulder as my eyes close.

As a mother myself now, I'm really beginning to understand why my mom said some of the things she did to me, so it's with that thought that I round my lips, and exhale, blowing the seeds to scatter free in the wind. To lay down their roots, and grow where they'll thrive.

My sweet, Lyla. May you always be as free as the birds, as wild as the flowers, and untamed as the sea.

ACKNOWLEDGMENTS

No book is completed without help from a lot of different sources.

Emily Wittig, you were the first person I told about this book, the first one to read it, and then you created the most artistic and stunning cover I've ever seen that perfectly captures Dani and how she sees herself.

Barbara you mean so much to me and I'm so lucky to have someone like you on my side. You're brilliant and amazing.

To my dog best friend Ollie, every book is completed with you by my side and I love you so, so, so much.

My family, thank you for your endless support. It means the world to me.

To everyone who reads a copy of this book, thank you for seeing something in this story. I hope you lived it every step of the way with Dani.

I hope Dani's story stays with you all for a very long time. It meant the world to me writing it.